P9-DTX-404

Buffalo Coat

By Carol Ryrie Brink

Harps in the Wind
Stopover
The Headland
*Strangers in the Forest**
The Twin Cities
Château Saint Barnabé
*Snow in the River**
The Bellini Look
*Four Girls on a Homestead***
*A Chain of Hands**

*Published by and available from the Washington State University Press.

**Published by and available from the Latah County Historical Society, Moscow, Idaho.

Buffalo Coat

Carol Ryrie Brink

With a Foreword by Mary E. Reed

Washington State University Press
Pullman, Washington

Published in collaboration with the
Latah County Historical Society
Moscow, Idaho

Washington State University Press, Pullman, Washington
99164-5910

©1993 by the Board of Regents of Washington State University
All rights reserved
Originally published 1944
WSU Press Reprint Series, first printing 1993

Cover illustration from a photo provided by Latah County Historical Society, Moscow, Idaho

Library of Congress Cataloging-in-Publication Data
Brink, Carol Ryrie, 1895-
    Buffalo coat / Carol Ryrie Brink ; with a foreword by Mary
E. Reed.
       p. cm.
    "Published in collaboration with the Latah County Histor-
ical Society, Moscow, Idaho."
    ISBN 0-87422-095-5 (paperback)
    1. City and town life – Idaho – Fiction. I. Title.
go3503.R5614B8 1993
813'.52 – dc20   93-17131
                                          CIP

Author's Biography

Carol Ryrie Brink was born in Moscow, Idaho, in 1895 and spent most of her life there until her junior year in college. Her youthful years spanned the settlement period of rustic one-story, wood-frame buildings lining Main Street to an era of paved roads and automobiles. At a young age her father died of consumption; a crazed gunman murdered her grandfather, one of the town's builders; and her mother committed suicide after an unfortunate second marriage. Carol's maternal grandmother and aunt raised her in their Moscow home.

Brink wrote more than thirty books for both adults and children. Her most acclaimed work, *Caddie Woodlawn*, won the Newbery Medal as the outstanding contribution to children's literature in 1936. It details and synthesizes in fictionalized form the stories her grandmother told her about growing up in Wisconsin. In addition to the Newbery Medal, Brink was honored with the Friends of American Writers Award in 1955, the 1966 National League of American Pen Women's award for fiction, and an honorary degree of Doctor of Letters from the University of Idaho in 1965.

Brink wrote three stories for children based upon her experiences growing up in Moscow. She also wrote an adult series of novels about her family in and around Moscow: *Buffalo Coat* (1944); *Strangers in the Forest* (1959); and *Snow in the River* (1964). In 1993 the Washington State University Press, in collaboration with the Latah County Historical Society in Moscow, Idaho, reprinted the latter three novels, along with Brink's previously unpublished reminiscences about characters she knew in Moscow, *A Chain of Hands.*

Carol Ryrie Brink died in 1981 in San Diego. Her home town recognized her posthumously with the naming of a building on the University of Idaho campus in her honor and with the naming of the children's wing of the Moscow-Latah County Public Library after her.

Among Brink's contributions to Western American literature are her works about her native state of Idaho. In view of the relatively few Idaho writers of this period, that is of interest in itself. But there are more important considerations for recognizing Brink, especially her portrayal of a West between two eras.

Although many writers concentrate on a colorful pioneer period and the heroic feats of those who plowed virgin ground, opened the first mines, and platted towns, the chronicle of those who followed is certainly equally or more important. These were the people who established the libraries, invested their lives and fortunes in the new communities, and generally created civic life as we recognize it today. Brink's portrayal of the lives and experiences of men and women in an Idaho town during this crucial period of growth and maturing serve as an antidote to numerous works about the wild American frontier. In her three Idaho novels and *A Chain of Hands* she shows us a small town whose citizens had to weigh justice with empathy, who had to learn that the resources of the West were not entirely at their personal disposal, and who discovered that the promise of these new lands was at times ephemeral.

Acknowledgments

In 1987 the Washington State University Press and the Latah County Historical Society collaborated in the publication of two books, Richard Waldbauer's *Grubstaking the Palouse* and Keith Petersen's *Company Town*. The recognition those two works received, including awards from the American Association for State and Local History, the Idaho Library Association, and the Council for the Advancement of Secondary Education, greatly pleased both institutions and led the two to seek ways in which to collaborate again. This reprint of *Buffalo Coat* represents another such venture.

Carol Ryrie Brink wrote more than thirty books for children and adults. Idahoans frequently point out that Ezra Pound was born in the state, although he left as an infant, and that Ernest Hemingway lived here for a while. Both writers were obviously accomplished, but neither wrote about Idaho. In seeking true regional writers—writers who knew the state and wrote about it— Idahoans have virtually ignored Brink.

In the late 1970s and early 1980s the Latah County Historical Society undertook several projects, including giving presentations about Brink throughout the state, with the goal of bringing recognition to this talented writer. Those efforts have largely been rewarded with renewed recognition for Brink in regional anthologies, with the recent publication of a biography of the author in Boise State University's Western Writers Series, and with the posthumous naming of two significant buildings in Moscow in Brink's honor.

In 1992 the Historical Society and WSU Press agreed to collaborate on a major publication venture that would bring back into print Brink's three adult novels about Idaho, *Buffalo Coat* (originally published in 1944), *Strangers in the Forest* (1959), and *Snow in the River* (1964). In addition, the two collaborated in the publication of Brink's previously unpublished reminiscences about characters she knew growing up in Moscow, *A Chain of Hands*.

This publication venture would not have been possible without the kind assistance of the Brink family, and we are indebted to Carol's son David and daughter Nora Brink Hunter for their encouragement and help.

The Latah County Historical Society has gained a national reputation for its publications program. Special thanks are due to its publications committee and board of trustees for their foresight in recognizing the importance of regional publishing in general and Carol Brink's work specifically. I would especially like to thank our two longtime friends, Carolyn Gravelle and Kathleen Probasco, who maintained unswerving faith in this publication venture for almost a decade. I have greatly profited from their encouragement and affection for our native author. I also wish to thank Bert Cross, who supported this project when others became discouraged.

At the WSU Press, I would like to thank my colleagues and friends director Thomas Sanders; assistant director, Mary Read; editors Keith Petersen, Jean Taylor, Glen Lindeman, and John Sutherland; designer Dave Hoyt; and promotions coordinator Vida Hatley. All of them proved not only receptive but also enthusiastic when approached about a possible Brink publication project. We at the Historical Society want them to know how much we have appreciated their support and collaboration over the years.

Mary E. Reed
Latah County Historical Society
Moscow, Idaho

Foreword

Carol Brink grew up with the conviction that someday she would write "something about the Moscow story" because of her family's intimate connection with the town. This novel of her grandparents' lives is the first of three Idaho novels connected to each other through the characters and events of this small western community. *Buffalo Coat,* published in 1944, was Brink's first adult novel. She wrote it several years after receiving the prestigious Newbery Medal for her classic children's book, *Caddie Woodlawn,* written in 1935. The second and third novels of the trilogy, *Strangers in the Forest* and *Snow in the River,* were originally published in 1959 and 1964 respectively.

The publication of *Buffalo Coat* created an uproar in Moscow as people quickly identified the fictional characters with the real ones. The reaction completely surprised the author, who thought she had been away for so long that no one would remember her.[1] Despite the local excitement, most of Idaho remained oblivious of their native author, even when the Latah County Historical Society reprinted the book in 1980. Yet *Buffalo Coat* is much more than a chronicle of local characters and events. As regional literature it expertly captures the essence of a particular time and place. Growing up in Moscow, Brink perceived that the impulse toward settled, civilized life could be challenged by another; that there was "still an atmosphere of wildness and of strangeness there that perhaps was in my imagination, but I felt that the mountains and the higher altitude had something to do with the kind of violent or strong reactions of the people."[2]

The vitality and tensions of the book are suggested in the title, which brings to mind the frontier and the free-roaming buffalo which human greed—disguised as sport—had almost destroyed. Its coat is a symbol of prestige and warmth, of masculine strength that has reduced this wild creature into a garment of utility. Placing the coat upon her grandfather's shoulders, Brink uses it as a vehicle to explore the motives of those who transformed the small frontier communities into respectable towns. But there is another side to the buffalo coat, and Brink uses her grandmother's character to question the conventional morality and motives of the inhabitants of the town Brink renames Opportunity.

Brink's grandfather, William W. Watkins, the Dr. Hawkins of the novel, came to Moscow in 1887 with his wife and three daughters to establish a medical practice after a distinguished career as a physician and surgeon in Missouri. A robust figure with "bristling whiskers" and "big, black eyes," Brink remembers him as "proud, confident, dynamic, single-purposed...someone you either loved or hated."[3] Dr. Watkins contributed to Moscow's growth by securing the state university for the little-populated northern panhandle of the state. He served as a university regent and also established the Watkins Medal for Oratory.[4] Along with his educational contributions, Watkins was president of the Idaho State Medical Society and the first permanent chairman of the first Republican state convention in 1890. As befit his position as a civic leader, Watkins was a prominent member of the Odd Fellows and Masons. Despite his medical and civic achievements, he lost two sons to diphtheria, a loss that haunted him even as his three daughters thrived.

Watkins's fictional counterpart, Dr. Hawkins, shares similar characteristics. He is a strong personality, a man guided partly by dedication to civic growth and partly by concern for his own reputation. The possibilities of Opportunity excite Hawkins, who has brought his wife and two young daughters to this raw town of shabby wooden houses and muddy streets. When his new assistant questions him about the purpose of his helping to build the new town, Hawkins explodes in surprise: "Why, for the future...for the boys and girls who are growing up, for the men and women of tomorrow!. . .God, for the fun of building!"[5]

The act of building also reveals a darker side of the Western experience, one that Brink explores through the character of Anna Hawkins, in reality her grandmother. It is Anna who feels "the danger and the hidden threat, the lure to suicide, the quick, wild urge to hurt and kill." She sees that the building up of Opportunity is only a thin crust of civilization over the pie which can easily crack to reveal the savageness underneath.[6]

Although *Buffalo Coat* is filled with the robust, masculine energy of Dr. Hawkins and the rapidly growing Opportunity, it is very much Anna's story. It is Anna who quietly mends the disasters that come to others, who offers the soothing words, who perceives the larger reality, like the landscape, behind the tangled lives of the other characters. So it was with Brink's grandmother, Caroline Watkins. Although Brink admitted that her grandmother was in every book she wrote, either as a character or as a source of inspiration, Caroline Watkins dominates *Buffalo Coat.*[7]

Brink had experienced the healing powers and strength of Caroline Watkins almost from her birth. After her father died in 1900, the four-year-old sought comfort and security in her grandmother's house. When her mother remarried in 1901, and then in increasing despair and shame committed suicide in 1905, Brink naturally turned to her grandmother whom she remembers as having all the "good solid virtues that are essential to a good life."[8] She lived with her grandmother until her fourth year in college. During these years Brink absorbed her grandmother's stories along with her sense of responsibility, resourcefulness, and making the most of life. In developing Anna Hawkins's character, there was little that needed to be fictionalized.

Anna fits the conventional mold of the woman reluctant to move West, allowing her husband to make the family's major decisions while she runs the household.[9] As Hawkins invests heavily in some municipal projects, Anna finds ways to save money, such as selling eggs, mending clothes, and growing and canning food. But she keeps this from Doctor as he is impatient with these petty economies.[10]

Caroline Watkins played a similar role in her household. At her husband's death, she found herself with numerous debts and few sources of income. But being resourceful and thrifty, she was able to keep her household together—a household that included Carol Brink and later two children of her youngest daughter, Winnifred—by renting rooms in her house and renting out her husband's office, gardening and preserving food, raising chickens, and leading a thrifty life.

Anna's role in *Buffalo Coat,* as well as Caroline Watkins's life, challenges our modern perception of men's and women's roles. Gram Watkins was very domestic and yet liked men's jobs, too. If a fence needed mending, "she got out there with hammer and nails," and she took pride in keeping her knives extremely sharp to make things like box elder whistles or tiny baskets carved out of cherry pits for Carol.[11] Gram dispensed with conventional female mannerisms and fashions. She didn't like parties and clubs, and after her husband's death didn't go out very often. Brink related an incident that illustrates her disinterest in personal appearance: "She went across the street to church occasionally and once she went with her kitchen apron. She put her coat on and didn't realize until she was in church that she had her apron on underneath."[12]

Although the lives of grandmother and granddaughter diverged, Brink's commitment to her home and family reflected Gram's influences. She also remarked that people often exaggerated how bad women's situations were in the past.[13]

Brink described herself as being a compulsive writer, but she maintained a schedule of writing in the morning when the children were in school or in the evening after they were in bed.[14] Like her grandmother, Brink was unconcerned about how others

regarded her. She commented that Macmillan's decision not to reprint *Buffalo Coat,* which had been on the *New York Times* best
seller list for two weeks, was fortuitous. "I think maybe I've been
lucky not to have made a great smashing success because you see
people who do that, on a first novel especially, and they're immediately involved in the speaking engagements and in all sorts of things
that they aren't supposed to be involved in if they're going to be
good writers. . . . But if you don't make a big smashing success
you keep thinking, well, maybe the next one will be better. . . .
I've just kind of pottered along and had a good time doing it."[15]

Brink's tribute to her grandmother and the connecting thread
between them is contained in her reminiscences, *A Chain of Hands:*
"She worked hard and managed her life with dignity and good humor. What did she get out of it? A step-by-step and day-by-day
satisfaction of daylight and dark, of turning seasons, of gardens
and flowers and friendly animals, of sharp knives and clocks that
were on time, of well-baked bread and a properly stuffed and roasted
chicken, of rich memories of a happy childhood. She took great
store in her happy childhood, and perhaps I, who have had so much
more happy and fortunate a life than she had, have inherited her
tendency to look backwards to my beginnings with appreciation
and understanding."[16]

Her grandparents formed two strong threads connecting Brink
with her novel. A third was the Idaho mountains. As a child, Brink
enjoyed the freedom of wandering into the countryside on her pony.
Her observations of the changing seasons with their progression
of wild flowers, native plants, birds, and other pleasures of the natural world became a reservoir for her writing when she was far
away from Idaho. Softly dominating the landscape were the mountains to the east of Moscow, the foothills of the Bitterroot Mountains, which in turn give way to the Rockies. The aesthetic
connection was also an emotional one, because they reminded her
of the wilderness where her Aunt Elsie Watkins had taken up a

homestead cabin along with other "refined" Moscow ladies. The
two summers she had spent in the white pine forests were ones
of both pleasure and appreciation of the dangers her aunt had
faced.[17]

The Idaho mountains play a major and unifying role in *Buffalo
Coat* through the gentle personalities of Anna Hawkins and Dr.
Hawkins's assistant, Hugh Duvall, who has come from France.
Since her arrival in Opportunity, Anna has been fascinated by the
mountains to the east. Catching her first sight of them from the
train window, she also noticed that "the light was sharper here than
in the South or Middle West. . . . There was a fine, red light on
the mountains at sunset."[18] As an interloper in the American West,
Duvall is also drawn to the mountains. As he enjoys long hikes
into the meadows and hills outside the town, Duvall also wonders
at how the townspeople built so that they did not look out at the
mountains, but faced their houses inward toward the streets. Instead of windows framing this beauty, they put family photographs
on their walls. At the end of the novel Duvall and Anna Hawkins
meet to say goodbye, and Anna turns again to the mountains to
find solace. "Ever changing, now blue, now purple, now pale as
silk; sometimes tremendous and threatening the sky, and sometimes dwindled to a gentle undulation around a peaceful valley,
the mountains seemed as fickle as water; and yet they were the
only permanence. In all of their variety, they were the only certain thing. . . . And birth and death, and gain and loss, and even
love itself, these were the shadows and the transiencies. . . . In spite
of all that had happened to her, she felt at peace."[19]

Buffalo Coat is important in providing an understanding of
a significant phase of Western history, the eager rush toward civilization. Although the Hawkins family arrives in Opportunity when
it is a cluster of one-story wooden buildings surrounded by mud,
the novel centers on the town's process of maturing through such
efforts as building a new university, ending the yearly typhoid

epidemics by installing a sewer system, and following the intricate social conventions and prejudices of the time. In conjunction with this, Brink gives us a portrait of a young town that is not the stereotype of a Western community. Murder is an uncommon occurrence that shocks and enrages the entire town, and the leading social event is the yearly commencement exercises of the new university. The two outsiders are not the gunslinger or the fallen woman, but the French doctor who cannot find solace for the death of his wife and the English wife of another doctor who finds the physical demands of the town and her status as a wife repulsive.

In this town struggling to become as conventional and progressive as any other in America, Brink skillfully fits the human pieces together. The result is a portrait of a community where generosity and selfishness mix in portions common to most human congregations. The vividness of her grandparents' personalities, the idiosyncrasies of her home town, Moscow, and the familiar themes of "birth and death and gain and loss, and even love itself" will insure the reputation of *Buffalo Coat* as a classic of regional literature.

MARY E. REED
Latah County Historical Society
Moscow, Idaho
June 1993

Notes

1. Interview with Carol Ryrie Brink by Mary E. Reed, July 1981, San Diego, California, transcript of tape 4, p. 8. The tapes and transcripts of a series of interviews with Brink in July 1981 are in the collection of the Latah County Historical Society library, Moscow, Idaho.
2. Brink oral history transcript of tape 4, pp. 6-7.
3. Carol Ryrie Brink, *A Chain of Hands* (Pullman: Washington State University Press, 1993), pp. 3-8.
4. Brink oral history transcript of tape 1, p. 10.
5. Carol Ryrie Brink, *Buffalo Coat* (Pullman: Washington State University Press, 1993; reprint), p. 33.
6. *Ibid.,* pp. 21-22.
7. *Chain of Hands*, pp. 27, 32.
8. Brink oral history transcript of tape 1, p. 9.
9. Brink oral history transcript of tape 2, p. 7.
10. *Buffalo Coat*, pp. 177-178.
11. Brink oral history transcript of tape 2, p. 7; *Chain of Hands*.
12. Brink oral history transcript of tape 5, p. 12.
13. Brink oral history transcript of tape 6, p. 7.
14. Brink oral history transcript of tape 3, p. 13.
15. Brink oral history transcript of tape 4, pp. 9-10.
16. *Chain of Hands*, p. 30.
17. Brink's account of a summer on the homestead when she was 15 years old is in *Four Girls on a Homestead* (Moscow, Id.: Latah County Historical Society, 1977). Her novel *Strangers in the Forest* (New York: Macmillan Company, 1959; Pullman: Washington State University Press, 1993) draws heavily upon her experiences and impressions on the homestead.
18. *Buffalo Coat*, p. 22.
19. *Buffalo Coat*, pp. 420-421.

Author's Note*

Buffalo Coat has sometimes been considered as a true account of early Moscow history instead of as a work of fiction. So much of the book is true that the mistake is a natural one. But on the occasion of a new edition it seems appropriate that I should set the record straight on what is fact and what is fiction.

As a child in Moscow I grew up hearing all of the town histories. They interested me as much as the novels that I read so avidly in the old Carnegie library. One of those true stories was particularly close to me as it concerned my grandfather, Dr. William Woodbury Watkins, who came to Moscow in 1887 and was killed there on August 4, 1901. Another tragic Moscow story was also close to me, as Mrs. Ledbrooke, the widow of Dr. Francis J. Ledbrooke, came to live with us after her husband's suicide, and she became a cherished part of my childhood. I was quick to see that these tragic stories were as fundamental and dramatic as anything I found in the library, and, when I became a writer, it was natural that I should think of using them in a book.

I first wrote a completely true story, using my grandfather's office on Second Street just off of Main as the link that bound the various stories together. Here is a brief history of that office and the men who occupied it in chronological order. I believe that my grandfather built the small brick building, although I am not sure of this. At any rate he was the first occupant, and he was later joined by Dr. Delapine, an early specialist in diseases of the eye, ear, nose, and throat. Dr. Delapine was a Frenchman who had formerly practiced in London and who had married an Englishwoman. Mrs. Delapine died young, leaving her husband with twin daughters and a small son. These children were later partly reared by my grandmother, who had a warm heart for anyone in need of care and affection.

It used to puzzle me that so many people in Moscow should have come from far away. There were all of the Scandinavian people; there were Chinese vegetable gardeners, a Hungarian shoemaker, and people from many countries in this very small frontier town. My own father came from Scotland, Dr. Delapine was French, and Dr. Ledbrooke was English. My grandfather and grandmother were of New England origin, although they had stopped in Wisconsin and Missouri on the way west. The explanation, of course, is that the American West seemed to offer unbounded possibilities in the 1880s and 1890s to people from all of the tired old countries of the world. In *Buffalo Coat* I have called Moscow Opportunity with the ironic thought that it seemed to embody opportunity for people from the Old World, while in reality it could offer them nothing new, only a rearrangement of the kind of life they had previously known.

Dr. Delapine returned to England before my grandfather was killed. Soon after my grandfather's death Dr. Ledbrooke and his wife Alice came from England and he rented the office from my grandmother. This is the chief difference between the real facts and the fictitious story. Dr. Watkins and Dr. Ledbrooke never knew each other.

After Dr. Ledbrooke's death on May 12, 1902, Dr. C. D. Parsons occupied the office for a short time. About a year later he fell from a packhorse while he was on a camping trip and died from a fractured skull. Three doctors had died violently in 1901, 1902, and 1903. After the third death the people of Moscow said that the office was hoodooed and no one would occupy it. It stood empty for a long time, and probably pedestrians crossed the street rather than pass near it. Then Dr. Delapine returned to town and evidently he had no superstitious qualms. He rented the office from my grandmother and practiced there for many years, a highly respected and competent physician. I believe that Dr. Clark and perhaps other doctors occupied the office later.

I sent my story of the doctors' office to my publishers, and they returned it with the criticism that it was not a novel but a series of short stories, and that I had "killed off" the most interesting character (meaning my grandfather) in the first story. To make a novel it remained for me to fictionalize the facts and dovetail the events, which I did by making Dr. Watkins (Hawkins) and Dr. Ledbrooke (Allerton) into contemporary rivals. I believe that the accounts of their individual fates are about as accurate as anyone living today can make them. The fiction is all in their relationship to each other and in some of the motivation and detail.

The newspapers at the time of the double suicide of Dr. Ledbrooke and Winnie Booth (Jennie Walden) shouted that he was a villain who had a malign hypnotic influence over an innocent young girl. I believe sincerely that it was simply a passionate love affair between two people who saw no possible future for themselves without scandal and harm to others. To understand their dilemma we must put ourselves back into the environment of the turn of the century. These were two very religious people who believed that, because he was married, loving each other was a sin. A divorce would have ruined his career and her reputation and would have wounded innocent victims. Yet they felt that they could not live without each other. Today there would have been various more-or-less easy solutions. In 1902 they saw no alternative but double suicide.

In making a fiction of all this, I have done an injustice to two characters. Alice Ledbrooke was one of the plainest—ugliest is an ugly word—let's say one of the least pretty women I have ever seen, but she was one of the delights of my childhood. She lived with us for many years after her husband's death, and we all loved her dearly. Dr. Delapine, I'm sure, was never an alcoholic, and the romance between him and my grandmother was much less real than

I have suggested in the book. I believe there was one time, when they were both in middle age and had gone through a number of troubles with understanding and sympathy, that he suggested marriage and she declined. But for the sake of a good story I have enlarged upon their steady friendship.

I hope that this will set the record straight for all new readers of *Buffalo Coat*. I am happy to see it once again in print.

CAROL RYRIE BRINK

*Carol Ryrie Brink wrote this author's note to the 1980 reprint of *Buffalo Coat* published by the Latah County Historical Society.

PART I

1888–1894

1

For a long time now the only moving object on the frozen road had been the purposeful figure of little Jenny Walden, going steadily southward away from the scattered, one-story houses of Opportunity. Between the empty stubble fields and against the immensity of snowy mountains, she seemed so small as to be hardly worth the attention of that meticulous Deity who watches for the fall of a sparrow. The mountains, which encircled this northern valley in Idaho Territory, were not high, but today they borrowed a deep solemnity from the storm clouds hanging above them. They were like slothful giants watching with an indolence too heavy for amusement the futile attempt of a little girl to make her escape.

Her thin legs, encased in homemade leggings which had been darned at the knees, moved quickly, for she had made up her mind to go a long way before dark. She was warm with an impulse and an inner vision which sustained her. In her coat pocket she had two pieces of bread and butter wrapped in a fringed napkin, and she had set out for San Francisco. Without a thought for the difficulties that lay between Idaho Territory and San Francisco, beyond the need for a couple of sandwiches and an extra muffler, Jenny had set out, and already she had covered three or four miles.

It was only when snow began to fall that some doubt assailed her. Still she kept on, going with the snow which fell at first in large, slow flakes at about her own speed. Soon, however, the flakes began to be smaller and more numerous. They flung themselves against her back and drove past her with ever-increasing speed and violence. Looking up, she saw that the mountains had disappeared behind a white curtain, and bit by bit the stubble fields melted and dissolved away into white nothingness. Presently there was only the road with

3

the rail fence on either hand, and the rails outlined now with a blowing fringe of white. Still Jenny kept on going southward.

Of course it was because of the blue dress in the missionary barrel, and of what Della had said to comfort her that she was here. Della, who was eleven, a year older than Jenny, had as keen an imagination as hers; but with Della the imagining was enough. She was safe at home in the parsonage now, sitting behind the warm stove on a hassock made of old carpeting and playing serenely with her paper dolls. With Jenny imagination was a part of action. She conceived and then she acted. Only it was a pity today that no one had seen her go out; that she had departed for San Francisco with no appropriate farewells.

The missionary barrel had arrived from San Francisco a month before Christmas at the end of the year 1888, and they had none of them been able to wait a month before opening it. Their impatience was partly due to necessity and partly to the unspoken knowledge, born of past experience, that it was better to be disappointed now than to be disappointed on Christmas. So the Reverend Mr. Walden, apple-cheeked and blue-eyed with his sparse hair a little on end, had fetched the hammer and hatchet and knocked off the head of the barrel while Mrs. Walden and the little girls stood by. There had not been any dolls or rock candy or storybooks, but there had been one wonderful thing. In among the patched coats and darned woolen underwear, there had been a little blue silk dress. It was made like a lady's dress with three tiers of ruffles looped up into a real bustle; and it was that color of blue which sings and dances.

Wild with delight, the little girls had clutched at it, and Della had got hold of it first, holding it up against her body so that everyone could see at a glance how ludicrously small it was. Still hoping against hope, Jenny had caught it to her breast, feeling the softness of the silk, and her mother had helped her measure it against her shoulders. The dress had been too small for her, too.

"If only it had been too large," Mrs. Walden said, "I could have cut it down."

Jenny had stamped her feet then and burst into tears. She could never hope to wear it nor have another like it. Della looked at her in surprise, because after all they were no worse off than they had been before. But for a moment Jenny had seen herself wearing the dress, and her sense of loss was violent.

"Tut, Jenny!" said her father. "There's no dress in the world worth crying for."

Jenny could not believe that. Tears were so cheap, and blue silk dresses so rare.

But Della, for all her surprise at Jenny's outburst, knew how Jenny felt, and when they were in bed that night she told Jenny a wonderful story to make up for their loss.

"Some day we'll go to San Francisco, where the barrel came from, Jenny," she said, "and that's a wonderful city where all the girls have silk dresses. Some are blue and some are pink and some are yellow and purple or any color you like, I guess. And I think maybe it's something like heaven in San Francisco—you know, with streets of gold and that—because I've heard people talk about the Golden Gate there. It's warm and sunny in California, too. And when we go we'll have a carriage to ride under the golden arch of the gate and along the beautiful streets, and we'll have silk dresses in any colors we want—"

"Is it very far to San Francisco?"

"Not so very."

"Let's go there, Della."

"Not yet," said Della. "I'm going to sleep now. But some day when we are big—"

Jenny had lain awake for a long while after Della was asleep, and the more she thought of San Francisco, the more she knew that she must go there. There was no use in saying anything to anyone, because she knew from the past that other people did not always sympathize with the things that she must do. She had learned very early that she had to do them alone and quickly or all sorts of useless barriers would be erected between herself and her passionate objectives.

So she had waited until her mother had gone out to the Ladies' Aid meeting and her father had lighted the Franklin stove in his study and closed the door and Della was busy with her paper dolls behind the baseburner in the dining room. She had had a moment of weakening almost to the point of asking Della to accompany her, and then she had heard Della making audible conversation between two paper-doll ladies about the respective merits of their babies and whether they had been baptized or not, and she knew instinctively that to tell Della about her journey would make the excursion impossible. She had hurried then to butter the bread quickly and to put another muffler around her neck before she went out and closed the door quietly behind her.

Jenny had seen the town fall away and the snowy fields envelop her with no misgivings, for she was not easily intimidated. The frozen road and the mountains, brooding under heavy clouds, were not terrible to a person with a vision. Jenny's vision of the Golden Gate was done after the manner of Gustave Doré, whose biblical drawings were familiar to her—except that her vision lacked the grimness of Doré. It was filled with golden light and the angels who went up and down the Jacob's ladder leading to the shining Portal all wore colored silk dresses with bustles.

Ever since the snow had begun, however, the vision had been growing dimmer. It faded and faded, darkening with the darkening day, and suddenly it was gone like a snuffed candle. Jenny's feet lagged until she was standing still in the road watching the snow hurtle by her; and the minute she stood still she knew with perfect understanding that San Francisco was an impossible goal. Now that she knew this, her feet ached with cold and her fingers felt numb. She had not noticed the silence before, but now it was all about her, a silence only deepened by the hissing of the snow. Softly, because of the silence, she began to cry. She tried to wipe her eyes, but her mittens were caked with snow which melted against her cheeks and mingled with her tears. She turned about and began stumbling back along the road she had come, but now the wind was in her face and the snow was driving harder and harder. When she came to cross-roads, she did not remember which one she had taken. She stood crying and bewildered, knowing with fatalistic clarity, unusual in a child, that she was lost and done for.

Thinking of Della, warm behind the stove with her paper dolls, she felt that she would never see her any more. By now they would have lighted the lamp and her mother would be slicing cold potatoes and onions and chopping the leftover soup meat for hash. She could hear the chopper against the wooden bowl and see the brown crust on the hash where the pancake turner turned it over. Probably there would be jelly and hot biscuits. She remembered that she had not eaten her bread and butter, but she no longer wanted it. In her pocket the butter was frozen and the bread stiff and hard with the cold.

She began to struggle forward again, but the wind and snow blinded her and took away her breath. She thought of the Babes in the Wood, but here were no robins nor any strawberry leaves. Her tears ran faster and faster down her cheeks. They froze in little icicles on her woolen scarf.

Then in the silence of the snowy evening came the faint chiming of sleigh bells and the muffled beat of horses' hoofs on the frozen road. The sound came nearer and nearer, making a most lovely music. Jenny began to run towards the sound and call out. Through the swirling whiteness she saw first the horse, looming large and terrible with flying hoofs and steaming nostrils; and then in a fury of bells the cutter was beside her, and it was big Doc Hawkins in his buffalo coat with his black muttonchop whiskers crusted with snow. He reined in the horse and stopped the cutter.

"Who's there?"

"It's me. It's Jenny Walden."

"No!" he roared in his great voice, his black eyes popping. "Well, gol-dang you little drowned rat, you! For the love of Harry! What are you doing out here?"

"G-going to San Francisco," she sobbed.

"Going t— For Lord's sake!" Doc Hawkins shouted with laughter.

Jenny began to laugh, too, a little mournfully, but now that Doc was here she could afford to laugh, for she knew that everything would be all right.

"Get in here, rat," he said. "My God! You're plastered with snow. Here, take off that coat, quick."

Jenny's stiff fingers fumbled obediently with the buttons. When Doc Hawkins said *Stick out your tongue,* you stuck out your tongue. When he said *Take off your coat,* you took off your coat, even in the middle of a blizzard on a November night four miles from town. He unbuttoned his own coat, and then he helped her out of hers and set her inside the buffalo coat against his warm body. The coat was big, and she was so thin and small that he could still button two buttons with both of them in it.

"So you were going to San Francisco." She could feel his laughter rumbling around inside the buffalo coat between the two of them.

"Yes," Jenny said, "but I changed my mind."

"The devil you did!"

Jenny was not ashamed. Her head relaxed against his breast. Inside the buffalo coat there was a warm and reassuring smell of tobacco and human kindness. Doc pulled the lap robe up around them and clucked to the horse. There was a beautiful ringing and chiming of bells as the cutter slid away towards town, smooth and silent behind the chiming and clopping horse.

Nothing that the Golden Gate had to offer could compare with this.

Jenny dozed the last couple of miles but, when the cutter stopped before the Methodist parsonage, she sat up with a start.

"I guess they won't like it because I went," she said.

"Look!" Doc said. "Don't you ever light out to go to San Francisco again, will you? or any other place?"

"No, I won't."

"All right then, I'll fix it up for you."

His big presence filled the bleak hall of the parsonage. She could see her mother and father and Della all staring at her with anxious, uncertain eyes, and from her to the doctor. But Doc Hawkins was laughing as if there was nothing to the whole adventure.

"Say," he said, "I hope I didn't have you people worried. I picked up Jenny on the road to give her a ride and I had a country call that kept me longer than I expected . . ."

It was all right now; and Jenny, as acutely aware of moral issues as any ten-year-old living in a parsonage in 1888 must be, saw that he had done it without lying. No one thought to ask why her coat was so wet and snowy. They were glad that she was at home, and so was she.

Later when she was in bed, warm in a plaid shawl, and eating hot milk toast, Jenny thought about Doc Hawkins and she was filled with love. She loved him even if he was a Presbyterian. Her love embraced the whole medical profession, which seemed to her a beautiful and noble calling. She was too familiar with the drawbacks of the ministry to give it this deep regard, and it is to be regretted, of course, that in both instances her reactions were materialistic. She did not admire the medical profession more than the ministry because she felt that the alleviation of bodily suffering was more important than the cure of the soul, but in part at least because sleigh bells rang and horses pranced for Doc Hawkins whereas only church bells tolled for her father.

She knew that Doc Hawkins' daughters, who were away at boarding school now, had silk dresses made up by the dressmaker out of new cloth, and that they did not have to wash dishes, because Doc Hawkins kept a little Swede girl to help Mrs. Hawkins with the housework. Jenny could not remember all the times when she or Della had happened to be looking in the candy-store window on

Main Street and Doc Hawkins had come by and dropped a nickel or a dime in one of their apron pockets. She knew that he hadn't sent her father a bill after he brought them all through the scarlet fever last year; and now he had snatched her out of the blizzard and saved not only her life but her pride as well.

Doc Hawkins had been a hero to little Jenny Walden before tonight, but now he approached the stature of a saint.

2

THERE WERE A GOOD many people who felt about Dr. Willard J. Hawkins as little Jenny Walden did, and then there were those who said that he was a hard man, as mean as the devil. His big, upstanding figure, with the fierce black eyes, the bristling eyebrows, and the muttonchop sideburns, was familiar to every person in Opportunity, and it was not a figure to which one could be apathetic.

Doc Hawkins certainly had a harsh temper which wouldn't stop at hurling dishes; but he had a good streak in him, too, that kept him watching all night beside an old woman's bed when he knew for certain that he'd never be paid for his trouble. The number of baby boys who were named Willard J. Something-or-other was increasing every year; and many a healthy child, growing to manhood in the new West, could thank Doc Hawkins for slapping or blowing the breath of life into him when it had looked as if he would be stillborn in some lonely mountain cabin with the storm howling outside.

Opportunity folks sometimes named the baby girls Anna, after the doctor's wife, and often she was there to bathe the baby or help Doc give an anesthetic. Anna was brave in an emergency, too, but she hadn't Doc's quality of impressing herself on the mind. Somehow she slipped off the imagination and was forgotten, while Doc, once known, was always remembered whether with love or with hatred.

It seemed now that Opportunity had never been without Doc Hawkins. As a matter of fact Doc Schilling had been there first; but he was so often drunk or hunting in the hills when an emergency came that no one counted on him. Old Schilling hadn't even owned a diploma to hang in his shanty, and tradition had it that he killed more patients than he cured. So the town had been a wide-open field for Willard J. Hawkins when he settled there in 1884. He came from St. Louis, Missouri, and he picked the town because he liked the name, *Opportunity*. Names were not empty to Doc. He took things for what they were called. He had already made half a dozen jumps westward from New Hampshire, where he was born. Time and again he would just get a nice practice worked up, and then he would have that itch to go farther west.

"By Golly! the future's in the West, Anna," he would say. "What are we doing here? Wasting our time, killing ourselves for nothing!"

It was the incurable fever of the period. Anna would pack up the household things and take the little girls' hands and follow him. To Doc the best place to be was always just ahead of him and a little out of reach; to Anna it was where she was.

So they had come to Opportunity with two little girls and a pile of trunks and baggage. Behind them in the places where they had been, they had left the graves of two little boys. If they remembered that, they never mentioned it.

Tonight Doc thought briefly of the Waldens as he drove away. He liked the Methodist preacher. Walden was a good man and he had to live and raise a family on next to nothing. The town was too damned full of churches, Doctor thought, they were springing up in all parts of town, too many for the population. You could have any flavor of sanctity you wished, from Episcopalian to Dunkard and Holy Roller. Doc took care of all sects without respect to creed. He went in his sleigh to fetch the priest and his Last Sacrament when the Dago switchman had both legs cut off under a train and they couldn't stop the bleeding. That was only one of a dozen times Doc had played coachman to the Holy Wafer. He knew, too, just what to do to bring around a Holy Roller who had frothed too long at the mouth, and he didn't object to damning out these newfangled

Christian Scientists, when they tried to interfere with a case of pneumonia. Doc called himself a Presbyterian because it was the best church in town and right across the street from his house, but he left attendance to Anna and the girls.

Temperamentally Doc felt most in harmony with the Methodists. They were good, sensible people, if a little touched on the subject of card playing and dancing, and he always felt easy with the Reverend Mr. Walden, Jenny's father. He thought of the child with a chuckle. He never saw her but he wanted to put his hand in his pocket and give her a nickel or a dime. She and her sister looked as if they needed it, and Lord! but they were pretty children even if their stockings were darned. They had wild, fairy faces, especially that little Jenny. Some man would lose his mind over her, six or eight years from now when she had grown up and put on a little more flesh. "If she don't kill herself first on some wild-goose chase," he thought, and laughed. "Going to San Francisco! My God!"

He drove down Elm Street to the office. His horse knew the way and stopped at the hitching post without being reined in. Doc got out and brushed the snow from the mare's back, flinging a blanket over her to keep her warm.

"Good girl!" he said. "Supper's going to be late, but you'll get it."

He stamped and shook the snow from his shoulders and went into the office. It was rarely locked, and he was not surprised to see a man get up from a chair by the stove and come towards him.

"My Lord," Doc said, "whyn't you light a lamp?"

"I didn't know if I should," the man said. "I been here since before it darkened. Doc, there's a man out here on the place where the road turns to the cemetery; he's hanged himself."

"Stevens?" Doc asked. "Elmer Stevens?"

"Ya, doc. I want you should come."

"Is he dead?"

"Ya, doc, he's dead."

"Then why in the name of the Old Harry do you come to me? You want the undertaker."

"Doc, they got the undertaker. He's gone already, if he gets through in this snow. But it's the Stevens kid. He found his old man hanging in the barn loft, and he cut him down. He's gone sort of rigid, like as if he was dead, and they can't bring him out of it. It looks like you had to come, doctor."

Doc pulled his big, loud-ticking watch out of his pocket and looked at it.

"Yes," he said, "but it's a damned shame. I was supposed to meet a train. It's important, too. I've got an assistant coming to help me with my practice, and somebody's got to meet him at the train. Look here, have you got a bobsled you can drive me out to Stevens' place in?"

"Sure, doctor. I'll drive you out there and bring you back."

"All right. You follow me out to my house now, will you? And I'll leave my horse and cutter for my wife."

Doc was hungry and tired, and it made him mad to have to go back out into the country again before the snow was dry on his shoulders.

"God knows I need an assistant if ever a man did," he grumbled to himself as he stepped back into the cutter.

The thought of the assistant doctor was troubling to him, too. Anna said he could never get along with another doctor in the same office, and, while he wouldn't admit it to her, he sometimes wondered himself. He wondered, too, if he had made the right choice among the many applications that had come to him. He had only written a few letters of inquiry to schools and doctors back East, and there had come this deluge of letters in reply. Every Tom, Dick, and Harry seemed to think that there was magic in the new West now that the first spadework had been done by the pioneers. They wanted easy money, and the name of the town undoubtedly attracted them as it had him. Well, there was money here all right, Doc thought, but on a night like this it wasn't easy money.

He remembered Anna's surprise when he had told her that he had decided on the Frenchman.

"A Frenchman?" Anna had said. "Does he speak our language?"

"Of course. Do you think I'd hire a fellow who talked like a frog? He's been married to an Englishwoman. She died, and I guess that's why he's trying to get clear away from everything he ever knew before. He has a brilliant record—studied in Paris and London, all those places. He's a first-rate doctor."

"London! Paris!" Anna had said. "Won't Idaho Territory seem strange to him after that?"

"Well, he wants to come," Doc said defensively.

"He must be running away from something pretty big to come this far, doctor."

"Damn your hide, Anna! You're always jumping to conclusions. All I know is, they say he's a first-rate doctor, and you don't pick up degrees from London and Paris every day. He may know more than I do; but, by Godfrey, I'm broad-minded, and I was in on the ground floor. I guess I can keep him in hand."

"Well, doctor, you know your own business," Anna said. And then she suddenly took his side: "Besides, you'll get along better with someone quite strange than with a man whose background is the same as yours."

Anna was sharp that way, Dr. Hawkins thought. She came out with things you wouldn't think of yourself, and then again she wouldn't say what she thought—only "Yes, doctor," and "No, doctor," like a nursing sister instead of a wife. He felt quite sure of Anna, and yet there were times when she puzzled him, too, and when she even shook his early-formed conviction that all women were fools.

Tonight she came to the side door when she heard his sleigh bells, and stood in the lighted doorway with a shawl around her shoulders. She was not a particularly striking or handsome woman, but she had a great mass of wavy chestnut hair which just missed being red. The lamplight behind her made it shine, and seemed to put a circle of light about her shadowed face.

"Anna," Doctor said sharply, "I've got to go out again."

"I know, doctor. They were here."

"It's that fellow Stevens, in the country. He's hanged himself, it seems. The boy who found him is in some kind of fit. Can you take the cutter and go meet Dr. Duval?"

"Yes, I can do that, doctor," Anna said. "But you must eat something before you go. You'll be a long time getting back."

"One of the neighbors is out front waiting to drive me there. He's been waiting in the office since this afternoon. I can't stop to eat."

"Don't be silly, doctor," Anna said. "I've got coffee ready for you and a bowl of hot soup."

"You'll have to bring it out then. If I get out of this damned buffalo hide for five minutes, I'll never have the gall to put it back on again tonight."

"Have it your way," Anna said.

She and the little Swede girl in their woolen shawls came out of the door with a steaming bowl and coffee pot and stood bareheaded in the falling snow while he ate. He was angry with them for this petticoat tyranny, but he was hungry and he enjoyed good food.

"Now, don't miss the train, Anna," he admonished. "It's due here sharp at seven-fifteen, and it may take awhile for you to get there with the snow blowing. He'll probably have a beard and a plug hat, so you needn't worry about not recognizing him. If he has yellow kid gloves, put a snowball into the plug hat for me, will you?"

The temperature of Doctor's spirits had risen several degrees with the hot soup and coffee.

"I'll do that, doctor," Anna said. Her mouth was unsmiling, but her eyes had a light that was next to laughter. She stepped into the cutter as he stepped out, and drove the horse to the barn. The chore boy whom Doctor kept now to look after the place ran after her.

"Mrs. Hawkins! Mrs. Hawkins! I'll take care of the horse for you."

Anna had never become accustomed to letting other people do things for her.

3

"WHY'D THE FELLOW hang himself, d'ye know?" Doc asked.

The man who was driving him had been working up a nice quid of tobacco while Doc ate his soup and drank his coffee. His mouth was full now, and he had to send a jet of tobacco juice into the snow before he could reply comfortably.

"Don't know exactly," he said. "Had a bad crop this summer, and he didn't get on too well with his missus, I guess. He used to be a bookkeeper back East before he come out here and took up this land. Like the rest of us, I guess, he thought he'd get rich soon as he come West and took land. Back East you hear about the gold and silver and copper out here; but you never hear about the claims that don't pan out or the crops that fail."

Doctor nodded his head. He had heard the same story before, but it never damped his own enthusiasm for the West.

"All the same, hanging's a damned desperate remedy," he said.

"Well, I think Stevens was kind of crazy myself. He let his place go ragged when a little elbow grease might just have saved it. They're a funny family anyway—never wanted to be neighborly with the rest of us out towards the Ridge. We wouldn't have known a thing was wrong today, only the woman rode over bareback without even a shawl around her, and you could hear her crying away down the road before she reached our house."

"Did you see the boy?"

"Ya, he looked like in some kind of fit," the man said, and spat again over the runner of the sled.

Doctor was silent. He knew the Stevens place, at the corner of the road where it turned to go up the hill to the cemetery. He should know it, by Gad! for he and the undertaker had ridden the country 'round to select a good place for the cemetery. The *Weekly Mirror* had had a funny paragraph entitled "They Get Us Coming or Going," in which it had lampooned Doc and Hank Briggs, the undertaker, for buying up cheap land so far out in the country and reselling it to the town for a cemetery. The article bothered Briggs a little, for he was a man who liked to be correct in everything, but Doc saw the joke and laughed as uproariously as any man in town.

"Lord!" he said. "The town's got to have a decent cemetery, and somebody had to start the ball rolling. Hank and I aren't getting rich on it, and, as for putting it so far out, this city is going to spread right out to the new graveyard before it's half filled. I've seen little towns in Missouri where they didn't have enough foresight for the growth of the town, and before they knew it the place had built up all around the cemetery and the graves had to be moved to make room for a new courthouse or a school. We don't want to go digging up our dead in ten or twenty years. Pick a good place a long way out and let 'em sleep in peace, that's what I say!"

So the hearse and the little black processions of carriages wound a long way out of Opportunity, through several miles of wheat fields, to the new graveyard. When the carriages returned to town, the dead could rest in peace, for there was nothing to break the silence but the humming of the wind in the pine trees, and in the spring the lonesome, seeking call of the meadow lark. On winter nights such as this one the snow blew and drifted across the little mounds, and in spring wild flowers and long grass ran riot.

At the corner where the road turned up to the cemetery, the Stevens house stood, narrow and bleak and weathered. It was built on the plan of a city house which has been forced into perpendicular lines because of close neighbors and narrow lots. It was the kind of house a city man would build, not a farmer. Yet there were no other houses for miles—only the flat yellow of stubble or the green of young wheat merging into the rippling gold of fruition or the long white undulations of the snow. It was brutal in its loneliness. A man's mind might grow strange and secret here, if he kept away from his neighbors. He might be troubled by fantastic thoughts which would not have occurred to him on a high stool in a narrow office with people passing to and fro.

The door of the house was open as they drove up, and there were people in the dooryard. Against the rectangle of lamplight Doctor could see the falling snow, and on the porch floor the lamplight spilled out in an irregular patch, illuminating the tramped and scuffed snow which no one had bothered to sweep or shovel away.

"Doc's come," someone called.

Doc lifted a hand in greeting, and sprang out of the sled just as it drew to a stop. Some histrionic quality in Doctor made him like dramatic entrances and exits. This pleasure in pageantry did not in any way detract from his skill or his integrity as a physician, and it endeared him to the common folks who liked a spectacle. He made a good entrance now, and the waiters and watchers who had begun to be a little apathetic towards the tragedy within the house, felt excitement and tension mounting in them once again.

"Doc Hawkins is here," they said in hushed voices. "The doctor's come."

Inside the house he heard the shrill, hysterical sobbing of a woman.

"She's been goin' on like that for hours. It don't do the boy no good, doctor," one of the neighbor women said.

Doc took Mrs. Stevens by the shoulders and shook her roughly.

"Stop it," he said. "For God's sake, stop it! You aren't the only woman in the world."

In the kitchen they had made a kind of makeshift bed of three chairs and laid the boy on it. He was probably about thirteen or fourteen years of age, with a pinched appearance of ill-nourishment and underdevelopment that was now painfully accentuated by the bluish pallor of his skin. He lay rigid and seemed unable to speak. Only the eyes moved sometimes, furtively, and as if they searched for something that had been mislaid. Doctor knew the boy as a shy, unstable child, and he was filled with pity for him now.

"Get me hot water," he said to the women crowding the room, "and some heavy cloths."

Mrs. Stevens had ceased to cry. She came now and stood at the boy's head wringing her hands.

"What are you going to do?" she whispered. "What are you going to do?"

"Bring him out of this," Doctor said briskly. "But first I am going to give you something to drink, and then you must go to bed."

"I fought with my husband," she said. "It was my fault. I've killed 'em both."

"Not both. The boy's just shocked. I think he'll be all right. Drink this, and get to bed now. You women, help her."

He sat by the boy's side holding the wrist between his fingers. It was a light, fluttering pulse that hovered uncertainly between this world and the next. A normal child would hardly have reacted so abnormally even to the horror of a family hanging, Doctor thought. There was an instant when it crossed Doctor's mind: *Why bring him back? Is it worth it to him or to anybody else?* The bare kitchen, the lonely house beaten upon by storm, a hysterical mother, a father who had hanged himself— There would be other crop failures, and the shame of trouble and defeat. Did the lad have stamina enough to stand up under it?

But Doctor was first of all an optimist and next a disciple of Hippocrates. *By God, the fellow may be President some day! Who knows?*

He began to strip off the boy's clothes and work the feeble circulation from the arms and legs towards the heart. The hot water and the heavy cloths came, and Doctor sweat and labored in the close room to bring a little warmth into the boy's cold body. At last it was as if the ice in the rigid limbs were dissolved, the tension slackened, the heavy head began to move restlessly to and fro, and the body shuddered into consciousness.

"It's all right now, Alf," Doc said soothingly. "Everything's going to be fine. You're going to be all right now. We're all here to look out for you."

Suddenly the boy began to sob, the terrible, hoarse sobs of adolescence.

Doctor rose and pulled down his shirt sleeves, taking his time with the moss agate cuff links.

"Keep him warm and quiet," he said. "Give him some warm milk when he'll take it, and don't talk to him. He'll sleep in a few minutes, I think, and I'll drive out to look at him tomorrow."

Half a dozen hands were ready to hold Doc's coat for him.

"Doc, it's a bad night you had to drive out here."

Doc began to laugh.

"That's not the worst of it. I haven't had my victuals."

"Stop by to our place, Doc. Selma will give you something hot."

"No, I thank you, Emil. Nobody makes such good bread and coffee as Selma, not even my wife; but I've got a new assistant coming tonight. Fellow from Paris and London. I got to go and take him down a peg or two."

They all laughed. The horror and the tension in the Stevens kitchen seemed to have gone.

4

ANNA STOOD ON THE station platform and waited for the train which had just been chalked up as half an hour late because of the snow. She did not go inside to wait, because she hated the hot, close smell of the small room with its hard benches and smoky stove; and, even heavy with snow, she loved the keen mountain air outside. She thought now that it had always been the mountains here which had made her happy. She had never wanted to go back to St. Louis or any of the other places. That was because the air was different and because there were mountains.

She stood composed and at ease while the snow and wind flurried about her. There was nothing in her plain, warm clothing that the storm could damage. She had no gift for ornate, feminine attire such as Doctor would have liked to see her wear, and tonight her simple dowdiness seemed eminently suitable to the weather and the station platform. A rich mind kept her company at lonely moments, and now she did not fret at the lateness of the train. In her thoughts she followed Doctor through the storm to the farmhouse on the road to the cemetery. She knew how it stood up stark and lonely in the empty fields and how the rushing snow would beat upon it tonight. The thought of suicide was distasteful to Anna, because she put great value on being alive. Loving this new, wild country and this high mountain air, she felt something in it which Doctor did not feel or would not admit. She felt the danger and the hidden threat, the lure to suicide, the quick, wild urge to hurt and kill. Sometimes in the first year of their life here, when she had ridden with Doctor in the hills, they had heard the scream of a cougar on a mountain road. The horse, neighing and frothing with fear, had bolted away through the darkness, and only Doctor's reassuring voice and firm hand on the reins had saved them from disaster. It was not the cougar nor the maddened horse that Anna feared, but something less tangible for which they stood. Doctor and other men with him were building civilization here, quickly and expertly, over the abyss; and on a night like this with blizzard and suicide in the air, she saw with quiet clarity how frail their building was. The men and women who came here were adventurers, the restless ones, the seekers after elusive bounties; and yet it was not only their recklessness and devil-may-care freedom which charged the atmosphere, but rather something untamed and nameless in the air itself. Call it altitude, thinness of air, what you would, it entered the lungs whenever one drew breath. She remembered once trying to put her feeling into words for Doctor.

"We don't half know this place, doctor," she had said. "All this building and planning, all the bustles and high hats and making social calls and going to church—that's not really Opportunity."

"Then what in tarnation is, Anna? We're building something here."

"Yes, you're building something, but it won't be finished for a long time. You've put a thin crust of civilization over the pie, but

crack the surface anywhere and it's still bear meat and venison underneath. It wouldn't take much to turn us all savage again, even the
men with high hats and the ladies with bustles."

"If that's a reflection on my new high hat—"

"Now, doctor," Anna had said, laughing. "It's not a reflection
on anyone. Just a sound remark."

But Doctor didn't feel those things. It was better not to, Anna
thought.

Standing here in the windy dark, she remembered the first time
she had seen this station, and even before that, the mountains. She had
not been one of the adventurous ones. She had come farther west
because Doctor wanted her to come, with no hope of anything
different.

It had been in the very early spring, and ledges of snow still lay
among the blue of the pines on northern slopes. The children had
been tired and fretful from the long journey on the hard plush seats
of the train. When they wiped their noses the handkerchiefs had
shown spots of black soot. The contents of the big lunch basket,
which had been so attractive on the first day, were almost exhausted
and had lost their charm. Doc had paced the aisles, torn between bad
temper at the tedium of the long trip with children, and the excitement and hope of a new venture. And then the high, sharp air of
upland places had suddenly set her blood atingle when one of the
long stops let it in to mingle with the stale air of the coach.

Looking out of the window, she had seen the blue of low mountains, and it had spoken to her. She had noticed with a catch of her
breath that the light was sharper here than it was in the South or
Middle West. Objects grew blue with distance, but they kept their
sharp, clear outlines. There was a fine, red light on the mountains at
sunset.

"Mama, will we stay here this time?" Mary had asked.

"I don't know. Perhaps." Her heart had felt a tug of hope.

The station at Opportunity had been an island in a morass of mud.
A drayman was backing and swearing at his horses. There was a

weather-beaten station hack, and a couple of leading citizens had come down to welcome Doc.

"This is Mr. Kessler of the Bon Ton Store, Anna, and Postmaster Peavy."

Anna had been polite, but she was used to letting Doctor do the talking. Her eyes had gone back to the hills, to the sharp dark outlines of blue pines against snow, to the red light that was still glowing from the sunset.

"Mama, do you think we'll like it here?"

"Yes, Mary. Look at the pretty color on the hills."

"Mama, I'm cold."

"Here, come under my shawl, Lita. We sat too near the stove in the train."

Sheltering the child under the warmth of her shawl, she could remember how she had drawn in great breaths of the thin, clear air, and she had known at once that there was a danger in the air here, some quality of tautness and high tension that she had not known elsewhere. Not fear but a detached clarity of vision had made Anna face the danger from the very start. Spring had not disturbed Anna for a good many years before she came to Idaho. But the moment she had stepped out of the train, she had felt the strangeness and the disturbing quality. Through the dirty windows of the hotel hack, as it strained through the muddy streets, Anna had looked at the one-story wooden buildings along the way. She had noticed with something of a shock how small and temporary was the town, how large and permanent the hills.

Doctor had found a little house for sale on the hill next to the new Presbyterian church. It was a considerable way back from Main Street with only a few scattered dwellings and a straggling muddy path between, but Doc had said: "Lord, the town will grow! In a couple of years this won't be far out at all." And he had been right, of course. Anna had been glad to settle down and unpack and wash out the children's clothes. Soon they were all at home there, and then the spring came on with a yellow rush of buttercups and lamb's-tongues and dandelions. Innocent as springtime anywhere, it had looked on the surface. Winter wheat was green in the fields and other fresh young green went running up to the place where the blue began on the hills. There were meadow larks on every fence post, western meadow larks which sang more joyously than any Anna had heard in the East. It was difficult not to be overwhelmed by the sense of newness and strangeness, by that quality of the air.

That spring the Indians had come and camped on the hill in front of the church and Doc Hawkins' house. It was the place they had always used for a camping ground on their way back to the river meadows for the summer and the camas harvest. Indians were still a menace in 1884. They had caused no trouble in Opportunity, but they were tricky and used to sell their ponies in the daytime and steal them back at night before they broke camp and moved on.

Anna fed them when they came around her kitchen. Some women were afraid of Indians, but Anna accepted things as they were. She had always accepted rather than knock her head against barriers. That is why it was odd that spring should ever again have made her restless. It was only the first spring in Opportunity that was unsettling, bringing back things she had almost forgotten, just as it was only that one spring that the Indians had come. On solitary days after that, when a Chinook wind suddenly melted winter into spring with a great roar and crashing of falling ice and water, the wild nostalgia of that first spring would sometimes seize her; but otherwise she fell into the routine, and no longer trembled at the thought that something she had longed for was just over the hill, or around the next corner. There was so much satisfaction to be had out of each day as it came, and it was foolish to tremble with expectancy for she knew not what. Only she never lost the feeling of threat and strangeness.

Doc had liked it here at once. He had left Missouri because there were too many people there and not enough room. It was not so much that he disliked people or small crowded places, as that he had caught the contagion of the day, Anna thought. He felt certain that just beyond were larger spaces, better soil, more golden opportunities. For the moment this northern bit of Idaho Territory satisfied him. Here there was rich soil and a moderate climate; there was the excitement of new enterprises beginning and of all kinds and conditions of people who wanted doctoring. And so they had remained, and now it was five years.

The wind whipped the snow against Anna's skirts, and she thought: "A Frenchman, a man who has known London and Paris! How will it seem to him? Will he understand it here? Or will he walk on the thin crust as the others do, without understanding? Or will he be lost and overwhelmed?"

Thinly through the blowing snow and darkness came the long, hoarse cry of the train.

There were not many passengers getting off the train tonight, and Anna picked out Dr. Duval at once, although he wore neither plug hat nor yellow gloves. He was not as she had expected him to be, for she had always heard that Frenchmen were short and quick and very voluble. She could not remember that she had ever met one before. Queer, too, she thought. There were Scandinavians and Italians and Poles in Opportunity. Europe was pouring a stream of immigrants into the new West—Bohemians, Chinese, Germans, a Russian or two, and a Greek; but the French didn't seem to come to new places as other foreigners did. She did not know why, but it made it all the more strange that this man with degrees from great European universities should be coming to Idaho Territory to be Doctor's assistant.

At a glance she saw that he was not as she had pictured a Frenchman, for he was tall and a little stooped, and he was slow and quiet in his movements.

Anna went towards him and held out her hand.

"I am Mrs. Hawkins," she said. "I am sorry that Doctor could not come for you. At the last moment there was a case in the country, and he asked me to come."

"Meeses Hawkins," he said. "It was very kind of you." There was just a tinge of accent in his voice, and a precise manner of speaking, as if he mentally translated and balanced each heavy English word an instant on his light Gallic tongue before he uttered it. Suddenly Anna heard the slovenly Western drawl and twang in the other voices on the station platform. She had not been conscious of it before, either in herself or in the others. She saw that there was also something in his eyes which was different from Opportunity, but she could not yet analyze the difference nor know whether it pleased or displeased her. He was as dark as Doc, but taller and thinner. She knew that he was somewhat younger than Doc, although gray had prematurely frosted his temples, and there were lines about his mouth and eyes. He did not wear a beard nor any of the complicated tonsorial effects which most men of the day achieved. His pressure on her hand was light and disinterested. It was the touch of a person who is unaccustomed to shaking hands with a woman, or who is generally averse to physical contact.

"I have the cutter here, if you will bring your valise," Anna said. "It is too bad that we didn't do something better in the way of weather for you, doctor."

"Weather does not distress me," he said.

"I hope your journey wasn't too uncomfortable?"

"No. It was no more so than I have expected." He was quiet again with the calm silence of one who retires into himself with no uneasy feeling of obligation to the general conversation.

So they walked to the end of the platform, and Anna untied the horse from the hitching rack. As she did so there was a sound of impatience from the train and the conductor's thin voice calling through the snow: "All aboard now. Al-l-l a-bo-o-ard!"

"If you don't mind," Anna said, "I'll stand by her head until the train's gone. Doctor likes his horses full of mettle."

"I do not mind."

He came and stood beside her at the horse's head, his hand resting lightly on the bridle. They were enveloped by the furious thunder of the departing train and the curtain of snow which shut them away from the familiar world. The horse flung up her head and trembled all over so that the sleigh bells shivered and chimed.

"Doctor wouldn't have waited," Anna said when the train had gone, "but I guess it's my nature to be cautious."

He offered her the back of his hand to assist her into the cutter, but Anna was unused to accepting common gallantries, and stepped in by herself, gathering the reins with one hand and offering half of the lap robe with the other. They rode in a silence of sleigh bells until they reached the main street of Opportunity, and then Anna said:

"This is the main street. You see the town's not very large, but you can't imagine what it was when we came here five years ago. Not a two-story building in town, and only a few straggling rows of houses beyond this street. I would show you the office Doctor built, but it's a couple of blocks out of our way, and this is no night to ride for pleasure."

"No? Still I have pleasure in this ride, Meeses Hawkins. There is a lightness in the air here, even in the snow."

Anna turned her head and looked at him curiously.

"You feel it?" she asked.

"Why, yes," he said. "I think that we are high here, are we not?"

"Only moderately so," Anna answered, "—three thousand feet or thereabouts; but we haven't yet civilized our air."

He laughed at that for the first time. When he laughed, his teeth showed white and even and his face looked younger.

"Doctor will have to help you find a buffalo coat," Anna said. "They are getting scarce now, but you need one in the winter here."

"You mean," he said slowly, "a coat of the hide of buffaloes?"

"Yes. That seems strange to you, doesn't it? Not that we see buffalo here any more, but there are still a few coats to be had. Doctor says a buffalo coat's better than an M.D. after your name to show the farmers and miners that you're a successful doctor."

"A successful doctor," he repeated. "Your husband is that, is he not?"

"Yes, of course," Anna said.

"And a buffalo coat, it is a badge of that success, eh?"

"That's what Doctor says."

"Then I will ask that he shall help me find one." His tone was light, and yet she felt a kind of gravity behind it.

She drove around the house to the side door, and gave the reins to the chore boy.

"Doctor hasn't come back yet?"

"No, ma'am."

"Dr. Duval, I hope you won't mind coming in the side door tonight? I think the parlor door is piled with snow. If you see the kitchen and dining room first, it will make you one of us sooner."

"Thank you, madame," he said.

The lamplight was warm and bright on the white tablecloth. There was a gratifying odor of cooked food. Red coals gleamed warmly through the isinglass panels on the door of the baseburner.

"Dr. Duval and I will eat now, Christina," Anna said. "And keep a plate hot for Doctor when he comes." She took off her hat and coat, and held out her hands for his. The melting snowflakes beaded her hair with many gleaming drops.

"I am afraid that you were obliged to wait for me a long time in the snow," he said apologetically.

She smiled a little bit as she said: "Weather does not distress me, either—nor waiting. I'm used to both."

5

ANNA AND DR. DUVAL still sat at the dinner table when Doctor came in. He took in quickly the peaceful domestic scene: the light-haired woman and the dark-haired man sitting beside the gleaming whiteness of a lamplit tablecloth; the warmth and comfort of the house; and the engaging smell of food. Duval sprang up when he saw him, and the two men shook hands, taking each other's measure in a first quick glance.

"Well, so you are here, eh?" Doctor said. "Sit down. Sit down and finish your coffee. I'll join you when I've washed my hands. *Christina*," he bellowed in the direction of the kitchen, "*food!*"

"Ya, doctor, ya." The little Swede girl came running with hot plates and steaming dishes.

"Doctor's a little short-tempered when he's hungry," Anna said pleasantly. It would do no good, of course, but she wished that some-one might explain them to each other before they got off on the wrong foot. She was anxious to see the two men get along together.

As if he had read her half-formulated thought, Duval said sud-denly in a quiet voice, "Madame, I shall make no trouble."

Anna was confused.

"Of course not," she said.

Doctor came back rubbing his hands, and he was not ill-tempered.

"By gad, I can use some food! Very inconsiderate of a man to hang himself on a night like this, eh, doctor? But you have to get used to things like that here. This is no nice society practice you're coming into, Duval. You know that, I hope? We're on the frontier here, and you'll find the life raw."

"I am not interested in a society practice," Duval said.

"Good!" Doctor cut himself a thick slice of roast beef and cov-ered his potatoes with gravy.

Two great tiger cats with leather collars on their necks had come in with him when he returned from washing his hands. They sat on either side of him now, looking at him with large, intense eyes. Doctor cut them each a piece of the beef which they caught in mid-air and then sank on their bellies to devour, growling as they did so and lashing their tails. There was something primitive in the sight, and Doctor looked at the Frenchman to see what he made of it.

"Nice cats, eh?" he said.

"Doctor spoils them," Anna said. "He won't let anybody feed them but himself. Their father was a bobcat."

"You mean—they are half wild?"

"That's what the fella told me who gave them to me," Doc said. "And they look it, don't they? Damned if I believed him at first!

It was a farmer out on the Ridge gave them to me when they were kittens. Anna didn't want them, said we could get plenty of nice tame kittens for the girls; but I said, 'Look here, Anna, any fool can raise up a couple of tame kittens, but you train these brutes up and you've got a curiosity.' "

"They are not dangerous?"

"Not a bit of it! They don't like handling the way an ordinary cat does, but they're good citizens. They're civilized. You know what I call 'em? Grover Cleveland and Thomas Hendricks. That's the way you do in this country. Take a thing that's half wild and give it a good civilized name, and half the battle's won. *Opportunity* now— that's a good name for a new town, isn't it? That's what I mean."

Doctor threw the cats more meat. He ate and talked, gesticulated and plied knife and fork with equal zeal and dexterity. "The thing I like about this country is, it's new. It's all on the make, and we're in on the ground floor. That appeals to you, doesn't it, doctor?"

"Yes, the newness, that appeals to me very much. To live in a new place, at the edge of civilization, that has seemed to me like to be born again perhaps."

"And the name of our town—Opportunity? No, don't tell me. I know. That appealed to you, too, didn't it?"

"Perhaps."

"*Opportunity* in the West. *Opportunity* in Idaho Territory. Yes, that's a good name for a new town. It packs the railroad train with ambitious men."

"Then I fear I am not of that company, doctor."

"You mean—"

"I am not ambitious."

"But you want to be born again?"

"Only that."

Doctor laughed. "I don't believe it, man; a fellow without ambition! But, assuming it's true, you'll be a curiosity in this country."

"A Frenchman is always a curiosity in a foreign country."

"Why is that?" Anna asked. "I wondered."

"The French stay at home, madame. They think that there is no place equal to France. The English now, they crawl like flies over the face of the earth, and yet they are always English wherever they go. But, no, the French, when they leave France, they become something else. Perhaps that is why they prefer to stay at home."

"That does not explain *you*, Dr. Duval," Anna said, smiling.

"No, madame, it does not."

He was silent again, and it was clear to them that he did not wish to explain himself. Yet his tone was so mild that one could not take offense.

"Well," Doctor said, "I need help here, and no mistake. I'm up to my ears in work. But, by the Lord Harry, it's work I love. I like having a finger in God's or Nature's pie, whichever way you want to put it; and this is the place for that. I can take a strong dose as well as give one, and Opportunity can spoon them out. You have to use your wits here, because you'll come across things that aren't in the medical journals."

"Now, doctor, aren't you bragging?" Anna said.

"No, I mean it. Take the time the plumber's wife had her gall-bladder attack. There wasn't anything I could do but give the old lady a sedative and tell her to quit eating cabbage and beans. But before she went to sleep she asked her old man to rub her stomach for her because she thought it helped the pain. Well, Lord! the old man was so pleased to do something for her that he kept right on rubbing her belly all the time she was asleep, and the next morning he was the first one in my office with the tears running down his cheeks because he'd rubbed the whole damned skin off her stomach with his horny hands. She was in a worse fix than she had been with her gallstones. If you can find a case like that in the Materia Medica— Well, it gave me a laugh."

"I hope you have a sense of humor, Dr. Duval," Anna said.

"I believe that I have."

"A robust one?"

"*Ah, ça!* Perhaps it will develop."

"And that Swede last winter," Doctor went on, helping himself to another slice of meat and a heaping spoonful of squash. "The ice got so thick on the saloon roof last winter that they were afraid the roof would fall in. So they gave Ole Arnesen an ax and tied a length of rope around his waist and sent him up on the roof to chop away the ice. Nobody thought to tell the damned fool to tie the rope to the chimney to keep himself from falling, so he just left it dangling while he chopped the ice away all around himself. There he stood on an island of ice on a sloping roof and no way to get down! He began to yell as the island began to slide. Right beneath the roof was a barrel of empty beer bottles. Well, it took me the best part of a day to get the glass out of that Swede, but, by George, it gave me a big laugh! And find a case like that in the records, if you can."

"Doctor will take a laugh instead of a fee, if there is any choice," Anna said.

"To laugh," Duval said gravely. "I think that it is of more value than much money."

"Now, don't get me wrong," protested Doc. "I like my laugh, but, by George, my mind is serious, too! I'm a builder, Duval, and that's why I came West where everything has to be done. Take this house, for instance. Comfortable, isn't it? Substantial? Well furnished?"

"It is a charming house to find upon the frontier, Dr. Hawkins."

"Thank you," said Doc. "But when we came here five years ago it was a two-room shack with a path leading up to it from a muddy two-wheel track road. I've added on the dining room, the parlor, the extra bedrooms, and a Gothic tower on the corner. It's as good as anything you'll find in the Middle West. And the lot? It goes clear through to the next block. When we came here it was just a bare hilltop, but I've laid it out on the lines of a little farm. I've got a barn any farmer would be proud of, and a horse lot, and chickens and turkey runs. Maybe I'll put in some rabbit hutches next year. And I've got an orchard planted now. I sent back East for my trees and I've got four different kinds of cherries, three different apples, a pear, a quince, a prune, and several varieties of plum, not to mention the berry bushes. Anna has some canning to do now in the fall and summer. From St. Louis I ordered me a honey locust tree and set it by the side of the house where the smell of the blossoms comes into the bedroom windows in late May or early June; and up and down the street in front of the house I've set out Lombardy poplars. I put a lilac bush in the center of the lawn on either side of the front walk, and the first year I was here, when I rode in the hills and saw a native syringa or spiraea that I liked, I dug it up and brought it home for Anna's garden. By God! I was never bored on my long rides, because I had this planting and building to think of when I wasn't worrying about a case.

"Anna thinks I'm bragging, doctor, but I'm not. I'm telling you all this, because it's the same kind of thing I'm trying to do for the town. I built the first doctor's office in town, and I've had a hand in putting up a town hall and an opera house. We're going to get the main street paved next year, and some of these days we're going to get an Academy for Higher Learning started in the dance hall over the Dry Goods Store. We're building, Dr. Duval, we're building."

"And for what are you building?" Duval asked in a mild voice.

Doctor was brought up short in the midst of his discourse. He looked at Duval in hurt surprise.

"Why, for the future," he said, "for the boys and girls who are growing up, for the men and women of tomorrow!" Then he added with a ring of surprised sincerity, "God, for the fun of building!"

"There!" said Duval. "That is a reason I can understand. For the future? What is that? Those men and women, they will want to build for themselves. But, if you have fun, that is another matter."

Doctor was uncertain for a moment, and then he began to laugh. He threw back his head and laughed loudly.

"Look here!" he said. "You take the wind out of my sails like that a couple of times, and you'll lose your job, eh? Aren't you afraid of that?"

"No, I do not think so," replied Duval. "I am an idealist as much as you are, but a less practical one. I think that I have never built anything in my life, but I shall not stand in your way. I have admiration for the idealist who also puts his visions into brick and mortar."

Doctor was surprised and a little puzzled, but he was not displeased.

Anna looked up and for an instant her eyes met Duval's. Seeing that he had already taken Doctor's measure accurately, her eyes slid quickly away. To meet Duval's eyes now was somehow like a breach of confidence. She rose quickly and went to the sideboard to get the decanter of claret which she set with a couple of small glasses at Doctor's elbow.

"Duval," Doctor said, "I'm what you might call a complete teetotaler. There are only two occasions when I allow myself intoxicating liquors. When I'm going on a fishing trip I like to take along a bottle of whisky for snakebite, as they say; and when I've had a long drive in the snow a little claret warms the lining of my stomach before I go to bed."

"I see," Duval said.

"Yes, I'm a complete teetotaler." He poured himself a small glass of claret, and set one before Duval. "And this is the exception that proves the rule."

"You are then a moralist?" Duval asked.

He was suddenly embarrassed and a little uncertain, Anna could see. She thought that he was not sure of his use of the word "moralist"; and "teetotaler" was probably not in his vocabulary.

"No," Doctor said, laughing, "you can take all your moral reasons and go hang, but the thing that is damned repulsive to me is to have my brain addled and my hand palsied for the uncertain pleasure of a warm stomach."

"I see," Duval said again.

"I decided a long while ago that a doctor has no business with liquor. Fellow named Schilling set himself up here as a doctor when this town was first started. He could have had everything his own way—the world by the heels with a downhill pull, as they say, but the damn fool drank his head off and left the whole field open for me. No, a doctor has no business with liquor."

"It is true," Duval said.

"But you're a Frenchman, and all Frenchmen like their liquor, they say; so drink what you like, doctor, but in moderation, in moderation."

Duval had pushed the glass at arm's length before him, his long fingers delicately curved about the stem. He was looking at it, and at the spot of ruby-colored light projected through the claret onto the tablecloth. He said in a quiet voice: "I, too, am what you call that thing—teetotalaire. I think I shall not taste your claret with you, doctor."

Anna looked at the two men curiously. In build and pigmentation they were singularly alike, but their differences were accentuated in the two hands which touched the claret glasses. Doctor's hand was square and ugly with short, blunt fingers and black, curling hair on the back; the Frenchman's hand was long and thin, beautifully modeled as a woman's and yet with a sense of latent power that a woman's hand rarely possesses.

"You're not afraid of the stuff?" Doctor asked. With his eyes still on the tablecloth Duval shook his head.

"Why should I be?"

A moment ago it had been Duval who was master of the situation; now, for some reason which she did not quite understand, it was Doctor who had the upper hand.

"Let's go and sit by the fire," Anna said. "Christina can clear the table then."

They went into the high-ceilinged parlor and sat in rocking chairs around the stove, which crackled and popped with freshly burning pine wood. Doc held out a cigar to the new assistant, but Duval shook his head and took a small pipe out of his pocket, which he carefully filled and lighted. After dinner Doctor's conversational powers were always a trifle slowed by his digestive processes. He lapsed into silence now, smoking and watching with half-closed eyes the dancing of the flames behind the isinglass of the stove door. Dr. Duval turned to Anna and said in a quiet voice:

"I wish that you will tell me a little about the mountains. Tonight I cannot see them for the darkness and the snow, but I have heard that they are beautiful."

"Oh, yes!" said Anna. "They are not very high here, but I like them best that way. It is so nice the way the wheat fields run right to the foot of them, all yellow, and then the pines begin, first green and then turning to blue as they go farther up. You will see, when the snow has stopped falling, how white they can be and how blue; and at sunset there is a light here and that I have never seen in any other place." She stopped speaking, and flushed a little, surprised that she had said so much.

"Can one go up in them to walk and climb?"

"Yes, I believe so, but people here don't often do it. Doctor used to ride there to see patients, and sometimes I went with him. But there are fewer homesteaders on the mountains than there were. The mining in these hills never amounted to much, and the people there have come down to the valley. I think that folks don't notice the mountains here any more."

"Terrible roads," said Doctor, puffing on his cigar. "But that's going to be changed now. We'll have a good wagon road to the top of Opportunity Mountain some day."

"That would be a pity," said Dr. Duval.

Anna laughed. "Do you like to climb, Dr. Duval?"

"I have done a little in the French Alps," he said, "but I am not a climber, no. I am maybe what you call only a stroller. I go to see, not to scale impossible heights."

"I know," said Anna. "It's more comfortable that way, isn't it?"

"But my little boy," said Dr. Duval, "he is one who will climb rather than stroll, I hope. It is only that he is more English than French, you see. The English are very determined climbers."

"You have a boy?" Doctor said. He took his cigar out of his mouth and opened his eyes wide. "Nobody told us."

"He is very young," Duval said, "only a little infant."

"How old?" Doctor was interested.

"He has about two years. He is with my unmarried sisters in my father's house in France."

"My God!" Doctor said. "You have a son, and you do not have him with you?"

"How could I?"

"No, maybe not. But when he's older, you want to send for him. This is a country for a boy to grow up in, Duval. A country for a boy. And I've got a couple of girls, doctor, a couple of scatterbrained females running up and down and giggling and simpering in their ribbons and laces. Good gals, yes. You won't find any better. I've sent them to San Francisco to the finest boarding school they've got out there, but, by thunder, when you finish educating them, what have you got? A couple of damn-fool females to find husbands for, and that's the end of it."

Anna sat quietly with bowed head, looking at her hands relaxed in her lap. She had not heard Doctor talk this way for a long time. She had almost forgotten how he felt. Would he bring himself to speak of the two little boys who had died?

"You have two daughters," Duval said. "Have you never had a son?"

"Yes, I've had two," Doctor said, his voice pitched to a lower key. "They both died of diphtheria when they were about two and a half years old. There were five years between them. And, by God, between the first one's death and the last I couldn't learn how to lick diphtheria! I don't know how yet, doctor. Lord help us in our ignorance!"

"What we do not know," Duval said, "it is so much vaster than the little knowledge we have."

Anna raised her eyes and looked at them, and for the first time she saw complete agreement in their faces.

Doctor cleared his throat and got up noisily.

"Well, tomorrow's another day," he said, "and I'm dead on my feet. Of course, you'll stay at the house a few days, Duval, until you know where you want to settle. We'll go down to the office first thing in the morning, and I'll show you the ropes. Anna, have Christina put a hot brick in the foot of Duval's bed. It's a damned cold night to sleep alone."

Anna showed Dr. Duval to the spare bedroom under the Gothic tower. On the bureau she had put a little silver filigree box which had belonged to her mother. The Frenchman took it up in his long fingers and looked at it, and, although he did not speak of it, she saw that he was pleased.

When she was alone with her husband, Anna said:

"Doctor, do you realize that you did all of the talking tonight? The new man knows all about you, and you know hardly anything about him."

"That's so," Doc said. He looked thoughtful for a moment; then his face cleared. "But, by Gad, I had a good time tonight! I believe I'll get along all right with that fellow!"

6

Dr. Duval fell into the routine of the practice with quiet ease. For the first few weeks Doc Hawkins took pleasure in showing him off to the town.

"Want you to meet Dr. Duval, my new assistant, folks. By thunder! He's something you haven't seen before—a specialist, that's what he is. Eye, ear, nose, and throat specialist, they call him."

"Can't he get below the neck, doc?"

"He sure can. He can saw off a frozen leg or bring you a baby as well as I can, but he's a specialist along those other lines."

"Specialist, huh? God Almighty! What finikin notions won't doctors get next! Well, glad to meet you, Dr. Duval. I'll remember you next time I get a earache."

It was true that Dr. Duval was not an ambitious man—Anna saw that at once. He had all of these degrees and handles after his name, but they didn't seem to mean much to him. An ambitious man wouldn't have gotten along so well with Doctor. As it was the two men shared the office with perfect amicability.

All eye, ear, nose, or throat cases, Doc turned over to Duval automatically; for the rest Duval was assistant and consultant. It was natural that way, because the people had confidence in Doc Hawkins, and Duval's accent frightened patients away or made them laugh. But if Doc said, "Here, you need Duval to handle this," then it was all right, and they trusted Duval to do it.

Yes, Doc and Duval got on together. They were friends. But they were so different that in many things their lives touched only externally.

Doc was what they called in town a "hail fellow, well met," and it followed, as the night the day, that he was a joiner. With his wild black eyes and his muttonchop whiskers, he looked mighty fine in his Mason's and Shriner's regalia. They had him for high potentate twice, and he saw to it that the brothers paid their dues and that the needy had Christmas baskets. Doc was careless about his own collections for professional services, but, put him in an executive position in a lodge, and all dues would be paid. When the Odd Fellows came to town, Doc joined them, too.

He tried to get Anna to go to the women's auxiliaries. She went twice, and then she rebelled.

"Listen, doctor," she said, "those women, with pasteboard crowns on their heads and sashes tied across their fat bosoms, they *drill* with *broomsticks!* They're old enough to have more sense. You join all the secret societies you want to, but I'll stay at home, thank you, doctor." There was no use arguing with Anna. And Anna soon saw that, like herself, Duval was not a joiner. The Odd Fellows, the Masons, the various churches and civic organizations knocked on his door in vain. He was polite but indifferent. When he had free time one saw him walking off across the fields toward the hills—a long rangy figure with an odd springing step, his shoulders a little stooped, his long hands swinging. He had not the brisk air of the purposeful walker with a destination in mind. He bought himself a buffalo coat, but he did not wear it with Doctor's authoritative swagger.

"Funny fellow," Doc said to Anna. "I don't understand him, but he's a good doctor. He knows more medicine than I do, that's sure; but what he don't know is how to get into folks' minds the way you have to if you're going to cure them."

After the first few days under Doctor's roof, Duval moved his bag and his small leather trunk to a couple of rooms over Skogmo's Drugstore. The rooms had been intended for offices, but the Frenchman proposed to turn them into an apartment. Doctor was sincerely shocked.

"My God! You aren't going to do your own cooking?"

"Yes, of course. Why not?"

"You can get decent board at the hotel, but a man doing his own cooking— The town will think you are crazy."

"In France the preparation of food, it is something which men do not despise. It is like an art," said Duval patiently.

Doctor laughed.

"Well, I like to eat," he said, "but, by the Lord Harry! I'd starve to death if I had to stew up my own concoctions."

Anna said: "Let me clean your rooms for you and help you furnish them. I think I can find you a woman to come in once or twice a week and set them in order."

"That would be very kind of you," he said.

So Anna helped to install him. She went with him to Hank Briggs' furniture store (with the undertaking business in the back), and helped him to select a bed, a table and some chairs, a bookcase and a couch and a couple of coal-oil lamps. In the trunk it seemed that he had brought his lares and penates with him. There were the little copper saucepans and casseroles in which he liked to prepare his simple meals. They were better suited to the preparation of good food than the heavy American skillets or the light tin pans, he said, and Anna saw that he was right.

He had a few medical books and a number of French novels in

yellow paper covers to put into the bookcase, and he had brought a few good engravings with him from France. He hung the large one of Notre Dame Cathedral over the bookcase, and on top of the bookcase he placed a little clay replica of one of the Tanagra figurines.

"She is dancing, isn't she?" Anna said.

"I think so. How did you know?"

"There is something about the draperies."

"It is like motion which has been frozen, is it not? Arrested motion, that is a restful thing to look at, I find."

Beside the figurine he put another curious thing. It was a woman's workbox, complete with spools of colored silk and a small silver thimble. He seemed to feel Anna's unspoken question.

"It is the workbox of my wife."

"She has not been gone long?"

"She died in childbirth."

"But she gave you a son," Anna said.

"That is small compensation," he said.

Suddenly Anna saw that she had stayed too long. She should not have watched him setting out his pathetic household gods.

"I must go now," she said. "I hope you're going to be comfortable. Christina's mother will come in twice a week and clean for you."

"Thank you, Meeses Hawkins."

So Constant Duval took up his residence in Opportunity in his own particular way, living what seemed a lonely life with little human contact outside his professional work with Doc Hawkins.

Twice a week Christina's mother came in while he was away and cleaned his rooms, and he did not need to see her. He left an envelope with her weekly pay in it for her on the second day she came, and he knew by the smell of soap and perspiration when he returned at night that she had done her work. Sniffing distastefully, he opened the windows to the mountain air, and in two minutes he was alone again in his own place.

One of the reasons he had selected the rooms over the drugstore was that he could see the mountains from his bedroom window. It was astonishing to him that the people of the town seemed to build their houses with the idea of shutting out the mountains. In a valley of such spectacular beauty, they turned their backs on the infinite variety of the hills and huddled together with their windows opening upon alleys and back yards, hedges and public buildings. Only a little planning and appreciation would have given them windows of changing beauty that no artist's canvas could have surpassed. Yet they seemed to prefer Pharaoh's Horses or enlarged photographs of deceased relatives. Was it fear, perhaps? A fear of something vast and strange which laid a blight of mystery and significance upon everyday living?

The one thing which Duval did not like about his living quarters was the dusty stairway that led up from the street at the side of the drugstore—"like purgatory before heaven," he said to Mrs. Hawkins, laughing. From the brightness of the street one plunged into almost total darkness, draughty and cold in winter and stifling in summer, and the steep, uncarpeted stairs, creaking and echoing underfoot, took one's breath before he reached the hall above. There was always the smell of the drugstore, too, to remind him that he was a doctor and on call night or day.

7

ANNA WAS BAKING BREAD on the day before Christmas. Her fruit-cakes and plum puddings and mincemeat, made according to old receipts which had come from England two generations before, had been ready for a week. But bread was a thing which could not be laid by weeks in advance. It was an everyday affair which continued like life itself. Anna enjoyed making bread, and she was proud of her loaves as she turned them out of the pans to cool. She scooped some butter from the crock with a bit of brown paper and rubbed the delicately browned crusts with it until they were golden and

shiny. Both she and Christina had been busy all day, because the girls
were coming home tonight for a week, and there was so much confusion when they were at home that it was better to have everything
done and time left for visiting.

She took the girls' homecoming calmly, just as she took everything else. It was Doctor who always got himself into a lather of
excitement over the arrival of their train, and then quarreled with
them the next day so that they were both in tears, declaring that they
wished they had never come home. Doctor's girls were wonderfully
like himself, with big dark eyes and flighty tempers. He went from
the one extreme of spoiling them by gratifying their whims to the
other of intermittently curtailing their allowances and damning them
out as useless females. Anna tried to stand between the three of them
and keep the peace, but on these short vacations the fur was sure to
fly. She knew that Doctor loved them, but that his disappointment in
the loss of his sons made him more bitterly exacting with them than
he would have been with any other girls in town. Still he was a good
father, and some heroic quality in him drew children to him.

Anna was thinking of this when a knock came on the side door,
and so she was not surprised upon opening it to see a small girl with
a parcel under her arm.

"Is Dr. Hawkins in?"

"Why, no," Anna said. "You might find him at his office, though."

"I went there first, and there was another doctor there. I was surprised. Is there a new doctor?"

"Yes," Anna said, "there is a new doctor."

"What's his name?"

"Constant Duval." It was the first time Anna had said the whole
name to anyone. She tried to say it in the French way as Duval himself did, and it seemed strange to her—like a plum in her mouth
instead of a cherry.

"He said to come here," the little girl said. "I guess maybe Doc
Hawkins is out in his sleigh."

Anna brought her attention back to the child with the parcel.

"You're the Methodist minister's little girl, aren't you? Is somebody sick at home?"

"No, we're real well," Jenny said. She stood uncertainly, poised like a bird about to take flight. *Like motion which has been frozen,* Anna thought. It was odd how she kept hearing his voice repeating things he had said. It was because it was so different from the Western drawl to which she was accustomed.

"Come in, won't you? Maybe you could tell *me* what you wanted," Anna said.

Jenny took another instant to decide which way to fly; then she came quickly in and shut the door behind her. Her rubbers made a wet spot on the kitchen floor. She took off her mittens and pushed back her cap so that her light hair fell forward about her face. She began very quickly to unwrap the paper parcel.

"I brought him a Christmas gift," she said a little breathlessly. "I made them myself. I made some for my father, too. They are not very good."

She held out a pair of carpet slippers, one in each hand. Anna could see that they were made with more enthusiasm than skill, but she was sincerely touched.

"You made them for Doctor?"

"Yes. Mother said I could."

"Well, he will certainly be pleased."

"I don't know about that," Jenny said. "He probably has better ones, but it was all I could think of."

Anna cast about quickly in her mind for a present to give in return.

"Wait a minute," she said. "Doctor would like you to have one of our fruit cakes to take home with you, Jenny."

Jenny was tempted, but she shook her head.

"I didn't bring a gift to get a gift," she said.

The last thing her mother had said to her as she went out of the door was: "Don't let them give you anything in return, Jenny.

I wouldn't want you to take him a gift with that in mind." And Jenny had been hurt and angry all the way, because this was different from making a bookmark or a pincushion for Grandma Waters or someone in the congregation. She had her own pride, too, and she had made the carpet slippers for old Doc Hawkins because she loved him, and not because she wanted anything more from him in return. It was to pay him back for all the good things he had done for her and Della, and if she accepted more from him, then the virtue of the gift was lost.

"I didn't mean it that way," Anna said. "I'd really like to give you something, you know. Perhaps a nice, warm loaf of bread?"

Jenny shook her head, but she did not move to go at once. It was pleasant to see Mrs. Hawkins admiring the slippers over which she had labored.

"Do you think they will fit him?"

"Yes, I think so. He will be very pleased."

Jenny looked at the floor. She said slowly, "I wouldn't want you to give me anything, but there's something maybe I could borrow."

"Why, yes," Anna said. "I wonder what?"

"Do you have any storybooks, maybe?" Jenny asked. Her eyes were suddenly eager. They were blue eyes with pupils which grew large and black when she was excited.

"Come into the parlor, and we'll see what's there. I think there are some old *Chatterboxes* and Christmas annuals."

"Oh!" Jenny said. "That's what I'd like."

In the parlor there were three big bookcases full of books. Anna scarcely knew what they were, for Doctor was an easy mark for every book agent who came to town, and when he found time he liked to read. That he found little time did not deter him from buying, for he had a great respect for books (the more respect, perhaps, the less he read). Many of his books had stood there for years with uncut leaves, but the children's annuals which he had bought for his girls were well thumbed. They filled a bottom shelf. Anna herself had never thought much about books. She read the newspaper carefully, because it presented for her the contemporary scene, and she had always lived in the present rather than the past or the future. She dealt with realities, and the world of fancy was a little out of her line. But the Methodist minister's girl fell on her knees by the shelf of children's books like a devotee before a shrine.

"We have lots of books at home," she said. "More than this, but they're mostly commentaries and concordances. What Della and I like are storybooks. We like the kind that make you laugh and the kind that make you cry—even the ones that turn out badly."

"You may have some of the old *Chatterboxes* to keep if you like," Anna offered. "The girls don't read them any more."

But Jenny could be strong when she made up her mind.

"No, thank you, Mrs. Hawkins. I'll take good care of them and bring them back," she said. She selected two and held them hard against her breast as she went out.

"Well, Merry Christmas!" she said, smiling a broad, rapt smile.

"Merry Christmas, Jenny, and thank you for Doctor's present."

When Doctor came in Anna showed him the carpet slippers.

"From an admirer," she said, smiling. "Little Jenny Walden."

"My Lord!" Doc said. "That kid made them for me herself?"

"That's right."

"What did you give her?"

"She wouldn't have anything."

"By George, I've got to go back to town and buy out the candy store."

"No, doctor, I wouldn't," Anna said. "She was very definite. She said she wasn't bringing a gift to get a gift."

"That kid beats all," Doc said. "A couple of weeks ago she was walking to San Francisco."

"Do something for her later. I think you'll hurt her pride now. What she wants is your gratitude."

"Well," Doc said, "what do you bet that's more than my own daughters do for me?"

Anna would have liked to bolster his faith in his girls' filial generosity, but she had seen them come home too many times with their allowances overspent and pockets empty. It would be enough to have them at home without presents.

"By the way," Doctor said, "Duval won't come to dinner tomorrow. I pretty near forgot to tell you."

"Why not?" Anna said.

"Good God! I'm his boss all week. You don't think I'm going to ask an accounting for his holidays, too?"

"No, of course not," Anna said slowly. "Only I thought—if he's cooking and eating alone in those rooms over the drugstore—it won't be very merry."

"He's not a merry fellow."

"No," Anna agreed. "No, he isn't."

It was odd, but suddenly all the baking and cooking she had done, all of the holiday preparations she had made seemed unnecessarily elaborate for Doctor and herself and the girls.

8

EARLY ON CHRISTMAS MORNING Dr. Duval set out for the mountains. It was cold but clear, and he could see a long way in the sparkling air. He was warmly dressed in such clothing as a European mountaineer might wear, and he had packed crackers and cheese in the knapsack on his back. Yet he did not look so much like a man upon a holiday excursion as like a man who is being pursued and must flee at all costs before he is overtaken. Some attitude of mind probably was reflected in the nervous, irregular stride, and the head which turned now this way, now that, as if to escape some inner struggle rather than to observe what passed around him.

He followed a clearly marked road out of town, which after a mile or two, he saw, led up to a cemetery on a hill. Beyond the cemetery hill were other higher hills, and beyond them the blue of a mountain. It was on the mountain that he had fixed his intention.

One last house at the turn of the road stood between him and the solitary fields and ascending hills. He would scarcely have noticed it except that its loneliness suited the present temper of his mind. He glanced at it as he passed and saw a half-grown boy standing just inside the fence watching him with an expression of intense curiosity. But when their eyes met a sudden change came over the watching face of the boy, as if a sponge had been wiped across a lettered slate or a curtain drawn upon a lighted room. The eyes grew blank and slid craftily away. The face grew dull and unresponsive.

Duval was shaken momentarily out of his own preoccupation.

"Merry Christmas to you," he said.

The boy did not reply, but suddenly turned and ran into the barn with the swift, darting movement of a frightened animal.

The Frenchman skirted the cemetery hill, and continued across open fields, to more hills. On the other side of every hill there was always a little valley to descend into and another hill beyond; but each hill mounted a trifle higher, and as he looked back he could see farther away and in different perspective. He began walking more purposefully now, and as if some inner tension had relaxed its hold upon his muscles. By noon he was high upon the mountain, where he could look over a great checkerboard of snowy fields to the dark patch of huddled buildings which was Opportunity, and beyond that to other hills and mountains. Sitting alone, he ate the food that he had brought. There was no sound at all except the wind in the icy branches of the pines. The pines were green, not blue as they had seemed from Opportunity.

When the cold became too strong for him, he started down again, following his own footsteps in the snow. There had been enough thawing and freezing since the big storm to make a firm surface to walk upon, and it was only occasionally that his foot chanced upon a flaw or rotten spot. The sun, which had shone fitfully all day, lowered as he himself went down, and, when he had reached the valley, he could look back and see the mountains turning to red and purple where they had been white and blue. He looked at them for a long time, and the peace that beauty often brought him laid hold of his heart. But there was the sadness, too. He walked back slowly, turning again and again to see the mountains as the light changed and deepened them.

"Always there is variety," he thought, "where one lives with mountains or the sea." He could think in generalities now that he had grown physically tired.

As he came into town he saw children sliding on one of the long hills. There were a great many children, and some climbed up drawing their sleds behind them while others slid down. Their voices rang out in the thin high air. It was always so in high places, he thought. Bells in the Alps rang clear and far in the silences of upland valleys —convent bells, the great bells of Alpine cattle.

Something familiar in the coasting picture made him stop to wonder. The snowy scene, the animation of moving figures, the cold clear light that illuminated everything, the red mittens and mufflers, the multiplicity of interest with no particular focal center. Surely he had seen a primitive Dutch painting of this scene hanging in some European gallery, a Pieter Breughel, perhaps.

"I have seen it all before," he thought, "all before. Nothing is new any more." It was the old thought which he so often had had.

When he reached the main street he was tired but tranquil, and whatever devils had plagued him at the beginning of the day seemed to have been laid low. He went up the stairway slowly, and his footsteps on the creaking wooden treads sounded hollow and lonely. The drugstore below was locked and deserted on the holiday, and only the stale smell of cheap perfume and drugs lingered in the dark well of the stairway to remind him of every day; but at the head of the stairs, heaped against his door, were a number of packages. Someone had been here from Dr. Hawkins' house and had left him fruit cake and pudding and a loaf of bread. He unlocked the door and went in. The rooms were cold, but soon he had a fire. He found that he was very hungry. He melted butter in his copper pan and made himself an omelet, and then he sliced Mrs. Hawkins' bread, and sat to eat. Physically and spiritually he was tired, and he knew that tonight he would sleep.

9

THE HARDEST THING for Doc to get used to, as the new year wore on, was having another man in his office. He was glad to share the practice, which was more than he could handle alone, and he much preferred dividing it with a partner to seeing it taken over by a competitor. Competition was a thing that tried his temper.

"By God, I don't want a rival doctor in this town! I'd rather have a half a dozen assistants underfoot."

But the office had always been his own place, where he could retreat when the girls were making a hubbub at home, or when he had worries or problems to work out alone. Winter or summer, at a regular hour he drove down the Presbyterian hill to Ash Street, along Ash to Washington, across Washington to Elm, and drew up at the hitching post in front of the office, where the horse would stand until he was ready to use her again. Folks who wanted to consult the doctor in his office could tell several blocks away whether or not he was in by whether or not the horse was standing outside.

On Sunday mornings Doc came down a little later, but before the Sunday crowd started passing his house to church. There wasn't much business at the office on a Sunday, but Doc liked to sit in the office. It was his own place that he had built to suit himself. He used to sit there, quiet, by himself, in summer looking out at the back of the Bon Ton Store across the dusty street; and in winter, with a good fire roaring in the baseburner, and his feet on the fender, watching the snowflakes whirl outside. Few people ever saw Doc silent like this, smoking a cigar or picking his teeth with a quill toothpick and thinking. If anyone came around, he began fussing with his drugs and instruments, or made an elaborate pretense that he had been reading a medical journal. Only the office shared his rare silences.

In his first year at Opportunity his office had been in a corner of his residence. He wasn't in it much of the time anyway, what with all the patients he had in outlying places; and Anna never let the little girls touch his things. Just the same, they were a nuisance around a doctor's office. Like the time he took that fishing trip with Peavy, the postmaster, and Larkin, the lawyer. He'd told Anna what to say to the patients who came to the house, and Anna could always say a thing convincingly.

"I'm sorry, but Doctor was called away for a few days on urgent business."

"Yes," one of the little girls had said, peeping around her mother's skirts, "an' he took a bottle of whisky along in case of snakebite, didn't he, mama?" That was the kind of thing he was up against with an office in the house. So when he had a chance to buy a little bit of land just off Main Street beside the new brick bank, he took it. They had opened up a brick yard down beyond the creek that year and were turning out pretty good bricks. At night you could see the fires glowing, warm and red in the darkness, when they were firing a batch of brick. Anna liked to walk by there sometimes at night and see them. She was funny that way. Things you'd never expect a woman to care about, she seemed to take a fancy to, and she didn't seem to care about clothes, the way he'd like to have her do now that he could afford to buy them for her. There was a good dressmaker in town, and the Bon Ton Store stocked materials as nice as you'd find in St. Louis; but Anna didn't care.

The office Doc put up was one story high and about a room and a half big, and it was all built of brick with a good-sized window and door in front, and a little side door on the alley. Doc had had a regular operating table shipped in from the East with a lot of nickel plate on it and all the latest gadgets. He even had a sink built in with running water, because he looked to the future and he figured that this office would be doing business for a long time in a growing town. He had shelves for his bottles and a bookcase for his books and medical journals, and a desk with a top that rolled up and down. There

was a big baseburner to keep out the winter chill, and from the ceiling hung a fancy coal-oil lamp that could be raised or lowered by
means of chains. He could even operate here at night if it was
necessary.

Buchanan, the house painter, had made him a shiny new black and
white sign to hang out:

Willard J. Hawkins, M.D.

Doc Hawkins had been like a hen with new chickens during the
time that the office was going up. He had rushed around, scolding
and admonishing, having this torn down and that done over. He
made a lot more fuss about the color of the wallpaper and the size
of the oilcloth pieces for the floor than he would over an amputation
or a case of smallpox, Anna said. He bought three kinds of curtain
material for the front window before he was satisfied. First, he
wanted the curtains ruffled; but then, when they were half finished,
he decided that they were not sufficiently businesslike, so that Anna
had been obliged to use them up in the bedroom at home, and start
all over on plain ones for the office.

He had been jubilant, but at the same time his nerves had been
pretty well frayed, by the time the operating table was unpacked and
assembled and the furniture in place.

Anna had come down with the finished curtains to see that they
were properly hung. They needed to be shortened a little, and she
sat quietly sewing with her head bent over the work. She had a peaceful face, the eyes set rather wide apart and the mouth straight and
calm under that abundance of chestnut-colored hair which she piled
on her head with neatness rather than art. Her clothes were undis-
tinguished by the bustles and drapings, the ruffles and cascades and
pleats that marked the woman of fashion. From her appearance she
might have been a schoolmarm or a farmer's wife rather than the
doctor's wife.

This lack of dressiness in Anna had often irritated Doc. The wives of the important men of Opportunity, all except Anna, had an eye to fashion. Doc knew, because he saw them on the street and at lodge nights and receptions, and, God knows, he saw more of their beribboned underdrawers and ruffled nightgowns than most men of town did! But Anna put the ruffles and frills on the little girls and went on looking dowdy herself.

It was the same way with the office. He had gone over the details of it with her a hundred times, bursting with enthusiasm, explaining this and that, and all she said was: "Yes, doctor. It certainly is nice."

"Yes, doctor"—she'd said it over and over in the same quiet tone, and sometimes, even, she might have been smiling at him inside. But of that he could never be quite sure.

That first day in the office, he'd spoken about something else which he had on his mind.

"Anna, now that I've got this nice place fixed up, I'd like you to go around calling on the women more. You know what I mean, sort of sociable, and maybe some dinner parties when we rebuild the house the way we will soon."

"Why, yes, doctor," Anna had said, looking up a little surprised. "I could do that. I don't like calling, though. It takes so much time for nothing, and I've got my churning to do and my bread to set; and you know the time I left the girls alone and Lita ran the sewing machine needle through her finger."

"I know," said Doc, impatiently; "but I'm going to get you a little Swede girl, so you'll have more time to go out. You know what they say about you in this town? Because you don't go around with the other women, they say you're proud."

"Proud?" Anna's eyes had filled with wonder. Her quick fingers had been quiet on the hem of the curtain. "No, doctor, I'm not proud. I don't care enough to be proud."

"There it is!" he had cried. "You don't care enough. You're cold. You're so cold, ice wouldn't melt in your mouth. I hate cold women, and, by the Lord Harry! I was fool enough to marry one."

Anna's eyes had become grave. He could see the look in them yet when he remembered.

"No, doctor," she had said, "I'm not cold, either. But I can't make myself get excited. I'm just not made that way."

They had looked at each other across the narrow breadth of the new office, and for the first time, perhaps, they saw how far apart they were in intangible things. Usually they stepped very carefully over this abyss, pretending that it was not there.

After that Anna had gone calling sometimes, in white kid gloves like Mrs. Kessler and Mrs. Peavy and Mrs. Larkin. She had her hired girl and she gave dinner parties. But somehow she always did it as if she thought that it was unimportant, as if she were laughing inside at a joke he didn't see. That made Doctor mad. It made him mad, too, to see how formal she was with strangers, and what a good time she seemed to have with Christina, the little Swede girl. He would come stomping into the kitchen to get the snow off his boots, and they'd have their heads together over a crock of mincemeat, laughing as if they were bosom friends. He wished she'd save her laughing and carrying on for the Peavys or the Kesslers or the Larkins. It was all right for *him* to hobnob with the lower classes, because that was part of his business, and a girl from the Bad House over behind the railroad station could suffer as much as the minister's wife if she got a bellyache. But Dr. Hawkins' *wife* didn't have to take her pleasure with her servants, when there was plenty of high society in town for her enjoyment. She was a home body, Anna was. Doctor liked that in her up to a certain point, but he would have liked a little exhibitionism in her, too. A leading citizen needed some of that in his wife, to make the combination perfect.

Yes, Doc missed the quiet times alone in the office, but there were compensations, too. Duval was a flattering listener, and Doc enjoyed talking.

"I told you that night you came, doctor, that this was no society practice; but, by George! I've got one case. Some of these times she'll come in, so you better know about her. It's Mrs. Kessler, wife of the proprietor of the Bon Ton Store across the street. My first case in town, too. Kessler met us at the train when we came to town and took us out to his house for supper. Good supper, too, roast prairie chicken and apple pie. All the way out to his house he kept talking about Mrs. Kessler's condition and hoping I could do something. In the family way, I thought he meant she was, but, Lord no, they hadn't chick nor child nor any sign of one on the way! You'll see her—she's kind of flabby and she's got an imaginative eye. The kind of female who enjoys poor health.

"'Doctor,' she said, 'I don't know what's the matter with me, but I don't feel right inside. I want you to prescribe for me.'" (Expertly Doc mimicked the complaining female voice.)

"'Do you have pain anywhere, Mrs. Kessler?' says I.

"'No, doctor. It's nothing so sort of crude as that. It's a kind of all-over feeling, if you know what I mean, and then spells when I get so depressed I cry. Just like a little girl, I cry—for days. I've tried a number of medicines I've seen advertised in the papers; but they taste so nasty, and they don't agree with my stomach. My stomach's very delicate, doctor,' she says. 'I read the doctor books, and I know you have to be right careful of a delicate stomach.'

"I could feel Anna kicking me under the table for fear I'd tell the woman she was a damned fool. I started a practice that way in Missouri, once, and Anna has never forgotten it. Well, I was too full of Mrs. K's good dinner to tell her she probably overate and didn't take enough exercise. No, I took her seriously, and I gave her a thorough examination—heart, lungs, kidneys, blood. God, how she enjoyed it! When I got all through, I didn't dare tell her there wasn't a thing the matter with her. She'd have been so disappointed she'd have fixed me up as a quack with all her friends."

"What did you do?" asked Duval.

He was standing by the window looking out. A farmer in a red muffler was driving a bobsled laden with wood past the office. The smooth side wall of the Bon Ton Store across the street was blue with winter shadows. Beyond it were the mountains.

"I told her I knew just what she needed to fix her up, and the next day I went into Skogmo's Drugstore and mixed up some sugar and bicarbonate of soda.

" 'Got some nice large capsules, Skogmo?' I asked.

" 'Sure, I got big capsules,' Skogmo says. 'That don't look like a very strong dose you puttin' in them. What is it, doctor?' "

" 'Skogmo, that's a doctor's secret,' says I, winking at him. 'This is going to kill or cure. It's an invention of my own.' "

"Why *large* capsules?" Duval asked.

"My God! to make her feel that she was suffering.

" 'Ma'am,' I said, 'I hope these don't gag you; but there's just a certain amount of this you ought to have every day, and you're a brave little woman.'

" 'I can manage,' says she, all eagerness. Well, by George! she's still taking those things, and she feels like a new woman."

Duval laughed.

"You call that ethical, doctor?"

"I call it my society practice," roared Doc. "I call it damned humorous, don't you?"

Doc's roar subsided to comfortable chuckling for a moment. Then he added: "Funniest thing about it, though, this Kessler woman is one of the biggest frogs in our puddle. I wouldn't miss one of her parties on a bet, although I know all the secrets of her ticker. Anna hates her, but she can put rings around Anna when it comes to dressing and setting up a stylish table."

"I think that you need not be ashamed of Meeses Hawkins' dress or table, doctor," said Duval quietly, turning away from the window.

"Lord, no!" Doc said. "Anna's a good woman, and I think she'll learn; but she doesn't care enough to put on style."

"Style!" Duval exclaimed contemptuously. "What is this *style* then? In Paris it is one thing, in Opportunity it is another. I am glad when I behold a human being who does not run after it."

Doctor laughed. "Yep," he said. "By God! I believe you and Anna are alike that way. Maybe that's why I like you both so well—and keep right on attending Mrs. Kessler's social functions."

10

DR. DUVAL's apparent loneliness troubled Anna. She hated to think of any man cooking his own meals and eating them in silence in a rented room. She was glad when he accepted Doc's urgent invitations and sat with them at their own table.

When the meal was over and Doctor stamped out to the stable to superintend the feeding and rubbing down of his horses, Duval sometimes sat on. Doctor's vigorous voice and personality dominated the room while he was with them. For a few moments after he left, it was as if they had been sitting in a cottage by the sea in which the roar and surge of breakers outside the open door made conversation impossible. With his going it was as if the door had been closed and they sat alone in the cottage with the sea shut out. They were both quiet people, and for a few moments neither knew what to say. They were embarrassed by the receding sound and fury, and the ensuing silence. Sometimes they were silent for a long time, Anna's head bent over some plain sewing, Duval sitting relaxed with eyes half closed. But sometimes he spoke to her of his work or of France. What he said was detached and impersonal, but she saw that to speak of France in generalities gave him a certain pleasure, and that to try to make her see it was also pleasing to him.

"Now that spring comes on," he would say, "I cannot help remembering Paris, for Paris is best in the spring. Out near the Bois there are long avenues of *marrons* (how you say horse-chestnut trees, but that is an ugly name). Some are white and some pink with bloom, and, when the rain comes down, the blossoms they fall in the streets like a pink and white carpet. And, where the blossoms have not fallen, there the wet pavement is like a river, and the street lamps make a long, quivering reflection."

"I thought it was an old gray city—all stone," Anna said.

"Oh, yes, that is so, but it is like country, too, with the great trees in the parks and along the avenues. On the corners there are stands where one sells flowers—violets and lilies-of-the-valley. There is a day in the spring, the first of May it is, when everyone in the city wears a sprig of lily-of-the-valley, because it brings good fortune."

"I don't know why you have come away out here, Dr. Duval. You still love Paris."

"My loves are in the past, Meeses Hawkins. It is better they be memories."

"I do not understand about you," Anna said.

"Why should you try? I think you are used to accept, *n'est-ce pas?* that which you do not understand."

"Yes," Anna agreed, "I've learned to take things as they come."

"Take me so, Meeses Hawkins. It will help me."

"You do not look like a man who needs help."

"One man can help me," he replied slowly. "That one is myself. But, if I may talk to you sometimes, like this—"

"Oh, yes. I am always here. I like to talk to you."

"Thank you, madame."

So in this way Anna caught glimpses of old gardens with gnarled trees and close-clipped lawns, and, deep in shade, gray statues etched with orange lichens. She walked with him briefly sometimes on the uneven cobbles of a foreign street and saw dark-haired children playing about a fountain in a village square. From the open doors of thatched cottages she smelled the bitter fragrance of generations of living and cooking and burning of faggots. Once for a moment she stood with him at an upper window looking into the courtyard behind a café, and saw the youngest *garçon* come out to swing a wire basket of washed lettuce up and down until all the excess water had been shaken away. At the same time she smelled the fresh, brown smell of roasting coffee from the café, and the more subtle odor of incense from the little shop next door which served the parish church.

They were vignettes, but almost as clear to her senses as the green and yellow tide of Idaho spring which she saw from her kitchen window.

Once in a few sentences he showed her the country château of his father, the plain gray stone house fronting on the tiny village square, and behind it the long garden where his unmarried sisters in their black dresses and garden hats sat to eat bread and soup and omelette in the open air beside the blossoming pear trees that were trained against the gray walls.

"And that is where your baby is?" she asked.

"Yes. I shall bring him here when he is old enough to travel. Before he is old enough to be hurt by talk."

"That is best," Anna said. "Children grow away so quickly. One year is like ten to them. In a few months you can lose them forever."

"I shall be a stranger to him. He has never known mother or father."

"You have something good in store for each other."

"Ah! if I were sure—"

"He will need a home. You will marry again, perhaps?" Anna said. It was not what she had meant to say, but some inner compulsion of curiosity about the wife he never mentioned drew it from her.

Something darkened in his face.

"I think not," he said.

"You never forget her?" Anna asked in a low voice.

"No," he said. "Sometime I shall tell you about her, when I have words."

When he was gone, Anna thought about the wife who must have died young. Or *had* she been young? It was strange not to know. She couldn't help wondering about her and trying to picture her. Had she been beautiful? Yes, surely. For she could see that the husband was still under her spell.

"Real love," thought Anna to herself. "Yes, it must have been real, true love." She tried to imagine that, too, but there! one must not remember those things. For a good many springs now, she had resolutely shut them out. Let the western meadow-larks sing, their voices bell-like in the thin, high air; let the sun draw forth again that shimmering tide of gold against blue—buttercups, lamb's-tongues, yellow bells, the flood of ragged dandelions, and later the goldenrod and the yellow wheat drooping with fruitful heads against the dark blue and purple of mountains; let the clouds pass like celestial dramas of strange, concerted movement and retreat above the valley; let the wind that stirred the heart ripple and sway the long grass; but never let the thought of love return with the spring. Not even the thought of love hallowed by death.

Anna put aside her sewing, and went to the kitchen to start her bread.

11

JENNY WALDEN skipped three steps, and hopped three steps, then she pirouetted solemnly and began the sequence over again. She was on her way with Della and Emma Dingle to do an errand at the grocery store, but she danced her small ballet in a circle of individuality which did not include the others. They shared their own preoccupations which involved avoiding the cracks in the board sidewalks

(*Step on a crack,*
You break your mother's back)

and keeping an eye out for white horses. The latter were counted and sealed by the ritual of wetting the right thumb in the mouth, pressing it into the left palm, and following it by a smart blow of the right fist. When each girl had thus set her seal upon a hundred white horses, the next man or boy she met wearing a red necktie would be her future husband. It was not good Methodist doctrine, but it excited the emotions just enough to be interesting yet not alarming.

Jenny took no part in this superstitious ritual. White horses seemed no better to her than black, and to watch for cracks would spoil the pattern of her dance. It was summer weather, and she was happy.

When she came near the principal saloon on Ash Street just before it joined Main, she stopped skipping and pirouetting and stood still listening. Someone in the saloon was playing the fiddle. It was a thin, scraping sound, but it intrigued her. She waited for the other girls to come up.

"Listen," she said. "Music."

They stopped, too, giggling a little. Then Della said, "Go on, Jenny, we can't stop here in front of a saloon."

Jenny trailed after them now, her feet slow, her ears full of the sound of fiddling.

"I wonder what it's like," Emma said, "in a saloon."

"Why don't you go in and find out?" said Della.

The two older girls burst out laughing at the risqué humor of Della's venturing such a remark.

"Why not?" cried Emma between gusts of laughter. "Oh, Della, you're a perfect clown!"

"Well, why not?" repeated Della. If a joke was good once, keep tossing it back and forth as long as there was laughter in it. Swaying against each other and shouting with helpless merriment, Della and Emma went along to the grocery store.

Jenny's feet moved more and more slowly. When she had gone a block she could no longer hear the sound of the fiddle, and she turned back.

The green slat swing doors of the saloon were closed, but there was a wide space at top and bottom through which the sound of fiddling came. It was a lonesome sound, almost a sound of sadness. Bending down, Jenny could see that there was sawdust on the floor inside, as on the floor of a butcher shop. Above the swinging door she could see only darkness in contrast to the sunshine of the street. A damp, cool smell, tainted with wickedness, issued forth with the sound of sad fiddling.

"Why not?" Jenny said, as the older girls had said. "Why not?" She pushed the door open gently and slipped inside, standing close against the door so that her black-stockinged legs and scuffed shoes could still be seen from the outside. She stood quiet and large-eyed, looking and listening with all her might.

The inside of the saloon surprised her somewhat, for it did not remotely resemble any of Doré's conceptions of the infernal regions. It was disappointing in that way. It was a long, dark room with sawdust on the floor and a few tables with stained tops. Along one side ran a bar, gleaming with bottles and glasses and shiny brass, and above it was an oil painting of a plump, pink lady about to take a bath. At the far end of the room there was a battered piano, and sitting beside it was an old man with long hair, sawing on a fiddle. One heavy boot kept time to the music. His eyes were far away and sad. Two men stood beside the bar with glasses before them. At a table back near the piano, sat the French doctor who had come to share the office with Doc Hawkins. He had a bottle and a little glass in front of him. His eyes were half closed, and he looked tired and as sad as the music.

Jenny stood very still and looked and listened. Suddenly one of the men at the bar glanced up and saw her.

"My God! Do you see what I see?"

"Ya. Whose little gel is it?"

"The Methodist preacher's."

"What the hell!" The men began to laugh. The man behind the bar in the white apron stopped polishing glasses and stared at her, too.

"Look," he said to Jenny. "You want something to drink?"

Jenny shook her head. She wanted to run away now, but her feet seemed glued to the spot. She could not speak. The bartender searched among his bottles and took one out from the back of the shelf. He selected a small glass and polished it carefully. Then he took the cork out of the bottle and filled the little glass with a dark red liquid. He came out from behind the bar and offered the little glass to Jenny. She shook her head again, for all speech had deserted her.

"You needn't fear, sister," he said kindly. "This here ain't fermented. I got a little gal of my own."

Mechanically Jenny took the glass and set it to her lips. It was good grape juice like that used in the communion cup at church. She drank it and returned the glass silently to the bartender.

"You hadn't ought to come in here, you know," he said.

"I know," Jenny said at last. Her voice was small and far away like the voice of another child speaking. "I heard the playing, and I wanted to see what it was like."

"Well, you know now," the bartender said. "Little gels don't come in here," he repeated warningly.

The men at the bar were still laughing.

The old fiddler stopped playing and looked at her, too. "Purty, ain't she?" he said.

Only the French doctor did not seem to notice her.

Della and Emma had missed Jenny almost immediately and had run up and down the street looking for her. They had asked several people for news of her, before Della happened to see the scuffed shoes and black-ribbed stocking legs under the swing doors of the saloon. Jenny was like an ostrich whose head is hidden while her nether regions are still exposed to view. Della uttered a cry of horror, and then she was in a quandary. The problem was how to get Jenny out without contaminating herself by going in. Emma was so shocked as to be of no use at all and kept crying out, "What shall we do—oh, what shall we do?" until quite a few passers-by began to collect and offer condolences or advice.

So, when Jenny finally summoned sufficient strength to her paralyzed limbs to come out, she encountered a ring of disapproving faces, the expressions ranging from cynical amusement to extreme shock.

"Jenny!" Della cried. "How dare you! How awful! You wicked, wicked girl!"

Jenny had been frightened in the saloon, but now for the first time she began to see that her action had moral implications as well.

As soon as they reached the parsonage Della plunked the cream of tartar and the laundry starch down on the kitchen table and cried in a voice of doom:

"Mama, Jenny went into a saloon!"

It was all brought out and told to Mrs. Walden, and then Mr. Walden was summoned from the study and it was repeated in its enormity to him. Jenny stood silently with hanging head. While the storm of their surprise and consternation broke over her, she passed gradually from self-loathing and repentance to a healthier state of questioning and rebellion.

"Jenny," her mother was saying sorrowfully, "no girl *ever* should go into a saloon, but it's worst of all for you! A preacher's daughter has to be more careful than any other girl. It's worst of all for a preacher's little girl!"

"But why?" cried Jenny.

"Because you're expected to do better," said her mother. "Because you have a moral responsibility to other people. You have to set an example. Because, if you don't do right, everybody in town will talk."

"Mother, that's a worldly reason," said Mr. Walden mildly.

"But it's the most important one. I haven't been a preacher's wife for fifteen years and not learned that."

"A better reason is to please God."

"Of course—that, too," said Jenny's mother.

Della felt herself left out of this conversation, dropped along the way as of no importance, whereas she was the one who had brought the culprit to justice and narrated the crime.

"Mama, it was awful of Jenny to do that, wasn't it? Next thing she'll be going to call on the divorced woman!"

"Oh, dear," said Mrs. Walden. "Don't bring that poor thing into it—just because she has short hair!"

Mr. Walden liked the truth at all times.

"It isn't because of her short hair, my dear, although I do hate to see that in a woman. It's because—"

"Come, Charles," said Mrs. Walden sharply, "we've said enough before the girls. Let's get back to the saloon."

"Mother, I think we'd better pray," said Mr. Walden.

Jenny was relieved to have the scolding ended and the talk with God begun. She loved to hear her father pray, for he was not presumptuous with God, neither was he servile. It was as if he and God talked together in a friendly understanding. Of course you could not hear God; but father's face, as he prayed, made it clear that *he* heard Him, and Jenny could imagine God saying softly, "Amen, brother!" as the deacons used to say it during the sermon.

"O God, help us to measure up to Thy requirements, help us to live as Thou wouldst have us live. Give us strength and a will to piety . . ." He did not name Jenny's name, nor call God's attention to her iniquity.

Jenny's hot rebellion faded into repentance. When the prayer was over she slipped away from Della and went into the clothes closet under the stairs. She liked being alone, and there were only two places where that could be achieved. One was the privy in the back yard, where one could latch the door and sit very quietly; the other was the back of the closet under the stairs. Of the two, the latter was the more impregnable because one could ignore a pounding on the door there, whereas one never knew but what the knocking on the privy door came from a genuine necessity.

The back of the hall closet was warm and close, smelling of rubbers and camphor balls. Sometimes, when she retired here, Jenny wept. But today she did not. She sat staring into the darkness, and she thought: "Why *do* preachers' girls have to be better? Why aren't they just the same as other people?" That they *were* different seemed inescapable, but she did not accept her mother's reasons why, nor her father's either.

There were a great many things in Opportunity which she did not understand. For instance about the saloons. There they were in plain sight, and you could see the men going in or staggering out as the case might be; and yet the righteous people walked by as if they could not see them. Apparently the righteous people could not, or would not, even hear the fiddling. And Della had spoken of the divorced woman. It was the same with her. She had a very bright and gay little flower garden in her front yard just where the stores left off and the houses began, and she looked nice with her short gray hair

that curled all over her head; but no one spoke to her. The people
going by to church on a Sunday morning, while she was working in
her garden, never saw her at all. Of course, working in the garden
on a Sunday morning! But that wasn't the only reason, either—as
Jenny's father said, it wasn't entirely the short hair nor the working
in the garden on a Sunday. It was the divorce that made her invisible
to the people of Opportunity. She never had any company, and that
was perhaps because she was too good for the people who frequented
the saloons and not good enough for the people who went to church.
It seemed as if there were only those two classes in Opportunity, and
Mrs. Shanley fell irrevocably between them.

Jenny felt sleepy in the back of the closet, and she stopped trying
to puzzle things out and began to savor her repentance. Yet, if she
was repentant now, it was not because she was the preacher's daughter
and owed repentance to God and the community, but because she
loved the preacher and wanted to please him. With Jenny love came
before reason.

12

ONE SATURDAY EVENING in the fall of the year Dr. Duval came
to Anna's door and knocked. Doctor had departed earlier, in full
regalia, for an evening at the Lodge, and Christina had gone to bed.
Anna sat darning stockings in a circle of lamplight, and the quick,
light knock made her lift her head in a motion of startled listening.
She rose without hurry and went to the door, and she was surprised to see him, for he had never come uninvited after darkness
fell.

He began speaking to her now in French, his voice full of dignity,
his eyes unnaturally bright.

"*Madame, je vous demande pardon. J'ai pour vous des sentiments
les plus respectueux et les plus distingués.*"

"I don't understand you, doctor," Anna said. "You must speak to
me in English."

He came in and closed the door behind him, leaning a little against it as he looked down at her. He was strange tonight.

"I am sorry," he said slowly. "You do not have the French, do you? Yet, I believe that you have great understanding . . ."

"Will you sit down?" Anna said. She was puzzled and a little troubled.

He continued to stand by the door, full of dignity, yet swaying a little as he stood. "I have come to confide in you," he said, "that all shall be plain at last between us."

"No," Anna said, "no, it must not be tonight."

Suddenly she knew what was the matter with Dr. Duval: he was drunk. The realization shocked her more than she could tell, remembering what he and Doctor had said on that first night with the decanter of claret between them. It was a first impression of him which she had not thought to question. She was used to the sight of drunkenness in a frontier town, but somehow this hurt her with a deep pain. "No!" she said again. "Not tonight."

"An-na," he said. It was the first time he had ever spoken her name. He said it carefully, dividing the syllables in his precise French way, so that each was equally emphasized. She saw that the liquor had not furred his tongue.

"Constant," Anna said in a low voice, "you have been drinking, I think."

"Does that make you afraid?"

"No, I am not afraid."

"Why not then? I think that you should be."

"I have never been afraid of people—only of circumstances and events."

"Oh—"

"But Doctor would be very angry. Don't you know that? I am afraid *for* you."

He came and sat in Doctor's armchair by the dining-room stove. There was a pathetic droop to his shoulders, and his chin fell forward on his chest.

"I will recite for you a poem," he said, "if you will be gentle enough to hear me—"

"No, Constant! No," she said. Her lips were trembling.

"Sit there for a moment," he said. "I promise you, I do not keep you long. You do not know how much I am alone . . ."

Anna sat down opposite him. Her mind was busy with means to get him back to his rooms before Doctor saw him. She was full of sorrow and pity for him.

"You wanted to recite a poem?"

"A poem? Ah, yes. It is something I heard long ago, and it is a thing like this, An-na:

> "*Dans la forêt chauve et rouillée,*
> *Il ne reste plus au rameau*
> *Qu'une pauvre feuille oubliée,*
> *Rien qu'une feuille et qu'un oiseau.*"

"It sounds very sad," said Anna. "I don't understand the words."

"It says like this: *In the forest, bare and rusty, there remains on the branch nothing but a poor forgotten leaf, only one leaf and one bird.*"

"And is that all?"

"No, there is more, but perhaps I have forgotten. It is something about love:

> "*Il ne reste plus dans mon âme*
> *Qu'un seul amour pour y chanter.*"

"I am sorry that I do not understand your language," Anna said. "It sounds very soft and beautiful."

"I have come to tell you about my wife," he said. "You have curiosity about her, *n'est-ce pas*, An-na? The little one with golden hair, who is dead?"

"Come into the kitchen," Anna said, "and I will make you some coffee. You'll feel better when you've had it."

He followed her quietly and sat on the big woodbox beside the stove, watching her while she rekindled the evening fire and measured the coffee into the pot.

"You will listen, An-na?"

"Yes, I will listen."

"It was in April, you see," he said, "and I had been working all the winter in London, arising in the darkness to hurry through the foggy streets to the laboratory, and half of the days working by gaslight all through the day and far into the night. I was very lonely in London, do you see? As I am lonely now, do you see, An-na?"

"No, I don't see," Anna said, bending over the coffee pot and keeping her eyes averted from his bright, entreating ones. "I've never understood why you left France."

"But I shall not tell you that," he said. "You must know there were sufficient reasons." He was silent, and she saw his slender, beautiful hands trembling and fumbling with each other. She was sorry for him again.

"Tell me what you wish," she said.

"In London it was only of my career that I thought, day and night, and that I should be some day a very great doctor, greater than all the others. Yes, I was vain—but they told me that, too, those others, the doctors, the professors. So they have always told me—I could have been great, if I had wished. But they are wrong, for it is not a question of will. *Non. Non. J'en suis sûr.*"

"Well," Anna said, "you were telling me a story."

"Eh, yes. And, when I have told it, An-na, it will be like something you have read in a book, eh? How do you know but it is something I myself have read, and recite to you like a poem?"

"I do not know," Anna said quietly, "but I think you tell the truth even when you are drunk."

"Thank you," he said courteously. He was silent, his trembling hands gripping the sides of the woodbox to steady himself. Suddenly he began to speak rapidly.

"I had not had a holiday for a long while, you see (I had not dared allow myself that), and one of my colleagues, he said to me, 'Look,

Duval, you must come down into the country with me this week end. I promised to bring my brother, and he is detained by business.' 'No,' I said at first. 'I cannot leave the experiment I have begun.' And I thought to myself: 'No. To meet socially new people whose language I do not well speak, that is not what I desire. I am better off here.' But he would not have a no. At last I said I would go. In the woods, when the train was out of London, there were yellow primroses in bloom. Is it that you have seen yellow primroses, An-na?"

"No, I have not seen them."

"They are very pale, then, not like the yellow flowers that bloom too furiously here. No, they are very pale. I cannot tell you unless you see them."

"I can imagine," Anna said. His voice always conjured pictures for her, and now she saw vividly dark woods and pale gold flowers.

"*Bien*—she was like the primroses," he said, "pale gold and transient as the spring."

Anna was silent. She thought, *The drink has oiled his tongue with pretty phrases. But now I know. His wife was beautiful and young.* At last she said to prompt him:

"She was a guest in the house where you were visiting?"

He considered a moment, coming back from a long distance.

"No," he said. "No, she was not a guest—a relative, a kind of a servant maybe. Governess—that is it—a second cousin and an orphan girl. Yes, she was governess to the children at that house. Almost a child herself, and who had learned a little French—only a little, you see, as one reads from a little primer in a simple tongue. But that was enough to link us in a kind of way. Figure to yourself how lonely one may be in a strange land where he has not for a long time heard the sound of his own language; and then a young girl with a very gentle face comes to him speaking haltingly and with shyness the little, peaceful words he knew as a child. No, you cannot understand what it was. It was spring returning. It was sunshine again after long winter. It had been long winter."

"I can understand, I think," said Anna.

"So we were married very soon," he said. His voice had grown thicker, the enunciation less delicate and precise. "But it is not very long I had her with me. So young she was, and her hair still the color of primroses when she died."

Suddenly he began to weep.

Anna poured out the coffee.

"Drink this," she said. "You will feel better." She saw by the clock on the wall that it was almost eleven. Perhaps they had an hour, but there was no telling. Doctor might come in at any moment. "While you are drinking it, I will go and hitch the horse. Don't go until I come."

In the windy darkness of the barn Anna's fingers fumbled with lantern and harness. She was desperately in haste. The horse snorted and blew at her, surprised but trusting her judgment. A colt in the box stall got awkwardly onto its long legs and whinnied, its eyes round and wondering in the lantern light. Anna found that she was shivering violently, for she had forgotten her shawl. When the horse was hitched to the light buggy, she drove to the side of the house, tied the horse, and went into the kitchen.

Constant had finished the coffee, and he sat now, staring at her, his hands relaxed between his knees.

"Come now," she said, "Doctor must not see you so."

He rose unsteadily, but he was as obedient as a child. He made no objection to getting into the buggy.

"You have no anger with me?" he said in a heavy voice.

"No," Anna said.

She took a way around quiet back streets, where they would not be likely to be noticed together nor meet Doctor with his Lodge regalia. When they were safely beyond the saloons, Anna drew in the horse on a dark corner near the drugstore.

"You must get out now," Anna said, "and go home to your bed. You'll do that, Constant?"

"Yes, I will do that," he said. He got down heavily, but then he turned and leaned against the side of the buggy. She could smell the sharp, sweetish odor of alcohol on his breath as he leaned towards her. "I remember now," he said. "It is like this:

> "*L'oiseau s'en va, la feuille tombe,*
> *L'amour s'éteint, car c'est l'hiver.*
> *Petit oiseau, viens sur ma tombe*
> *Chanter, quand l'arbre sera vert!*"

"I will hear it another time."

"No, there was something else. It was I who killed her, you know. Yes, it was my own fault, because I had been drinking that night, too. It was the same in France, too. That's why I cannot go back there."

Anna sat very still.

The horse was uneasy in the windy night, feeling the weight of unreason against the wheel of the buggy. But Anna's firm hands held the reins steady.

"Go to bed now, Constant," she said at last. "You will have tomorrow to sleep." She sat still and watched until he had disappeared in the direction of his rooms. Then she turned the horse and drove quickly back to the barn and unharnessed in the dark. As she came in the back door, Doctor came in the front.

"My God!" he said. "What are you doing outdoors in a shawl at this time of night?"

"I was afraid the boy had forgotten to bed down the colt again," Anna said.

"You're a damned good farmer's wife, aren't you, my girl? Do I smell coffee?"

"Yes, I just made a cup. Will you have some?"

"Think I'd ever turn down a cup of coffee? How about that pie we had for supper? Any left?"

Anna brought a slice of apple pie from the cupboard, and watched silently while Doctor loaded it with black pepper.

"Good Lord!" Doctor said. "This coffee is so strong you could cut it with a knife. A body'd think you'd been using it to sober up a drunk."

"Doctor," Anna said, "just put the dishes in the sink. I think I'll go to bed now."

On Monday afternoon Doctor had to make a call in the country. While he was gone Duval came to the front door and rang the bell. Anna answered it, and they stood and looked at each other thoughtfully for a moment.

"Will you come in, Constant?"

"No, An-na, thank you. I have come to say I regret what passed the night before last."

"It is forgiven."

He stood uncertainly, his hat in one hand, his small black bag in the other. He looked pale, and his eyes haggard.

"It was kind of you that you have not spoken to Dr. Hawkins, but you may do so, if you wish, because I am going away now, on farther west."

"No," Anna said, "you are not going to run away any more. This is the last place. You're going to turn around here; and, if you ever leave, it will be to go back to those places you have come from."

"That is impossible."

"Nothing at all is impossible except in your own mind."

"But that is where it is," he said, smiling a little.

"Listen!" Anna said. "Stand and face this thing. You can't go much farther west. You'll come to the Pacific Ocean, and what will you do for your next jump after that?"

"There are ships, of course, and, if I never reach the other side, it will be of little consequence to anyone—a small splash in a large pool."

"You are a fool," Anna said, "as well as a coward. I had thought so much better of you, Constant."

"So now you know me."

"But you are worth saving. Try again, please. Stand around and face it. I will do all I can to help you."

"You do not know what it is to be weak and full of a terrible hunger of despair. You are strong, An-na."

"Yes, I am strong," Anna said quietly. "I am strong enough for two."

"How can you help me, An-na?" he asked, looking curiously at her. For a moment he had stepped outside himself to wonder about her.

"By believing in you, Constant."

He was silent for a moment, then he said, "My heart is buried in the past."

Anna flushed hotly.

"I have not asked you for your love," she said. He, too, flushed and drew himself up straighter.

"I beg your pardon again, An-na," he said. "I have for you a great respect, but it seems I can offer you only insults."

"I've never taken them that way."

"I know. You have great goodness."

"And you will not run away?" she asked.

"I will think again if I can stand and face myself," he said.

She watched him as he walked away between the empty flower beds with the wild leaves blowing, and she knew that for this time, at least, he would stay and try again. But her heart was heavy for him, for he had left too many ghosts behind him in the places where he had been. What they all were, she did not know nor care to know. It was enough that they were there.

13

With Duval to take over much of the practice, Doc Hawkins gave more and more time and thought to the town. He knew everybody up and down the street and had his finger in every enterprise. He ran a sort of placement agency for the benefit of his patients and the good of the community.

"Say, Pete, you need a bright young fellow to help you in the feed business? I know just the lad: Old man Smith's boy out south of town. Crop was bad this year, and they're living on cornmeal and turnips out there. Boy's smart as a whip, and you'll never regret giving him a lift."

Or maybe it was a girl from the other side of the tracks who needed help.

"You out of a girl again, Mrs. Kessler? A smart woman like you never ought to want for help. You know the Widow Fifer, the other side of the tracks? Her Maria has just turned sixteen, and say! I had a slice of her cake the other day! Even *your* delicate stomach, Mrs. Kessler, couldn't take offense at a cake so light and delicate of flavor. Her reputation, you say? Good Lord, woman! What's a person's reputation got to do with the lightness of a cake? I thought you were looking for help in the kitchen, not a Sunday-school teacher. But I guess Mrs. Peavy can use her, if you can't. She's been talking to her."

Doctor was prospering now, and whatever money was left over from his open-handed mode of living he put into town land and real estate. The country did not particularly appeal to Doc. There was nothing of the gentleman farmer about him. But he saw in his imagination how Opportunity would grow, how it would become a city, the best one in the state, perhaps even in the Northwest.

Anna watched Doctor's accumulation of vacant corner lots and tumble-down shacks in Swede town and Italian town with mild interest. Sometimes she made involuntary suggestions.

"Doctor, why don't you tear down that old rattletrap that rents for ten dollars a month and put up a decent cottage? Let me plan it for you, the way a woman would like it inside, with cupboards for dishes and a copper sink that drains outside."

"My God!" Doctor said. "And get ten dollars a month for it?"

"No. Ask more."

"Listen, Anna, you're a mighty fine housekeeper, but leave the business end of this to me, will you? It takes a man to work a deal like this."

Doc had never trusted Anna's level head with the details of his financial arrangements. He had formed the firm conviction as a boy that all women were fools about money, and fifteen years of life with a thrifty wife had brought him no enlightenment. Anna had seen a number of Doctor's wildcat enterprises make off with lumps of his capital, but she had learned to say nothing. She did not care enough to make a scene, and, after all, she thought, Doctor was the one who made the money. Let him do what he wanted with it, so long as she and the girls had a good roof over their heads and plenty to eat and wear.

There was only one time when she felt worried. She was sponging and pressing Doctor's black and gray, pin-stripe trousers once when she found a notice in his pocket from one of the insurance companies. Apparently he had stopped making payments on his insurance, and the company had sent him a last warning. The last warning was dated a month back. Of course, Doctor must have sent in the money since, but it made her a little uneasy.

That time she said to Doctor, "Are you sure you ought to be putting so much in land, Doctor? I wonder if you can afford it?"

"My God, Anna! I'm making money hand over fist. Of course, I can afford it."

"A man can be property-poor. You're keeping up your life insurance, aren't you, doctor?"

"What makes you ask that?"

"I found a notice in your pocket."

"By the lord Harry!" he said. "Do you go through my pants every time I take them off?"

"No, doctor," said Anna. "But I want an answer."

"Anna," he said, "I never felt better in my life. I come of a long-lived family, and you don't. There's not a one in my family but sees the better side of eighty-five or ninety. The girls will marry, and there's every chance that I'll outlive you. I'm keeping one policy, but I've got damned tired of paying out that money every year for something I'll never enjoy."

"You saw it differently when you took it out."

"I had sons then, Anna."

Anna was silent. She had never been one to ask for security for herself. But apparently Doctor still felt that his position needed justifying.

"I see enough death in my business, by thunder! I don't want to think about it for myself. I'm a vigorous man, and I've got thirty— maybe forty good years ahead of me. I'd rather invest my money in the future of this town. If I do pass away before you do, Anna, you'll be a rich widow. From now on I'm going to put everything I've got into land. I may be a gambler, but I'm betting on a long life and a booming town. Does that satisfy you?" He put his arm awkwardly around her shoulders and kissed her cheek—something he did not often do any more.

"Yes, doctor," said Anna. He had answered her question, and she could think of no more reasonable arguments to move him.

In the summer of 1890 Idaho Territory became a state. There had been talk of sending Doctor to the constitutional convention in Boise City the summer before, but, much as he would have enjoyed dabbling in that pie, the practice came first.

"Politics are like hard liquor," Doctor said jovially to the delegation which waited upon him. "Neither one goes well with the practice of medicine." But he was flattered, nevertheless, and he was glad that his northern county was to be a part of the new state rather than attached to Washington or Montana as some folks had advocated.

"I'm for building up something new, by Gad! not for being stuck onto what's already built, like a fifth wheel on a rickety democrat."

The same year that Idaho became a state Doc Hawkins started campaigning for a bell for the new Presbyterian church. Doc was not a churchgoing man, but the Presbyterian church was almost on his own doorstep, and, when he had rebuilt his house in good style, it was natural that he should want the Presbyterians to keep up a prosperous appearance also.

The Baptists started things first by putting a bell in their tower—a little, plaintive thing that could be heard only five or six blocks; and immediately afterwards the Catholics and the Methodists and the Lutherans put in bells, too. Dr. Hawkins began to get excited. What in thunder were the Presbyterians thinking of to let these other churches get ahead of them?

The elders were sitting around in session drawing up plans for a new Sunday-school room and a larger tower, but no one said a word about a bell.

"By thunder!" said Dr. Hawkins, going around to Larkin and Peavy and Kessler and all the other influential Presbyterians he knew. "We've got to have a bell here that is a bell. Are you going to let a Catholic or a Methodist ring louder than we do? Are you going to be content with a tower and not have the biggest bell in town? Opportunity is going to grow, we're building for the future. Are we going to live to be ashamed of a small, cheap bell, or are we going to have future generations thank us for our courage and foresight?"

After he had talked about it for a while, Doctor became so enthusiastic that he started a subscription list, and he put his own name at the top with a donation of fifty dollars. "The Biggest Bell in Town" Fund captured the popular fancy. Even some of the freethinkers and atheists contributed fifty cents or a dollar towards the Presbyterian bell, just because they liked Doc Hawkins and were swept off their feet by the controversial spirit of the thing.

Before long it seemed certain that the Presbyterians would, indeed, have the biggest bell in town if they could build a tower to hold it. And so this summer of 1890 another delegation, this time of Presbyterians, called upon Doctor and asked him to head the committee which should go East to select the bell.

Doctor was mightily tempted this time. He had been made official railroad doctor for the district several years before, and consequently he had free passes for himself and his family all over the country. He had always thought that he would take advantage of the passes to do some traveling, but the damned practice never gave him time. Now he contemplated the trip East to select a big, loud bell with considerable longing. There was no reason why he couldn't leave the practice with Duval for a few weeks, he thought. Then, just as he had about decided to go, typhoid fever and something which Doctor called cholery morbus broke out in town, and he had to change his mind. Every summer there was this flurry of typhoid in Opportunity, and he knew he couldn't leave the burden of it all on Duval's shoulders.

He saw the committee off on the train with a good deal of regret.

"Now, don't forget to get the bell *big*, and a deep, rich tone," he admonished.

"We won't, doctor. We'll get the best."

"*Big and loud!*" he called as the train pulled out.

Dr. Hawkins used to have bad attacks of indigestion, probably due to his fondness for black pepper. From observing so many ailments in other people he had acquired a fatalistic attitude with regard to himself, and he used periodically to succumb to soul-searching waves of nausea and headache without ever submitting himself to the sort of diet and regimen he would have insisted upon for a patient. One of these attacks coincided with the hanging of the new Presbyterian bell.

Doc had been awake half of Saturday night groaning, vomiting, and cursing. Along towards morning a deep, sweet sleep of exhaustion overtook him. The attack was over, all he had to do now was to sleep and recover. Anna and the girls tiptoed around the house and conversed in whispers. It was half past nine o'clock and Doc still slept like a baby.

Full of pride and jubilation the Presbyterians began to ring the first call to Sunday school. The sexton threw the full weight of his enthusiasm and triumph over other religions into his ringing. There was a brazen thunder of sound that vibrated Doc's bedsprings. The whole hill was filled with an intolerable noise of ringing. The eardrums crackled, the mind reeled. After each tremendous clang there was a hum of sound that filled the interim until the next clang came. Even when the ringing was over, the air seemed to hum and vibrate for a long time.

Doc sprang out of bed, his hair on end, his eyes wild, his whiskers bristling.

"Stop it!" he yelled. "My God, Anna, do something!"

He came out in the parlor in his short nightshirt with his hairy legs exposed to the view of the girls and Anna and the little Swede girl. His eyes were bloodshot and his face a sickly, greenish white.

"God in heaven!" he shouted. "I never thought. I have to live across the street from it!"

Anna was holding her hands over her ears, and, by thunder, the woman was laughing at him!

Jenny Walden, twelve now, and going to Sunday school in a starched white dress which scratched the delicate pale skin at the base of her throat, stopped in her tracks to listen to the bell.

"Della, listen! It's Dr. Hawkins' new bell."

"I don't think it's nice of him," Della said. "He's just trying to outdo the other churches."

"Don't you wish you were a Presbyterian?"

"No, and it's bad of you to say a thing like that, Jenny. You know it's better to be a Methodist."

"I don't know anything for certain," Jenny said dreamily.

"Not even your Sunday-school lesson?"

"Well, it's something about Samuel, but I don't care if I don't know it. All I have to do is smile at Mr. Dunbar and nod my head. He thinks I know."

"I don't see how I can keep on being shocked at you, Jenny. You wear me out."

Jenny smiled her elfin smile, but she was listening to the new bell, loud amidst all the clamor of the other bells.

"Oh, sounding brass!" she said, feeling biblical, and doing a solemn skip and hop to emphasize her words. "Oh, clashing cymbals and sounding brass and bells and bells and bells . . ."

Still skipping, she was engulfed by the wide dark doorway of the Methodist church, and the sunny street was lonely without her.

14

THE RAILROAD PASSES were still burning a hole in Doctor's pocket at the end of that summer. The girls were at home for their vacation, and the usual peaceful regime of Anna's well run household was broken by amateur theatricals, mandolin serenades, and a clutter of adolescent young men underfoot. Besides his own two girls and their harebrained company, there was Christina and the boy who worked for his board and room, all around the kitchen, laughing and cutting up, and shouting at each other around the dining-room table. Most of the time Doc didn't mind it, for he was fond of an uproar; but sometimes after a hard day with typhoid cases he blazed out like summer lightning and shouted them down until the females were all crying except Anna, and the chore boy and miscellaneous young men had ducked out to the barn or run home. They got so they waited to see Doc's mood before they let fly with any monkeyshines. Doctor wanted peace.

So it seemed to him a propitious moment to use the railroad passes.

"Anna," Doc said, "I'm going to send you and the girls back to St. Louis for a visit. It's been about seven years since we left, and I'd like you to go back and show the folks we knew there how well we've done out here."

"How would I show them, doctor?"

"Good God, Anna! by wearing some stylish clothes and exhibiting the girls and telling them about our place here."

Anna laughed. "You'd be a better one to do that than I would, doctor."

"You know I can't spare the time, and I've got these free railroad passes. It would be damned foolish of us not to use them."

"All right," Anna said, calm as usual.

"Now, look, Anna, you get the dressmaker in and tell her to do her damnedest, will you?"

Anna did not tell Miss Mead to do her damnedest, but she said with her easy smile, "Miss Mead, Doctor wants us to have some real nice clothes this time, just a little flashy, I think. Do you know what I mean? Just go ahead and plan them for us, will you?"

Miss Mead was in her element with *carte blanche*, as you might say; and Mary and Lita ran up and down town matching threads and ribbons and crying out with delight or vexation as the mood struck them. Clothes had already become more interesting to them than they had ever been to Anna. Anna was pleased to see the girls happy and excited, but she had to give them little responsibilities that would calm them down and take their minds off the journey. Their expectations, like Doctor's, so often led them astray, that she was afraid they might burst into tears of vexation and disappointment at the sight of a real St. Louis after all the air castles they had been building.

"Mama, aren't you excited? Aren't you in a dither? How do you sleep at night?"

"I sleep real well, thank you," smiled Anna.

"Mama, you're so funny. You act as if you were just going across the street to church instead of to St. Louis."

"Then I'll be that much more surprised to find myself in St. Louis."

Anna was busy in the last days teaching Christina how to make bread just as she made it, so that Doctor would not feel the difference in his meals. She gave her careful directions about how full to fill Doctor's mustache cup, and the temperature of his shaving water, and when to pick the summer apples, what to feed the cats, and how long to scald the sour milk for the best cottage cheese.

She thought about Constant, too, and she would have liked to make a hundred little arrangements for his welfare as well as Doctor's. But what she could do for him had no name, and it could not be placed in the care of anyone else.

From the station platform she looked back at the mountains. On this August day they were blue and solid, like a crudely painted backdrop for a Western drama. She was sorry to part with them, even for a month, to breathe the heavy air of a lowland region.

Doctor had put on his best clothes to see them off on the train. He had a bag of horehound sticks for each of the girls and a book of favorite quotations as a parting gift for Anna.

"Now, Anna, hang onto that pass," he said, "and don't let the girls leave their purses on the car seat when they go to the privy. And, if you want anything, Anna, telegraph. Remember that, *telegraph*."

"I'll remember, doctor," Anna said.

Looking over Doctor's head as she stood on the car step, she met the amused eyes of Constant. He had come, too, to see them off. Their eyes clung a moment with a humorous understanding.

"Take care of yourselves, both of you," Anna said. She was still looking at Constant.

When the train had started, Lita said: "It was nice of Dr. Duval to come down, too, wasn't it? But he didn't bring us anything, and look at these nasty little bags of candy papa brought us! He still thinks we're little girls."

"He's awfully distinguished-looking," Mary said.

"Who—papa?"

"I meant Dr. Duval."

"I'll bet he's going to miss mama more than papa does," Lita teased. "Didn't he look it, Mary?"

"That's silly," Anna said gravely.

"No, but he does come often, doesn't he? And sits there talking about France. You must know as much about France as any woman in Opportunity, don't you, mama?"

"Maybe I do."

"It must get tiresome. Doesn't he ever make pretty speeches, mama?"

"Only about his poor, dead wife."

"Oh, what a dreadful bore!" cried Mary, dismissing the subject to put her new straw hat into a clean pillowcase, and settle herself for the journey. Anna leaned back and closed her eyes. She did not care a great deal about traveling.

Doctor heaved a sigh as the train pulled out.

"Now, by George! I'll have a little rest and quiet. Maybe I'll even treat myself to some kind of spree to celebrate. You join me, doctor?"

"No, I thank you," said Duval.

"So much the better. You look after the office if I don't show up tomorrow, will you?"

"Yes. I will do that."

But Doctor was only a little later than usual at the office the next day.

"By God!" he said. "It's a funny thing, but I have more sport living my daily life than trying to go off on a debauch. Either I'm a damned poor sport or the life I lead is exactly suited to me. I don't know which."

"Possibly you are a victim of habit," said Duval mildly. "Another, what you call, spree, perhaps—"

"No," Doc said, "I'll be damned if I try it again."

The sunshine lay warm and languid on the sidewalk outside the office; the flies buzzed. There was a great emptiness and stillness throughout the town for both of them.

By the second week of Anna's absence the silence of the house began to fret Doctor's nerves. He asked Duval to dinner, and afterwards they sat on the front porch in the darkness which smelled of Anna's roses and mignonette.

"Duval," Doctor said, "do you know anything about Spiritualism?"

"A little," Duval said. "Why?"

"You know that Litowsky girl who died last week? On her deathbed she had some kind of vision, describing heaven and some kind of celestial music she heard. Said she was coming back, too, by Gad! Do you believe she could?"

"No, I do not believe so, doctor. After my wife—died, I read about Spiritualism, because I wanted her back. I gave it a fair trial, I think. There is nothing in it."

"I don't know," Doctor said. "The house is so damned quiet these nights, I can't help thinking about that girl's vision. Looked to me as if she really saw something. You got a book on Spiritualism? Lend it to me, will you?"

"You may have it. I shall never look at it again."

"You think I'm a damned fool?"

"No. Everything is worth investigating."

Dr. Hawkins liked to read in bed, and now with Anna gone he could read all night if he liked and no one to say: "Doctor, you're wasting coal oil." He would have been a little ashamed to take a book on Spiritualism to bed with him under Anna's humorous and sensible eye. He saw that, if he were ever to make any psychic investigations, this was the opportunity to do so. Therefore he took Duval's book to bed with him that week, reading late while the moth millers flew about the lamp and summer beetles bumped against the ceiling.

The silence of the house during that second week was particularly propitious to spirit visitations. On Friday night he read himself to sleep on the case of the deceased music master who returned after death to play ghostly nocturnes on the family piano. Doc had scarcely blown out the light and rolled over to sleep, when he was brought wide awake by the striking of a note on the piano in the parlor. It was followed by another and another in stately procession. Doc sat up in bed with every hair bristling. There was one wild moment when he was sure that the Litowsky girl had come back. His eyes popped out in the darkness. His breathing came with difficulty. Up the scale—down the scale the spirit fingers moved.

Then suddenly Doc flung off the sheet and plunked his feet on the floor. It had just occurred to him that he had forgotten to put Grover Cleveland out for the night.

But that was enough of doing without Anna. While Christina was making coffee in the morning, Doc put the book on Spiritualism in the cookstove.

"Vy, doctor, you burning up a good books?"

"Mind your own business, Christina," said Doc, not unkindly. "You know what I'm going to do this morning? I'm going to telegraph Mrs. Hawkins to come home."

"She ain't hardly gone, doctor."

"She's gone long enough. A man can't have much peace with a houseful of women, but he's a fool without them. Give me a cup of coffee."

The day Anna and the girls came home, he paced the station platform for an hour before the train came in. Dr. Duval was there, too, lounging on a baggage truck.

"These damned trains!" Doc said. "It's six whole minutes off schedule."

"Eight," Duval said, consulting his watch.

15

IT WAS AUTUMN again when the young wife of the Swedish carpenter lost her baby and died in labor.

Doctor came home after long hours of watching and ate a good dinner, but he was a little depressed.

"She was a pretty girl," he said, "—one of these pink and white Swede girls with yellow hair; but she wasn't formed right for giving birth to a big nine-pound kid. Maybe if we'd had some safe way of easing off her pain—but the thing went on for forty-eight hours until she hadn't any strength left. Duval wanted to perform a Caesarian— maybe I should have let him, but, by God! I never saw one of those Caesarians that didn't die anyway."

"Dr. Duval wanted to try that?" Anna asked.

"He's a funny fellow," Doc said. "Sometimes I think he's too full of himself to make a good doctor. He knows all these scientific facts and methods, but usually he don't care enough to put himself into the patient's shoes the way you have to do. But this case—by George! it knocked him over somehow. I thought he was going to cry when she died."

"His wife died that way, you know."

"I s'pose that's it. Last time he came on the case to relieve me— well, by God! if I didn't know the fellow was a teetotaler, I'd have thought that he'd been drinking—"

"Surely not," Anna said quietly. She stood very still beside the table where Doctor was eating.

"Well, he knows I won't stand that," Doctor said, his mouth full of bread and butter. "I won't have our office getting the name Doc Schilling's has, not on your life! We may be powerless to save what the Lord didn't intend to be saved, but, by thunder! it won't be said of us that we went around our patients under the influence of liquor."

"Of course not, doctor."

"Of course not! Of course not! My God! I'm tired. I'm going to bed now and sleep—if I don't hear that poor, yellow-haired girl yelling and yammering in my dreams." He pushed back his plate, and banged his chair against the wall.

"Good night," he said. "If any more calls come in, you or Christina wake me."

"This town needs a couple more doctors," Anna said.

"Keep cool, Anna. I can handle everything that comes. This is my town. We don't need any other doctors, see?"

Anna walked quietly back and forth between dining room and kitchen, clearing the table. Christina was crying over the dishpan in the kitchen. The girl who had died was her second cousin.

"Mis' Hawkins, you tink I die, too, ven I have a baby?"

"No, of course not," Anna said, patting Christina's shoulder. "Answer the door, Christina, if anyone comes for Doctor, won't you? And wake him if it's urgent."

"You going to bed, too, Mis' Hawkins?"

"No. I am going out a little while."

She put on her hat and coat and went quickly down the hill. It was a clear, frosty night full of stars, and she could see the mountains like purple shadows against the starlight.

First to his rooms, she thought. *If he isn't there, how am I to know which saloon he's in? How am I to get him out of it?*

She felt her way carefully up the dark well of the stairway. The uncarpeted stairs seemed loud under her feet. She could smell the stale drugstore smell and hear a rumble of men's voices in the room below. When she felt the doorknob under her fingers, she turned it without knocking. The door was not locked. It swung open slowly upon a dimly lit room, and, in a warm surge of relief, she saw that he was there. She would not have to hunt the town for him. Once more, perhaps, Doctor would not have to know, nor all the babbling and censorious town.

She went quickly to him, but she did not put her hand on his arm as she had felt the urge to do.

"Constant!" she said, looking steadily at him. His fingers twitched on the glass he held, and he rolled his head a little from side to side but did not raise it to look at her.

"*Comment ça va? Comment ça va?*" he muttered thickly.

She drew another chair to the table and sat beside him, still looking into the averted face.

"This is nothing, Constant," she said eagerly. "You have only to start again, do you see? I'll take the bottle away, and tomorrow you will be sober. Nobody's going to know. It's not going to happen again."

"Like a little beast crying," he said, jerking up his head and shaking it a little, the blurred eyes trying to focus on her face. *"Une petite bête blessée.* Did I tell you then I have killed her? The yellow hair all spread upon the pillow—"

"Stop it!" Anna said. "You did all you could to save her. Now you are making a fool of yourself."

He did not answer, and presently Anna got up and went to the kitchen to make coffee. She took the bottle with her and poured the liquor into the sink. She hated women who did melodramatic things like that, but she didn't know any other way.

When she returned with the coffee, she sat beside him again. It was going to be a long struggle, she saw, a struggle which she had not yet won nor ever would perhaps. Yet something urgent impelled her to try.

"Constant," she said, groping for his wavering attention. "Constant, listen. Life is like a wild horse: either you're in the saddle and riding high or you're under its feet and being ground into dust. A man must ride, Constant—don't you see that? A man must ride."

The urgency of her tone brought his eyes to rest on her face with a shadow of comprehension in them. He said with a melancholy dignity:

"It is a long time that I have been under its feet."

"I won't accept that."

"You think it is wrong to drink? to ease a little bit the awful darkness?"

"Constant," she said, "you know how it is with Doctor. He won't have you here if he finds out."

"Then I will go on."

"No. I have made up my mind. This is the turning place for you. Either you stay here, or you go back to the places where you have been."

"No, I cannot go back."

"Then you must stay here."

"Why do you care, An-na?"

"Because there is no one else who does."

"That is not the answer. It is true, but it is not the answer."

"Well, then I bother with you because of someone I knew— before I married Doctor. That is the truth, that is the answer."

His hand shook as he raised the coffee cup to his lips, but his eyes rested on her face with a melancholy lucidity. When he had drunk it, he set the cup on the table. Anna took it up and restored it to the saucer.

"Two shipwrecked persons," he said distinctly, still looking at her. "It's so, is it not? A great, dark ocean full of storm, *n'est-ce pas?* And we are two who float together clinging to wreckage of the past."

"Come," Anna said. "I will open your bed for you. You must sleep now, and not think at all. Tomorrow you will go on again."

"Yes, yes," he said. "Tomorrow I shall go on." He laughed a little foolishly and dropped his head forward on his arms. Anna had to shake his shoulder and make him get up. She put her arm around him and helped him to the bedroom. She unfastened his shoes and helped him with his coat and trousers. Her hands were quick and expert with his tie and collar and shirt. She stopped at his underwear, and pulled the covers over him.

"I thought that you were going to sleep with me," he said in the voice of a disappointed child.

"No," Anna said. "Sleep with your memories."

She folded his clothing neatly on the chair. Before she left the room, she lifted the lamp to look at a photograph on the chest of drawers. A little dark-eyed boy, dressed in a kilt and a white blouse with a wide collar, leaned against the arm of a chair. His dark hair fell in long ringlets about his serious face. Behind him was a painted backdrop of woods and clouds with a little temple of love. Anna took up the photograph and looked at it. The photographer's name and address were French. On the back was written in slanting, pointed handwriting in very black ink:

Eugène à quatre ans, trois mois.
Pour son papa.

She put the photograph back carefully. Constant had already fallen asleep. But she knew now that she had been neglecting the best tool she could have used in the rehabilitation of a man.

It was not difficult to make Dr. Hawkins believe that the idea of sending for Duval's boy was his own. Anna dropped only a few well placed remarks here and there to both Doctor and Duval, and they were presently planning the whole thing together.

Doctor was a little apologetic about it to Anna. "You wouldn't mind a little kid around the house again—a *boy*, would you Anna? The girls are away so much. They'll be getting married. The house is damned empty without little ones—and Duval needs something—"

"Wouldn't it be better if he had the boy to himself, doctor?"

"Well, maybe. But how could he, while the kid's so little? A housekeeper couldn't be depended on, but *you* know how to handle young ones, Anna. He could see the kid every day."

"I'd be willing," Anna said, "but Dr. Duval ought to come to me about it himself."

"He thinks it's an awful favor to ask. I told him the favor was all on his side to let us keep the kid for him."

"Well, let him come and ask me," Anna said.

Duval had been constrained with her ever since the night she had gone to his rooms. She did not know how much he remembered, but she did not care. It was enough for her to see that he had pulled himself together again.

She was making bread when he came to ask her. He had been going the round of his patients, and he smelt faintly of carbolic acid solution. He was very meticulous about cleanliness and the new use of antiseptics, which Doctor still dismissed as poppycock when he was in a hurry. He put his bag on a kitchen chair, and came and sat on the edge of the woodbox as he often did. It was high enough to suit his long legs.

Without looking at him Anna talked pleasantly as she worked; but she did not introduce the subject of his little boy. She wanted it to be their own idea, his and Doctor's. For a long time they skated awkwardly on the surface of generalities. He watched her kneading and molding her loaves. Finally he said:

"You like fashioning and shaping things, eh, An-na?"

"Perhaps."

"A man's life?"

"I like it better to see him shape it himself."

"Yes, I think so. But then, if he is too lazy or weak, then you will take a hand yourself. You have shown me that."

"Sometimes."

"And a little boy, perhaps? You would enjoy to help him grow into a good man?"

"You mean Eugene, don't you?"

"Yes, Anna."

"He is with his aunts in France, isn't he?"

"Yes, but they are older than I and not very broad-minded, as one says. That little narrow-mindedness of a provincial French town, that can set a boy on the wrong track, you know."

She looked at him pityingly.

"Yes?" she asked.

"I would like that he be an American."

"I think that is good, too," Anna said. "But you, Constant, aren't you ever going back yourself to face that provincial French town?"

"Not yet," he said. "Only you, Anna, know how great a coward I am. No, not yet."

"How will he come here?" Anna asked. "You won't go for him?"

"No, but there are French families traveling to America quite often in these days. He shall be put in the care of one of them, and, if he must travel alone some of the way, they will put a label on him that makes plain his destination."

"Poor little thing!" said Anna. "Does he know English?"

"Somewhat, I hope. I have had the parish priest teach him for the sake of his English mother."

"And you would like him to stay with us?"

"I can think of no better way until I find a suitable housekeeper."

"Or marry again?"

"No, not that."

"Yes, I'll keep him for you," Anna said. "I'm glad that you have decided to have him come."

"I don't know," he said hesitantly, "whether it is for myself or for him that I am causing this to be done—nor how it will end."

"It is a good thing!" Anna assured him warmly. "I'm sure it is right, Constant. I'm sure it is right." She arranged her pans of dough in a warm place and covered them with a clean cloth. "Now you are going to live again, Constant."

"You find it so?"

"Yes."

"Then I shall hope."

16

IT TOOK A LONG TIME for letters to go and come between Idaho and France; the French aunts had to be persuaded and convinced; the suitable emigrant family had to be found. It was spring of 1891 before Gene came from France, and he was five years old. He was a dark, handsome child, full of a roving curiosity and energy which bubbled through the surface crust of pretty manners that had been superimposed upon him. He had been stared at and petted and commented upon throughout his long journey, and he was at ease with strangers.

Doctor had wanted to go to the station to meet him, but Anna dissuaded him. "No. Don't do that. His father is a perfect stranger to him. Let him be there first and establish a little contact with him before he meets the rest of us. It's only fair."

Dr. Duval brought the child directly to them from the railroad station, and Anna saw with some amusement that although he was flushed with happiness at Gene's safe arrival, he was also a little uneasy until he could pass the responsibility of the boy's care along to someone else. He had never learned, in the gradual and normal way that family men learn, to be a father.

Well, he must learn now, Anna thought, *for both their sakes. This first constraint of meeting will soon pass away.* She knew how much thought Constant had given to the child's welfare before he came. He had bought a small bed for him and put his mind on proper mattresses and blankets, on how much air he should have while he slept, and on the kind of clothing he should wear. He had discussed and planned Gene's food very carefully with Anna, for Duval had notions about children's food. He believed that they should have eggs and milk and fresh fruits and vegetables. Common-sense food, Anna called it, but it was odd for a doctor to think so seriously about food, as if it were a kind of medicine. He had been quite definite that there should be warm milk and soft-boiled eggs for Gene's first supper.

"Doctor will have his roast," said Anna. "You don't think the boy will be disappointed not to have some too?"

"No, he will not be disappointed. European children are taught to obey. It is best so."

But Anna wondered. Gene had had a lot of liberty, traveling all that long way, now with one group of people, now another. A winsome small boy with a label marked "Idaho" would probably have been offered odd delicacies from all sorts of lunch baskets and platform coffee stands. A planned juvenile diet might have to be imposed upon him gradually. Yet she was so eager to do everything as Constant wished that she made no objection. Although he was to live with them until his father could make a home for him, she was determined that from the very start he must be Constant's child. She and Doctor must never come first, or the whole experiment would be a failure. The bond of language would tie father and son together at the beginning, she thought, until a firm, warm tie of affection bound them.

But Gene's first words showed her that he was already bilingual. He had no great need of his father as translator and interpreter. What the parish priest had begun in the way of Shakespearean English, the riffraff in American boats, trains, and railway stations had completed with a salty complement of slang.

"How do you do, madame?" Gene said, shaking hands with Anna. She could see that he was tired, but excited.

"Did you enjoy your long journey, dear?"

"I have a helluva time, thank you," said Gene gravely.

Doctor roared with laughter, but Constant was sincerely pained.

"It is something he has heard, you see."

"Of course," said Anna. "We'll take care of that. How about something to eat, Gene?"

"That is very bully, madame."

"And shall we wash first?"

"I expect."

"Make an American of him?" cried Doc. "Listen to him talk! He's a full-fledged Yankee already, ain't you, Gene?"

"Bet you boots!" said Gene, grinning. He and Doctor eyed each other, and both were pleased.

They sat at the table, and Christina put a roast in front of Doctor and soft-boiled eggs and warm milk in front of Gene.

"Can't he have meat?" asked Doctor.

Anna shook her head warningly.

"This is nicer for Gene," she said, smiling at the child.

But Gene had already pushed the bowl of eggs away. "I eat meat, if you please."

"Eugene," Duval said, "I prefer that you shall eat your egg. I have asked Meeses Hawkins to prepare it especially for you."

Anna saw the look change on the child's face.

"No, papa," Gene said, "I do not wish the eggs." His childish lips were set in a firm line of resistance.

"Whether you like them or not," said Dr. Duval gravely, "you will eat this one."

"No."

This is a bad beginning, Anna thought. Doctor went on carving the roast without saying anything, but there was a new air of tenseness all around the table.

"In France you have learned to obey when you are spoken to, n'est-ce pas, Eugène?"

"Oui."

"Et alors, en Amérique tu obéiras aussi, n'est-ce pas?"

"Je n'aime pas des œufs, tout de même, papa."

"We shall not leave the table," said Duval firmly, "until Gene has done Meeses Hawkins the courtesy of eating this egg."

The meal seemed very long.

Anna tried to bring the conversation around to pleasanter things; but through all lighter matters brooded the grim determination of two human beings. When everyone else had finished, Christina cleared away the dishes and brought the dessert; but Dr. Duval would not allow Gene's plate to be changed.

"He will eat his egg," he said.

"No," replied Gene.

"You see, Gene," said Anna, "if you ate it quickly, you could still have your dessert."

"I do not wish dessert, madame."

Doctor had kept quiet as long as it was possible.

"Oh, for God's sake," he shouted, "give the boy his dessert! Carry out that damned egg. It gives me dyspepsia just to look at it."

Anna rose quickly from the table.

"Doctor," she said, "you haven't rubbed down your horse. Now that you've finished dinner, you go to the barn. This has been a long, hard day, and Gene has come a long way. Tomorrow when he has

helped me feed the chickens and has gathered his own egg, I think
that he will eat it. Is that right, Gene?"

"*Oui, madame,*" Gene replied. The hard line of his mouth suddenly broke into a tremulous ripple. After all he was little more than
a baby.

"Shall we go to bed now? When you are all in your nightclothes,
I think you'll have your milk with some bread in it, won't you?"

The child made a little rush and thrust his head against her skirt,
clinging to it on either side with his two hands. She could feel and
hear his stifled sobbing. She put gentle hands on his dark head. The
long hair which she had seen in the photograph had been cut for
the journey, and the short, brown curls were thick under her fingers.
The two men got up awkwardly, their chairs scraping on the floor.

"Come, Gene," Anna said.

Still hiding his face against her skirt, the child let her lead him
away.

"You damn fool!" said Doctor to Duval. He turned and tramped
out through the kitchen to the barn.

When she returned to the dining room the table had been cleared,
but Dr. Duval sat on in his place beside the lamplit tablecloth. Doc
had not returned from the barn.

"I am sorry," Duval said. He looked troubled and humbled. Anna
came and stood beside him. She had an impulse, which she resisted,
to touch his close-cropped hair.

"Doctor was wrong to interfere," she said.

"It is only that I love him. I am his father. It is I who must see
that he is obedient and polite and that he eats what is good for him."

"He hasn't had a father for a long time," Anna said. "It's as
strange for him to have a father as it is for you to have a son. You
must remember that he's come halfway around the world alone,
making a good many of his own decisions, and for what? Why, to
have a strange man make him eat eggs when he's been used to deciding that he didn't like them."

"You are angry with me, as Doctor was," he said humbly. "But he has no mother, and I—I am a little bit ignorant about children."

"You will learn," Anna said. "Let your heart teach you. He isn't asleep yet. Tell me, can you sing anything, Constant—in French, I mean?"

He looked at her, appalled.

"Yes, of course," he said, "but why?"

"Go in then and tell him good night, and sing him something he might know, something you knew when you were a child."

He looked at her a moment without speaking. She could almost see the sweat breaking out on his forehead. She was not sure whether she wanted to laugh at him or cry. Then he turned around and went into the bedroom. After a little while she heard him singing. He had a warm, deep voice.

> *"Et ron, ron, ron, petit patapon*
> *Il était un' bergère*
> *Qui gardait ses moutons*
> *Ron, ron,*
> *Qui gardait ses moutons."*

Anna heard Doctor coming in the back door, scraping his feet on the doorstep and noisily banging a few sticks into the woodbox. He came and stood in the dining room door, lifting his head to listen to Duval's singing.

"My God!" he said. "What's the fool doing now?"

"Be still, doctor," Anna said. "I sent him in to sing to the child. The boy is his, not ours. We've got to see that they come together—in the right way."

Doctor was silent, his eyes moody.

"It beats all how this world is planned," he said at last, lowering himself heavily into his patent rocker. "If I had a kid like that—"

"I know," Anna said, "but we don't. We must always remember that."

"Yes," Doctor said. "Yes, I know that, Anna. I'm going to keep my hands off, and remember."

After a long time Duval came back and joined them. The sharpness of his face was misted over, his eyes were a trifle vague after the darkness of the bedroom. He did not immediately straighten his shoulders from bending over the small bed.

"I think that I must apologize," he said to Doctor in a low, formal voice, "first for that I behaved badly myself, and second for the behavior of my little boy."

"Listen!" Doctor said. "Don't ever apologize, Duval. You've got a boy there, a live one, a kid with some guts. Thank your lucky stars, that's all."

17

It was not Dr. Hawkins' fault that almost from the start Gene loved him best. He had propinquity on his side and a kind of childlike forthrightness that spoke to the child.

Gene loved Doc's great cats, and Doc allowed him to help with the feeding of them. He liked to follow Doc to the barn and imitate Doc's way with the horses. When Doc had a long country drive to make, he took Gene with him and let him stand between his knees, holding the ends of the reins and feeling that he drove. If Doctor wanted Gene to be quiet and not get into mischief while he made a long call, he gave the boy the responsibility of holding the horse. Gene took this seriously, even if he knew that Doctor had snapped a hitching strap around the post before he left them alone. There were always interesting encounters connected with these country trips. Sometimes a woman gave them new-made gingerbread or cookies; sometimes they stopped to "gas," as Doc said, with a farmer at a crossroads; sometimes they picked up passengers—a tramp, a boy hiking to town, an old prospector coming down from the hills. One day they had a race with the wheat buyer in his democrat wagon. It was a wonderful experience—the two horses running neck and neck in the narrow country road with Doc and the buyer both yelling and cracking their whips and the dust billowing out behind. Doc beat the buyer by a few feet to a narrow bridge and the other rig had to fall behind; but they went over a bump at the other end of the bridge and broke one of the traces, so that Doctor had to stop and mend it.

"Beat you just the same, by Gad!" Doctor shouted, as the grain man thundered by.

Gene jumped up and down in the buggy, shouting: "Beat you just the same, Mister! Beat you just the same!"

When Doc got back into the buggy, he said to Gene, "Don't you tell your father or your Auntie Anna how we broke that trace, will you, bub?"

"No, I won't," Gene said.

They looked at each other and laughed.

One day they picked up Jenny Walden out beyond the cemetery on a country road. She had a bunch of drooping wild flowers in her hand, and her straw hat was pushed on the back of her yellow hair.

"Going to San Francisco?" Doctor asked, as he stopped the horse for her.

She shook her head, smiling a little shyly at him. "No, just walking."

"You're a funny little gal," said Doctor. "Just walking! You know you oughtn't to go out so far alone."

"Look what I got," Jenny said, holding up the flowers.

"Something special?"

"Black-eyed Susans," she answered. "You have to walk a couple of miles for them."

"Are they worth it?"

"I thought so," Jenny replied. She looked at them now critically. They had begun to droop. "They'd be all right, if I had some water."

"Now you see if I'm not an accommodating man," said Doctor. He turned the horse in at the gate of the Stevens place and drove up to the watering trough.

"Uncle Doc was going to water his horse anyway," said Gene.

"You shouldn't tell that, Gene," Doctor protested. "We don't get so much credit for being accommodating."

Jenny jumped out of the buggy and ran to wet her handkerchief to wrap around the stems of the flowers. While the horse sucked deep draughts of the water, Doctor went to the back door of the house and knocked.

Mrs. Stevens came to the door. She looked dark and secretive.

"If it's about Alf you come," she said, "he's all right. He ain't done nothing untoward."

"No," Doctor explained, "I just wanted to water my horse. I thought I'd stop to see how you were making out while I was here. Everything going all right? You got some help with your harvest?"

"We're about as usual," Mrs. Stevens said, unsmiling. "Summer— winter, that's the only difference here. Ya, we can still pay for harvest help. We don't get nothing free."

Doctor laughed easily.

"Nobody does in this world, ma'am. It's pay as you go."

"Some folks get neighborliness at least," said the woman bitterly. "Seems like a hanging scares away any friends a body might have. All they do now is bear tales about my boy."

"I haven't heard any," said Doctor, "except that he rides his horse hell-bent and breakneck all over the country."

Mrs. Stevens did not answer. She was a small, stony-faced woman. She looked beyond him towards the bleak expanse of wheat fields, and Doc saw that the interview was closed.

"Well, good day to you," he said.

He went back to the watering trough and fastened up his horse's check rein. Jenny was still dabbling her flower stems in the water, and he saw that young Stevens had come out of the barn to watch her. The boy had shot up in the years since his father's death and he was almost a man in his proportions, but there was something in his face that Doctor did not like. He held a whip in one hand, and the dog that skulked behind him looked as if it might have known the lash.

He waved the dog back now with a threatening motion of the whip as he moved slowly towards the horse trough with his eyes on Jenny's face.

"You want flowers?" he asked in a voice that sounded rough and hoarse from disuse.

"I have some," Jenny said. "They're wilted but they'll be better with some water."

The boy went to the side of the house where an untended flower-bed flourished raggedly between the path and the pump. There were yellow tansy—"old man," as the country people called it—and an ubiquitous pink flower known as Bouncing Betsy. They were proof against negligent gardening. Among them grew dog fennel and clover. Alf snatched handfuls quickly and carelessly until he had a large bouquet. The broken stems of the tansy gave off a pungent odor that compelled the nostrils without exactly pleasing them. He went close to Jenny and thrust the flowers into her hands. Jenny was fastidious about flowers. She had walked a long way to get the ones she wanted. But she was also good-natured, and she did not like to hurt people's feelings. She gave Alf one of her exquisite smiles.

"Thank you," she said.

The boy lifted a dirty hand as if he were going to stroke her hair, but Doctor's voice snapped out like the report of a pistol.

"All right now, Alf!" and "Get in, Jenny," he added. He didn't like a half-grown boy looking at a little girl like that.

Alf swung his head around quickly and looked at Doctor as if he had not known that he was there. Then his eyes slid away from the older man's like the eyes of an animal which has not had gentle handling, like those of his own dog.

"I hope you don't mind our watering up here," Doctor said, pleasantly enough now. "Most folks don't."

"*I* do," Alf said in a rough voice.

"Oh, come now, bub," Doctor said easily. "I pulled you out of a fit once. Remember? I thought we were good friends."

"I want no friends," Alf said, and, with a quickness which went side by side with a heaviness in his movements, he disappeared into the barn.

"Kind of grumpy," Doctor remarked cheerfully, driving out into the road again. "Look here, Jenny, you keep away from this road in your rambles for wild flowers, will you? That's a mean-looking kid to have around."

"He gave me flowers."

"Just the same you keep away from him. He might harm you."

"What would he do?" asked Jenny.

"H'm-m," Doc said. "He had a whip, didn't he? You saw that."

"I don't think he'd whip me," Jenny said. "He doesn't look at me that way. Lots of people look at me. I don't care."

"Well, you might, some day. You've got to watch out for yourself, a kid like you—"

"I know."

"*What* do you know?" Doc asked in exasperation. "Nothing very much, I'll bet."

"I've read a lot of books," said Jenny defensively. "I know a lot of things."

"How old are you now, my girl?"

"I'm thirteen."

"That's right. You had the measles when you were nine and that's four years ago."

"No, it was scarlet fever."

"My Lord, you're right! And so you read a lot of books? How far you got in school?"

"I'll be in the eighth grade when school starts. I'll be through next year."

"And what'll you do then? Would you like to go on?"

"Oh, yes," Jenny said, "but there's only money enough to send one of us away. Della's going away in the fall because she's the oldest. She's going to be a school teacher. But I've got to stay home and help mama keep house." She wrinkled her nose and stuck out her tongue at the prospect.

Doctor and Gene laughed, but Doctor was excited, too. He had forgotten the Stevens boy already and begun thinking of his pet project.

"You know what I'm going to do, Jenny?" he asked. "I'm going to get an academy started here next year, so you kids who want to go on from the eighth grade can do it. It isn't right that we have to send our kids away to get them educated, is it, Gene?"

"You bet you boots!" said Gene.

"You mean I could go on to school for a long time?" Jenny asked eagerly.

"Maybe two years to start with, then three or four or more as we get money and buildings and teachers. Would you like that?"

"Oh, yes!"

"By thunder!" said Doc. "I'll get it started so you can begin in the first class, Jenny. Shall I do that?"

"Oh, yes!"

"You'll have to study hard this year then, my girl, so you'll be a credit to the Academy's first graduating class, eh?"

"Oh, I *will*," Jenny promised.

"And me? Me too?" asked Gene.

"Yes sir! You, too, Frenchie, when the time comes. Your Uncle Doc will see to that, by Gad!"

"For that Stevens boy, too?" Jenny asked doubtfully.

Doc laughed. "Well, I don't know. Maybe higher education wouldn't take with that kid, like some young ones won't take the mumps or the smallpox when everybody else has them. But we'll see —we'll see."

They clattered into town with bright eyes in their sunburned faces. And Dr. Hawkins was started on his campaign for the Golden West Academy.

18

SOMETIMES, thinking of the new Academy, Jenny did work hard that year. Education was not a matter of course or a social expedient in those days in the West; it was something rare and desirable, too often just beyond reach. And Jenny was one of the "sharp" children who would benefit by education, so her teachers thought—that is when she didn't go dreamy and remote with sudden vacant eyes. The trouble was, perhaps, that learning came too easily to her. Often her eyes were out the window while the class droned on with something which she had already leapt at and lost interest in. But she liked to understand things, and when the teacher tried to introduce them to poetry by way of some of Mr. Longfellow's earlier efforts, Jenny was annoyed and impatient. She liked things to make sense, and she seriously questioned whether poetry made sense.

> *Wondrous truths, and manifold as wondrous,*
> *God hath written in those stars above;*
> *But not less in the bright flowerets under us*
> *Stands the revelation of his love.*

Why wasn't it better to say: *God has written wonderful truths in the stars and revealed his love in the flowers?* There was much less fuss and the result seemed clearer and more satisfactory.

She took the question home to her mother.

"Mama, why do people write poetry?"

"I don't know, I'm sure," said Mrs. Walden. It was a question which had never troubled her.

"Well, I wondered, because it seems so much easier to say things straight. There must be a reason."

"I suppose it's something like singing. You don't say things straight in singing."

"No, but that's not the same either. I don't like poetry if there's no reason for it except to make things hard to understand."

"Don't they tell you at school why people write it, Jenny?"

"No, they just tell us to read it. Mama, do we have any books of poetry here? Some of the children have. I'm supposed to read some."

"There are the Psalms, of course."

"No, I don't think so," Jenny said. "They don't rhyme."

"Well, ask your father, dear."

The Reverend Mr. Walden was even more vague. He was in the midst of preparing a rather trying sermon, and his ideas on secular literature were not easily brought to the surface. He rumpled his thin hair and looked at her with his kind blue eyes preoccupied and unseeing.

"Later, my girl," he said, "later. Papa's busy."

Jenny caught up one of her mother's shawls and started up the hill. There would be books at Dr. Hawkins'.

Halfway up the hill Jenny saw Mrs. Shanley, the divorced woman, working in her little patch of garden. All summer it had been gaudy with flowers, and now she was clipping withered stalks and spading and mulching in preparation for winter. Mrs. Shanley's short gray curls glistened in the autumn sunlight; her face was soft and full of little undecided lines. Jenny had never exchanged a word with her before, but now she had a sudden impulse to speak to her.

"Good morning, Mrs. Shanley."

"Hello, there."

Leaning on the picket fence, Jenny was suddenly embarrassed to know what to do with the conversation which she had initiated.

"Well? You want something?" Mrs. Shanley asked.

Jenny laughed. "I'm trying to find out why they write poetry."

"Did you think I'd know?"

"I guess not."

"You're a pretty girl, ain't you?"

Jenny was used to that. "Oh, nothing extra, I guess," she said, laughing again.

"Yes, kind of extra. I hope you'll be happy."

"Well, I am," Jenny said.

"I know. I meant later. Look, here's the last rose in the garden. I'll give it to you. There's a song like that, *The Last Rose of Summer*. Do you know it?"

"Yes, the soprano in our choir sings it—I don't mean in church, but if there's a concert. She takes a rose and tears the petals off one by one while she sings."

"It's a pretty song. I used to sing it. Well, there you are. It matches your cheeks."

"Thank you, Mrs. Shanley."

Jenny went on up the hill, thinking: *She's just like anybody else. I don't see any difference.* But then she thought, as she went farther, *I'll throw the rose away before I get home. Mama and Della wouldn't want me to have a rose from a divorced woman.*

The little French boy was playing in the large yard at Doctor's house. Jenny could not make out whether he was an architect or a horse. He had made an elaborate labyrinth of low walls by raking leaves into windrows, and now he ran between them, prancing and lifting his feet in the air and tossing his head. Sometimes he stooped and caught an armful of the leaves which he tossed upward to the wind. Anyway he was having a good time.

Indoors Mrs. Hawkins and Dr. Duval were sitting by the dining-room table which had a crocheted doily on it and a plate of red apples. Mrs. Hawkins was darning some of the little boy's stockings; and Jenny saw by his hat and bag on the chair beside him that Dr. Duval was only there in passing. She did not feel at ease with Dr. Duval as she did with Dr. Hawkins. Perhaps she resented him a little because he did not notice her as other people did and say, "Isn't she a pretty child? and smart, too!" She looked at Mrs. Hawkins and said, "I wonder if you have any poetry books I could borrow?"

"I wouldn't be surprised," Mrs. Hawkins said. "Doctor has a little of everything there. Do you want to go and look?"

"Poetry?" said Dr. Duval. "Does anyone in Opportunity read poetry?"

"I guess not," Jenny replied, "except for school. I think it's silly to twist words all around just so they make a rhyme, when you can say it plainer without. Do you know why they do it?"

"Yes," the French doctor said. "I can tell you."

Jenny was surprised.

"Why?" she asked.

"It is to make you feel what they say with your heart as well as your mind, I think."

"But I don't understand—"

"Have you read Shakespeare?"

"No," Jenny said. He had spoken to her as if she were an adult, and Jenny was ashamed that she had not read Shakespeare. "I thought he wrote plays."

"Ah, yes, but the poetry also. Forget the little, silly words that rhyme. There are bigger things than that in poetry, are there not, An-na?"

Mrs. Hawkins laughed.

"We have a book of Shakespeare, if you want it," she said. "I guess Doctor has Robert Browning, too."

Dr. Duval went with Jenny into the parlor where the books were kept, and ran his long brown finger up and down the shelves until he found the book of Shakespeare's plays. He pulled it out and opened it, running through the pages as if in search of something.

> *"Oh, speak again, bright angel! for thou art*
> *As glorious to this night, being o'er my head,*
> *As is a winged messenger of heaven*
> *Unto the white-upturned wondering eyes*
> *Of mortals . . ."*

He broke off in the midst of the reading, his eyes sad.

"It is a long time since I have read it aloud," he said. "No, no! Poetry, it is not for the schools to teach. Wait until you have a lover, Jenny." He put the book roughly into her hands.

"*Romeo and Juliet,*" Jenny read. "I know about them. They died, didn't they?"

"They died for love," said Dr. Duval solemnly.

"For love," Jenny repeated, wondering a little how that could be.

"Listen, Constant," Mrs. Hawkins said. "Start her on something else. She's too young for that. She's only a little girl."

"I am nearly fourteen," Jenny said, drawing herself up. She did not like Mrs. Hawkins when she spoke of her as a little girl. Dr. Duval had made her feel grown-up.

"*La petite Juliette* had only fourteen years, An-na," the French doctor said, smiling. "Love is for the young. Why should we deprive them of it?"

They were looking at each other now, and not at her, Jenny saw. There was something different about their eyes.

"Perhaps you are right," Mrs. Hawkins said in a low voice. "Why should we?"

Jenny took the Shakespeare and the Browning which Mrs. Hawkins held out, and went away with them under her arm. At the foot of the hill she opened the first one to the *Romeo and Juliet,* and began to read as she walked slowly along. Much of it was dull and hard to understand, but still there were parts which said things better than they could be said in prose. It was not the same as taking a common sentence and twisting it out of shape so it would rhyme. This was different. There seemed some reason for it. And it was beautiful, too, to think of anyone dying for love. "They died for love," Jenny said to herself. It gave her a strange sensation of pleasure. It was the kind of thought you could keep inside yourself and take out to look at once in a while. She did not speak to Mrs. Shanley as she went back because she was too engrossed to see her.

Walking home from school, when things had been dull and tiresome all day, Jenny could say to herself, *They died—for love,* and there was suddenly that feeling of mystery and happiness. *For love— for love.* The world was beautiful again and full of a secret promise that nobody else shared or understood. *They died—for love.*

It was Jenny's introduction to poetry. Reading in the books she had borrowed from the Hawkins' parlor, she forgot to ask why poets went such a long way around to say simple things. She didn't take the books to school as she had thought she would at first; but she learned some of the lines by heart to say to herself on nights when the wind blew so that it shook the house and she lay awake to listen to it, or on clear afternoons of winter when to look at the blue of the mountains was to ache for words which expressed beauty.

"Poetry is not for the schools to teach, Jenny," Dr. Duval had said. "Wait until you have a lover."

Would she have a lover? she wondered. But he had said: "Does anyone in Opportunity read poetry?" No, she must go away somewhere, when she could, where there were blue silk dresses and lovers who would recite poetry, where the sun would always shine, and she could be free and beautiful without the congregation having to be thought of, and where she could weep if she wanted to without having to hide herself in the privy or the little closet under the stairs.

In the midst of her natural gaiety and good nature, Jenny was still a rebel and a hungry seeker for something which she did not have.

19

Doc Hawkins talked about the new Academy now wherever he went. Aiming a jet of saliva expertly at the spittoon in the drugstore, while he waited for a prescription to be put up, Doc regaled the bystanders with the pleasures of higher education. He slapped Postmaster Peavy amiably on the back and said, "By God, Peavy, it's influential citizens like you who ought to be behind this thing." To Larkin, the lawyer, he said: "We've got to stand for the intellectual life out here at the edge of the wilderness, Larkin. If the professional men don't hang together on a question of this kind, there'll be no intellectual future for this state."

He dropped in on Mr. Walden and sat for an hour with him one evening in his little study. The preacher did not often smoke, but that night they both puffed comfortably on Doctor's expensive cigars.

"I promised Jenny I'd have an academy ready for her when she stepped out of the eighth grade," Doctor chuckled. "Wouldn't want to disappoint the kid either."

"She's counting on it, doctor," Walden laughed. "I suspect that you come next after God in Jenny's scheme of things."

"Well, she's a little gal with a future, I believe, as far as any woman can have one. She's sharp, Jenny is. It's almost a pity she's so confounded pretty, if you'll excuse me saying so, Walden."

Mr. Walden's eyes grew tender.

"She's a good little girl," he said.

"Well, drop a few hints with regard to generosity and the life of the mind in your sermons, will you, reverend?"

"I'll do that, doctor. I think some higher education might do a lot to counteract the influence of the saloons in this town. I suppose the Presbyterians stand behind you in this, too?"

"By George, they'd better!" Doctor said. "Look at the bell I got them."

Doctor sat with Mrs. Kessler by the stove in her parlor and balanced a teacup skillfully on his knee. Here was a woman who knew how to put on style. In a pale blue cashmere tea gown with lace at the neck and sleeves and a little train to sweep across the garlands of roses on her Brussels carpet, Mrs. Kessler was like something out of *Leslie's Ladies' Journal*. She lay back languidly in her chair with a stylish little black and tan thoroughbred dog on her knee. Doc didn't particularly like black and tans. There seemed to be more yap than dog to them. Replete with cake, this one alternately yawned and shivered, his eyes half closed in his narrow, ferret face. But Doc appreciated that he was in the height of fashion just as the blue cashmere was. When she wore a gown like that, it didn't particularly matter to him that Mrs. Kessler was pale and flabby and a scandalmonger.

Her house had the same effect on Doctor. He looked at the Moorish corner in her front hall, at the fishnet draped above the red plush lounge in the parlor and stuck full of photographs, at the enlarged crayon portraits of her mother and father in massive gilt frames, and, as always, he was impressed. It is true that the eyes of the portraits had a piscine quality which went well with the fishnet, but, if the crayon artist had not quite caught the human expression, he had more than done justice to the diamond earrings and shirt studs of his sitters.

Doctor leaned forward and patted the blue cashmere knee of his hostess.

"And how is our patient today?"

"Rather poorly," Mrs. Kessler said. "Oh, doctor, you're the only one who knows what I suffer. Even Mr. Kessler—a businessman, you know—how could he understand?"

"You're a brave little woman, my dear. The capsules holding out all right?"

"Yes, but I'm wondering if you couldn't make them just a little stronger, doctor? I tried to go without them a few days as you suggested, but oh, doctor! the frightful gnawing in my vitals! the sense of giddiness! the palpitations of the heart! I wonder sometimes if you have put some fearfully insidious drug into my capsules, doctor. I'm so utterly helpless without them."

"No, ma'am, I'll swear there's no habit-forming drug in 'em," said Doc. "But you just need a little bracer, and this mixture seems to give it to you."

"Oh, it does indeed, Dr. Hawkins. Sometimes I wake up in the night and think, 'What if Dr. Hawkins should die without leaving a record of my medicine? How could I go on, facing the rest of my life without it?' You *will* leave a record of it, won't you, doctor?"

"I've written it all out in my record book at the office," Doctor assured her. "It goes like this: *Patient, Mrs. Kessler: Tendency to lipothymy and hysteria, general debility, pallor, and a slight flaccidity. Prescription: sucrose et sodium bicarb. capsules magnum. This*

*has been most helpful in Mrs. Kessler's peculiar case, and treatment
should be continued as long as needed."*

Mrs. Kessler listened with morbid pleasure.

"Oh, thank you, doctor! I feel so much safer now that I know.
Although, of course, it's silly for me, with my frail constitution,
even to think of the possibility of surviving anyone. God knows, I'll
be the first to go."

"Come, now, cheer up, ma'am. You know that's what we all
admire in you—your courage, Mrs. Kessler—your courage!" Doctor
helped himself to a second slice of Mrs. Kessler's admirable pound
cake. "Have you ever thought of some kind of memorial to yourself
and family, Mrs. Kessler? Something permanent and on a high
plane?" He glanced respectfully at Mrs. Kessler's father's diamond
studs. Sometime Doctor meant to have studs like those, and earrings
for Anna, too, by God!

"Well, yes," said Mrs. Kessler cautiously. "You mean a stained-
glass window, I suppose?"

"No, ma'am, I don't. One well aimed rock in the hands of a small
boy, Mrs. Kessler, and your stained-glass memorial has gone to
blazes. No! but a part in putting books and the power of knowledge
into that small boy's hands instead of a rock. There, Mrs. Kessler—
there you have a real memorial!"

"You mean—"

"I mean an endowment for an academy, Mrs. Kessler. I mean an
investment in the intellectual future of a city in a great new state.
God didn't grant you children of your own, ma'am, any more than
He granted me the favor of living sons, but He *has* put into your
hands and my hands the power to mold the lives of hundreds of
young people in Opportunity today and of generations upon generations as yet unborn."

"You think so?" Mrs. Kessler asked.

Doctor's dark eyes snapped. The room blazed and crackled with
his oratory and the fervor of his convictions.

"*Think?*" he said. "My dear lady, I *know* it." He set his cup and saucer dangerously near the edge of the marble-topped parlor table, and shook the crumbs from his napkin onto the piece of zinc under the stove. Mrs. Kessler moved the teacup back a few inches to the safety of the red chenille tablecloth, but in spite of her housewifely caution, she was deeply moved. A stained-glass window did not seem important at all now, compared with this vision of power and influence.

Doctor rose abruptly and reached for his hat and bag; but he set them down again immediately and turned back to take Mrs. Kessler's plump, limp hand in both of his.

"Well, I've given my little patient something to think about, haven't I?"

"Indeed you have, doctor."

"But don't forget the afternoon rest, my dear. Don't let the old fool doctor keep you awake with his impossible notions."

"Not impossible, doctor! Not impossible!"

Doctor went away feeling optimistic and in excellent spirits.

"That was damned good cake," he said to himself. "Anna ought to get the receipt. Damned good cake."

Jenny Walden saw how Doc Hawkins went about his campaign for the academy, and she was as smart as he was about getting what she had set her heart on.

"Look! Don't you want to go on to school next year?" she said to the other pupils. "Tell your parents to go to the meeting Doctor's having in the courthouse next week. Maybe my father's going to speak. Tell them to write to the Governor at Boise City about an appropriation for the school, and maybe they can give something themselves." She smiled particularly at the boys when she said it, and her smile took the intellectual curse off the subject matter. She and Doc Hawkins were a pretty good team, she thought. Doctor probably would have agreed if anyone had called his attention to the fact that Jenny was campaigning, too.

So the Golden West Academy started temporarily the next fall in an empty store building, and all the preceding summer the brickyard had been busy turning out piles of brilliantly red brick for such a new building as should shed glory on the town. At Doctor's urging they put the building on a hill across the railroad tracks where everyone could see it and feel pride. It would be the first and last thing in town to be seen by travelers on the railroad. They had the Governor up from the south to lay the cornerstone; and Doctor in a high silk hat headed the delegation that received him. The building went up perpendicular and Gothic, and also very red, with an abundance of decoration in white limestone as if the builders had been over it with frosting in a pastry tube. There were many steps to climb to it; and, inside, more steps mounted and mounted to a final small observatory in the tower.

"Hitch your wagon to a star," was one of Doctor's favorite sayings, and something of this intention had gone into the building of the Golden West Academy. It was an achievement of which the town was proud.

20

THE YEAR OF Doctor's great triumph in the founding of the Academy gave him also two disappointments.

He had sent his two daughters back to San Francisco to boarding school again that year, because they were already past the point where the infant academy could do their education any good. Mary was to graduate in the spring and Lita the next year, and Doctor was planning how he and Anna would use the railroad passes to see Mary graduate. The girls would be proud to show off their parents to the other girls—their father, the prominent physician of the new state, looking still young and handsome in his high silk hat and frock coat with his gold-headed cane. As soon as they were educated, Doctor planned, he'd begin to look around for husbands for them. He didn't want them to be schoolmarms; he could afford to make ladies of them. He could afford it. But how long could he stand their living at home, playing the piano at night when he wanted to sleep or acting plays in the parlor, leaving their fans and parasols on his desk or in his favorite chair, and having their tantrums across his dinner table? Not very long, he thought. No, as soon as they were graduated he meant to pick the right young men to husband them. There would be a big, fine wedding for each of them. It would cost a lot, but he could afford it. He'd invite all of his patients, every one, by God! And that meant practically the whole town. It would be a high-class Presbyterian wedding he'd give each one, and the sexton could split himself ringing the bell for them. Yes, Doc's girls would be married right!

In the fall of '92 Doctor came home in the middle of the morning with a face like thunder. Hearing buggy wheels, Anna looked out of the front window and saw him coming up the walk with a yellow envelope in his hands. He was white to the lips, and his dark eyes more prominent than usual; and Anna knew that something terrible had happened. Her woman's heart cried: "Death!" And, when she met him at the door, her face was almost as pale as his. Sensing disaster in the air, Gene followed her to the door, his hand on her skirt.

"What's wrong, doctor?" Anna asked.

Doc stalked past her as if he could not hear, and flung the telegram on the dining-room table.

"There's your daughter," he cried. "Seventeen, and she's gone and eloped! By God, if I could get my hands on that man who ran away with her, I'd beat the life out of him!"

"Mary?" Anna said. "Eloped? Oh, is that all? Thank God!"

"*Is that all?*" roared Doctor. "Isn't it enough? Isn't it enough?"

Anna read the telegram silently. It was hard to believe that Mary would have married without telling them. It was only a few weeks since she had gone back to school with Lita. Her father had paid her tuition until the next spring. Why, she was only a little girl, Anna thought—and she had eloped.

"Did you know about this, Anna?" cried Doctor. "She calls him Harry. Harry who? For God's sake, *Harry who?*"

"There was a boy named Harry she talked about this summer," said Anna. "His father had a hardware store, I think, and his sister went to the boarding school. I never thought that it was anything."

"*You never thought that it was anything,*" cried Doc. "By thunder! you pretty nearly eloped yourself when you were a girl, didn't you? A dozen people told me so when I was courting you."

"Are you annoyed with *me*, doctor?"

"You? No! I'm mad at that girl. I'll disown her, that's what I'll do. Never let her show her face at this house again! Never let her darken my door!"

"Doctor," said Anna, "you're talking like something in a novel. Come down to earth before you've vowed more than you can keep."

"My eldest daughter! Run away at seventeen and married a no-account."

"How do you know he's a no-account? He's got a job in his father's store, I'm pretty sure. Maybe she's done better than if you'd picked the man yourself. Besides she'll get play-acting out of her mind now with a husband to cook for. What I was afraid of this summer was that she wanted to be an actress."

"Confound you, Anna! You always make the best of everything. You can't let a man enjoy a decent fit of anger without sticking your oar in."

"Doctor, I guess I feel as bad about this thing as you do. I'm trying to argue with myself, too."

"All right," he said irritably. "What do you want me to do? Forgive them both? Give them my blessing?"

"What else is there to do now without making a bad job worse? What's done can't be undone."

"You're so damned logical," said Doc. "It's the one thing I can't forgive you—always being so damned right."

"I think I was right, too, when I wanted to keep the girls at home with us more. But you were always for sending them away, doctor.

Yet now you are surprised that one of them has met a man you
don't know, and married him."

Doctor was silent. Anna didn't often talk back, but when she did,
by George! there was no worsting her.

They looked at each other for a long moment across the crumpled
yellow paper on the table. Gradually both of their faces softened.
Then Doctor came around the table and took Anna by the shoulders
and kissed her cheek. For a moment they clung together, Anna's
heavy chestnut hair sweet against his cheek and on his shoulder. Her
breath came quickly, somewhere between sobbing and laughter.
Doctor began to laugh, too, the kind of laughter that hurts a long
way down.

"Look here, Anna," he said. "We'll be grandparents before you
know it. Maybe a boy—"

"That's more like you, now, doctor, counting your chickens before
they're hatched."

"Yes, by George, it might even be a boy. We've got a fifty-fifty
chance. I might even get a boy—"

Gene, who had been watching this scene with considerable bewilderment, cried suddenly, "*I* am your boy, Uncle Doc."

Doc's laughter didn't hurt so much now.

"By George, you are, young feller!" He caught Gene up and
tossed him to the ceiling. "Maybe I'll have a half a dozen boys
before I'm through, but you'll be the first, Gene, you'll be the first."

Gene shrieked with the suddenness of his ascent and the delight
of Uncle Doc's approbation. He was much happier here than he had
been in France with the old aunts.

Mary settled in a small northern California town to be a hardware clerk's wife. It wasn't what Doctor had planned for her, but,
seeing Anna accept it without questioning, he gradually reconciled
himself to it. They talked of bringing Lita home, but after all it
seemed foolish to do that now. Another year and a half and she

would be "finished," as the head mistress of her boarding school put it.

"Let her be finished," Doctor said. "Few enough things are ever finished in this world. By God! let the girl be finished."

21

THE OTHER DISAPPOINTMENT which Doctor had that year was perhaps not so much a disappointment as an irritation, a something which he felt unable to cope with satisfactorily. Doctor was usually so sure of everything, particularly himself, that to doubt for a moment his own wisdom and ability was distressing to him. The case of the Stevens boy lay heavily on his mind, and what he did in connection with it vexed and troubled him more than most of his cases did.

For a year now reports had been coming in to him about Alf Stevens' crazy actions. He'd seen the boy himself riding his horse breakneck through the Saturday night crowd on Main Street, licking the poor brute with a whip to make it go faster, and watching out of his sly little eyes to see the furor he was creating.

Any young buck from the hills will do that sort of thing on a Saturday night after he's had a glass or two of whisky, Doc reflected; but still there were these repeated complaints from the neighbors, and at the back of his mind Doc kept the memory of that look the boy had had for little Jenny Walden when he gave her the flowers. The neighbors complained that Alf mistreated his horses, that he prowled about their places and looked in their windows at night, and that he did a lot of other queer things. Some of them even claimed that he was brutal to his mother, that he struck her as often as he did his dog or horse. However that might be, her voice was never raised against him. She might be hard to live with, but she was loyal to her son. People avoided them more and more, and began pointing the house out to strangers. "That's where Alf Stevens lives. Don't go in there, or they'll have the dogs on you. Queer folks, they are. His old man hanged himself."

Doc just laughed a little to hear people talk. He didn't want to get mixed up in it.

Instead of riding straight into town from the south, Alf used to cut in through Swedetown and the residential district, galloping, hell-bent, down past the Methodist church and parsonage and so to Main Street. The winding route he had laid out for himself took him past the Kessler residence, and Mrs. Kessler never heard him clattering by without resentment for the noise he made and the unnecessary dust he raised to soil her lace curtains or lie in an unpleasant film on the bright surface of her rose mahogany. Her little dog was frantic when he heard Alf riding by, and rushed up and down the inside of the picket fence barking his shrill displeasure. One day he found the gate open, and Alf's horse trampled him and killed him.

Kessler came to Dr. Hawkins then.

"Hawkins," he said, "that boy is crazy. You know it as well as I do. Next time it's liable to be a child instead of a dog."

Doctor considered. He had been out twice to give Mrs. Kessler sedatives since she had lost her little dog, and he was slightly tired of the whole affair.

"What can I do, Kessler?"

"Well, *you* should know that better than I do, doctor. Give him an examination, commit him to the new asylum over to Orofino."

"By God, I hate to shut a young human being up in one of those crazy houses," Doctor said. "I'd rather see the fellow dead."

"I know," Kessler said, "but you've got to think of the safety of the sane folks in this town."

"I'm no authority on mental troubles," Doc said crossly.

"You're the best we've got," said Kessler jovially.

That snapped Doc out of it. He wouldn't have anybody question his authority to act for the best interests of Opportunity.

"I'll see what I can do," he said.

Sitting in the office later, he talked the matter over with Duval.

"The kid is not quite normal, that's a fact," Doctor said, "but still it's a border-line case. I hate to shut the fellow up with a lot of God-damned loonies, when he might pull out of it and make a useful citizen."

"I should not have too great an optimism," said Duval. *"Dementia praecox,* I should say it was, coming on with adolescence, after an emotional shock, as you say. One never knows at what moment the fellow may become violent."

"I s'pose you're right. The fellow's always making threats of violence, too, I hear. It don't seem safe to leave him running around loose."

Kessler made the formal complaint against the boy and had Peavy sign it with him, and the law had its finger in the case with Sam Larkin making out commitment papers. Doc gave Alf as thorough an examination as he could, according to his lights; but after all, as he himself said, a doctor who's had to concentrate all his efforts on delivering babies and setting bones and preventing gangrene and fighting diphtheria hasn't had much time to go into the fine points of these mental diseases. Alf certainly acted crazy, and Doc signed a report to that effect and gave it to Larkin.

Doc went down to the station when the deputy sheriff took Alf away. He said: "Look here, Alf, this is just a kind of rest cure we're giving you. You're going to a hospital for a while. You be good and quiet and do what they tell you, and you'll be coming back one of these days, all cured up. You see?"

Alf did not reply. He was sunk in a heaviness of despair and resentment. Doctor did not know how much the boy understood of what was being done to him.

Jenny Walden, coming home past the depot from the new Academy with a boy on each side of her carrying her books, saw Dr. Hawkins on the platform. "Give me my books," she said to the boys, "I'll ride uptown with Doc."

The boys were disgusted. Lester Davis grumbled: "Oh, shoot! What do you want to ride with that old fogy for?"

Jenny was arch. "He's my best fellow."

"We'll stay, too."

"If you do, none of us will get a ride. Go on. I'll see you tomorrow."

Reluctantly they gave up her books. "Silly!"

"Silly yourselves."

Jenny came to stand beside Doctor and watch the train go out.

"Hello, little one," he said.

"Hello, doc."

She looked up to the open car window and saw Alf Stevens sitting beside the deputy sheriff.

"What's he done?" Jenny wanted to know.

"He's sick," Doctor explained. "Going away for a little change of air."

"Oh, I'm sorry!" Jenny exclaimed. Stuck in her belt she had a sprig of juniper which she had broken from one of the hedges along the way. She pulled it out now and tossed it into the car window. "Here, Alf," she said. "That's for you. I hope that you get better soon."

Alf leaned forward to pick up the fallen bit of green, and suddenly he began to sob, a terrible, hoarse sobbing that shook his shoulders. A moment later the pitiable sound of his crying was drowned in the noise of the departing train.

Jenny looked at Doctor with troubled eyes.

"I never meant to make him cry," she said. "How terrible!"

"It's not your fault," said Doc. "The poor kid's crazy. They're taking him to Orofino."

"Oh!" Jenny said. "I didn't know. I guess I shouldn't have spoken to him."

"Sometimes it's good for them to cry. It loosens up the knots inside. Forget about him now. That's what I'm going to do."

"I'll try."

"Want a ride as far as Main Street?"

"Yes. That's why I stopped when I saw you. I knew you'd give me a lift, Dr. Hawkins."

"The hack drivers and liverymen are going to run me out of town," Doc laughed. "I'm a menace to their business."

"A very nice one," Jenny said archly.

By God, the child's a coquette already, Doc said to himself. *But with a face like that, maybe she can't help it.* Aloud, he said, "School going pretty well?"

"It's fine," Jenny said. "It's really too easy. I thought the Academy was going to be hard."

"All you have to do is smile, eh?" Doctor teased.

"That's about the size of it," said Jenny, treating the old Doctor to one of the most disarming of those smiles.

"Well, don't forget that a little elbow grease is a good thing, too, my girl!"

"I won't," said Jenny.

She got down at the corner of Main Street and Elm, and tossed him a careless kiss off the tips of her fingers, her eyes demure under her long lashes. Doc let the horse stand a moment while he watched her swinging up the hill, her schoolbooks over her shoulder. All of her angles had suddenly—overnight, it seemed—become curves.

"My God," said Doctor, "there goes a charge of dynamite, if ever I saw one!"

He slapped the reins over the mare's back and let her take her own way to the office.

That autumn Doc saw to it that Mrs. Stevens had all the groceries that she needed to take her through the winter. He got the Masons interested in the case, and they hauled and cut her winter's wood for her. Her husband had been a Mason and Doc said they owed it to her.

22

ANNA HAD BEEN feeding the chickens when Dr. Duval came through the back door looking for her and Gene.

"He's not home from school yet," she said. "It won't be long, though. I'm going to the barn to mix up some bran mash for the colt. Will you come along?"

Dr. Duval set his bag on the back step and went to open the barn door for her.

"The chore boy doesn't get home from the Academy until five," she said apologetically. "Doctor doesn't like me doing this, but the colt gets hungry!"

She had on one of Doc's old hats and a man's coat over her house dress. In one hand she had a measure of bran, and in the other a steaming kettle. She looked as if she were enjoying herself.

"You make me to laugh, An-na," Duval said.

"Doctor says I was cut out for a farmer's wife. He doesn't like that."

"I believe that I do."

"Only to laugh at?"

"It is more than I could do when I came here—to laugh, I mean."

He followed her into the barn. Doctor had built it on the same scale as he would have built a country barn. There were vast hay-mows, room for the sleigh, the phaeton, and a light buggy, shadowy harness racks and grain bins, and several empty stalls besides those occupied by a cow, two horses, and a colt. Duval paused by one of the empty stalls and looked over the end, which had been half boarded up, into a big box of dusty wooden forms.

"What do you have in here?"

"Doctor calls it Anna's Folly," she said, laughing a little. She had begun to mix the mash, and the colt was already whinnying and stamping his feet.

"I did not know that An-na was ever foolish," he said lightly.

"You know, of course, that Doctor thinks all women foolish."
She was still laughing, but he could see that it went deeper than the
surface. "Well, I proved him right that time. I invented a new kind
of butter mold, and I talked Doctor into helping me get it patented
and a lot of samples made up. But then I never could sell them.
There it is: Anna's Folly!"

Dr. Duval reached over and picked up one of the molds, turning
it critically in his long fingers.

"I think that it would march very well," he said. "Why not?"

"Oh, of course, it will work. I'm not such a fool as all that. But
there was no market for them. Doctor was justly annoyed."

"Anna, why did you marry Doctor?"

He asked it suddenly, and Anna stood very still, her kettle poised
over the mash which she had been stirring. Then she set the kettle
down, and said in a low voice:

"You see, I had been in love before, but he was what my folks
called a drunkard. I could have lived with that. I could have helped
him."

"Yes, you could," Duval agreed. "I understand you now a little
better."

"You think you do?"

"Yes. I am sure. But tell me what kind of man he was."

"Oh, I don't know. He had a nice, gay way with him, irre-
sponsible perhaps, but I was in love. We were both real young, and
mother and father were dead-set against him. I had my things all
packed to elope."

"Like Mary, eh?" said Duval with a smile.

"I've never been so headlong as my children. Sometimes I'm sorry
for that."

"Tell me, my friend."

"I was just about Mary's age. Yes, I can understand her eloping.
And at the same time I know now better how my parents felt than
I did then. I guess we do learn a little bit from life. Do you think
so?"

"I have hope."

"The only reason I gave in then was because I loved my father very dearly and I respected his opinions. He came to me and he said: 'Anna, this is not the marriage for you to make. All your life you will regret it.'"

"And all your life, Anna," said Dr. Duval quietly, "you have regretted *not* making it. Is it not so?"

"No," she said, "I have had a happy life. Doctor has been good to me. It is only sometimes in the spring that I remember."

"And Doctor, does he know?"

"I have been a good wife to him."

"Yes, I can see that."

"My father liked Doctor for his ambition and his enterprise and the fact that he didn't drink more than was good for him. He was quite a bit older than I was. I guess I married him on the rebound, as they say. I was shelling peas on the side porch at home when Doctor proposed to me. It was only a week or so after I had planned to elope. I felt very desolate. He wasn't very romantic about the proposal, and at first I said 'No'; but then I said 'Why not?' I have loved Doctor, too, you see. It is odd how a woman can do that. It has often bothered me. I loved them both so differently."

"Love comes but once, Anna," Dr. Duval said gently. It was almost as if he were reassuring himself on a conviction which had been shaken. "I am glad that you have had that one great love."

Anna began stirring the mash. She went into the box stall to feed the colt. He came nuzzling against her and bumping the rough old coat sleeve with his nose.

"Take care now," she said to him. "You are greedy, aren't you? Look now, you will make me spill your dinner. That wouldn't please you at all, would it?" She stood beside him for a moment while he ate, and absently stroked the soft hair on his neck. Then she looked up at Dr. Duval.

"I think you are wrong, Constant," she said, "about love."

"I only know from myself, Anna," he replied.

The hungry feeding of the colt sounded loud in the quiet barn. There was a noise of pigeons cooing and fluttering in the loft above, and Anna heard Gene clattering down the board walk from the house.

"Auntie Anna! Papa! Where are you?"

"In the barn, Gene," Anna called, "feeding the colt. Do you want to help?"

"No," said Gene. He stood in the doorway, red-cheeked and breathless. "But I'd like some bread and butter with brown sugar on it."

"Tell Christina to give it to you; but first, Gene, have you nothing to say to your father?"

"Hello, papa," Gene said.

"Go with him to the house, Constant. Help him to get his bread and butter," Anna urged. "I will be there later."

Constant seemed to rouse himself from a deep preoccupation. Awkwardly he took Gene's hand, and the two went toward the house together.

23

"Now, CONSTANT," said Doc, pronouncing Duval's Christian name as if it were the common adjective—for he had no patience with the subtler, nasal twang which Duval and Anna gave it—"now, Constant, maybe you can give me some advice. You've seen all the civilization of London and Paris, and you ought to know the best of it. I've seen Boston and a little of New York, and I know St. Louis like a book; but I'm open-minded. I want the best."

"What had you in mind, my friend?" asked Duval.

"I want to inject some culture into this town. You know, give it a hypo," said Doc.

"You have given it a fine academy, doctor. What more is there to do?"

"That was the first big step, but, by thunder! we can't stop because we've gone that far. We can't rest on our oars or we'll go drifting back."

"You are going to establish a rival academy maybe?" asked Duval, smiling.

Doctor gave a sudden roar of laughter. "No! No! My projects ain't always so big. No, we'll let the Academy rest in peace. This is just a little afterthought to give a flourish to the first commencement. The kids have got this building and all, but has it really roused their mental faculties? What I want is to jack them up to a higher level somehow. We've got past the pioneer stage here, and I'd like the young folks to begin to think of something besides keeping a roof over their heads and filling up their bellies."

"Are they not happy here as they are?" asked Duval mildly.

"Well, they shouldn't be," cried Doc angrily, "not by a long shot, they shouldn't. No, they've got to build America out here in the West. And, by golly, it's about time they began to think about it!"

"Already you have an idea, perhaps, which is better than anything I could give you?"

"I have in a way. It's not such a remarkable one maybe, but it ought to be a start in the right direction." They sat in the office, at their ease, Doc filling the atmosphere with smoke from his usual cigar.

"So you wish to do something special for the first commencement?" said Duval.

"That's it," said Doc. "I worked pretty hard to get the town stirred up enough to establish this Academy. Now the first class graduates in June, and I feel like doing something handsome for them. I think it'll be a medal, and a cash prize—something to make 'em feel that scholarship's worth while."

"Why do you not establish a little laboratory for science?"

Doc Hawkins laughed.

"Rats and guinea pigs, eh, Constant?"

"Rats and guinea pigs," Duval repeated gravely.

He had made a little laboratory of his own in the back room of

the office where he carried on desultory experiments when the practice was slack. This may have gratified Doc secretly, but it afforded
him ample material for boisterous joshing on the surface. Now, however, Doc did his friend the honor of entertaining his suggestion
before deciding against it.

But finally he said: "No, by God! When I make a public-spirited
gesture, it don't always have to be a practical one. The practical side
of my nature gets enough damned exercise every day in my work.
I don't claim to have any of this culture myself, but I can make
obeisance to it in other people, and I'm damned determined that the
next generation in Opportunity is going to have it, whether they
want it or not."

Duval laughed, showing his white teeth in the dark face. He liked
to hear Doc Hawkins running on. It gave him a good deal of pleasure and amusement. He did not bother to express his own ennui with
culture, nor the conviction which was growing in him that simplicity
was after all the only end worth striving for.

"No," Doctor continued, "I want something kind of classical
and high-cultured and at the same time patriotic. I thought maybe
an essay contest—an essay on the future of our state. We're nearing
the turn of the century. These young people will make the new one.
What kind shall it be? I want to make these young folks think about
the future and what they're going to build here. Ideals, that's what
we want here, Constant, ideals!"

"Ideals are very good," said Duval noncommittally.

He was still smiling at Doc, but at the same time he felt a twinge
of envy. To care so much about an abstraction like the future, to be
so warm and passionate over a grabbag labeled *Ideals*—that continued to amuse Duval, and yet it also gave him a sharp pang of
nostalgia. It was good to be so full of vitality and to believe in something, however ridiculous, with warmth and certainty. Yes, he recognized that it was good to be able to believe.

Doc could make the decision about amputating a gangrened hand
or probing for a deep-lodged bullet very quickly and accurately, and

he could go ahead with the execution of it calmly and with perfect confidence; but he spent the rest of the winter in a dither of excitement over the essay contest. In a sense this was to be Doc's own commencement.

Doc liked ceremony, and it had always been a disappointment to him that he hadn't been present at his own graduation exercises. He had been the youngest of a large family of children, and, after his mother's death, an older sister had brought him up. His father was a hardheaded old customer with very little money and less will to give it up, and Doc had had to get out and rustle for what he got. When he was ten they had moved to Missouri from the family home in New Hampshire. He liked horses, and after school he used to hang around the stable of the local doctor because the doctor had a fine, high-stepping filly. When he was about twelve, the doctor gave him the job of tending his stable after school. Old Dr. Frost it was, in Plainsville, Missouri. After a year or so Dr. Frost got another boy to do the stable work and took young Hawkins on to sweep his office and keep his bottles straight, and, when the boy had finished the local school, the old man said to him:

"Look here, Hawkins, I'll advance you the money to go to medical school, and you can work it out by helping me in my practice as soon as you graduate. I'm taking a long chance, but I think you're my man."

Doc often thought of that. He could hear the old man's voice yet: *I'm taking a long chance, but I think you're my man.* It was one of the big moments of Doc's life, and it had shaped his whole future. Now, when he saw some boy struggling to get ahead, it was as if he saw himself, and he always had the feeling, when he did something for a youngster, that he was somehow repaying old Dr. Frost. Although he'd worked out the actual money years ago, there was still the obligation, too great ever to be repaid, for the self-confidence those words had given him.

Old Dr. Frost had fallen sick in the midst of a scarlet fever epidemic, and the young student had had to leave school just before the graduation ceremonies, so he'd never worn a mortarboard nor marched up to get a sheepskin. They had mailed him the sheepskin later, and, by George! he'd been too much in the thick of the epidemic even to open the paper tube and look at it. He had it framed now over his desk, but whenever he looked at it he was sorry he had missed the ceremonial.

"It was a shame," he used to say, "a God-damned shame!"

24

JENNY THOUGHT about the essay contest as she walked to and from school, and she was determined that she was going to win it. She was sorry that it was not a poetry contest, because she would have liked to try her hand at an elegy or an ode, and she knew that she would have had less competition. As it was, every one of the sixteen members of the graduating class was writing an essay. Jenny thought also that if the contest had consisted of a list of the best ways to spend the hundred-dollar prize which Doctor was offering, she would have been certain of winning, for her ideas on that subject were almost inexhaustible. The medal would be nice, but she could *use* the hundred dollars.

President Martin, announcing Dr. Hawkins' essay contest from the pulpit in the Academy chapel, had said that they were to write on their ideas for the future, the future of the West.

At first it seemed very nebulous, but once Jenny began seriously to think of the future, ideas came thick and fast. The fact that for a long time she had been critical of her present situation in Opportunity lent color and fantasy to her vision of what might be; for she was too young then to know from experience that there is no future in actuality, only one day of the present following another day like beads on a string.

Jenny wrote four different essays before she was satisfied. But the final one came like an inspiration. *Women,* she thought—did anybody ever write about the future of women? The future of the state, the future of boys and men, but why not something better than they had for girls and women? Yes, she would write on the future of Idaho, but there should be women in it, too. They would vote and hold office and write histories and march shoulder to shoulder with the men. It was an intoxicating idea, and, in her innocence Jenny thought, quite new and original, for she had never happened to hear or read such natural and sensible sentiments put into words before. Why not? Was it possible that women had not dreamed of liberty? Nor men in their generosity conceived of making women their equals?

Whatever Jenny did, she did quickly, and the fourth essay was written in no time.

"It's good," she thought. "It's really brilliant."

In senior study hall the essay was the chief topic of conversation.

"I don't think it's much use us girls competing against the boys," said Sarah Peavy, glancing archly across the room at the male contingent of the class. "They ought to have a special ladies' contest for *us*. It isn't hardly fair with gentlemen so superior intellectually."

Jenny, fresh from her vision of a woman's future, cried belligerently: "I won't admit that. That's just a prejudice."

"Oh, come now, Miss Walden," Russ Porter said, "won't you admit that men are a superior class of beings?"

"I think they're quite inferior," said Jenny, but her smile took all the sting out of her brash sentiments.

"Oh, now listen, fellows," Lester Davis said, "Jenny's got to be persuaded. We've got to make her see the light."

"She's gone and written half a dozen essays," said Maud Peters tartly. "You boys had better look out. For all her softy smiles, she's out to beat you."

"Now, Miss Walden, you wouldn't be so heartless as that, would you?" begged Russ, his eyes soft on Jenny's face.

"Bet your boots, I would," said Jenny.

"You're so slangy, Jenny," Sarah said. "If the judges hear you talk, you'll certainly never win."

"Old Doc Hawkins likes slang, I bet," said Jenny audaciously, "and quite a lot of profanity, too."

"Jenny! And you a preacher's daughter!"

"Well, Doc Hawkins isn't the only judge. There's President Martin and Mrs. Kessler and the mayor," one of the boys said, "and the essays have to be turned in with no names on them."

"That's good anyway," said Maud. "Jenny can't pin a smile on hers."

Myrtle Peterson said nothing. She had had a struggle to get through school at all, and now to have to top off the struggle with an original essay was almost unendurable. Of course, one didn't have to compete, but every other member of the graduating class was doing so; not to do so was to lose face hopelessly. Her brain was numb from cudgeling, her eyes red-rimmed with worry, and nothing at all had come of it.

She fell into step with Jenny as they walked home from school. She admired Jenny very much as a superior kind of being who dared say or do almost anything. Some of the girls hated Jenny—for no good reason, it seemed; but Myrtle sincerely admired her, perhaps because she had never been in competition with her. She had no ulterior motive now as she said:

"Oh, Jenny, did you really write a half a dozen essays?"

Jenny laughed and linked her arm carelessly through Myrtle's.

"No, only four," she said. "Silly to do that, wasn't it? But I kept getting better ideas."

"Oh, glory!" Myrtle said. "And I haven't one idea, not one! Oh, I wouldn't mind, but everybody thinks I'm so stupid already. If I don't hand in an essay it'll be—it'll just be—awful." It was the first time Myrtle had told her troubles to anyone, and now suddenly to hear them put into words in her own voice overwhelmed her. She began to cry.

Jenny stopped and looked at her.

"Why, Myrtle, I didn't know you cared so much. Why, Myrtle—"

She took out her handkerchief, since Myrtle's seemed to be missing, and helped the girl dry her tears.

"Oh, I'm awfully silly," Myrtle said. "Please don't pay any attention to me, Jenny. I don't know why I should have cried."

They walked along in silence for a few moments, and Jenny was wrung and torn by pity. When they came to Myrtle's corner, Jenny stopped and opened her book satchel.

"Look here, Myrtle," he said, "here's the next to the last one I wrote. I was going to throw it away. Why don't *you* hand it in? It's badly scrawled, but you'd have to copy it over anyway; and you'll probably have to look up some of the spelling."

"Oh, Jenny—you mean?—honestly?" Myrtle's face was flooded with pleasure. Jenny pulled out the scrawled sheets of the third essay. It was the one which began, "Bright angel of the future, let us glimpse your scroll." Myrtle read a few words and cried: "Oh, Jenny, how beautiful! how beautiful! Are you sure you want me to have it?"

"It's much too fancy," Jenny said. "I don't know why I ever started with an angel. I had an overdose of them in Sunday school. The essay I'm going to hand in begins: 'O pioneers, we are here to keep faith with you. We are here to carry out your visions of the future. The women are here, too, standing shoulder to shoulder with the men.'"

"How wonderful!" cried Myrtle. "Oh, Jenny, how can you think of so many things? And I needn't be ashamed, now that I have one to hand in, need I?"

She caught Jenny's hand, and before Jenny knew what she was going to do she had kissed it. Jenny was embarrassed, but she was happy, too. Life being what it was, she seldom had anything to give away; but she took great pleasure in the act of giving.

She had no question in her mind but she had selected the best of her essays for herself. She had put the most thought and feeling and truth into the one she had kept.

They all sat in study hall on the day the judges were deciding.

They knew, because someone had seen Mrs. Kessler drive up, and a moment later Doc Hawkins had arrived without his little black bag and looking important as he always did when he attended a board of regents' meeting or was on some business of the intellect.

After a long time Miss Paine, the English and Latin teacher, came to the door. Her face wore a slightly bewildered look. She said:

"Myrtle Peterson. Miss Peterson, will you step into the hall a moment, please?"

Jenny's heart gave a frantic bound.

"It can't have anything to do with the essays," Sarah whispered. "I don't think Myrtle even wrote one."

"Yes, she did," Jenny said. "It was a darned good one, too." She had a tight, hard feeling in her throat and all across her chest. *You fool*, she thought to herself, *you little fool*.

It was a long time before anything else happened, and then Miss Paine came back.

"Jenny Walden? Miss Walden, please." Jenny followed her out. There was a singing in her ears, and she wondered if, under the circumstances, a perfect lady would not faint at this juncture and save herself a lot of awkward explanations. But her legs were quite steady and she kept on down the hall behind Miss Paine until she reached the President's study. She could hear Myrtle sobbing in the small adjoining room where Mr. Martin kept the chalk and his academic robes and ate his lunch out of a newspaper. Before she had time to recognize them individually Jenny was aware of several people looking at her from various parts of Mr. Martin's study. Instinctively she flashed around on them her most enchanting smile, and she added a look of gentle questioning as if she did not know why she was here.

"My dear Miss Walden," President Martin began in his shrill, timid voice, "Miss Peterson tells us that she did not write her essay at all—that it was you who wrote it for her."

For an instant Jenny could not think of anything to say. Before she had gathered her wits together, Doc Hawkins' big bass voice broke like a bomb shell over her.

"How many more of these essays did you write, Jenny? Come on. Tell us. All of 'em?"

"No," Jenny said, "that was the only one besides my own. I wrote this for myself first, and I was going to throw it away; and then Myrtle couldn't think of one, and I felt sorry for her."

"Jenny, you damned little fool, you! You've got to stop wearing your heart on your sleeve," cried Doctor.

His words stung Jenny onto the defensive. She threw back her shoulders and cried: "You're a nice one to talk, Doc Hawkins. Where do you wear your own heart? If I'm a damned little fool, you're an old one!"

Mrs. Kessler uttered a faint cry of horror, and President Martin, whose bread and butter depended upon holding his tongue when Dr. Hawkins swore, cried feebly:

"Miss Walden! Miss Walden! Please!"

"Let the girl talk," roared Doc. "My God! she's earned the right. She's written the two best essays in the class."

"Is that so?" Jenny asked, her anger melting away in a rush of triumph. "Is that really so?"

"What do *you* think?"

"Yes, I think it's true."

"Conceited, aren't you, my girl?"

"Haven't I got the right to be?" They looked at each other and grinned. All about them was a cold atmosphere of shock and horror.

"All right," Doc said, "so you win the hundred dollar prize and the gold medal. But don't tell it around until the night of the graduation, will you?"

"You aren't going to punish me?"

"What for? I'm giving this thing, and you took first and second places. The only reason we decided against the second essay was the subject matter. We liked the angel of the future better."

"I'm sorry about that," Jenny said. "But, look, I don't want any shame put on Myrtle. Let her claim the second essay then."

"There's no money for that."

"All right, but a little glory will be good for her."

"You're a card all right, Jenny," Doctor said. "Well, give Myrtle the credit. No one will believe it anyway, probably. But when it comes to reading the essay on Commencement night, you're to read the one that starts with the angel, see?"

"The pioneer one is much better, doctor," Jenny said. "I put a lot more thought on it."

"Yes, but what's it about?" cried Doctor. "A lot of feminist twaddle about women ruling the state."

"Not ruling—just taking their place alongside men."

"Look here, my girl, when you're a little older you'll realize that woman's place is in the home. The hand that rocks the cradle rules the world. Ain't that enough for you?"

"Well, no," Jenny said, "if men aren't afraid of women, why don't they let them vote and hold office and be lawyers and doctors and all the rest?"

"By God, you talk like a suffragist. That's the way that second essay sounded, too, just like it was written by a damned Bloomer girl."

"Much better than a Bloomer girl could have done, I think," said Jenny archly.

"You go to blazes, girl, and be sure you read the angel essay, see? This time I'm telling you!"

Jenny went out demurely, with a last conciliatory smile around the room.

"By Gad, that girl's got more spunk than any other female in town," cried Doc admiringly. "We've got to keep her in hand, but I'm glad she won! I'm glad she won!" Mrs. Kessler and Miss Paine, even President Martin looked as if they were not quite so sure.

Out in the hall Jenny's knees turned suddenly to water. The spunk was all out of her. Instead of going back to study hall, she went to the cloakroom and took her hat and cloak off the hook.

A hundred dollars! she thought. *Oh, glory! glory! What were some of the things she had planned to buy?*

The country roads were still muddy, but when she came to the railroad station the tracks invited her. Balancing herself delicately on a rail, Jenny began to walk swiftly out towards the country. It was something between dancing and flying to walk on the rail, her arms spread to keep the balance. The air was keen and fresh, smelling of earth, and the mountains were the color of autumn grapes. For a time the tracks ran along beside a stream which was full of freshet water and made a joyful noise. As she walked, the phrases she liked best in her essays kept repeating themselves over and over again in her mind. They sounded better to her than they had ever done before. Even the bright-angel essay sounded good to her. But as she walked an audacious plan formed in her mind. No matter what Doc Hawkins said, she was going to read the better essay on Commencement night. She smiled as she walked, balancing herself so lightly and swiftly on the narrow steel rail. The mountain air was sweet in her lungs. She had never, never been so happy, she thought. No, never! She wondered if she could ever, ever be so happy about anything again.

25

LARGELY DUE to Doctor's enthusiasm and his flair for publicity, the essay contest and the first Academy Commencement became the proud concern of the entire town. Just as Doc had sold the Presbyterian bell to the freethinkers and atheists, so now he sold a yen for the intellectual life to the stupid, the vulgar, and the uninformed as well as the aesthetes and intellectuals. It soon became apparent that the small chapel of the new Academy would never be able to accommodate the crowd, and Doctor and President Martin went to the mayor about securing the Opera House. The mayor was delighted to let them have the Opera House for such superior entertainment. As soon as they heard of it, the Masons and Odd Fellows both volunteered their large silk flags with the new Idaho star on the blue fields.

Several ladies' auxiliaries offered their services to weave evergreen garlands of boughs which the Academy boys should bring down from the mountains, and Kessler donated three bolts of bunting from his store. Hank Briggs, the undertaker, offered the potted palms and the rubber plant which he kept alive in the front windows of his furniture store for use at high-class funerals. The Presbyterian Ladies Aid, urged on by Mrs. Kessler, planned a collation to be served at the reception after the graduation. Everyone in town contributed something, if only good will.

And all the week before the graduation Mrs. Walden sewed on yards of thin white muslin for Jenny's dress. Most of the girls had white mull or organdy or dotted swiss, but muslin was the best the preacher's family could muster.

"But it'll be all right, Jenny," Mrs. Walden said, "with the ten yards of lace I ripped off that underskirt from the last charity box. No one will know but what it cost as much as Sarah Peavy's, and you're a lot prettier than Sarah."

"Mama, you're a jewel!" Jenny cried. "I love you! I adore you! Will you have the next waltz?" And, disentangling her mother from a confusion of muslin ruffles and newly starched lace, she began to waltz her around the parsonage dining room. They enjoyed themselves very much for a few moments, and then Mrs. Walden broke away and said:

"Goodness! What if someone in the congregation saw us!"

"Let's kill the congregation."

"Jenny! How awful! And listen here, wherever did you learn to waltz?"

"Where did you, little mama?"

"Well, I wasn't always a preacher's wife, dear—but *you*, Jenny—"

"Yes, yes, dear! Always a preacher's daughter! But one doesn't have to be taught to waltz, mama; the knowledge falls from heaven, like manna or whatever it was."

"Jenny, you're simply terrible."

"I'm incorrigible, mama," said Jenny happily.

"Well, see you behave yourself on the stage of the Opera House, dear."

"I'll be too scared to do anything else," said Jenny. "I'll probably be praying harder for divine support than I ever do in church."

Jenny was not the only one who suffered qualms of nervousness before Commencement night. Doc Hawkins was as restless as a witch. He had been asked, of course, to make the presentation of the prize, and he walked the floor several nights before, mouthing resounding phrases.

"Come to bed, doctor," said Anna calmly. "I don't think they'll expect you to say more than a few words, will they?"

"Anna," he said, "you don't understand the importance of this. It's the beginning of an intellectual life in this town."

"Yes, doctor, I know," said Anna. "But don't forget to blow out the light when you do come to bed, will you?"

Doc had had the tailor make him a new suit, and he insisted that Anna get a new dress and hat.

"Really, doctor, I don't see why," said Anna. "You're giving the hundred dollars, and the gold medal will cost you quite a lot, too. It seems like this would be an excellent time for me to wear my old hat that feels so comfortable."

"You talk of comfort at a time like this!" cried Doctor. "No, Anna, I won't have you sitting on the platform with me and looking like a hayseed from the Ridge."

"The platform?" Anna said. "Oh, doctor, I'll get the new dress and hat. But please don't make me sit on the platform. I'd so much rather be in the audience."

"Mrs. Kessler is going to sit there, and she'll be dressed to the gills."

"But she gave all that money to the Academy, and she's one of the judges. Besides, she likes that sort of thing, doctor."

"Anna, this is an occasion," said Doctor. "After all, you're my wife. I want you to sit on the platform with me."

Anna did not laugh, and she seriously tried to do her best to get a becoming outfit, but she did not look very well in the prevailing leg-o'-mutton sleeves and bustles; and the stiff, small sailor hats with their bird-wing ornaments sat very badly on her abundant hair. And, oh, how she hated to sit on a platform in front of all the critical eyes in town!

Duval watched her in amusement as she went about her preparations. She had never breathed a word of how she felt, but it was as if he read her mind.

"Never mind, Anna," he said, "there will be two who feel as you do on the platform that night."

"No!" said Anna. "You are to sit there, too?"

"Yes, indeed," said Duval smiling, "that privilege has also been extended to the doctor's assistant."

"I am sorry for you," said Anna, "but I guess there is no help for it."

"How do you say in the proverb? Two will make company, eh?"

"Yes," said Anna, "that's right. But, please keep an eye on me and try to help me to behave as I should. I am very serious in wanting to please Doctor in this. It's so important to him, and I have a talent for doing the wrong thing in public. I have no gift for the public eye—and I do try, for his sake."

"You will do very well, Anna," said Duval. "You have that natural dignity which comes with a tranquil mind. It is something to envy."

Anna smiled at him.

"You say things prettily, Constant."

"No, no," he said. "Do not turn an honest sentiment into a mockery. I have no wish to make the pretty speeches."

The day of the Academy Commencement was very dark for Anna in spite of irreproachable May weather. Doctor was in and out of the house all day, unable to settle down to any sort of peaceful occupation. His temper was in a lamentable condition, and his nerves were raw. As late as five o'clock he looked over his shirts and flung his best linen one, whose stiff bosom Anna had hand-tucked for him herself, onto the floor, crying out that Christina had not properly washed and ironed it. Anna hurriedly built up the kitchen fire to heat water and boil starch.

Christina herself was of very little use, because Doctor had insisted that she and the chore boy should attend the ceremonies, too, and anticipation of an evening in society had turned her completely upside down all day. Now, when she found that Doctor was in a tantrum about his best shirt, she burst into tears and fled to her room, where her sobs could be heard echoing mournfully through the house.

"I'll kill that girl," cried Doctor, "as soon as I can think of a painful enough way to do it. Where in hell is Lita? Where's Gene?"

"Lita went to walk with Arnold Larkin. She should have been home by now."

"What business has she to go gallivantin' off at a time like this?"

"There's no reason why she shouldn't," said Anna calmly. "Life is pretty dull for her with nothing much to do now that she's out of school."

"Nothing to do!" cried Doctor. "Nothing to do! You might teach her to launder a shirt, if the hired girl can't do it."

Stalking out of the kitchen, Doctor saw through the dining-room window that Lita was hanging over the front gate in the throes of a lingering farewell with a young man. Doctor could hear their giggles and the creaking of the gate, and he was enraged almost to the point of apoplexy. He went out onto the front porch in his undershirt and bawled: "You break that front gate of mine, and I'll have the law on you."

"Be careful, papa," said Lita pertly. "His father's a lawyer and probably knows a lot more about the law than you do."

"You come in here, you brass-faced hussy," roared Doctor, "and as for you, you young whippersnapper, get the hell out of here, and I don't care if I never see you back."

Now Lita was in tears.

"Papa," she sobbed as soon as she was in the house, "you're always asking me why I don't get married. That's why! That's why! Do you think he'll ever come again? You won't let be me a nurse, and you insult my gentlemen friends. I might as well kill myself and be done with it all!" She stormed upstairs, stamping her feet and slamming doors behind her.

For a while there was the sound of two separate sets of sobbing; and then Christina, recognizing the violence of a grief greater than her own, sat up, washed her face, and went downstairs to set out the cold supper which Mrs. Hawkins had planned.

Through the turmoil Anna continued quietly to wash, starch, and iron the shirt. There was no use trying to comfort Lita for a little while yet, and Doctor was better left alone. In a few moments Gene, sunburned and dirty, came in the back door with a dead bird in his hand.

"Look what I found, Aunty Anna. I am going to give it a big funeral. Can I? Where's a box to put it in? Do you know?"

"I'll find you one first thing in the morning," Anna said. "Remember, this is the graduation night?"

Gene dropped the bird in the woodbox and began to unbutton his shirt.

"Hully-gee!" he said. "I pretty near forgot."

"I'm glad you could, Gene."

"Will I be late?"

"No. Put the bird outdoors and start to wash. I'll help you."

"I want to see Uncle Doc."

"No, no," Anna said hastily. "Not now. He's busy."

"Who's crying?"

"I'm afraid it's Lita. Get washed now. Everything will be all right."

The incident of the shirt had put them behind schedule, and it took Anna longer than she expected to get Gene dressed and Lita into a tolerable state of mind to appear in public.

"I *can't* go, mama. I might see Arnold. I can never face him again."

"Of course you can, Lita. That's just what you *must* do. I'll be extra nice to him, too, and you know Doctor will be all over his nerves by tomorrow. I'm sure we can patch it all up."

"Oh, mama, never! never! We were having such a good time. It can never be the same."

"Don't say the word 'never,' Lita. It's too final. We've always got to compromise a little in this world, dear. We have to do what we can."

"Papa has ruined my life."

"Your life is just beginning, dear. Other people may spoil things for you temporarily; but it's *your* life, after all, and you can do a lot with it, if you have strength and courage. Tonight may be a wonderful evening for you, Lita. You never know what's around the corner."

"Well, mama, thanks, dear. I'll try."

Anna saw Gene and Lita, Christina and the chore boy started towards the Opera House to have an early choice of seats, before she herself got around to the task of dressing. Duval was to come by for Doctor and her, and the three of them would join the graduating class and the other platform ornaments behind the scenes. She was already tired when she went to her bedroom to dress. Doctor had made a shambles of it, his old clothes flung here and there in unrelated heaps; his razor and strop and military brushes in places where they did not belong.

He stood in the midst of his chaos with Jovian fury in his eye, trying to tie his cravat.

"Here, let me help you, doctor," Anna said.

Her fingers were expert with his tie. When she had laid it smoothly in place, she gave his shoulder a gentle pat.

"You look magnificent," she said.

"It's going to be a damned poor speech," he said in a small, tight voice, "a damned poor speech."

"I don't believe it, doctor."

She had only time now to sponge herself a little and brush her hair before she rushed into the tight new dress with the ugly sleeves. Doctor was finished now, and he really looked splendid with his fierce dark eyes shining, his chin all freshly shaven, and his mustache and sideburns combed and clipped. The new suit fitted him beautifully, and he had his high silk hat and the gold-headed cane that his friends had given him when he left St. Louis.

"Now, let's not be late, Anna," he said. "Where's that damned Duval?" He stamped out into the hall.

Anna dusted some rice powder hastily over her flushed face, and pinned on her new hat. She could hear Doc's cane tapping impatiently in the hall, and then she heard Dr. Duval coming in the side door to join them. She thought with an upward curve of her lips that Constant's tie would probably need arranging more than Doctor's had; but Constant would not care how it looked himself, and so it wouldn't matter.

She ran out into the hall before Doctor should lose all patience. He turned to her and took her all in at one critical glance.

"*My God*, Anna!" he cried. "Your hat is on crooked."

Terribly dismayed, Anna stopped to straighten it in front of the hall mirror. Her level hazel eyes looked at herself critically and despairingly. She saw that her face was still flushed in spite of the powder and that the hat was not quite in place. She put up her hands and pushed the small, stiff, ridiculous concoction backward and forward, trying to find the fashionable angle at which the milliner had advised her to wear it.

Doc stamped out of the door without her, bringing his gold-headed cane down *thump! thump!* on the front porch and sidewalk.

"Don't be late," he shouted.

Duval stood in the dining-room doorway and watched Anna. Her face, usually so competent and serene, was full of anxiety. It made Duval unexpectedly angry to see this. He found himself wanting to lift the silly hat from the abundant chestnut hair and fling it into a corner of the room. He came up behind her and looked at her eyes in the mirror. He had never touched her before. In all the hours they had spent together, he had scarcely felt the swift brush of her dress against the back of his hand in passing. Now he put his hands very lightly on her shoulders.

"Anna," he said quietly, "you are beautiful."

She looked quickly into his eyes reflected behind hers in the mirror. Her own eyes were startled, questioning, then suddenly swimming in tears. They looked at each other thus for a long moment. It was the first and last time that Duval ever saw tears in Anna's eyes.

"Thank you, Constant," she said finally, in a low voice. "You don't know how I needed that. Perhaps we had better go."

26

THE OPERA HOUSE was packed, and it was certainly not all out of deference to the sixteen graduates. Their families and friends were there, of course, and the upper stratum of Opportunity society, which felt duty-bound to support the Academy in whatever it did; but the great mass of the audience had only one thing in common: they had been Doc Hawkins' patients. Doc had been talking about this graduation for weeks. He had rubbed it on with liniment and poured it down with ipecac and salts. Tonight's audience was largely a demonstration of good will and friendliness for Doc Hawkins.

When Doc came onto the platform with his cane over his arm and his high hat in his hand, there was a burst of applause.

"The babies had better wait tonight, eh, Doc?" shouted a voice.

"You're darned right, Eddie Gallagher," replied Doc, lifting a hand in salutation. After all the empty fury of the day, he was suddenly perfectly at ease, like an actor in a play who has spoken his first lines.

It was like that when he performed a dangerous operation. Sometimes he worried about it a lot in advance, and was nervous and irritable at home before it started. But, once he had begun the operation, he was suddenly sure of himself and perfectly cool. His hands moved quickly and efficiently, and whether the patient would eventually live or die, he knew that he was using all the skill he had in the best way that he could at that moment. So now, after all the fussing and irritability, he was suddenly calm and happy and having a damned good time. He looked all over the audience, nodding to friends as he sat down. He saw Lita and Gene and Christina and Jim. They were sitting well to the front and looking proud and excited. Suddenly he was terribly sorry that he had shouted at Lita's young man. Gene was bouncing in his seat and trying to get his attention. Doc gave him a sly wink that put him into an ecstasy. Doc looked behind him at the expectant graduating class, and at the small and anxious faculty. He looked sidewise at Duval and Anna. The hat had slipped slightly to one side again, but it no longer irritated him. He thought: "By George! Anna's not a bad-looking woman when you get her dressed in stylish clothes."

There was a long invocation by the Episcopalian rector, during which Doc crossed and uncrossed his legs. They had selected the rector, not because he had a large following in town, for his chapel was almost as small as the Catholic Church, but because his vestments lent an air of distinction to the occasion. It was thought that the Waldens were sufficiently in evidence with Jenny taking off the prize, and so the Presbyterian minister, representing as he did the better element in Opportunity society, had been selected for the final prayer.

When the invocation was completed, the President of the Academy offered the graduating class some well chosen advice and then turned to the real business of the day, which was introducing Dr. Hawkins. Doc listened with no attempt to conceal the interest he felt in the praise which was being heaped upon him. He smiled at the jokes and looked gratified at the eulogies. He almost clapped his hands when the audience burst into applause; but just in time he remembered and got to his feet.

"Ladies and gentlemen," he said, "—and friends! I'm glad to see so many of you here tonight, because to me this is an occasion of great importance, and I hope that it will be so for you, too, after you've heard what I have to say. President Martin, here, has said some mighty kind things about me, and I won't deny that it makes a man feel pretty good to sit by and hear himself praised. But some of you know me better than President Martin does, and I don't expect you to swallow what he says, hook, line, and sinker, without a little struggle. You've got to take me as I am, and, by George! if you can still like me, I'll be mighty gratified."

"Yea, doc!" shouted a voice, followed by applause.

"Now, what I had to say about Idaho tonight is something to the same effect. We're a brand-new state here with everything ahead of us, and I'm going to let our essay winners tell you about that in just a few moments. But first I want to look back at our history as a territory, and, if I'm not as flattering to Idaho as President Martin was to me, it's because I want you to see her failings and love her in spite of them, *God bless her!*"

"*Yea! Yea!*"

"Here in this new state of ours we have gold and silver, copper and lead, hidden in the mountains; we have acres of ripening grain, as golden as anything that comes out of the mine; we have mighty forests that will build the ships and cities of the future; we have rushing rivers that will bring water to the desert places. All these things were here for the taking when the first explorers came West. The first explorers went back East and told about these riches, and then came the next white men, the fellows who were looking for what they could take out of this country and not what they could put in. All they wanted to do was to load a couple of mules with gold dust and get back home again. Some of you remember those fellows, don't you?"

"You bet your boots!"

"All the riffraff in the United States poured into Idaho Territory for a while. Law and order? They never heard of such a thing. Murder and robbery stalked hand in hand through this beautiful country of God's. Some of you old fellows remember the Magruder murder and how Hill Beachy had to take justice into his own hands to avenge the cold-blooded murder of his friend. That was only a sample of what went on here. Some of you were members of the Vigilante committee in the south that had to go out capturing and hanging men because the officers of the law were themselves aiders and abetters of the criminal element. Those wild days of disorder are still fresh in our memories, but, thank God, they are over and done with forever! Mob rule is dead in Idaho! You pioneers who have stayed here, and we others who have come since those days, have come to Idaho to make homes. We have come here to put something into the state, not to carry it away on pack mules. We have built our homes and established our businesses. Churches have been built, and in clear weather you can hear this town ringing fifteen miles away on a Sunday morning."

General laughter.

"We've built schools, and the one-room log schoolhouse has flowered into this fine Academy whose first graduates we are about to honor tonight. These young people are a symbol of the future of Idaho. They point for us the direction which our growth must take. We have achieved law and order here, now we must go ahead to advancement of the intellect and the spirit. We must not only satisfy our material cravings, but we must see that this new state shall also lead in scholarship, in literary and scientific pursuits. I sought for a quotation from the poets, and, by thunder! I wished I might have found one to give you from the pen of a native son of Idaho. But that will come, friends, that will come! In the meantime I give you the words of one of the eastern poets, Henry W. Longfellow:

"Life is real! Life is earnest!
And the grave is not its goal."

"Dang it, doc! I thought you medicos was all in cahoots with the undertaker," shouted a voice from the audience.

"My good fellow," thundered Doc, "the undertaker has his eye on every one of us. The only fellows who are in cahoots with him are ignorance and complacency; and you and I are here to put those two fellows under the sod where they belong."

At this point there were cheers, and such a storm of applause that Doc had to raise his hands for silence before he could go on.

"All right! All right!" he said, laughing. "We'll leave the poet and the undertaker out of it, but, by the Lord Harry, I'm going to get some culture into this town, if I have to stuff it down your throats along with the calomel and paregoric!"

There was another long roar of amused approval from the audience.

"And now," shouted Doc. "I've tried to give you a look at the past of this young state. Our past is not very long and not always glorious, as you see, but the future stretches ahead of us, long and shining, like the shining mountain, E-dah-hoe. The essays in this contest were written on the future of our state by the young people who are going to take part in that future. Now, I don't know what the boys in this class were doing, but, by George! they've let a woman get ahead of them. Yes, sir, my friends, our best essay has been written by a young lady. One of the prettiest little girls in town, too, and one whose future should be as bright and shining as the Idaho mountains. Ladies and gentlemen, I give you the Methodist minister's little girl, *Jenny Walden!*"

All during Dr. Hawkins' speech Jenny had been holding herself rigid so that she would not tremble. She sat among the sixteen seniors of the Academy, clutching her essay, which was rolled and tied with a piece of ribbon that matched her blue sash. She had brought only the one essay with her, the one about women, and now she was desperately wishing for the other. The great sea of faces, like so many hundreds of pale oval eggs arranged in neat rows and waiting to be candled, filled her with unaccustomed awe. Dr. Hawkins' speech had moved her, too, and now she was ashamed that she had planned so gleefully to defy him. But there was no help for it at all. In her extremity she could not remember a word of either essay; the only thing she could do was to read the one she held in her hands.

She found herself on her feet, in the center of the stage, and gradually her knees were growing strong again, for the audience, which had howled and thundered with Dr. Hawkins, was quiet now, waiting for her to begin. Particularly in the eyes of the men, she saw that thing which she had so often encountered of late. She did not entirely understand the look, but somehow it was reassuring and raised her own opinion of herself. She took her time now and looked all around, giving the audience one of her confiding smiles.

"Ladies and gentlemen," she said in a clear voice, "my essay is called 'Our Future Is Full of Promise.' Now I will read it to you." For an instant the clear voice hesitated, and then she went on quickly:

"*O pioneers, we are here to keep faith with you. We are here to carry out your visions of the future. The women are here, too, standing shoulder to shoulder with the men . . .*"

Her eyes slid around to Dr. Hawkins. If he had clutched her by the collar and cried out against her in his great voice, she would not have been at all surprised. What did surprise her very much was that he had not even heard what she was reading. He was looking over the audience with a benign expression, and what he was hearing was his own speech, coming back to him in his own voice through flattering space.

Jenny continued her essay in a firm voice, remembering it now, as she went along; but much of her satisfaction was gone. Doc Hawkins was not even listening. He did not know that she had defied him, and there was no shock or hope or mental turmoil discernible on the faces of the audience, either. They looked at her tenderly, and what they thought was not how woman's lot would be improved in a better world, but *Ain't she pretty, the little thing? Good enough, too, to have the hundred dollars go there. The Waldens need it.*

Jenny read on, but somehow she felt that her intelligence had been insulted.

27

AFTER THE GRADUATION Doc and Anna stood with President Martin and the graduates and shook hands. The meeting had almost taken on the character of an ovation for Doctor, and everybody wanted to shake his hand and have a word with him. Jenny's disappointment vanished, too, in the flood of congratulations and good wishes which flowed over her. She was almost as well known in town as Doc, and most people liked her. She was different in many ways from the other girls, but so good-natured that most of them were fond of her. Only a few of them had begun to be jealous of her; and, if she seemed giddy to the older women, she was still so young that even the deacons' wives had not begun to take offense. If she had been better dressed, they might have worried earlier; but, as it was they felt that their own daughters' prospects were secure. Jenny was so radiant tonight, however, that several mothers felt the first sharp twinges of dissatisfaction with her: *She's pretty forward for a preacher's daughter. I don't like how the young men look at her.*

When the reception line broke up, there was dancing, and of course Jenny wasn't allowed to dance; but she could use her eyes if not her feet, and after all, most men hated dancing, Jenny learned.

It was a glorious evening. *Commencement!* she thought, and the word had a beautiful sound of promise and expectancy. *Ladies and gentlemen, our future is full of promise!*

To teach school now, to get away from the eyes of the congregation, to meet new people and begin to live the splendid, the mysterious life of the future—Jenny's heart swelled at the thought of that beautiful unknown which lay before her.

Lester Davis, his father one of the deacons, was pestering her to dance.

"Come on, Jenny, up on the stage, behind the scenes, where it's dark. No one will see us."

"Up on the *stage*, behind the *scenes*, where it's *dark*? Why, Lester Davis! You don't expect I'll go and dance with you there, do you?"

"Come on, just for a minute, Jenny. I'll perish if you don't."

"What a loss to the world, Mr. Davis!"

"Come on. I'll never tell a soul."

"Mr. Davis, you amaze me!"

"I don't believe you know how to dance," Lester said. "I bet you were bragging."

"Of course I know how," Jenny protested.

"Come on then, blue-eyes."

"I'll try anything once," said Jenny, "but only for two minutes."

"Two minutes in heaven," said Lester into her ear as he dashed away after her. He was a rawboned youth, with a nasal tenor voice and a long jaw.

Jenny was laughing at him as she ran.

Doc Hawkins slapped her father on the shoulder and said: "Well, man, you can be proud tonight. Your daughter's topped the class. And what'll she be doing now? Teaching school the next thing, eh?"

"Well, I don't know," said Mr. Walden slowly. "That's what she wants to do. It seems like she's crazy to get out of this town and into the world, as she calls it. But her mother's not very strong, and we need one of the girls at home. Mother and I have talked it over, and we think Jenny's the one to stay. Della's already got a good situation, and she's dependable. Jenny's so young, and she's always been the wild one of the two—"

He paused and smiled apologetically.

"Maybe there's a little selfishness in it, too, because I love her best. She's a good girl, too, but impulsive, you know. We thought to keep her here and work her into the life of the church."

"You told her yet?" asked Doc.

"No, we thought we'd let her graduate first. She may not like the thought of staying home."

"Well, by George, I think you're right!" said Doctor. "Girls get too many notions nowadays. My Lita now, she's got it in her head to be a nurse. You think I'd let her? My God, a doctor knows the kind of thing that means: washing and lifting men in bed, all kinds of men, as naked as they were born, their vital organs floating on the breezes—"

"Doctor!" Anna said.

"Well, Reverend Walden gets my meaning. No, by thunder! That's not the way to make a lady out of a young female, not like that!"

"Of course, school teaching's more respectable," the preacher said; "but still a young girl away from home—an impulsive young girl—"

"Sometimes it makes you wonder," Doctor said, "all this educating up of women that we do . . . Well, have a cigar, reverend. I'm spoiling for a whiff of smoke, and, by the Lord Harry, I believe that I smell coffee brewing!"

Yes, Jenny had a glorious and triumphant evening. At the end of it four different boys asked to take her home; but Lester got his invitation in first, while they were dancing in the dark behind the scenes. Jenny laughed at him when he kissed her under the dark pines just before they got to the church. She had never thought that she would laugh at her first kiss, but there was something about Lester's long face and twitching upper lip that reminded her irresistibly of a sentimental horse. Whenever she thought of Lester for days afterwards she wanted to laugh, and she wondered if it was love—this excitement that ended in laughter.

Jenny had often been told that nice young girls never allowed themselves to be kissed until they were engaged. What puzzled Jenny was how they could avoid it.

28

As soon as the exercises were over Duval had gone down into the audience to find Gene. Gene made him an excellent excuse to get away from all this fury of hand-shaking and slapping on the back. It was well that he had come for Gene, because Christina was having a difficult time to persuade him to go home. Lita had already found the consolation of young company and intended to stay for the dancing; and Gene had almost convinced Christina that they had better stay, too. Duval took Gene's hand.

"Come, my son."

"Let me shake hands with Uncle Doc."

"In the morning, you may do that. You see now how he is busy. What a long line of people! You would have to wait."

Reluctantly Gene abandoned his aspirations for a grown-up evening, and let his hand rest quietly in his father's. At the door of the Opera House, Duval turned and looked back as if he were searching for a face. Anna was just coming down the steps from the platform, and her eyes had found them across all the crowd. He half lifted his hand in a gesture of encouragement, and she smiled.

Gene was wide awake and excited. He swung on his father's hand and his talk flowed endlessly.

"Papa! Didn't Uncle Doc make a good speech, papa?"

"Magnificent," said Duval truthfully. He thought that he had never heard a speech which was better integrated to the audience.

Gene was pleased with the word. "Yes, it was very magnificent. It was a magnificent speech, wasn't it, papa? Yes, it was a very magnificent occasion all together, I believe. Uncle Doc will be pleased with that, too, because I think he was a little worried."

"He vas cranky plenty before supper," said Christina. "He be all right now."

Gene was too much excited to walk sedately. He dropped Duval's hand and pranced about them, lifting his feet high and snorting and neighing.

"This is the way Doc's horse goes when it trots. Now it is shying. Now it is being magnificent. See, papa, how a horse looks when it is magnificent."

Duval went into the house and helped Christina put Gene to bed, but he was anxious to be gone before Doctor and Anna returned.

"Papa, you must sit down and sing, or tell me a story now."

"No, no. Tonight it is too late. You must sleep now, *tout de suite,* like a little rabbit."

"Papa, please! please!"

"Not tonight."

He went out into the still spring night and began to walk in the dark streets. A fine rain that was scarcely more than a mist had started falling. It was warm, and it smelled of lilacs and newly turned earth. There was the fresh smell of pines, too, which one always had here, as in France one always had the old smell of hearth-fires, kept burning for so many generations that they were like a kind of incense perfuming the ancient towns and villages.

"France!" he thought. "It is there that I belong, I suppose—not here. In me are too many burned-out fires, the incense of too long a past, for me to be of use here. This new country is for men like Doc whose minds are not complicated by too many subtleties. Yet I cannot go back."

There were dark areas in his mind on which he rarely let himself look. They were like windows opening upon desolation which are kept hidden behind the tapestry of everyday living. He knew that they were there, but he did not often draw aside the hangings to look out. When he did rarely lay them bare to memory, he saw events through them in a kind of dark chiaroscuro and the faces of the actors were unreal and shadowed as faces reflected at the bottom of a well. He saw himself as a young man performing the charity operation at the *Hôtel-Dieu* upon the man who had every right to live. The fog which had enveloped his brain that day clung around him in memory like a paralysis. That was the first time that his drinking had betrayed him into negligence. Before that he had thought it gave him skill and confidence. Even afterwards he had told himself: *Just enough of it at the right time—I need that. The trouble was I took too much, too soon before I started to operate.*

Then in the half-light of memory he saw the trial for malpractice, and the widow and the half-dozen badly nourished children sitting below him while he testified; and darkest of all, perhaps, was the verdict which had exonerated him. He had been free then, and there was nothing he need do for those pitiful victims of his mistake, nothing he *could* do without admitting the guilt which he had denied. And then he saw the other time when he had been so worried for his wife, Elizabeth, so worried that he had had to drink to quiet his shaking hand.

Elizabeth! Tonight somehow he could not visualize her at all. Her primrose hair, her little innocent face would not come back to him; but he could hear her crying, and then he could hear the silence after she had ceased to cry, and the breaking of that silence by the hungry baby's wailing in the next room. Everyone had pitied him so, and no one had blamed him. That was the bitterest part. It was always himself who had had to bear the solitary agony of knowing that he was to blame.

There were other somber pictures in which he saw himself ingloriously, always running away to a new place, and then once more stumbling into the insensate flood which washed over him. The futility of escape had made a kind of nightmare of his life until he had found this place: Opportunity in Idaho and Anna Hawkins.

He walked a long way in the dark street, smelling the western pine and lilac, and his troubled mind sought other images. As he had made himself lift the curtains upon the dark hours of his life, so now as antidote he set his mind upon the innocent familiar objects he had known, making himself see again the scenes of his childhood. It was a trick which he knew how to play upon himself. When he was worried about a case, or could not sleep at night—when he was afraid of loneliness—he voluntarily reached out for peaceful scenes and built them up again around him. These happier pictures he saw clearly and in colors which were brighter than the originals. He saw old gardens with fruit trees espaliered upon gray walls, old stone calvaries encrusted with moss and yellow lichen, and tree-lined paths where little children spooned sand into their buckets beside their nurses. The peace of inanimate things which have been in existence for a long time brought him peace. The remembered music of water falling from ancient fountains into ancient basins soothed his tired mind. It was a kind of drug which usually deadened the present for him and wiped out once again the other things.

But tonight there was a turmoil in him which would not be silenced by remembered peace. The mental pictures were thin and unsubstantial even in the darkness and the emptiness of the streets. He tramped on doggedly in the soft rain until he came to the edge of town where he could see the brickyard beyond the stream, and suddenly he could no longer stay himself with memories of other places. For here a stream rushed darkly with a great noise of freshet, and beyond, across a field, the fires of the kilns were glowing orange in the night. This was more real to him at the moment than anything he could remember. He stood still in the dark and let the soft rain fall upon his face. He held out his hands to it, and over his mind flooded other things which he had been trying to put out. Anna, looking at him in the mirror; the color of her eyes with tears brimming them; how smooth her shoulders were under his fingers; the clean smell of her hair.

For the first time since he had come to Opportunity, he was afraid —not for himself, not for Anna, not for Dr. Hawkins—but he was afraid for his dead wife, Elizabeth. The whole dark past bound him to her in a way that must not be broken. In death she held him more closely than she had done in life; and, whether through love or faithfulness or remorse she held him, he knew that it was a strong bond. The first wild twistings of his heart to free itself, filled him with alarm and set his will on guard.

He walked for a long time in the rain. Gradually he shut out the soft new feelings he had had; and, when that was done, he grew angry with himself, for he had almost been a traitor to the passion of his life. He turned and walked quickly towards his dark and silent rooms. He was very tired, his shoulders were wet, and he was cold; but once more he was resolved.

"Why the devil won't Duval come out to dinner every week the way he used to?" Doc asked, that summer. "It's not because I don't invite the fellow. You think he's courting somewhere?"

"No, I think not," Anna said. "He likes to be alone, I guess."

She was more troubled than she cared to admit. Such a little thing had passed between them, and now the long hours when they talked together were a thing of the past. It seemed that their friendship could not survive the touch of flesh or the meeting of eyes in a mirror. But had it been such a little thing after all? she wondered again. It is difficult for a woman not to think of the man who has told her that she is beautiful; perhaps it is even more difficult for the man who has spoken the words.

It was not until early July that they mentioned, however tacitly, that slight encounter. Doctor had prevailed upon Duval to go with them to a community Fourth of July picnic on Opportunity Mountain. Just before they started Duval and Anna were left alone on the side porch among the picnic hampers while Doctor and Gene were supervising the hitching of the horses to the large carriage. Lita had already departed with younger company.

They stood in silence for a few moments, and then Anna said in a low voice: "You know it would never have made any difference to me, Constant. I am not a fool."

He did not reply at once. Then he said slowly, "You will not understand, perhaps, how a memory, an ideal if you wish, can be more tyrannical than a living thing."

"You are stubborn, aren't you?"

"Faithful, I think, not stubborn."

"I prefer honest words that say what they mean. 'Stubborn' is a live and rugged word to me. 'Faithful' is something out of an old song."

"Well, I am stubborn then," he said.

"I wish that I could help you."

"There is no help anywhere, I think."

"Yes, it is in yourself."

"Then you need not concern yourself with me," he said roughly.

29

THE JULY SUN flowed liquidly among the branches of the pine trees, dappling the brown, needled ground, falling upon the light dresses of the women, upon the rough plank stand draped in yards of bunting, upon the flags, and the trestle tables with their white cloths and crocks and platters of food. Between the trees one caught occasional glimpses of the wide, sweet valley below, which was checkered at this time of year with green and yellowing fields of grain. At this height it seemed removed from actuality and became an allegory or an abstraction, unrelated to the daily life which they lived there.

It is good to go up in mountains, Anna thought, as she busied herself with the preparation of the tables; *a person gets a little perspective that way.* A yellow jacket which had been attracted by an open jam jar settled momentarily on the back of her hand, but she continued her leisurely movements without attempting to brush it off.

"Mama!" Lita cried. "Look at your hand. A yellow jacket! Ugh! Mama! Look! Brush it off."

"The way to get stung," said Anna quietly, "is to shout and jump around. Let it alone—there won't be any harm done."

After the picnic luncheon, there was a galaxy of spread-eagle speeches from the bunting-draped stand, and Jenny Walden had been asked to read the Declaration of Independence. The speeches were long and tiresome to the young folks, who wandered off in pairs and quartets through the pines. When the time came for the reading of the Declaration, Jenny was nowhere to be seen, and a hue and cry had to be raised. Presently Jenny came running down one of the woods paths, her hair loose and shining, her laughing mouth red. Laughing, she climbed the rostrum and spread her hands in a naïve little gesture of supplication and apology. Still breathless from running, and trembling on the verge of giddy laughter, she began the solemn Declaration. People took the Fourth of July orations seriously in Idaho in 1894, and a good many of them were annoyed by

Jenny's heedlessness. The fact that, in her white dress with a strip of bunting looped across her breast and knotted under her arm, she looked fresh and wildly beautiful only served to turn some people more against her.

After the oratory was over, there were races and contests for the young folks and the hardier oldsters who wanted to compete. Jenny was in the thick of all the ladies' contests, and she and Julie Schwartz, a girl from the other side of the tracks, even allowed their ankles to be tied together in a three-legged race, competing with the boys.

"And now the gunny-sack race!" shouted the judge of events. "Miss Walden, are you entering that, too?"

"Of course!" cried Jenny, breathless and laughing.

Half a dozen boys were there to help her stuff her long white skirt into the gunny sack, all of them hoping for the light touch of her hand on an arm or shoulder as she balanced herself in the sack before the report of the cap pistol which should start the race.

Mrs. Kessler leaned to Mrs. Peavy.

"That little Walden girl is having altogether too good a time today. Look at her! Absolutely shameless."

But, if Jenny was able to forget herself in a riot of merriment, there was still beneath the surface that little gnawing of frustration and discontent which had lain there like a canker ever since the end of school.

When it was time to go home, she avoided Lester and Russ and Harvey Tillotson, because she was tired of them after a long day, and seated herself among the girls for the hayride back to town. Her eyes were dreamy for the long shadows of the trees and the golden dust haze that made a mystery of the valley.

Myrtle Peterson, sitting beside her, looked at Jenny wistfully and with affectionate admiration. Shyly she reached out and took Jenny's hand.

"A penny for your thoughts, Jenny."

"I don't have them any more," said Jenny, her eyes still on the valley.

"You're such a funny girl," said Myrtle. "I know you have a lot of thoughts."

"I cut them off, *swish!* as fast as they come up."

"Listen, Jenny, what are you going to do in the fall? Have you got a school?"

"No. I have to stay at home."

"Honest? I've got a country school out on the Ridge. I'll earn some money for myself that way, and Mama says it's a good place to meet a rich farmer." Myrtle giggled.

Jenny didn't say anything. Her head and body swayed with the jolting of the wagon, but her eyes were steady on the valley below.

"Why won't they let you go out to teach, Jenny?"

"Somebody has to stay at home," said Jenny in a flat voice, "and it seems I've been elected."

"What'll you do?"

"Learn to cook, and copy papa's sermons, and sing in the choir, and teach Sunday school."

"Yes, and have a lot of beaux," said Myrtle enviously.

"That's nothing," Jenny said. "They come a nickel a dozen."

"Oh, Jenny! Not for all of us! What in the world do you want then?"

"I wish I knew, Myrtle."

"You were so brilliant at Commencement, Jenny!"

Jenny lay back on the straw and looked up into the yellow evening sky.

"Commencement," she repeated. And then she added bitterly, "Commencement of *what?*"

Someone in the front of the hayrack began to sing *Sweet Marie,* and gradually the others took it up. Jenny lay quiet, listening. Presently they went on to *After the Ball* and *Sweet Bunch of Daisies.* Jenny sat up and patted her hair. They had begun to sing *Tarara Boomdeay,* and suddenly Jenny's voice joined the others. In a moment she was laughing again and throwing handfuls of straw at the boys in the front of the wagon.

By the time they reached town it was dark enough for fireworks. Dr. Hawkins and Gene had a big night before them. Piled on the stone mounting block in front of Doctor's house was a small mountain of rockets and pinwheels, nigger chasers, and Roman candles, volcanoes, and fountains of stars.

"Look out now, Gene. Mind you don't let the womenfolks touch those things. Where's that damned punk now?"

"Here it is, Uncle Doc. Uncle Doc, can I get the trough we made for the skyrockets now? Can I, Uncle Doc?"

"Sure thing! Bring it out. I'll watch the pile for you while you're gone. And bring another box of matches, Gene."

Other children on the Presbyterian hill began to gather at Doc's hitching block, because he always had more fireworks than any other father in the neighborhood and they seemed to go off with a louder report and rain more colored balls.

"Step back now, kids, before I set this off. I don't want any powder burns to salve or fingers to amputate. This one is going right over the steeple and, if it shakes the damn bell down, I'll get my sleep on Sunday morning. Here she goes now! Keep your eye on her!"

There was a rush, a hiss, a boom, a burst of colored stars, and the long ah-h-h! of blissful satisfaction from the watchers.

"Oh, say, doc! That one was a lollipaloozer!"

"Lollipaloozer! Lollipaloozer!" sang out Gene, capering and shrilling with enjoyment.

Lita sat with a young man on the porch, both too consciously adult to allow themselves much interest in the fireworks. Anna and Constant stood by the front gate where they could watch without having to participate. In the west there was still a faint, clear greenness which remembered tenderly the day in the mountains; and through the greenness stars pricked out, minute threads of white light that were lost in finding, and found again on losing. A warm, fresh smell of earth came up from the garden, and the evening flowers gave off a faint perfume, soon lost in the acrid tang of smoke and powder. Rockets from other parts of town had begun to pierce the sky with sudden showers of light. When Anna and Constant spoke at all, they spoke about the rockets.

"That was a very bright one!"

"Look! Green and red balls together."

"Those large ones must be coming from the fair grounds. They are having a special celebration there."

At last Duval said in a low voice: "I did not mean the last I said today. I am sorry."

Anna did not reply, and presently he added: "Somewhere long ago I lost a thing that was precious to me. You are the only one who has ever succeeded in making my loss seem not so great."

"Can't we leave things as they were?" Anna asked. "Surely we are strong enough." There was a kind of anguish in her quiet voice.

"Yes, as they were," he said. "Let us try, An-na—just as they were."

Anna's lips curved upwards in the darkness. She had never asked for much, and now she only knew that she was happier than she had been in the morning. Tonight each rocket that went up awoke an answering rain of stars in her heart.

PART II

1894–1895

1

"ANNA!" Doctor called. There was a note of anxiety, almost of fear in his voice.

Anna had been helping Christina bottle the late pears, and she came out of the kitchen now, rolling down her sleeves.

"What is it, doctor?"

"Anna, there's some damned quack come to town and opened up an office the other end of Main Street."

"How do you know?"

"Well, first thing I knew, I heard them talking in the drugstore. The fellow never wrote to ask me."

"I mean, how do you know he's a quack?"

"Good Lord, my intuition tells me so!" cried Doc.

"I'm really not surprised, doctor. The strange thing is you haven't had more competition in a town like this."

"You don't seem to understand, Anna. Duval and I can handle the work in this town. We don't need any other fellow sticking his horns in."

"There's more than one grocery store here, doctor, more than one lawyer, more than one dry-goods store, and look at all the churches."

"Well, there are lots of ways to get to heaven; but, by thunder, one doctor's office to save you from it, ought to be enough."

"Still, I'm not surprised."

"By God, I am. But I can tell the fellow this much, he'll have hard sledding. He won't find the going very easy. People are loyal to me here. It won't take long to freeze him out, I guess."

Jenny Walden could have told Dr. Hawkins a month before that a new physician was coming to town. She was angry about it herself. What right had a stranger to come in and try to take over a practice which belonged to old Doc Hawkins? When her father had first shown her the letter, she was scornful and incredulous.

"You aren't going to help him, papa, just because he's written you this letter?"

"But of course I am, Jenny. He's a Methodist. He's asking my protection and support. It's a preacher's duty."

"You mean to tell me it's your duty to desert Doc Hawkins, after he's doctored us for years without any charge, after he's done so much for us and the whole town? and fall on this fellow's neck because he is a Methodist?"

"Now, listen, Jenny. See things reasonably. A professional man writes to the minister of his church and asks his advice, tells him he means to open an office in the minister's town. What is the minister to do? Why, the only thing that he can do is help the man the best he can. Dr. Hawkins knows the world. He'll understand if anybody does."

"I don't know," Jenny said, "he's a big man, but I doubt if understanding is his strongest point."

"Well, dear, I have to do the best I can."

"All right," Jenny said, "go and toady to this new man, if you want to, father, but old Doc Hawkins is still *my* doctor."

"I like the photograph of him," Mrs. Walden said. "He looks serious and purposeful. It's harder to tell about the wife with her face turned to the side, isn't it? Did you see the picture, Jenny?"

"I don't want to, mama," Jenny said. "I dislike the man already."

"You're too opinionated, Jenny," said Mr. Walden mildly. "A young girl ought to accept other people's views sometimes instead of always insisting on her own."

"Oh, papa, what's the use of having views, if they must always be suppressed?"

"I should think that Mrs. Allerton might be older than he," continued Mrs. Walden, still looking at the picture which had come in the letter; "but then you never can tell about a light-haired man, and Englishmen always look younger than they are—I don't know why that is. The women usually have buck teeth and are quite plain, and the men have that rosy, boyish look even when they're quite old."

"Oh, mama!" Jenny said impatiently. She had flung on her hat then and gone out the door for one of her walks. She hadn't meant to slam the door after her, but there were some days when she had to do things violently. It seemed to ease the pent-up life and tension in her which did not find release in any other way. It was hard to see autumn come again with no more school to go to, and nothing to occupy her mind except the daily round of church and household duties. Even in those she was not the initiator, only a minor executor in a routine which others had established according to their own beliefs and inclinations.

"If I got married," Jenny thought, "I could at least manage my own house—" But she did not want to be married and settled yet. She wanted to see things and people. She wanted to use her mind and be her own master. Besides, which one of the boys did she care enough about to marry? Lester? Russ?

Lester's kiss had not been the only one forced on Jenny that summer in the darkness under the pines or in the narrow passageway between the Sunday-school room and the organ loft at choir practice. The more of them she had, the less she laughed, not because they no longer amused her, but because she was no longer surprised. Her merriment began to subside into a kind of smiling cynicism that man should want only that of woman and be so sly and insistent on getting it. Love? she wondered. Was that it? Was that what Shakespeare had written about? what Mr. and Mrs. Browning had? She laughed and shrugged her shoulders. By autumn people had begun to say that Jenny Walden was a flirt and a coquette.

2

Dr. Hugh Allerton had been working all week to get the old barber shop cleaned out and repaired and turned into a respectable doctor's office. Katherine, of course, had been of not the slightest help to him, because she was still upset by the long journey; and, if she could manage to get them settled into some kind of living quarters outside the hotel, he thought she would be doing very well. He left the living arrangements entirely to her, for all he cared about was establishing himself in the new practice. They had told him at the drugstore that a Dr. Hawkins and his assistant had all of the practice in town, and that fact had surprised him a little. In England a town the size of this would have had half a dozen doctors.

The barber shop with its running water had been quite easily converted to his use, and he had gone down the street to Buchanan, the painter, and had the man make him a sign.

Now Dr. Allerton stood in front of his new office, his light hair blowing in the November wind, and watched his sign go up. He was satisfied with the formal black and gold paint and with Buchanan's neat workmanship.

Hugh Allerton, M.D.

There was no other doctor's name ahead of it, no *assistant* written after it. He breathed the free air of the mountains with a sense of pleasure and release.

It was a windy day for hanging a sign. Buchanan on a step ladder wrestled with the wires that held it in place. Dr. Allerton stood on the sidewalk below and directed or made suggestions. He had a quiet, English voice, and he gave his whole attention to the hanging of the sign. He did not speak to the small group of children which had gathered, either to joke with them or to send them about their business. He did not look at the girl who presently joined them.

"A trifle more to the right now, Buchanan," he said. "No! No! That will be too much. Ease it back now. Only a trifle, I said."

Jenny put her hands on her hips and set her feet sturdily apart, bracing herself against the wind. She was watching Dr. Allerton instead of the house painter and the sign. Her eyes were critical and appraising.

"*Hugh Allerton, M.D.,*" she said in a mocking voice. "So *you* are the one, are you?"

Dr. Allerton noticed her for the first time.

"I beg your pardon?" he said.

"So *you* are the one," she repeated. "You're the one who's come to crowd Doc Hawkins out?"

"I have no desire to displace anyone," said Dr. Allerton stiffly. He did not care for forward young women.

Jenny dropped her mocking tone, but her eyes were still steady on his face. The wind had whipped the color into her cheeks and it had stirred and roiled the sediment of rebellion which was always just beneath the surface in her these days.

"You know, someone ought to tell you," she said, "just what you're up against. Doc Hawkins has done everything for this town. He's nursed it through all its ailments and given it ideals along with the medicine. He's been everything to the town, and he's been a kind of god-out-of-a-machine to me. He pulled us through scarlet fever without ever charging us a cent, and he saved me from freezing to death in a snowstorm; and it wasn't only winning his essay prize either, but, when I was little and used to stand in front of the candy-store window with my stomach gnawing against my backbone, Doc Hawkins was the one who always put a nickel in my hand. He's a Presbyterian, too. That's the kind of thing a child never forgets."

"You seem to have been especially favored by your friend," said Allerton dryly.

"No," Jenny said. "He's been that way to lots of people. I didn't think it would do you any harm to know."

Dr. Allerton was silent a moment.

"Thank you for telling me about Dr. Hawkins," he said formally. "I shall try to give him worthy competition."

Jenny continued to stare at him, as if in some way he surprised her.

"You're not very old, are you? I expected someone older."

Dr. Allerton was disconcerted.

"I am not young either," he said defensively.

"I think," she said, "that life is long according to how much you crowd into it."

Dr. Allerton was betrayed into a smile.

"One crowded hour of glorious life—" he quoted mockingly.

"Is worth an age without a name," she finished fiercely. "That's why I want to get away from this town and go where life is. I want to go where life is! Well, hang your sign, why don't you?"

She spun around and went quickly up the street, her back straight and narrow, her hips swinging a little as she walked.

Dr. Allerton could not help watching her walk away. Then he was conscious of Buchanan sitting on top of the step ladder and regarding him with humorous eyes. The painter shifted his quid of tobacco from one cheek to the other and spat expertly into the mud just beyond the sidewalk.

"It's a good thing you're a married man, doctor. She'd be out for *your* scalp, too, if you wasn't."

"The sign is still a little lower on the right side, Mr. Buchanan," said Dr. Allerton severely.

But the painter was used to having his say. "She talks about life!" he said. "For a Methodist preacher's gal, I'd say she had plenty of it."

"You mean, that was Mr. Walden's daughter?"

"That's right. Just into long petticoats since last spring, and she don't care what she says to any man in town. She's spoiled with her good looks."

"Her good looks?" Dr. Allerton repeated.

"Ya, didn't you notice?"

"I'm afraid I did not."

"Oh, come on, doctor. They all notice that, and the men at the poolroom can tell you what kind of ankles she's got, too, if you didn't notice for yourself on a windy day."

"I am more interested in getting that sign up, Buchanan, than I am in your description of a young lady's ankles."

Dr. Allerton went into the office and closed the door firmly. One thing he had not become accustomed to in the West was this familiarity of artisans and tradesmen. They seemed to feel themselves on an equality with professional men, even to the point of coarse jocosity. It was the American way, he supposed, and he must accept it as well as he could along with its better aspects; but he wouldn't have a woman's reputation brought into it, no matter how lightly she might value that herself.

He probably would not have thought of Jenny Walden again had it not been for the painter; but Buchanan's words fretted at his serious mind. Beginning with the frank blue eyes, he reconstructed her face. It did not seem to him a bold or bad face. There was something elfin about it with the pointed chin and delicate eyebrows. His professional sense told him that the color of lips and cheeks showed unusual health and vigor. Probably good circulation, plenty of red corpuscles, and a general condition of eupepsia. But she was young to be talked about by the men of town. It was her mobile, discontented mouth that caused talk, perhaps, and the way she looked full in one's eyes and said what came into her mind to say. She had a pretty woman's audacity. He did not like women of that sort, but still it angered his sense of propriety that any woman, however young and careless, should be the butt of a house painter's loose remarks. He considered speaking to her father, who had impressed him very favorably; but his acquaintance with the Reverend Mr. Walden was still slight—he had better wait, he thought, until his letter came from the chapel in Manchester before he broached so delicate a subject.

Anyway, he thought, Miss Walden was a person whom he could easily avoid. She did not look as if she would ever need his professional services, and the social life of the town in which she might move did not interest him at all. He was sure that it would not interest Katherine, either—so few things did.

3

Doc Hawkins and Duval both happened to be in the drugstore a few days later when the new man came in. Doc was waiting for a prescription to be put up, and Duval had gone around behind the counter to help himself to some tobacco. Skogmo kept a little of everything in his drugstore. He'd even put in a line of schoolbooks and tablets and pencils to accommodate the new academy, and Duval liked his brand of pipe tobacco better than the kind they carried at the cigar store.

Dr. Allerton came in with that air of serious detachment which always surrounded him, as if he were the sole inhabitant of a small planet with its own particular orbit.

Doc looked the new man over with his keen black eyes. It was the first time he had had a real good look at him, for some deep-seated resentment had kept Doc from going around to call on him or making his usual affable advances. Doc made no move now to speak or hold out his hand. He saw that Allerton was a man of medium height, sturdily built, somewhere between twenty-eight and forty probably, although it was difficult to put a finger on his age. He was fair-haired and good-looking in a serious, clean-cut way. A man with preconceived notions and ideals, Doc thought, and not a spark of humor or the devil in him. But maybe not a quack, no, not a quack. Doc could have learned to like him, had he been a quack.

Skogmo, behind his little prescription window, called out: "How are you, doctor? Say, you fellers ought to know each other, the three of you here in town. By George, am I to have the honor of making you acquainted with each other? Dr. Hawkins, this is Dr. Allerton; Dr. Allerton, Doc Hawkins. And here behind the counter there is Dr. Duval. Dr. Duval, Dr. Allerton."

Doc held out his hand.

"How are you?" he said shortly.

"I have been hearing about you, doctor," the new man said. "You have a great many admirers in this town, it seems."

"You're damned right, I have," Doc said. He had a good, hard grip when he shook hands. The two men looked at each other over their strong handclasp. There was a little pause, and then Doc said, "And how are your patients, Dr. Allerton?"

"Principally nonexistent as yet, Dr. Hawkins," said Allerton quietly.

"You haven't killed any of 'em yet, eh, Allerton?"

Skogmo laughed boisterously.

"No, I've not yet killed any of them," repeated Allerton, smiling.

Duval, leaning on the tobacco counter, filling his pipe, could see that Allerton was feeling his way, uncertain of the direction which American humor was likely to take and desirous of giving no offense. Duval understood, for he, too, had been obliged to learn the idiom of the West, with the difference perhaps that he had cared less how he got along. Allerton appeared to him to be a man who was used to going ahead professionally, and who would not enjoy being brought to a halt.

Duval said now in a friendly voice:

"You are from Manchester, doctor? I took some of my training in London, but outside of London I did not so well know England."

"I practiced in London, too, a few years," Allerton said, turning to Duval as if he were glad of the diversion. "I was assistant to a doctor there in a rather unsavory district—the Elephant and Castle district. Probably you recall it."

"Yes, I know it."

"And what decided you to come to Idaho?" Doc asked.

"A great many things," Allerton said, his voice cool with reserve. "I have always admired the freedom of the West. I had a desire to be—to be my own man."

"Dr. Hawkins," said Duval, "he has a theory—*n'est-ce pas*, doctor?—that it is the name of this town which draws men to it from a long distance."

Allerton smiled, and a light flush mounted his cheek, giving him a guileless, almost boyish appearance for a moment.

"I must confess," he said, "that I went over a map of the western states with a reading glass and a pencil. When I found Opportunity, I made a small mark with the pencil. I dare say that was the little factor which decided me."

"Well, Allerton," Doctor said indulgently, "we'll have to see that you get a little practice here, as long as you want to stay. How about it, Duval? That chronic heart case in the country—wouldn't a little change of doctors do that fellow good? I s'pose you have a horse and buggy, doctor?"

"I have made arrangements with the livery stable for the use of a horse," Allerton said uneasily.

"Shall we let the new man in on that case, Duval?"

"As you wish, Hawkins," Duval said.

He had lighted his pipe now, and he continued to lean on the counter, watching the two men with the detached amusement of a spectator at a play. Allerton's face had flushed even more under the thin, light skin. His voice was very gentle and polite when he spoke.

"I thank you very kindly, Dr. Hawkins. But perhaps you will need your chronic country cases also one day. I should dislike very much to deprive you of them."

"The devil you would!" cried Doctor. "So, it's to be war then, is it, my man?"

"Surely not," the Englishman said. "Such an unequal struggle could hardly be called war, doctor, for you already have the whole town on your side."

"He's got you there, Willard," laughed Skogmo.

Jenny Walden came in the door just then, closing it after her with a bang.

"I'd like a packet of that foolscap paper papa uses for his sermons, Mr. Skogmo; and I'm in a big hurry for it, too. The congregation is panting for a little enlightenment on Revelation, and I've got a cake in the oven that's likely to burn."

The four men looked at her as if a small whirlwind had suddenly entered with the opening door. Dr. Allerton turned abruptly and went out of the store and down the street without saying why he had come in.

"That damned upstart! He better not try to fight me," Doctor said. Jenny looked at him and laughed.

"Why, Dr. Hawkins, you sound as if you had a grudge against him."

"Grudge? No! I just tried to do him a favor."

"Mees Jenny," Duval said lazily, puffing on his pipe, "Doctor has just offered the new man a very kind and friendly insult, and the new man has refused to take it."

"He was smart enough for that?" Jenny said. "I'm surprised."

"God damn him!" Doctor said. "He's nobody's fool."

4

SOMETIMES, when she couldn't get hold of a workman for a small piece of repair work on one of Doctor's heterogeneous properties, Anna took hammer and nails herself and went out to fix a few loose boards in a sidewalk or replace pickets which the neighborhood dogs had knocked loose. She liked seeing things neat and in shipshape condition, and she enjoyed working with her hands even at menial tasks. She would have liked nothing better than to have full charge of Doctor's scattered properties, to rebuild and redecorate and make paying concerns of them. But Doctor would not listen to her. What did a woman know about business or real estate?

"A woman's like a skittish horse," he said. "Give her her head, and she'll run you into the ditch." It was a good saying and made Doctor laugh at his own acuteness.

Anna was fastening a loose *For Rent* sign on the gate of the big Swedetown house which so often stood empty. Anna knew what was wrong with that house. It was loosely built and hard to heat in winter, and it had no running water nor any of the modern things, such as sink or bathtub or cupboards, which tenants had begun to expect.

In the thin Indian summer sunshine, Anna paused, with hammer in hand, to look at the ungainly pile of clapboards and dream of what she would do with it if she had permission and a little money. She had come bareheaded from home with an old coat tossed on over her morning dress, and her hair shone in the autumn sun. The morning light picked out the few gray hairs at her temples, but the glossy sheen of her abundant hair indicated her evergreen vitality. She leaned her elbows against the fence and thought: *That whole back part that's so shabbily built should come down, and some of the material could be used again to make a wide front porch. The walls should all be reinforced outside and plastered inside, and water should be piped into the kitchen and a bathroom on the first floor. I'd tear down the old privy and have a toilet in the bathroom, and I'd build in cupboards all around the kitchen.*

A woman came hesitantly along the street, and, when she saw the *For Rent* sign, she paused and looked uncertainly from it to Anna for a moment before she summoned courage enough to speak.

"I beg your pardon," she said at last, "but might I see the house?"

Anna turned leisurely about and smiled.

"Why, yes," she said. "There's a man downtown who's supposed to handle it; but I have a key, and I'd be glad to show you."

She led the way into the house, feeling some curiosity about the woman, because most of the women of Opportunity she knew by sight, and this one she had never seen before. The face was one to remember, not for any impressive quality in feature or expression, but because of an accidental prank of nature which had set a heavy purple birthmark down the left temple and cheek. Anna noticed the birthmark first, and later the nervous and apologetic mouth, the irresolute, dark eyes, and the little petulant crease between the brows.

"I'm so dreadfully sorry to trouble you—but I saw the *For Rent* sign. We're obliged to find a house to live in."

"It's no trouble at all," Anna said.

The house had a stale, closed smell, and after the autumn sunshine it felt cold and damp; but Anna did what she could to make it sound attractive.

"The south exposure is very nice in wintertime, and, you see, there is lots of room. There's a nice view of the mountains from the upstairs bedroom windows. That's the part I should like best myself, I think."

"You like them? The mountains, I mean."

"Oh, yes," Anna said, "I'm very fond of them."

"They're so vast," the other woman said. "I've not got used to them."

"You haven't been here long?"

"Oh, no!"

They went on from room to room, but Anna could see that the stranger's interest was only perfunctory.

"It's so tiresome not having gaslight, and I dare say I shall miss the coal grates as well. I've brought no coal-oil lamps at all with me, and I suppose I shall have to go out and purchase those."

"You've come from a city then," said Anna, "probably a long way off."

"I've come from England, from Manchester."

There was a homesick note in the voice that brought Anna up sharply. She turned and held out her hands.

"Why, I know who you are! You're the new doctor's wife! You're Mrs. Allerton."

There was withdrawal and retreat in the dark eyes.

"I dare say my accent betrays me," she said. "I've not become accustomed to your way of speaking."

"But I'm so glad to meet you," Anna said. "You see, I'm Dr. Hawkins' wife. I've wondered quite a lot about you."

"You are the wife of one of the other physicians?" Mrs. Allerton said uncertainly. "I'd no idea—"

"There are only two other doctors here, you see. The other one is a widower and shares my husband's office. I've been the only doctor's wife here for a long time." Anna laughed. "But if you're looking for a house, Mrs. Allerton, you don't want this one. My husband owns it, to be sure; but it's not a good location for you, and it heats very badly."

"I've looked and looked," the other woman cried. "Things are so different here, and it's very trying to be obliged to turn dollars and cents into pounds and shillings and pence before I understand the rental." Suddenly the frightened eyes were full of tears. "It's all so difficult, so difficult."

"Well, won't you let me help you?" Anna asked. "I'd like to, if I could. I think it would be better for you nearer the center of town, wouldn't it? so that your husband could get home for meals in the odd hours doctors keep?"

"Yes, if there is anything to be had. Perhaps your husband has another house to let which is nearer to Dr. Allerton's office?"

Anna smiled a trifle dryly. "Maybe it's just as well your husband shouldn't rent from mine—professional men, you know."

"I dare say," Mrs. Allerton said. Behind the dark eyes Anna could almost see the timid mind shuttling back and forth. *Should I let her help me? It would be so much less difficult. But would it be dignified after meeting her so casually? Would she think ill of me for accepting her help? Yet what a relief to have it!*

"There are several smaller places that I know of nearer town. But perhaps you had your heart set on something large?"

"Oh, no, really! There are only just the two of us, Mrs.—"

"Hawkins, Anna Hawkins. If you like, I'll go with you this afternoon."

"Oh, would you, Mrs. Hawkins? You wouldn't think it odd of me to let you?"

"I'll tell you a secret," Anna smiled. "I love looking at houses, and, do you know, I've never in my life picked out my own place to live."

"How strange! And why is that?"

"Well," Anna said, laughing, "you see the Doctor's such a good provider. He likes to choose the house and furniture and then move us all in on top of it helter-skelter, and say, *Here you are now. Make a home out of it.*"

"Oh, Dr. Allerton is not at all like that. No, not at all," said Mrs. Allerton.

Anna could see as they went from house to house that afternoon that it was indeed different with the Allertons. The doctor apparently did not care where he hung his hat so long as his office was as he liked it, and the wife was vague and undecided. Anna saw that she was frightened by responsibility, and haunted by the fear that her husband would not be pleased.

"But, if he isn't interested in helping you select things, why should he be critical of the result?" asked Anna sensibly.

"Oh, he will not be critical," said Katherine Allerton quickly. "It's not that. But I want things to be right for him, and sometimes I feel so—inadequate, so very inadequate."

So they tramped the town together, looking at houses, and Anna found herself doing the bargaining and suggesting the repairs and improvements to be made. For Mrs. Allerton did not know what questions to ask about the houses, and she was easily beaten down by people who thought her an easy mark. Anna began to have a maternal feeling of pleasure in defending her.

"Things are all so strange to me in this country," Mrs. Allerton said, "and I've never been clever at getting on with people. I can't tell you how I appreciate your helping me, Mrs. Hawkins."

It was difficult to find just the right place, for houses worthy of the dignity of a professional man were always built on a large scale, presupposing a family of children. In spite of her having blundered into one that morning, Mrs. Allerton seemed to be terrified by big houses.

"Oh, they are so lonely, Mrs. Hawkins, with all the empty rooms! And besides I do my own housework. I like it so much better that way. I can't have a servant about waiting for me to tell her what to do. Oh, I can't bear that feeling of someone watching me, and criticizing me in her mind, and waiting for me to give orders which she must obey whether she likes it or not."

"The best way with a servant is just to be friends with her, I think," said Anna. "She's a human being like yourself. If you wanted, I could get Christina's cousin for you. Christina is the girl I have. She'd know what to do and go right ahead without making you feel awkward."

"Oh, no!" said Katherine Allerton. "Really I couldn't. Thank you so much! But I couldn't."

They finally settled on a small house not far from the doctor's office, and Anna talked the owner into making a number of improvements.

"Wouldn't you like to have your husband come and see it now before you sign the lease?" asked Anna.

"Oh, no!" said Mrs. Allerton. "I think he'd rather not be bothered."

5

"What's this I hear, Anna?" asked Doctor at dinner that night. "You trailing all over town with the new doctor's wife, looking at houses? What in thunder has gotten into you?"

"I don't know, doctor," Anna said. "I just did it, that's all."

"Well, *why,* in the name of the Lord Harry? *Why?* Don't you think it makes me look a fool to have you running around like a bosom friend with the new man's wife?"

"It seems to me the most appropriate thing, doctor. We'll be better off as friends than enemies."

"But why?"

"Well, she blundered into the Swedetown place while I was there this morning. I couldn't help seeing how lost and forlorn she was. I was sorry for her."

"Sorry?" Doctor asked. The look he bent on her was not so much angry as curious. "You're a funny woman, aren't you? I think you'd rather be sorry for folks than proud of them, wouldn't you?"

This was the last that was said between them concerning Anna's friendship for Katherine Allerton, for, oddly enough, Doctor let it alone to flourish as it might.

Anna felt from the beginning that there was a strangeness about the Allertons, for man and wife. Perhaps it was because they had no common sense of humor. Both of them seemed serious and very much in earnest. When she saw Dr. Allerton she was a little shocked by the apparent discrepancy in their ages, for she had taken Katherine to be somewhere near her own age.

Katherine was the swarthy type of woman who grows gray young, and whose face is sown and harrowed by time and the nervous seething of elements within her, while there was nothing in the light hair, the strongly cut features, the steady gray eyes of the man to indicate the mark of time.

Anna liked Mrs. Allerton because there was no artifice in her. There was repression but no artifice. Anna saw that she was painfully shy, but also that she was kind and simple. Anna admired kindness and simplicity, for they were qualities which she herself had, and which she understood. Definitely there were limitations to Katherine Allerton's character, but there were none of the devious subterfuges, the advances and withdrawals, the pretenses and coquetries of the designing female in her. Anna did not feel that she must be on guard with her for fear of treachery. Almost immediately they were friends. But Anna's feeling for Hugh Allerton was not so clear-cut. It was perhaps because he was not a simple person, she thought. She did not at once understand him, and she wondered if this, too, were because he did not quite understand himself. She saw at a glance that he was a serious man with a definite purpose; and in parentheses she thought that life was harder on a man with a definite purpose, because he was never ready for the unexpected emergency which lay in wait for him along the course he had drawn for himself. He would lay his plans calmly and without passion, but he would have no sense of humor to make the best of the unforeseen which would inevitably at this point or that interfere with these plans. It was not dislike that Anna felt for him, but a kind of uneasiness and distrust of him. She could not quite see all around him. "But he is good," she said to herself. "I think that both of them are good." Goodness was important to Anna.

Perhaps she would have understood them better, had she been able to see what lay behind them.

6

IT WAS TRUE that Hugh Allerton had rationalized his life. His father, a laborer in a Manchester cotton mill, had lost his life in a mill accident. Hugh had been the only support of a widowed mother. So he had been early chastened in a stern and upright poverty that had crowded out laughter to make way for ambition. He had brought himself up from poverty and ignorance by the power of his own concentrated effort. In everything, he had been grave and sensible and taken at every crossroads the most advantageous turning.

His mother had wanted him to be a minister. She had reared him in a strong Methodist chapel atmosphere, and this had furnished his chief emotional outlet in a world of whirring mills and foggy streets, ugly with gaslight and corner pubs. After his mother's death the urge to go into the ministry was somewhat relaxed, and he went through a period of drifting and indecision. The only thing clear in his mind was that he must lift himself out of the ugliness of mill life by any means he could find. At this time he had read anything he could put his hands upon—oddly assorted and trivial reading, often enough, but his mind was retentive. The clamor of awakening scientific thought which was beginning to beat in great waves upon an unwatered shore had reached him faintly and excited his fancy. While he was still at this moment of indecision about his life, there had been an ugly accident in the mill, and Hugh had given first aid to the girl who was hurt until they could fetch a doctor.

"Where did you learn how to do that?" the doctor had asked, his sharp, dark eyes kindly above his great white beard.

"Out of a book, sir," Hugh had replied. "My father was killed in a mill accident, and I remember what I read."

"You're a bright-looking lad. Come to see me some evening after the mill closes. I can give you something to do in your spare time, if you want to better yourself."

"Yes, sir, I'd like to do that," Hugh had said.

So, at the end of a long day in the mill, he had begun spending his evenings and sometimes half of the night in the little laboratory which the old man maintained at the back of his house behind his office. The old doctor also read a good deal and was full of theories with which he had not time to experiment alone. The simpler processes of these tests and experiments he began to turn over to the bright lad from the mill, and he began to lay out more thoughtful reading for him, and to point his future. The way was soon clear again. Hugh set aside his ambitions for the ministry, which had after all been his mother's rather than his own, and bent all of his efforts towards a medical education. The struggle upward had been a life in itself, absorbing and satisfying. He did not pleasure himself with frivolity, for he could not afford it. His one relaxation was the Sunday singing in chapel choir. He had a fine baritone voice, and all of the emotion, the art, the realization of beauty which lay quiet in him during the striving week, flowed into the majesty of Sunday hymns. He marveled sometimes that singing could so stir and shake him, as if some inner force lay sleeping in him, which was touched only by music. Sometimes he went to concerts and sat alone in a high seat; but after a time he gave that up, because the music troubled him with a strangeness of feeling which was not good for his work. Music was an unplanned thing that did not clarify the straight, clear course he had set himself. It asked him unanswerable questions, and he liked to be able to give answers. It frightened him because it stirred feelings in him which he could not govern nor explain.

About the old doctor's house, never in the office nor in the laboratory, but looking out of windows, shaking a duster at the back door, fetching the letters from the carrier, or airing the rugs and pillows, were his wife and his daughter, Katherine. They were like shy ghosts, but they were always there, flitting through the background of a domesticity which seemed somehow incongruous with the busy life of the old doctor. They were completely Victorian in their detachment from the intellectual life that went on in the laboratory; and Dr. Jamison was equally Victorian in his determination to keep his females pure and innocent of the world even to the point of ignorance and superstition. Along with the recipe for roast beef and Yorkshire pudding, Mrs. Jamison had taught Katherine modesty, shame, resignation, and repression. They lived very quietly. Hugh Allerton had always respected them as women in a higher sphere than the one to which he had been born; further than that he thought very little about them. But the old doctor, who liked to arrange everything, had his own ideas about his daughter and the bright assistant; and when the time came to make a decision, Hugh took the turning that led upward, as he always had done. He and Katherine were married quietly one winter afternoon in the Methodist chapel. When he took her hand and turned to kiss her after the brief ceremony she burst into tears and ran down the aisle to fling herself into her mother's arms.

"Give her a little time, Hugh," Dr. Jamison had said, winking a fatherly eye.

Hugh had given her time.

Hugh was fond of Katherine, for he knew that she was a good woman, and he was glad that he could in some measure repay the old man's kindness to him by cherishing and caring for her. She had never complained at giving up her comfortable home to live in the odd lodgings they could afford as he progressed from student to intern to assistant in one town after another. With the assistantships there came a pause in Hugh's career. He could have gone back to Katherine's father and settled in with him to be his assistant until the old man was ready to give up his practice to his son-in-law. This was the logical and sensible thing to do, and it was what all of them urged upon him; but, as life slipped past him, some of the restlessness which should have had its fulfillment in his adolescence began to trouble Hugh. Was this the sum total of all that he had striven for and pushed to achieve: to see himself settled for the rest of his life in the ugly mill district where he had grown up? All of his striving as a boy had been to get away. Now should he come back voluntarily to something ugly and drab? It was a life sentence which he could impose upon himself. The more he thought of it, the more something deeper than his reason said "No!" There seemed to him then only one alternative, America. The eyes of the dissatisfied and the ambitious among the lower middle classes of England were all turning to America and the opening West.

When he had suggested America as a land of greater opportunity, Katherine had only once shed tears over the prospect. She had had one of her difficult nervous headaches afterwards, and he had had to give her a sedative as he often did, because she had so little resistance to pain. When she was better, he had said: "Of course we won't go, my dear. I'm doing well enough here, and some day there will be your father's practice. There was only something about the new West that appealed to me——"

And she had said: "Oh, Hugh, of course we must go. I was silly and upset the other day at the thought of leaving England. You've gone ahead so rapidly, and I know the past few years have been a standstill for you, being assistant when you should have had your own office."

"It's only that England is old and overcrowded from a professional man's view. I'm still young enough to want a place where I can go forward. It's been my life, you know."

"Yes, I know. And I don't mind going, really," Katherine had lied. "No, really I don't."

And so they had come to America, to the new country where he could establish a practice of his own with no older man over him. It was the sort of challenge which he loved and the opportunity of which he had dreamed. He had never felt more alive than he did now in this high, bracing air, so different from English air, and with everything to build by the skill of his own hands and brain.

He tried to open his mind to American ways and his ears to the idiosyncrasies of American speech, for he was determined to make a success of this venture.

When Dr. Allerton drove in the country he looked at the mountains, and they loomed large in his thoughts. Lines from the Bible which he had passed over without constructing a mental image of their grandeur returned to him now.

I will lift up mine eyes unto the hills, from whence cometh my help. . . .

Give glory to the Lord your God, before he cause darkness, and before your feet stumble upon the dark mountains . . .

The mountains and the hills shall break forth before you into singing, and all the trees of the field shall clap their hands.

He thought that one must live with mountains in order to understand them. One could talk in Manchester of "everlasting hills"; but he could not know their strangeness and their majesty, that they were sometimes a dark menace and sometimes a mysterious promise of things to come; in Manchester he could not conjure up whole ranges receding into a misty infinity of time and space at the sound of a single word.

When he was alone on a hill road Hugh thought these things, and was surprised at himself, for he had never been a dreamer nor a philosopher. He drew in deep breaths of the thin clear air, and, instead of appeasing and lulling him, it filled him with the kind of restless excitement which had begun to fret his blood in the last years in England. Driving home as the yellow leaves were falling, he was filled with an almost physical aching for something nameless, something he had missed along the way. The feeling kept recurring in him. He tried to bring it out and examine it, but he could never quite put his finger on what it was that he had missed nor where he had missed it. He tried to keep too busy to be conscious of the feeling, but on lonely drives it sat beside him and looked at him with quiet eyes. It was in the pungent smell of the dry leaves which rustled underfoot, and in the smoke of autumn fires. It hung, jewellike, in the clusters of orange berries among the lacy, yellowing leaves of the mountain ash. It trembled in the Indian summer haze on the purple hills; and, when a fleet of colored leaves drifted across the dark background of pines, the feeling tightened in his throat. It was a pain which was not altogether an unhappiness.

"When the practice is established, I'll not have time for it," he told himself.

7

LITTLE BY LITTLE cases came to the new doctor. People who had been offended by Doc Hawkins' profane forthrightness came to Allerton and liked his reticence. There were times when Hawkins and Duval were both busy and the emergency caller ran down the street to the renovated barber shop. The Methodists, finding him a steady, religious man who added a warm baritone to their Sunday choir, began to call him in. The restless and changeable element in town went to him out of curiosity or a desire for novelty.

Yet the change in Dr. Hawkins' practice was after all so slight that, after the first few weeks, his Jovian resentment against Dr. Allerton began to subside.

"By thunder, what's the difference?" he said. "I'm still the cock of the walk. Looks like I always will be."

Mrs. Kessler's was the test case, and the outcome of that filled Doctor with tremendous laughter. When Doc could laugh, he could begin to forgive.

Doc had not been surprised when Duval reported seeing the Kessler phaeton tied in front of Allerton's office.

"Sure," Doc said gloomily. "I knew she'd want to try him, the old fool. It all depends on what he gives her now. If he can produce a bigger capsule or make up a pill with a prettier damned color to it, he'll be her man, and I might about as well pull up my stakes and find me a new pasture."

Dr. Allerton gave Mrs. Kessler a thorough examination. She had not been so amused and titillated for a long time. She said: "Doctor, I've been taking these dreadful, big capsules for so long, and while, of course, they help me quite a lot, I simply *know* you'll have some new remedy that will be less offensive to my sensibilities. My sensibilities are very delicate, Dr. Allerton. Perhaps you've never had a patient like me, doctor."

The Englishman did not pat her on the back and roar at her as Dr. Hawkins did.

"Yes, madam," he said in his quiet voice. "I've seen a number of cases just like yours—not in the slums of London either." That dashed her just a little, but, as she thought it over later, his "not in the slums" made a certain appeal to her class consciousness, and her spirits rose again. By the next day, when she was to return for his final diagnosis, she had worked herself into a fine peak of excitement and expectancy.

"He's very quiet," she told her husband, "but, you know, still water runs deep. I'm sure he'll have a really novel method of treatment for me. Oh, I can't expect to be relieved in a day, of course. It's bound to be slow, even with the latest methods; but I'm filled with boundless hope."

"I thought you were so satisfied with Willard's treatment, Evelyn."

"Anything will wear out with time," said Mrs. Kessler irritably.

The next day she lowered herself heavily into the chair beside Allerton's desk, panting a trifle from exertion and excitement, and Dr. Allerton said quietly:

"Madam, I am very happy to inform you that there is nothing whatever the matter with you. My only suggestion would be that you take more exercise, eat less heavy food, and interest yourself in some charitable organization outside of your home."

Mrs. Kessler felt that she had been struck across the face with a heavy glove. She could scarcely totter out to the phaeton because of the shock and the humiliation. At home she took three of Doc Hawkins' capsules and lay down in a darkened room with a cold, wet cloth across her forehead.

She was well enough by the next day to go to the Ladies' Literary and Uplift Society, but she could not keep silent there. To everyone who would listen to her she said that Dr. Allerton was a charlatan and a mountebank and ought to be run out of town for incompetence.

"How do you know?" they asked.

"Didn't I subject myself to his crude methods of examination to find out? for the good of the town?"

"Evelyn! How public-spirited!"

"What did he tell you?" Jenny Walden asked.

The girl had been taken into the exclusive Literary and Uplift Society last spring on the strength of her commencement essay, and now, frankly, they did not know what to do with her, because she had an opinion on everything and was forever asking embarrassing questions.

"Well," Mrs. Kessler said reluctantly, not having meant to go into needless details. "Well, he showed himself absolutely ignorant of my case. Imagine! After all I've suffered, he said there was not a thing the matter with me."

"How horrid of him!" Jenny cried, and burst into one of her wild, irrelevant fits of laughing.

"I was not amused," said Mrs. Kessler coldly. "I know what I've suffered, and so does Dr. Hawkins."

"And I should think it would be even worse to have to take off your chemise and drawers for a new man than for an old one," volunteered Mrs. Peavy with quite unnecessary frankness. "Poor, dear Evelyn! You've been a martyr for us."

When Mrs. Kessler came by Dr. Hawkins' office the next week for a fresh supply of her capsules, he was astute enough to reconstruct the course of events, and he knew that his society practice was safe. The laugh that he got out of the affair softened his disposition towards the new man, and eased the tension of his nerves.

8

IF ANNA HAD thought that, after the renting of the house her relationship with Mrs. Allerton would cease, she was mistaken, for after the house came the need for furniture. Katherine was as helpless there as in the matter of the house, and Anna found herself not only interpreting prices but helping in the selection and the arranging of it. By the time they came to unpacking Katherine's English china and pictures they were on a sound basis of comradeship. The big barrels were placed in the new kitchen, and Anna watched with interest while Katherine unpacked the straw and papers from around the delicate china. Most of the well-to-do women of town had Haviland china imported from France; but Katherine's cream-colored Belleek with its pale green shamrock was new to Anna, and she was delighted by it. She held one of the fragile cups in her hand and turned it slowly around, admiring it.

"What a lovely thing!" she said.

"It was a wedding present."

"A nice one."

"From my parents."

"They are still alive?"

"Only my father. We could have stayed with him. Hugh could have been his assistant ahd had his practice after he was gone. I've never understood why he must come so far—"

Anna smiled.

"Women accept a lot of things without understanding. It's the best way." She held out the cup again for Mrs. Allerton to take. "It's beautiful."

But Mrs. Allerton did not take it; instead, she picked up the saucer and wiped it clean of straw and dust.

"Here," she said, "I should like you to have the cup and saucer, Anna—if you will let me call you that."

"Oh, do call me that, Katherine!" said Anna. "But I couldn't take your cup and saucer. They are part of a set."

"We have no use for a set. There are only the two of us. Please take it. I feel that you are my friend. I have had so few friends, Anna."

Anna hesitated. But she had a strong feeling that she could not take the cup and saucer.

"No. Thank you, Katherine, but I'd always feel bad to think I'd broken your set. Some day it will be an heirloom—for your children perhaps."

A strange look came into Katherine's eyes, something hunted and harried.

"Listen," she said. "You are my friend, Anna. I will tell you something that I have never told before. I think now that we will never have any children. It was my fault, because I was so frightened at first. No one had ever explained all about marriage to me, and it seemed horrible to me that he should want me to do things— things that I had always been taught to abhor. I don't know whether I can make you understand, but later—later when I was willing to do anything for him—even *that*—then he didn't care for it. I don't think he ever really loved me or wanted me. Oh, sometimes I think it was only to please my father—"

Anna put the teacup on the table and went to the window. She said in a quiet voice:

"Have you noticed that you have an apple tree in the back yard? It will be beautiful in the spring." Katherine sprang up, and the tears were running down her cheeks. Her face was white and blotched. The purple mark stood out strong and dark against her pallor.

"You are angry with me for talking like this. But I know it's true. He never really loved me—"

"No, I am not angry, Katherine," said Anna, still looking out of the window. "But there are some things one woman never tells another—even her best friend—because she will be sorry later."

"I couldn't help it," said Katherine. "It's been lying there in me so long now."

She was trembling all over, and her mouth worked pitifully. Anna was moved, too. She came and put her hand on Katherine's arm.

"I have a very bad memory," she said. "By next week I'll have forgotten everything you said. But I *will* take your cup and saucer, because we are friends now and always will be, I hope."

"Oh, I hope so," cried Katherine, pressing her hand, "because I am so cruelly alone."

Anna hesitated. "You'll think I am cruel, too," she said slowly; "but I've found out for myself—we're each of us alone in this world. We touch each other outside—but inside, each one is alone. It's kind of appalling sometimes."

They stood for a moment in silence looking at each other, and then Anna said: "Let me help you wash the dishes now. The water is hot."

9

ALONG IN NOVEMBER, as was her annual custom, Anna took Doc's buffalo coat out of the cedar box in the attic, and hung it to air on the line.

"By George," Doctor said, "that damned thing's getting mighty tacky! Worn along the seams, isn't it? Don't look like a prosperous physician's coat any more, Anna. It might belong to any jackleg."

"Why, doctor, it has years and years of good service in it yet. You look fine in it."

Still, knowing Doctor, she was not surprised to see him come home a few days later in a brand-new coat, a beaver coat that must have cost him a pretty penny. He was in such high good humor that Anna did not have the heart to reproach him for his extravagance.

"Take a good look at me, Gene," he said. "You see anything new? You see anything you never saw before?"

"A new coat, Uncle Doc! Golly, what a beaut!"

"The old Doc's a pretty slouchy-lookin' feller, eh, Gene? Run down at the heel, wouldn't you say?"

"Oh, no, I wouldn't say that, Uncle Doc. I think you're beautiful!"

"Feel of it," Doc said. "It beats your damned tough buffalo hide all to pieces. This is a piece of fur, I tell you! This is a gentleman's coat."

"Oh, soft!" cried Gene. "Let me try it on, Uncle Doc."

"Hey lad, you'd drown in that coat. You've got to grow up to it! You've got to be a big man, Gene."

Nevertheless he took the coat off and draped it about the child's shoulders, holding him up to the looking glass to get the full effect. The house rang with their merriment.

Anna watched them with quiet amusement. Then she asked:

"What did you do with the old buffalo, doctor?"

"Oh!" said Doctor, his face flooded with satisfaction. "You'd like to know, wouldn't you? Well, I'll tell you: that old buffalo has come to a God-damned good end, too. It's going to keep me laughing for the rest of my life. I sold the old buffalo, Anna, worn seams and all. Yes, sir, I sold it for a fair price and, God Almighty, how I laughed!"

"*You* sold it, doctor? Who to?"

"No. Kessler sold it, really. Said there was a feller in looking for a buffalo coat the day before, a feller who wasn't prosperous enough to buy a beaver, by Gad, and anyway he had his heart set on a buffalo. Kessler hasn't had a buffalo in stock for two years, but he told this chap he'd try to pick him up a secondhand one. And, by the Lord Harry, he's sold him mine!"

"Who was the man, doctor?"

"Allerton!" Doctor roared. "Did you ever hear a better one? *Allerton,* by George!"

Anna smiled, but she did not join in Doctor's roars and Gene's shrill shouts of merriment. When she could be heard, she said:

"Doctor, I should think that you would be superstitious about that coat. You started your practice here in it."

"Superstitious? No. Are you?"

"No. Only sentimental, perhaps."

"No, by God! It's the best joke I ever played on a man. He's a little too small for that coat, and it's worn along the seams. He's not used to this climate, and I can just see him, his English nose kind of blue with Idaho cold, warming himself in *my* coat!"

"Well!" said Anna. "The joke?"

"The joke?" roared Doctor. "My Lord, you're English yourself, aren't you—a few generations back? Do you think there's a man in town or within a radius of forty miles around who won't recognize that coat? There ain't a man or child in this county but will see the new doctor riding by and say: 'Look what he's got on! Doc Hawkins' cast-off hand-me-down.' "

"And Kessler didn't tell him?"

"Of course not! Let him find it out himself. And don't you go and tell his wife either, will you?"

"No, I won't," said Anna.

Doctor took a double pleasure in wearing his new coat.

And Allerton took pleasure in wearing his. Slipping his arms into the old buffalo coat, he saw that it was a trifle large for him, but not too much, and he liked the feel of it. A buffalo coat! It dovetailed with his boyhood dreams of America—a country of redskins and buffalo! He thought of himself as he had been, a little millhand, almost too young to bear the responsibility of supporting himself and his mother. With the detachment of one who visualizes a character in a book of fiction, he saw this boy hurrying through the reeking fog and the slimy streets of Manchester with a copy of Cooper's *Deerslayer* from the Chapel library wrapped under his jacket. A little boy with a great dream of the West at the back of his serious mind. A little boy who meant to get ahead.

"You are in Idaho, Hugh, wearing a buffalo coat!" he said to himself. It came as near making him laugh as anything ever did.

Eagerly now he looked forward to the western winter as an experience of which he had dreamed in his boyhood. There would be snow before long, and the sound of sleigh bells and the creak of runners on hard-packed roads. It would be the antithesis of winter as he had known it in England. The high, rolling wheat fields would be blanketed in virgin white, and they would shine and sparkle in the keen, light air. When he drove in the country now, he felt strong and prepared for any eventuality. In the anticipation of his first western winter he had moments of exaggerated happiness, when he was uplifted to the mountaintops.

He tried to get Katherine to drive with him sometimes when he had a long trip to make. He wished in some way to share his exhilaration in the mountain air. Sometimes she had used to bicycle with him in England when he had a case in a near-by village; but she was reluctant now. As a girl she had never become accustomed to horses, and they terrified her.

"No, Hugh. Oh, thank you for asking me, but it's so cold and the horse so—so unpredictable. I'm much better off by the fire with my crocheting."

Hugh reflected bitterly as he rode that Katherine had always retreated rather than advanced. Her first reaction was always "No"; then, when she had thought over his request and accustomed herself to the idea, she sometimes changed her mind and brought him a belated "Yes." By that time his own interest had flagged, and he cared very little whether it were "Yes" or "No." They did not pull well in harness because he was always quick to say "Yes" and firm to go forward. He did not have time to wait for a reluctant mind, and so they often passed each other on the road instead of keeping step. More and more they were slipping beyond each other's reach, he saw; but, if he had known what to do, the will to do it was not very strong. He gave Katherine every opportunity, he thought, and her first reaction was always to flee.

He was glad to see that Katherine took some comfort from her friendship with Mrs. Hawkins. He wanted Katherine to be happy, and he thought he made her so. That she had never been a wife to him, he accepted as part of her character. It was a period when people believed that the physical aspects of a man's emotional life were relatively unimportant. They had always seemed so to Hugh Allerton, because he had his career and his religion.

He had his religion. It was a warm and vital thing to him which pulsed with a mystical longing and humility. It was enough for any man.

The earth is the Lord's, and the fulness thereof, and that was what these western mountains were trying to say to him, he thought. His voice rang out in the little Methodist choir loft with a vigor which had not been heard there in a long time. The voice was clear and moving, and it asked a question which hung unanswered in the air even after the organ had ceased playing.

"Dr. Allerton, you sing as if you really meant it," said Jenny Walden, laughing up at him from her seat below him in the choir.

"I do," he said seriously.

He did not like Miss Walden, nor her flippant ways, nor the young men who obviously belonged to the choir because she sang in it. She had a thin, sweet soprano, as elfin as her face, but he distrusted both the face and the voice. And yet he could not help seeing her at every service and at choir practice, for she sat below him and directly in front. She wore her light hair brushed up into a knot on the top of her head, like a small girl playing lady; and on her neck there were little golden ringlets which escaped the stern intention and were soft and shining as a baby's hair.

10

PAST MIDNIGHT early in the winter there was a hurried knocking on the Hawkinses' side door. Doctor continued to sleep, breathing heavily through parted lips. Anna was Doctor's ears in the night.

"The Humphry baby on its way," she thought. She arose quickly, shoving her feet into slippers and her arms into the sleeves of the woolen dressing gown which hung on a chair by her bed. She had a candle and matches on the bedside table, where they would be quick and easy.

But it was not Tom Humphry's face in the shaken light of the candle. The knocker was one of the Italian girls from the boxcar shanties across the railroad tracks. The girl was white to the lips, and her great dark eyes held urgency and terror. Her breath came in painful gasps as if she had run the whole long way across town, and Anna could see that, even in the chilly night, she was sweating under her shawl.

"What's the matter?" Anna asked.

"Da doc—I gotta have da doc—an' queeck, too, meesus, please."

"All right. I'll call him. Can you tell me what it is?"

"It is a man—is hurt. You tell da doc come queeck—queeck."

Anna shook Doctor awake, and he stumbled out of the bedroom buttoning his trousers and swearing. Anna had his coat and his medicine kit ready for him.

"Some kind of accident, I guess," she said.

"Why, hello, Gina," Doctor said, when he saw the girl. "You got some trouble down to your place? What's the matter?"

"Doctor, you come. I tell. You see, but come."

"We'll save time to hitch the horse."

"All right, doc. But queeck."

While Doctor rushed the horse between the shafts and fastened straps and traces, the girl stood beside him wringing her hands and crying.

"*Madre di Dio,*" she said, "it ain't my fault dey fight, doc. I don' wan' two. I got one man—is enough."

Presently she was silent, and, looking up, Doc saw the wave of nausea coming over her. Just in time he got the horse pail to her and held her head. When she was better, Doctor said:

"What's the matter with you, Gina?"

"Not'ing," she answered sullenly.

"Look here, my girl—you got some fellow's baby growing in you?"

"Oh, doc," she said, beginning to cry again, "Pietro going for marry me! Honest, he is. But now he have to keel dis fella. What we do now, doc? *Mio Dio,* what we do now?"

"Get in the buggy," Doctor said. "We'll see what we can do."

"Oh, Mudder in heaven, if Pietro ain't dead, too!" the girl sobbed. "Such a cut he got, doc, witha blood run down like water."

The boxcar shanty was silent in the moonlight. Nothing stirred around it, and there was only the wintry sound of restless air in the frosty branches of the pines. Doc tied the horse to one of the trees and followed the girl in.

"Look out, you don'-a step on Luca's face," she warned. The door came only halfway open, and Doc saw that the obstruction was a man's body.

"Luca!" he said. "That devil mixed up in it, eh? What was he doing here?"

"He come for make me da love, doc. Honest, I never wanta him for come. He know my pap gone on da long run wit' da freight train east. T'ink I'm alone here, see?"

"I see," said Doc.

He closed the shanty door and leaned a moment over the body. The ugly face leered up at him in the uncertain light of a smoky lamp. The eyes and mouth were open, but the eyes would no more covet nor the mouth kiss. A knife was wedged expertly between the ribs where it would stop the heart most quickly, and his blood had flowed around him darkly on the shanty floor. The small, hot room reeked heavily of human blood.

"Oh, doc, don' waste da time. He dead. Look at Pietro, doc."

"Ya," Doctor said, "he's past all help."

He was careful not to step in Luca's blood. The girl had flung herself against the bed, crying again and calling on Pietro. Doc went to the bed and looked at him. Pietro was little more than a boy, and Doc remembered having pulled him through the smallpox in the first winter he had been in Opportunity. He could see the little pockmarks now in the dark skin which seemed more gray than brown against the girl's pillow. Doctor liked Pietro.

"Well, kid," he said, "the old goat nearly finished you up, too, didn't he?"

Pietro's eyelids fluttered open, and the white teeth flashed in a fair imitation of that smile which had stirred the female pulse all up and down his section of the railroad line.

"I gotta get away, doc." Pietro's stiff lips formed the words. "You sew me up, doc. Then I gotta get away."

"One thing at a time. One thing at a time. Get me some water, Gina. Do you have some hot?"

"Sì. I t'ink."

The girl had put a rough tourniquet on Pietro's arm before leaving the shanty, but the blood still oozed sluggishly down a long rip in the forearm and dripped from the hand that hung off the bed. Doctor saw that he would have to take five or six stitches, possibly more. He opened his satchel and took out his carbolic acid and cotton lint and rolls of bandages and sponge. He laid out the catgut and the scissors and the suture needle.

Gina held the lamp for him, and he worked quickly and thoroughly. In that hot small room with lamp and open fire, ether was out of the question, but Pietro did not cry out. The sweat stood in cold beads on his forehead and upper lip, but he shut his mouth hard and endured the pain.

When Doc had finished, he straightened his shoulders and looked around the room.

"Now what?" he said. "Shall I call in the town marshal or the sheriff? They got a comfortable bed for you up at the courthouse jail, Pietro."

The girl caught Doctor's arm in both of her hands.

"Oh, doc!" she begged. "Oh, doc!" Her eyes were liquid with anguish and fear.

"All right," Pietro said sullenly. "So I am a murderer. Yes, it is true. It don't matter if he try to kill me first. So I will hang then. You sew me up to hang, eh, doc?"

"That's about the size of it," said Doc, "unless you know what else to do."

"I know! I know, doc. I got me a shack back in woods. Da night freight she come t'rough in 'bout twenty minutes. Gina an' me—"

"Well, keep it to yourself," Doc said. "My God! It's enough if *you* know. I don't want the knowledge, too."

Doctor began to gather up his things. He left the bottle of carbolic acid on the table with a roll of bandage and some lint. "Be sure to take that with you. You saw the way I mixed that stuff with water, Gina? Not too much of either, and keep the wound clean, see?"

"Oh, doc!" She caught his hand and kissed it, and he felt her tears.

"Don't be a fool," he said angrily. "And as soon as you can, marry her, see, Pietro? Tell the priest everything, and start off right in a new place. Give the baby a fair chance."

"*Sì*, doctor, *sì*. An' some day I send you da beeg money, doc, for sure."

"Forget the money," Doctor said, "but get the hell out of here, and see you do a good job of it. Don't let them pick you up halfway down the line."

He didn't look at Luca again as he went out. The fellow had been a troublemaker for years. He had no relatives by blood or marriage to grieve for him or weep for his support. Opportunity would be more tranquil and law-abiding without him.

It was not the first time that Doc had used his own judgment about reporting a case of death. In a few days someone would look in a window of the shanty and see the corpse; and then he would be called in as a matter of course, and they would start out looking for the murderer. If they never found him, justice would be done, in Doctor's estimation.

The streets were lonely and deserted. Not even a dog barked as he drove homeward. Just as he turned in at his own driveway, he heard the whistle of the night freight, drawing in to a brief stop at the water tank. When he crawled into bed, Anna was asleep.

In the morning Doctor said: "Anna, that call that came in last night—that's one of these calls we never mention. See?"

"All right, doctor. But some day you're going to get yourself into trouble."

"Well, it's my own damned business if I do," said Doctor. He went in to breakfast and bellowed at the top of his lungs: "Who the hell filled my mustache cup too full? By Gad, Christina, next time you do that, I'm going to make you burn your own lip on it. See if I don't!"

Few things put Doctor into a greater rage than finding a slop of hot coffee in the china mustache guard on his cup.

11

MORE THAN a week passed, and there had been no mention of the finding of a body. No one had run breathless along Main Street to beat on Dr. Hawkins' door, calling: "Doc! Doc! Somebody's killed a man!"

Doctor began to feel a trifle restless about the affair. Even in winter a corpse will tend to disintegrate as the days go by. Luca would not be nice to handle if the thing dragged on too long. Doctor was not squeamish, but he liked to get the dead buried as soon as circumstances would permit.

And then they brought Art Foley in from the Ridge with an ax cut in his foot, and when Doc looked in his surgical kit for his suture needle it was not there. He had more of them in his desk drawer, but as he sterilized and sewed Art's foot his mind kept going back to the last time he had used that needle. Had he left it in the shanty? If so, how and why? He was always careful to put everything back into the bag before he left a place, particularly a place like the shanty where he had dealt out his own brand of justice. As he thought it over, he knew, of course, that it was because he had not put all of the things back into his bag. He had left the bandage and the bottle of carbolic for them to dress the wound, and somehow the needle had been overlooked too—under the bandage maybe. Well, a person discovering a dead body was not likely to notice a small surgical instrument in his first excitement. He'd be seeing only the comprehensive aspects of the thing at first. He'd want to get away quickly and call the doctor and the marshal. The needle could be easily retrieved as soon as Doc entered the shanty. But another thought came to Doc's mind: as the days slipped by, would even the layman make his first call on the doctor? There would be no doubt of the fact of death certainly, and perhaps the one who discovered the body would only call the marshal or the sheriff of the county. That another doctor might be called did not enter Doctor's thoughts at all.

It was waiting and silence that irritated Doctor beyond measure. Why didn't some of the neighbors think it funny that the shanty was so quiet and go down to investigate? Wasn't it time for Gina's father to be back from his eastern freight run? Doctor thought of sending Duval down there. He could say casually: "Haven't seen old man Torelli lately. His heart isn't too good. Why don't you stop by the shanty next time you're near the depot?" Or: "Gina Torelli's going to have a baby in a month or two. Stop by the shanty next time you're near there, and look her over, will you?" But Duval would think that odd in the first place, and odder still if he found a body there.

I could go down myself, Doc thought. *But better not. No, better not. Just hold your horses, Willard. Sit still, and let things work out naturally. It will be all right, whatever happens. I'm solid in this town.*

As the days wore on Doctor stayed more closely at the office and sent Duval out on the long drives. If they came for him, Doctor did not want to miss the call.

It still lacked a day of two weeks from the midnight call, and Doctor was sitting tipped back in his swivel chair, smoking a cigar and nervously chewing the end. Duval came in from a drive, and hung his buffalo coat with neatness and exactitude on one of the pegs behind the door.

"Getting colder," he said, rubbing his hands together towards the baseburner.

"Yeh?" said Doctor absently.

"You know, Hawkins, I think you are too optimistic, my friend, about the state of civilization of this town. In the commencement address, you say mob rule is dead in Idaho. Maybe, doctor, but the wild hearts, they are still here. For a town of this size there are a great many killings, I think. No, we are still the wild and—what you call it?—woolly West, here, I believe."

Doctor turned his head slowly to look at Duval, his interest suddenly coming to focus.

"What do you mean?"

"Only another killing, doctor—down in a shanty by the railroad. An Italian section hand, they say, who has been lying there for a long time with a knife sticking out of him and people passing to and fro only a few hundred yards away and never knowing he was there."

Doctor got to his feet.

"Were you there, Duval? Did they call you in?"

Duval shrugged his shoulders.

"No. You and I were out of it this time, doctor. They have told me in the drugstore. It seems the new man was driving by in a livery stable rig, and the person who discovered the body hailed him in. There was no question but that the Italian had been dead a long time. I think that you and I are well out of it, doctor. For myself I prefer a good Roquefort or even a Limburger to a two-weeks-old body. Let the new man have him."

"By God!" Doctor cried. "I don't feel that way. Allerton had no business on that case! That case belonged to me, by God!"

Duval looked at Doctor in surprise. He stopped warming his hands and began to rub his chin.

"It is hardly a *case*, doctor," he said slowly. "With a knife sticking out of the fellow's ribs, even an autopsy should not be necessary, I think."

"Just the same, he had no business—" Doctor cried.

"You speak as if you knew about this thing?"

"Of course not! Of course not! How would I know?"

They looked at each other across the stove, and their eyes held steady for a moment. Then Doctor's voice fell to a lower key.

"Just keep your mouth shut," Doctor said. "That's all *I* did. There are times when that's the best thing to do. You know that, Duval. Any doctor knows that."

"Yes, there are times. But was this one of them?"

"Yes, it was, damn it!"

"Very well, doctor. I take your word for it."

There was an uneasy silence between them. Presently Duval went into the back room to attend to some of the various small inquiries which he conducted there. "Duval's playroom," Doc facetiously called it. Doctor began to pace up and down the office. The cigar went out, but he continued chewing the end until it was a ragged pulp; then he threw it into the waste basket, put on his hat and his fine beaver coat, and went out. He did not have a definite destination in mind, but he was sick and tired of the stale atmosphere of the office.

When he turned the corner onto Main Street, he saw the marshal coming along the street towards him. He raised his hand in cordial greeting.

"Hi, George," Doctor said. "Haven't seen you in a month of Sundays. What's the good word?"

"We've had another murder down here, doc," Marshal Fridley said. "Fact of the matter is, I was just coming round to your office to chin with you a bit. Know anything about this killing, Willard?"

"Not much, George. Duval just told me he'd heard something at the drugstore. I was going out to get the facts. There's a new doctor in town now, George, in case you didn't know. If they call him on a case, you'll have to ask him what *he* knows—not me."

Doc laughed. But Fridley's face remained serious. He took something out of his pocket.

"Look here, doc," he said, "do you know what this is?"

Doc's eyelids flickered. He hesitated just an instant.

"By God, it's my suture needle!" Doctor said.

"You know where they found it?"

"Who found it?"

"Dr. Allerton. The rest of us wouldn't have known what it was, I guess."

"The devil he did! What's he going to do about it?"

"See here, doc, this looks like trouble for you. You know I didn't ask you if it was yours, and I'm warning you now, anything you say may be used against you."

Doc's anger rose in a red tide.

"You think you're going to shut me up that way? Not by a damned sight! I'm not ashamed to tell you what I had to do with that case."

"Now, hold your horses, Willard. Don't go and hang yourself."

"Hang myself!" roared Doc. "Since when have they begun to hang doctors for sewing up a wounded man?"

"I didn't mean it literally, doc. I only meant, sometimes the least said, soonest mended. There's this other doctor here, this Allerton, says a doctor who lets a criminal get away and doesn't report a murder is an accessory after the fact."

"Why do you quote *him*?" Doc demanded. "Don't you know the law yourself, George? So the new doctor has to tell you what it is, eh?"

"No, Willard," Fridley said, "and I don't want to be ugly.

Everybody knows you'd always do the right thing by this town; but the law's the law. If they ever catch the fellow who killed Luca Pozzetti and try him for murder, they can try you, too, doctor, as an accessory after the fact. I'm damned sorry, Willard, but if the murderer's caught it looks like trouble for you."

Doctor's voice rose defiantly.

"By God, I like a little trouble once in a while! It clears the atmosphere. Sure, I was there that night. Sure, I let the fellow get away. I won't tell you who the fellow was, but bring it to trial if you can catch him. I'd rather have it that way. I'd rather have it out in court where I could tell the whole town, than to have folks salve it over on the surface, and go around whispering behind my back. Sure, I was there! Sure, I let the fellow get away! Sure, it's my suture needle!" Walking away from Fridley down the street, he had a gratifying sense of lightness and relief. He liked things open and aboveboard, and the past week's silent waiting had been more agonizing than he had realized. He liked a good open fight with plenty of clean, hard slugging on both sides. If it ever came into court, he'd be fighting Allerton—not the law or the courts, but the rival doctor, the upstart and the challenger. Damn Allerton, damn him!

Doctor felt confident and exhilarated.

12

MOST OF THE town shared Doctor's opinion that Luca Pozzetti had been no good, and that, if the murderer could get away and make a fresh start somewhere along the frontier, it was fair enough. That the killing had occurred at the Torelli shanty, and that Gina was missing, pointed either to her or to Pietro, her lover, as the murderer; a case of attack and self-defense, no doubt. Western justice might have let it rest at that, but there was this new doctor from England who took another view of justice. To him there were no palliating circumstances. Murder had been committed, and an impartial punishment must follow.

A little shamefaced at his own lack of enthusiasm, the sheriff took the affair in hand and began to spread his deputies out over the county, and to get the search going in other counties beyond. There was a lot of wild country in which a man could hide, even a man and a woman, if the woman were young and used to an active life. Back in the hills there were any number of deserted cabins which had belonged to prospectors and homesteaders. A couple could easily lie quiet there over the winter. Some of the cabins might still have food cached away; certainly there would be traps and an abundance of game. Or, if the fugitives had money or friends on the railroad, all the towns and cities of the coast were open to them, and they had had a good two weeks of freedom for the flight.

So the belated dragnet went out over the hills and mountains and into the heavy timber and the waste places; deputies made inquiry over the bar in frontier saloons, and questioned packers who came out of the white-pine forest where the only sound had been the wind in the trees and the jangling of the bell on the neck of the lead horse. At the long table in country hotels where the lumberjacks ate silently, reaching long arms for the platters of beans and salt pork in milk gravy, there was low-voiced question and answer.

"Ya, I seen a man on the old Lewis an' Clark trail up by Freeze-out last week. Maybe he done it, a mean-lookin' cuss. Sure, he was totin' a gun. Who don't? But he wasn't no Eyetalian. Swede, I guess."

And then the snow began to fall. It had held off for a long time this year, as if it wished to give justice a fair opportunity. It fell slowly and heavily in the gray air, blotting out, shutting away, reducing the world to a single town, and then to individual streets, and at last to individual firesides. It is difficult to hunt a man in the snow. Sometimes justice was snowed in here in the winter and had to wait until the chinook wind came roaring through the hills at the end of February or March before it could function again.

Dr. Allerton watched the snow fall with a strange elation. Already he was very far from England.

13

THE HAWKINS HOUSE had never witnessed a more elaborate Christmas. Doctor had Christina's father cut and sled them such a tree as swept even the high ceiling of the parlor; and the banisters were hung with evergreen, and the tall clock crowned with it.

"Make twice your usual lot of cakes and cookies, Anna," Doc had said. "We'll have some people in this Christmas. By Gad, there's no use living like hermits. We'll have some toddies and eggnogs, too, by George, and open house on New Year's Day."

That year Doctor bought expensive presents for everybody. He bought the diamond earrings he had so long coveted for Anna, and a fur-trimmed dolman for Lita. He gave Christina a twenty-dollar gold piece, and Dr. Duval a set of studs and fine gold and moss-agate cuff links. But he took the greatest pleasure in buying for Gene. There was a shiny new sled by Gene's bed when he awoke in the morning. Ever since coming to them he had used Lita's old sled; but now he had a new one with steel runners, and its name was painted on it, *King of the Hill*. And that was only the beginning: there were skates and a ball, a *Chatterbox* and a tinsel-trimmed cornucopia of bonbons and lemon drops, and over behind the tree the climax of all, a red bicycle.

Gene was wild with delight. The games and books which his father had given him lay untouched on top of the piano, while he balanced himself precariously on the new bicycle, wavering up and down the parlor, leaving behind him the curved lines of his progress imprinted in the parlor carpet.

"It might have been better to wait until spring for the bicycle," Anna said. "It'll be of no use to him in the snow."

"Keep still, Anna," Doctor said. "You've got your diamonds. Let the boy enjoy his bicycle."

Anna smiled a little wryly to herself. The diamonds had been Doctor's ambition, not her own. She had never had her ears pierced

as a girl, and now she had to submit to the piercing and keep the holes
open with bits of broomcorn until they were completely healed and
ready for the cruel little screws behind the diamonds.

"You must wear them on New Year's Day, Anna," Doctor said.
"I want the Kesslers to see you wearing them. They're just as fine as
Mrs. Kessler's got—by Gad, every bit as fine!"

Constant came to all of the festivities at the Hawkins house during the holidays. He rarely walked alone in the hills any more, but
he was quiet and withdrawn, watching with the eyes of an outsider
his son's excitement over the new red bicycle.

After the Christmas dinner Doc and Gene took the bicycle into
the icy carriage drive, and Constant and Anna stood at the window to
watch them.

"The best bike in town," shouted Doc, "and, by gum! the best boy
on it. Some day this thing is going to supplant the horse, you know
it, Gene?"

"You bet your boots, Uncle Doc!"

Doc had never learned to ride a bicycle himself, but that did not
prevent him from giving Gene the most minute instructions as to the
proper manner of mounting and keeping his equilibrium. Together
they spent a happy afternoon.

Watching them, Anna said lightly, "You'd think Doctor had
something on his conscience this Christmas, the way he's given
presents."

Constant turned and looked at her curiously. Then Doctor hadn't
told her what was hanging over him?

"You deserve better than you have, Anna," he said seriously.

"Better than diamonds?" Anna mocked. "Surely that is the last
pinnacle, Constant."

People went from house to house on New Year's Day, making
calls and eating cake and drinking the punches and eggnogs that
filled every bowl. Lita stood with her mother and father to receive
callers during the early part of the afternoon, and then a group of
young folks hailed her out to go the rounds with them. Gene, in a

new suit with tight, short trousers and a white shirt with a ruffled collar, let people in at the door and performed the duty of butler by shrilling their names the length of the parlor.

The entertainment at the Hawkins home amazed and delighted people this year, and Doctor was loudly cordial, slapping old friends on the back and giving boisterous greeting. If Anna held herself back with quiet reserve, it did nothing to spoil the picture. Doc's patients liked his cordiality, and the stillness of her dignity made a nice foil. Her black silk dress might have looked drab; but she had drawn her hair back from her ears to display the diamond earrings, and, blazing above it, they transformed the drabness into a magnificent simplicity.

Constant came in late with the last of the afternoon callers. He went to Anna and said with a half-smile and in a voice that was only for her ears: "I find that I approve of them, *mon amie*. You are really regal."

"They hurt like the devil," Anna said, her eyes twinkling, "but thank you, anyway."

Doctor came and flung his arm around Constant's shoulders: "Why so late, doctor? Where have you been all day, eh? Sampling the punch bowls all over town, I'll bet!"

"No, I was reading," Constant said. "I have forgot the time, and that it was a day of celebration."

Gene came and swung upon his father's hand.

"You should have been here sooner, papa. All sorts of people have been here: the Presbyterians and the priest, and all the patients, and Gibbs, the plumber. But he had had too much to drink, I think."

Doctor shouted with laughter.

"There's observation for you! Will anybody say that youngster isn't smart?"

"He walked like this," said Gene gleefully, imitating Gibbs's tipsy swagger down the length of the parlor. "And Mrs. Gibbs, she took him by the arm and hustled him, like this."

They stood around Gene, laughing and admiring him. Then Doc turned suddenly and slapped Constant on the back.

"*Reading!* By God, man, your whistle must be dry! Come and have a drink. Did I tell you I was a teetotaler, doctor? Well, this year I'm celebrating. New Year's comes but once a year, and all the fences are down. I've got a little dish here that will warm the cockles of your heart and put the spirit of auld lang syne into you. Try it, Constant, try it."

"No, I thank you," Duval said.

"By God," cried Doctor, "you don't turn me down like that! It's New Year's, man, it's New Year's."

"That is so."

"Well, come then. Do our hospitality justice."

"Don't force it on him, doctor," Anna said. "There's coffee, Constant, and you'll find the fruit cake good, I think."

But Doc was jovially persistent.

"No, sir, I won't tolerate drinking during the year, but today I say you shall." Laughing, he ladled a cupful of the heavy punch and held it out. It had a delicate, pervasive odor. Anna saw Constant's face darken and the nostrils dilate.

"Give it to *me*, doctor," she said. "I've been standing for hours, shaking hands. I'm very thirsty."

"Well, in a minute. This is for Constant."

"Papa," cried Gene, swinging upon his father's hand, "what is the matter with you? Are you afraid of it?"

Constant took the cup from Doctor and drank it hungrily.

"It is a small cup, doctor," he said. "I will have one more."

"No, try the coffee," Anna urged.

"Meeses Hawkins seems to be concerned about her punch, doctor."

"There's lots of it," cried Doctor. "The crowd's all gone. Leave the man alone, Anna, for Lord's sake!"

Duval's hands were trembling as he set the second cup on the table.

"A very good punch, doctor."

"Have another one?"

"Not for the moment. Later, I think."

"Moderation," Doctor said. "Moderation in everything, that's what I always say."

"Yes," Duval said dreamily. "Moderation, it is such a tidy virtue, *n'est-ce pas?* It is a kind of anchor—isn't it?—to hold one steady on the tide." He laughed, and although he did not look at her Anna saw that his eyes were bright.

As they stood so, the front door opened with a blast of wintry air, and Lita stood a moment on the threshold framed by the cold blue of early evening and falling snow. Her cheeks were very red, and her eyes, large and dark like Doctor's, were full of anger.

"Mama!" she cried, slamming the door behind her. "Is it true what they're saying about papa? Is it true? Why didn't somebody tell me before they let me go out to parties—to hear people laughing and making fun?"

"Why, Lita!" Anna said. "I don't know what you're talking about, dear."

"You're trying to keep it from me, all of you! It's horrible! I won't be treated like a baby!"

"Lita! What are you talking about?"

"Ask him! Ask my father. I heard them talking. Mama, he's let a murderer escape, and, if they catch the man, they'll try papa, too. That's what they said. We'll all be mixed up in a murder trial. Oh, it's too horrible!"

"Hold your tongue, you little fool!" cried Doc. "You're talking about something you don't understand at all."

"It's true then!" Lita cried. "But if I don't understand it, it's because I have to go away from home to learn the family shame. Oh, heavens! to go out gayly to a party, and then to learn that I'm the daughter of a criminal."

"Damn you!" Doctor shouted. "You stand there and call me a criminal—you stand there in a fur dolman that cost me a hundred and fifty dollars—"

"Take your dolman," Lita cried. "I'll never wear it again as long as I live." She took off the fur-trimmed cloak and flung it across the room at Doctor, bursting into a storm of tears as she did so.

Gene sprang to Doctor's side, his face white and his hands clenched. "You're not a criminal, Uncle Doc. That Lita is a little fool."

"Listen!" Anna's quiet voice cut through the turmoil. "This is like something out of a play. Pick up your coat, Lita, and stop crying. If there is something to face, let us face it quietly."

"It's horrible," sobbed Lita. "I'll never dare to lift my head in this town again."

"I've heard you say that before, Lita. Suppose you trust your father now. I don't believe he's ever failed you."

"I only did what was right," Doc said, "if that damned Allerton hadn't interfered—"

"Maybe you'd better start at the beginning, Doctor," Anna said. "It must have been the night that Gina Torelli came for you."

The guests were all gone now except Constant, and mechanically Anna began to unscrew her earrings. The little holes in her ear lobes were still sore, and the weight of the earrings had become unbearable.

"Yes, it was," Doc said. "I'll tell you, but I'll be damned if I'll stand for any hysterics."

"There will not be any more hysterics, doctor," Anna said.

Constant moved uneasily. A smile of embarrassment twitched at his lip.

"It is better I leave you, I think," he said. "Good night, and, if it is not too late, a Happy New Year." But, before he left, he went to the table and poured himself a third cup of the drink. It had an indescribable aroma which promised peace and forgetfulness and pleasant dreams.

14

DR. ALLERTON's sleigh skimmed over the frozen road, and the bells sang in his ears. The white austerity of field and mountain lay about him on every hand, a cold and terrible beauty.

He was about three miles out of town, lost in a kind of waking dream, when he saw a woman walking in the road ahead of him. She had a brisk, swinging stride, and he saw her for quite a distance before the horse and sleigh overtook her. He was familiar with the straight, vigorous line of the head and back, and the slight swing of the hips. He had seen a good deal more of the Walden girl's back than of her full face, he thought.

He considered driving by her with a nod; but, after all, a woman walking this far in the country in winter weather must have need of assistance. He reined the horse beside her.

"Aren't you a long way from home, Miss Walden?"

"Yes, I am," she said, "and I'm beginning to regret it."

When she smiled, her teeth flashed white between the red lips. Walking in the freezing wind had stung her cheeks to scarlet. She had a little dark fur hat and her hands were hidden in a small round muff. She stood in the road and laughed. She did not look like a woman who needed to be rescued.

"Get in," he said, not very graciously perhaps.

His voice was rough from having ridden so far in silence. He held back the lap robe and indicated the seat beside him. Jenny stamped her feet and scraped the loose snow from her overshoes against the runner.

"No use carrying a melting snowdrift with us," she said. When she stepped into the cutter, she was light and quick. She settled herself beside him without looking at him.

He said, "Do you often walk so far?"

"Yes," she said. "People around here are used to me. They don't stare any more."

"Did I stare?"

"I'm afraid you did."

"I beg your pardon."

"I don't mind."

Dr. Allerton did not say any more, for he expected to be drowned by her chatter. At choir rehearsals she was always chattering—not to him, of course, but to the other people: to the reedy tenor with the faint attempt at a mustache, to the paunchy bass. But today she said nothing at all, and they rode a long way in silence. The sleigh bells jingled in rhythm with the beat of the horse's hoofs. Without looking at her he felt her beside him, alert and warm and silent. At last the silence which he had desired began to oppress him.

"I dare say I am dull company, Miss Walden."

"I hadn't thought of that."

"Your thoughts were farther away."

"Yes. If you can call them thoughts."

"You seem to have a low opinion of them."

"It's one of those days," she said. "You wonder why you were born. That's when I walk."

He looked around at her then, because he was surprised.

"Don't tell me that you have days of that sort," he said lightly. "You were born to delight the town, Miss Walden."

"That's almost a pretty speech, doctor, but I know the way you mean it. I delight the town all right. The Ladies' Aid has been after mama to tone me down again. Am I to be myself or what they plan for me?"

"I think you had better be yourself—or is that bad advice?"

"I can't be sure. I think that it is." She laughed in one of her sudden shifts of mood, and Dr. Allerton found himself smiling with her.

"An unreliable character," she said, "and born into a threadbare Methodist parsonage. What a combination!"

"You see yourself objectively."

"I try to. Sometimes it's difficult."

They rode again in silence. Her eyes rested on his hands holding the reins. Katherine had knit a pair of heavy brown woolen mittens for his country driving. They were just a shade lighter than the fur of the old buffalo-skin coat.

"Is it true," she asked, "what they say about you and Doc Hawkins? That you found something of his at the scene of that Italian murder!"

"I'd rather not discuss it, if you don't mind."

"You're a funny man," she said. "You'd rather not discuss it—and there you sit in Dr. Hawkins' coat. How do you feel in it, in Dr. Hawkins' coat?"

Hugh looked around at her with startled eyes.

"Hawkins?" he said. "What do you mean? This coat is mine."

"I wondered if you knew," said Jenny. "Everyone in town knows you're wearing Doc Hawkins' coat—but you."

"I bought the coat at the store. It wasn't new, of course, but I wanted a buffalo coat. They don't have new ones any more."

"No. And so Doc Hawkins sold you his. I guess he's had some laughs at your expense."

Hugh Allerton reddened. "How do you know that this is true?"

"I've heard people talking, but I'd have known anyway. I love that old coat. I know every seam of it, inside and out. It's part of my childhood."

"Part of your childhood, Miss Walden?"

"Once," Jenny said, "when I was a little girl I lit out to run away—to San Francisco. I guess I've always had ideas that were too big for me or this town. Anyway it was something about seeing the Golden Gate and getting a blue silk dress that I had in my mind. But after I got way out in the country it began to snow, and I was lost, honestly lost. It was no joke. I'd have frozen to death and been covered by the blizzard. I saw it all real clearly. There didn't seem any help for me at all. And then Doc Hawkins came driving out of the storm and took me in his cutter. He made me take off my wet coat and he set me inside his buffalo coat and buttoned it up around us (I was a little, skinny, frightened thing then), and I went to sleep with my head against his breast. I like this old coat better than the fancy new one he has."

Dr. Allerton was silent, looking between the horse's ears at the frozen road ahead. At last Jenny said curiously:

"Now that you know, what are you going to do? Go on wearing it?"

"Of course," he said. "What do you think? If they have laughed at me for wearing it, wouldn't they laugh more if I were suddenly to abandon it? No, I have paid for it; it is my coat now."

"Are you angry with me for telling you?"

"No, I am not angry."

"But you don't like me, do you?" persisted Jenny. "I shouldn't have told you about my running away, because it makes you see me as a silly, discontented little girl. But that's what I was, and that's what I am. There are plenty of people in town like you, who despise me for knocking my head against the wall. But Doc Hawkins was never one of them, and I appreciated that. How are you ever going to get out of walls, if you don't knock your head and try?"

"Are the walls so bad, Miss Walden? I had my own walls in England; but, now that I am in Idaho, I believe that I have found freedom."

"Do you? Do you feel that?"

"Yes, I do. Perhaps it is the mountain air—I don't know. More likely it is because I have my own practice and there is no one over me to ask for an accounting."

"Oh, you *are* a human being after all!"

"You thought that I was not?"

"I had been wondering."

"Miss Walden, you are a very strange young lady."

"I know. So many people tell me that, that I have almost begun to believe it myself."

"I didn't mean to offend you."

"You haven't. If I ask you to let me out now, you won't think it's because you have offended me, will you? We're almost to town, and I'd rather walk the rest of the way in. Thank you for giving me a lift."

"I could take you directly to the parsonage."

"No, don't, please. The Ladies' Aid *would* have a morsel then! I'll walk from here."

"Good luck, then," he said—he didn't quite know why.

He stopped the sleigh, and let her get out. In a lonely jangle of bells he went on, not looking back again at the erect, small figure following briskly along the frozen road.

Dr. Hawkins' coat, he said to himself. That was why he had seen people looking at it, smiling and sneering a little, perhaps. Nothing he touched in this town seemed to be free from the taint of Doc Hawkins. Katherine had even tried to rent a house from Dr. Hawkins, he had discovered, and in that terrible Italian shanty reeking with murder and corruption, he had found Doc Hawkins' suture needle. He would have preferred friendship with this man; but it seemed increasingly difficult—and now he found himself wearing Hawkins' cast-off buffalo coat, and people in town were laughing at him. But Hugh was stubborn, and he meant to wear the coat in spite of everything.

15

KATHERINE STOOD in the window watching for Hugh to come home to supper. She felt at home now in the small warm house. To keep it clean and orderly had become a deep preoccupation with her. Through the fall and early winter she had spent her spare time in crocheting tidies for the backs and arms of the chairs, so that the red plush could be kept clean and fresh. She missed the neat coal grates of England with their glowing embers in winter and their pleated paper fans in summer, and the mantelpiece which offered a woman such an outlet for her artistic ingenuity. Sometimes, when she was alone, she opened the door of the baseburner to give herself

the feeling of an open fire, and she had contrived a shelf between
the parlor windows on which she could put the draped velvet
lambrequin with its gold tassels that had always ornamented her
mantelshelf in England. On it were arranged the Staffordshire dogs
which had belonged to her mother and the Carrara marble urn with
the doves. She liked everything well clothed and draped, and her
windows were hung and looped with yards of Nottingham lace and
dark red velveteen, edged with ball fringe and tied back with ribbon
bows. She had a cupboard for Hugh's books, because she did not like
to see them lying about on open shelves where they could collect dust.
Now that the bewilderment of her first settling in was over, she had
enjoyed very much working out these small details of her housekeeping.

Hugh seemed pleased with all she had done, too, she reflected.
There was only one thing that she was sorry about. She had bought
the large coal-oil lamp for the marble-topped center table without
consulting Hugh, hoping that it would surprise and please him. In
England there had always been gas, and she had brought no lamps with
her, so that buying one for the parlor had become a major enterprise.
She hadn't even asked Anna's advice because she felt so sure that she
was right about the lovely lamp with the round oil globe and the
matching round glass shade. The roses on· the shade were hand-
painted and just the right color of pink to go with the roses on the
Brussels carpet. The lamp threw such a subdued light over the
chenille table cover and the rich binding of the family Bible which
her mother and father had given them on their first anniversary.
Beside the Bible she liked to have the pressed-glass paperweight and
the shell from the South Seas to rest just at their proper angles, with
the rosy lamplight over everything.

Hugh hadn't noticed the lamp at all at first. When she had called
his attention to it, he had said: "Oh, Katherine, couldn't you have
found a lamp with a wide, plain glass shade—a student lamp, you
know—something a man could read by?"

It was too late to change it then, and every time she looked at

the rose lamp now, instead of the lift it had given her at first, she
had a sinking feeling.

"Oh, dear! I have failed Hugh again somehow. I never know
until it's too late."

But this evening she was not thinking of her housekeeping arrangements. She had half of a cold steak-and-kidney pie on the table with
boiled potatoes and buttered cabbage simmering on the cookstove
and her stoneware teapot filled and steeping on the oven door.
Everything was ready for supper, and Hugh was late. She worried so
when Hugh was late. The icy roads, the western horses, the mountains, they all filled her with dread and anxiety. Particularly the
mountains. She had never told Hugh how she felt, because, although
she could not fancy why, he seemed happier here than in England.
But to Anna Hawkins she had said once: "I am afraid here, Anna.
I don't know why. But it's not like England. England was so safe."

Anna's lips had curved into something that was not quite a smile.

"Sometimes I am afraid, too, Katherine. This is a place for the
strong."

"But, Anna, you *are* strong."

"I used to think that I was," Anna had said. "Sometimes I'm not
so sure."

Now at last, when Katherine saw Hugh walking home from the
direction of the livery stable, wearing that barbarous fur coat, she
was flooded with relief. Her anxiety of a moment before turned
quickly to annoyance that the tea had been obliged to steep so long.

She left the window and went to the kitchen so that he should
have to look for her when he came in. She heard him moving around
the hall, taking off his coat and hat. She served up the cabbage and
potatoes, setting the dishes and the teapot on the dining table beside
the cold meat pie, the jar of jam, the butter, the two slices of bread,
and the two slices of pound cake.

But instead of coming out to her, he had gone into the parlor.
She could hear him moving about by his book cupboard. *His books,
his books*—she was more jealous of those than of any woman. She

went to the parlor door and said in a fretful voice: "Hugh! At last, dear!"

It was his small, worn Bible which he held in his hand. He looked up at her and began to read aloud.

"And the people asked him, saying, What shall we do then?

"He answereth and saith unto them, He that hath two coats, let him impart to him that hath none."

There was a rare glint of laughter in his eyes.

"Oh, do come now!" Katherine said fretfully. "I've worried so, and the tea is too strong and the vegetable all dried, and now you must read the Bible. Why can't you come on time, Hugh?"

The gleam of humor left his face.

"You were the daughter of a doctor, Katherine. Now you are tied to one of them. Can you never realize that the time for a doctor's meals is when he comes for them?"

"But you could try, dear. Instead of coming directly to the kitchen you had to stop here to read your books! You didn't even look at the clock, dear. You didn't think how I had waited and worried."

"It is quite tiresome of you to worry, Katherine. I had a country call. What did you suppose would happen to me?"

"Oh, so many things could happen. How should I know? But come now, dear. The tea will be quite, quite cold."

He followed her to the table, his finger still between the pages of the Bible; and, when they had exhausted the thin supply of small talk which the day had furnished them, he laid the book open on the tablecloth and continued reading to himself as he ate the cold meat pie:

Then came also publicans to be baptized, and said unto him, Master, what shall we do?

And he said unto them, Exact no more than that which is appointed you.

And the soldiers likewise demanded of him, saying, And what shall we do? And he said unto them, Do violence to no man, neither accuse any falsely; and be content with your wages.

"Neither accuse any falsely," he thought, and he searched his heart and mind to see if they were clear in this respect. He found that they were.

But after supper a restlessness seized him. He walked up and down the tiny parlor, unable to concentrate on Carlyle's *Life of Schiller* which lay on the table in the subdued glow of that irritating lamp which Katherine had purchased.

Once, a voice said, *when I was a little girl I lit out to run away . . . I guess I've always had ideas that were too big for me or this town. . . .*

After the dishes were done Katherine came with her crocheting to sit in the parlor, and he settled himself in his chair then and took up the Carlyle.

"Hugh," Katherine said, "you know, I think we should have gone to call on Dr. and Mrs. Hawkins on New Year's Day. It must have looked very strange to them that we didn't. The grocer's boy said that they had a great gathering there that day. I wanted to go at the time, you know, dear; and you didn't care to."

"Perhaps we should have," he said absently.

"I so seldom care to go out in crowds, and that one time when I wished to go, it seems you might have humored me, dear."

Hugh laid the book on his knee and said patiently, "I'm sorry, Katherine, but I don't think that they would have welcomed us."

"Why not, dear? Anna Hawkins is the only friend I have here."

"You know that her husband and I are rivals professionally."

"You used to be good friends with other doctors."

"I know, Katherine. The situation is a little different here."

"I don't understand why."

"Then I will tell you. In the first place Dr. Hawkins has openly resented my coming here. In the second place I've had the misfortune to be the one to discover that he is somehow implicated in an unpleasant affair, an Italian killing in a shanty by the railroad."

"You mean he killed a man, Hugh?"

"Oh, no, Katherine, not at all. But it seems that he was called in, and did not report the death, probably in order to let the murderer escape."

"How horrible!" Katherine cried.

"I had not meant to tell you."

"Oh, dear! I wish you hadn't."

"It need not make any difference in your friendship with Mrs. Hawkins unless she feels that it must."

"But how did you know, Hugh?"

"I found his surgical needle."

"Couldn't you have left it where it was?" cried Katherine. "Couldn't you have overlooked it, Hugh?"

"No," he said. "I could not do that."

"Oh, dear!" said Katherine. "How horrible, how horrible!"

Hugh rose and put his book on the table.

"I think I shall walk a little while before bedtime, Katherine. Do you mind?"

"Oh, no, if you must. But it's so cold, Hugh. I'd think you would rather stay in by the fire."

"I must put more coal on the stove at the office. I'd not like the drains to freeze."

"Well, dress yourself warmly, dear. Oh, how horrible that you should be mixed in an affair of this kind! If only you needn't have seen his needle, Hugh!"

He put on the buffalo coat and went out. The stars were like millions of diamonds which sparkled frostily in the heavens, and the snow creaked and scrunched under his feet. The air was a sharp, quick blade into the lungs, but good, so good. He noted the outline of the mountains by an absence of stars. The streets were quite deserted, and tonight he owned them.

But, walking in the cold streets, he was strangely not alone. Inside Doc Hawkins' coat, warm against Hugh's body, was a thin, lost child, her head against his breast. It was a sensation rather than a thought, and he did not try to analyze it. Enough that it warmed him in his loneliness, and surely it was an innocent thing to let the imagination hold and comfort a lost child.

16

BEFORE WINTER BROKE, the sheriff had a tip from a trapper in the hills. He and two deputies went in on snowshoes, and found Pietro and Gina in a cabin deep in the woods. They had to make a litter of branches to bring the girl out, because she had an infant at her breast. The fugitives were cold and hungry and not reluctant to give themselves up, even to face a charge of murder.

Sheriff Wall summoned a grand jury and the indictments were made. The blow fell on Dr. Hawkins, too, as accessory after the fact, but Doctor was ready for it now, and he did not falter. There were at least a dozen people willing to go his bail, and Larkin came around to Doc's office to offer his services as counsel. Doctor shook his head.

"I'll be calling on you for advice, Sam, but, by the Lord Harry, I'm going to plead my own case!"

"You've got the gift of gab, doc," Larkin said, "but you're damned hotheaded for the law."

"I know it," Doctor said, "but I won't let myself get out of hand. This thing is blamed important to me. That's why I want to handle it my way."

"You know," Larkin said, "they could have had you up there before this. There was a statute passed in the Territory in 1887 that says an accessory to the commission of a felony may be indicted, tried, and punished though the principal may be neither indicted nor tried."

"They couldn't do that to me, by God! I wasn't accessory to the commission of the crime."

"Maybe not, but you gave the fellow comfort and assistance afterwards. You let him get away. You failed to report a death."

"Whose side are you on, Sam? If you're on the other side, you get the hell out of this office before I throw you out."

"Hold your horses, man. I'm on your side, and you know it. But you need a little legal counsel all the same. The state has got to prove that you *knowingly* assisted the felon to escape. There's our loophole, Willard, there's our loophole."

Doctor spat a remnant of a chewed cigar into the brass spittoon.

"Spin out your legal cobwebs if you want to, but, by God! there's another aspect to this case, the human side. You get me any jury in this state and let me tell them my own straight story in my own way, and the state won't have a leg to stand on."

"Well, just keep calm, doctor, and we'll work this thing out. I can put you on the stand, and give you your head. But you've got to remember you're walking on eggs."

"By God, I'm good at that!" Doc said.

17

JENNY HURRIED ALONG with the crowd towards the courthouse. Her mother had said: "I know you're interested, but I really don't think a nice girl ought to go there every day, Jenny, with all those men and everything. All sorts of horrible things are sure to be brought out."

"Oh, mama, I *won't* be wrapped in cotton wool! I've got to go to this. It's so tiresome of you to keep telling me what nice girls ought to do, when I really care so very little."

"I wish you cared more, Jenny. I know you're a good girl, but so many things you do look odd to people."

"Poor little mama!" Jenny cried, taking her mother's shoulders and kissing her on both cheeks. "You're the hen that hatched the duck's egg, dear, and nobody is sorrier for you than I am." She laughed, and Mrs. Walden laughed, too, reluctantly. Their home had always been a happy one, and it had been easier to let the girls have their own way than to insist upon rules and regulations. Della was the one who liked things regular, with discipline and seemly conduct for all; and this year, since she had been away teaching school over the mountains, the three who were left behind had lived so easily. Besides, Mrs. Walden knew Jenny's bitter disappointment over being kept at home. If she wanted to attend a trial in the courthouse—well, why not?

Jenny put on her little fur hat and thrust her hands into her muff. She almost ran up the long hill to the courthouse. The air was like wine, and her feet felt light as they did when she danced. *Oh, the joy and pain of life, jostling against each other or locked together in an incongruous embrace!* She laughed as she ran.

It was the second day of the trial, and she knew that, if she did not hurry, she would not get a seat. Yesterday half of the town had come surging up the hill to sit or stand packed into the small, close room, listening in sweating silence to the selection of the jury and to testimony which most of them already knew. For the case had been talked over thoroughly in Opportunity, the more so because Doc Hawkins was involved, and, whether they cared what happened to a couple of shanty Dagos or not, people cared what happened to Doc Hawkins. It had been hard to find a jury which was ignorant of the case, but they had haled them in from the hills and the surrounding farms.

The courtroom excited Jenny and gave her a feeling of strangeness as if she had left Opportunity for an unfamiliar town. The room was inextricably mixed with her emotions, for as a little girl she had been there before. Curious and enterprising as ever, she had followed another crowd into the courthouse when she was nearly twelve and had sat in breathless silence through part of another trial for murder. At that time it had been a homesteader who was accused of murdering his neighbor in a dispute over a boundary line. They had held up the dead man's undershirt, bloodstained and with a bullet hole in it, for evidence; and Jenny had looked at it, thinking for the first time in her life with an unclouded consciousness of death. A man had worn this shirt. It was still stained with his blood and sweat, and creased with the crook of his elbows, and the man was gone while the bloody shirt remained.

When she entered the courtroom now the other trial came back to her. In some ways it was even more vivid to her than the one which was going forward today.

She found a single seat at the side of the room and slipped quietly into it, looking about her with faculties alert and mind open. Oh, the delight of change, even the change of a trial which involved people she knew! The jury was filing into the box now; all the principals were here; the judge would be here in a moment, looking more like a farmer than the farmers in the jury box. Judge Hoffman was famous for the early potatoes he grew on his place at the edge of town, and he had sent all the way back East for a thoroughbred Jersey cow. Once he had adjourned court during sessions for half a day while the Jersey calved.

She saw Doc Hawkins sitting by a table with Sam Larkin. He was laughing at some remark the lawyer had made; but when he was not laughing his brows were puckered over the fierce, dark eyes with an expression of intense concentration. His wife and Dr. Duval were in the audience. They sat together very quietly, and a strange thought crossed Jenny's mind: they looked more as if they belonged together than Mrs. Hawkins and her husband did. An odd impression, yet it was as if something bound them together as it does old married couples. Lita Hawkins was absent, and Jenny remembered that the weekly paper had mentioned a visit to her married sister. So Miss Lita had run away and left her father when he needed her! Jenny's lip curled. Her loyalties were fierce and strong, and she had never liked the Hawkins girls.

Her eyes moved slowly about the room, and she saw that Dr. Allerton was there, too, half facing towards her. He was reading out of a little book which he had taken from his pocket, and she thought that the noise of the rapidly filling room washed against him as the waves of the sea wash against the stillness of a rock without making any impression upon it.

Now the sheriff came in with Pietro. Doc Hawkins raised a hand in greeting to the Italian boy. The gesture was a little defiant, as if Doc said to the town: "Sure, I know the fellow. Sure, I wish him well. You think that makes me his accomplice? Think again. You know me better than that, damn you!" But the gesture was lost on the sheriff's prisoner. Pietro had changed a good deal in the weeks which had elapsed since the killing. The women up and down the line, who had hung out of their windows for a glimpse of him when he had had a bright and roving eye, might have been obliged to look again to recognize this lean, unshaven fellow with the hanging head. He glanced up only once, and that was to look quickly around for Gina. His eyes rested on her for a moment with a melancholy brightness, and then he let the sheriff lead him to a seat facing the bench.

Jenny continued to watch the Italian girl after Pietro had been seated. She could see the back of the girl's sleek, dark head. The head was inclined a little towards the left, and in the crook of the left arm she held her baby, a baby born in a cabin on the mountain to a girl without a wedding ring and a man who had murdered. The trial had begun now, but Jenny's thoughts continued to dwell on this girl who sat so quietly holding her baby. As she watched them, the baby began to move restlessly in its blanket, and, cutting thinly through the lawful sounds of the courtroom, came the cry of the newly born. It was a cry of hunger, but Jenny thought: "He's tired of the world already. He doesn't like it." She felt great pity for him. The Italian girl opened her dress and gave the baby her breast. The crying ceased, and there was a little sound of sucking satisfaction. The dark head was turned to the side now, looking down, as the mother watched her child.

This girl had sinned; because of her a man had been killed, another man was on trial for his life, and a good citizen was involved as an accomplice. Yet in spite of all this Jenny could see that the girl was happy. She was happy because a hungry mouth tugged and fed at her breast. For her all the rest had paled into insignificance.

Jenny raised her eyes, and across the courtroom her eyes met those of Dr. Allerton. She did not know how long he had been watching her. For an instant their eyes clung, staring, wondering, and then he turned his head aside and looked away.

18

THE PROSECUTING ATTORNEY was a noisy fellow. He made the room ring with accusation and quiver with sentiment. "Here we have murder," he cried. "*Murder*, my friends! High Heaven recoils from the perpetration of a crime like this, and the innocent among us turn away their heads in anguish and shame. Has the time come in this fair city of ours when an innocent man can no longer dare to enter the house of a friend? when a man cannot safely go about his business without fear of being stabbed in the heart? God forbid, my friends, that this should ever be the case. Yet such a thing has transpired in our midst. I am going to show you today how Luca Pozzetti went in innocence to the house of a friend, and how he was there set upon and horribly murdered by a young man who had no business to be there, and how this young man was then aided and abetted in his escape by one of our leading citizens. I am going to show you, gentlemen of the jury, how this innocent man, Luca Pozzetti, was not only murdered in cold blood, but how his mutilated body was allowed to lie without decent Christian burial for a matter of two weeks although at least three people knew that it was lying there. Those open wounds cried out to heaven for justice, but there was no response. Fourteen times the sun rose and set upon this tragic spectacle of death, and nothing was done. An innocent man, lying in his blood, abandoned by his fellow men! I think the very moon, looking in at that cottage window, must have hidden her head in shame for base humanity. I think she must have wept to see the loneliness of that *corpus delicti.*"

The prosecutor paused an instant for breath, and Doc Hawkins' admiring voice was heard by the people on the front rows as if he were thinking aloud.

"*Corpus delicti,*" Doctor said. "That's a damned literary name for something that stinks."

The people on the front rows roared with laughter, and those behind them leaned forward and asked what Doc had said. The remark ran like a ripple to the back of the courtroom. Judge Hoffman rapped sharply with his gavel.

"Willard, for God's sake, keep your mouth shut," he said in an aside to Doc. "I'll have you for contempt."

Doctor subsided, but the prosecutor's "*corpus delicti*" had been robbed of its dignity and pathos. Murder is a grim business, and people are glad to get a laugh out of it if they can.

There were not many witnesses to be had. The prosecution produced a couple of character witnesses to speak for the blamelessness of the deceased's life, but they were both of so doubtful a character themselves as to make their testimony questionable.

But Hugh Allerton made a witness of a wholly different sort. No one could doubt his sincerity, his uprightness, and his honesty. He took his seat in the witness chair quietly, a reserved man who had no doubts of himself. When he took the oath, his voice sounded strange to western ears. After the noisy bombast of the prosecuting attorney and the uncultivated voices of the preceding witnesses Dr. Allerton's precise and unemotional testimony, together with his English accent, made him seem somehow effeminate. There was nothing effeminate in the sturdy shoulders and the clear-cut masculine features; but the voice was not familiar in a western courtroom. It set him apart. Sitting so quietly in the witness box, he seemed to be a lonely figure.

"Dr. Allerton, you were called to view the body of the murdered man?"

"Yes. I was driving along Spruce Street just beyond the depot. I was returning from a rural call. I saw a man running from the group of boxcar dwellings between the railroad tracks and the river."

"The man called to you?"

"Yes. He said: 'Doctor, doctor! Pull your horse in and come here.'"

"You went with him?"

"Yes."

"What did you find?"

"I found the body of a man."

"The man was dead?"

"Yes. He had been dead a long time."

"How long, doctor?"

"I believe that that would have been difficult to say with exactitude. The weather was cold. My guess was about a fortnight. I believe that you have since established that guess to be correct."

"And what was the cause of death, doctor?"

"A knife wound which must have been immediately fatal."

"What was the exact location of the wound?"

The questions and answers went on for some time—the booming voice of the questioner, the quiet and meticulous reply. At last the prosecutor asked:

"Doctor, before you left the shanty did you find any evidence which was of interest to you?"

"Yes, I did."

"What was it?"

"On the table was a suture needle."

"Will you explain that to the jury?"

"A suture needle is a small curved instrument which a surgeon uses in sewing up a wound."

"Had it been used upon the body of the deceased?"

"No, it had not."

"Then why was it there, doctor?"

"I can only conjecture why it was there."

Sam Larkin sprang up.

"Your honor, I object. They've no right to introduce conjecture."

"Objection sustained," said the judge. He was glad to put a word in. He had been up early to see to repairing a corral fence before he came to court, and the warm, close room was making him sleepy.

"We intend to show," said the prosecutor, "that this needle belonged to Dr. Willard Hawkins, and that he was in the cabin on the night of the murder and used this needle to sew up the arm of the accused before he let the accused escape."

"Dr. Allerton," cried Larkin, "do you consider it ethical to testify against another physician?"

"Mr. Larkin," replied Hugh, "I found a surgical instrument at the scene of a murder. I did not know to whom it belonged. I believe that Dr. Hawkins has since laid claim to it; but I cannot testify in any manner as to that. I have no bias one way or the other in this case; but my ethics consist in this: that I desire to see justice done. I have a deep respect for abstract justice, Mr. Larkin."

"Thank you, Dr. Allerton. You may step down," said the prosecutor. This was better than he had expected.

19

It was late afternoon before Doc Hawkins was called. In the meantime Pietro had given a poor account of himself. Humbled and frightened, he had become confused in his testimony and made contradictory statements. He did not always have a clear understanding of the English idiom, and that contributed to the confusion of his remarks. His lawyer was pleading self-defense, but under cross-examination Pietro did not make a good impression. Now he admitted, now he denied, and once he shouted: "By God! I done a good job. Dat fella oughta be keel!" Things did not look very bright for him.

Doctor had been nervous all the afternoon while he listened to the muddled testimony. He picked at his fingers and twiddled his mustache. Sitting inactive was enough to drive him wild, and when a boy came in for Duval and Duval hurried away he knew there was business to attend to. "By the Lord Harry, am I a doctor, or am I a God-damned benchwarmer?" he asked Larkin.

"Sit still," said Larkin. "Today you've got business here."

"I'd give a ten-dollar gold piece for a cigar!"

When at last they put Doctor on the stand, a little sigh of relief and expectation ran through the courtroom. Whether one liked Doc Hawkins or not, he was sure to be amusing.

Doctor's demeanor was suitably grave. He took the oath in a resonant, deep voice.

"Dr. Hawkins," said Larkin, "I'm not going to question you. I'll leave that to the prosecutor when you are through speaking. But I want you to tell the jury your own story in your own way. Go ahead, doctor."

Doctor looked all around the courtroom solemnly before he turned to the jury. He cleared his throat.

"Gentlemen of the jury, and friends," he said, "I'm going to tell you what I know of the murder of Luca Pozzetti. It isn't very much, but I believe it may help to clear things up. But first I'd like to say a word of praise for Dr. Allerton, whose testimony you heard this morning.

"You have a new doctor in town, gentlemen, a doctor who believes in abstract justice. I want to congratulate you on that. There's nothing finer than abstract justice, gentlemen, nothing. And at last you have a man who will give it to you. You have all seen the cartoonist's idea of abstract justice, haven't you, gentlemen? She's a fine, deep-bosomed woman with a pair of scales in her hand—and a blindfold over her eyes. That's as it should be, my friends. Justice is blind. Her bounty falls without prejudice upon all. She does not see the little individual who cries and prays to her. In her blindness she deals out the wherefores and whereases with impartiality. In that respect she differs from God, who is said to temper justice with mercy and to number the very hairs of our heads. But we are not dealing with God in this courtroom, and we are grateful for the blessings of abstract justice. I am reminded of what one Irish immigrant said to the other, after they landed in New York. 'O'Connor, me lad,' says O'Toole—"

"Doctor," interrupted Judge Hoffman, "this court will take care of justice and also of any stray Irishmen. Proceed with your testimony."

"I beg your honor's pardon," Doc said. "The Irishmen will keep, gentlemen."

The gentlemen of the jury looked a little disappointed. It would have been a welcome change after a long day to hear what O'Toole had had to say to O'Connor.

Someone at the back of the courtroom called out. "Let him tell it," but the judge rapped for order, and order was restored.

"Gentlemen, on the night of Luca Pozzetti's death, I was waked up out of a sound sleep about 12:45 A.M., by a pounding on the side door. A doctor's used to that, gentlemen—it don't very often mean murder. It's usually a new citizen at that hour of the night. It's damned inconvenient for a doctor that so many babies come at night, but a medical man has got the habit of taking what comes and keeping his mouth shut. So I thought nothing strange about a late call, until I saw Gina Torelli's face. I found out then she was going to have a baby, too, but her time hadn't come yet—it was something else.. *Gina Torelli*," Doctor said thoughtfully. "I've known her since she was a little girl. Most of you have, too, I guess. I've seen her running around town in her little patched dress with her big eyes and her long black braids— She hasn't had a mother for a long time, poor kid! It's no wonder she got into trouble while her old man was away on long freight runs. She didn't have a mother to look after her. Love's all right when there's a wedding ring around it, but we all know damned well it's sin without the ring. Old Luca Pozzetti thought that, too, I guess. He was an expert in sin of one kind and another."

"Your honor, I object," cried the prosecutor.

"Confine yourself to the events of that night, doctor," said the judge.

"Yes, I'll go back to that night. Gina told me what happened as we drove down to the shanty. I've been wondering why you haven't had her up here before this to tell you. Is it because she's the wife of the defendant? Of course, you're right there, I've no doubt. Before she had her wedding ring she was a sinner, and now that she's got it she can't testify. That's abstract justice, and Dr. Allerton and I want to see abstract justice done. Well, I can tell you what she told me that night, and if you want to hear it from her maybe some woman who's compassionate enough to forgive sin will hold her baby for her while she comes up here. She told me that night that Luca came to her house to force his attentions on her, knowing that her father was away from home. She says: 'I've got one man, and that's enough. Pietro's going to marry me.' Well, you can judge about that for yourselves; maybe a sinful girl would accept the attentions of Luca Pozzetti, I don't know. You all knew Luca—at least you did if you haunted the alleys behind the saloons; and you know Pietro. He's a clean, upstanding, good-looking young man. I'd be willing to leave it to any woman's judgment if this little girl encouraged Luca Pozzetti's salacious advances when she could have the attentions of a man like Pietro."

"I object, your honor," cried the prosecutor. "There are ladies in this courtroom, and the witness is using unnecessarily suggestive language."

"Objection overruled," said the judge. "Proceed, doctor, but spare the ladies as much as you can."

"Thank you, your honor," Doctor said. "I might add that according to my personal observation a good many ladies are also human beings."

The judge rapped down a rising tide of titters.

"I'll try to stay on the track," promised Doctor, his eyes glinting. He was going well now, and he felt the audience and the jurors going with him.

Only Jenny Walden, listening to him, remained untouched by shock or amusement. She thought: *He talks about ladies, about compassionate women, but all he's trying to do is save himself. He wouldn't give me permission to read my essay on women's rights. He's making fun of Dr. Allerton's abstract justice, too.* It was as if she saw her idol for the first time in the light of day, and he had become a stranger. She was the only one who sat unmoved by Doctor's eloquence.

"When I entered the Torelli shanty, the first thing I saw was Luca Pozzetti's body," Doctor was saying. "It didn't take me over two seconds to see that he was dead. A doctor gets to know death when he sees it. There was likely to be another death, too, if I didn't act quick. To save life is the first rule a doctor learns. It gets to be instinctive with him. He doesn't stop to call in the police if a man's bleeding to death. Ask Dr. Allerton, and he will corroborate my statement, gentlemen. At least, I think he will. Maybe he'd call in the police.

"I had to take eight stitches in Pietro's forearm, gentlemen. I know now I did wrong. The law tells me I was giving aid and comfort to a felon. Maybe it would have served abstract justice better if I'd let Pietro die, gentlemen. Then you'd have had another case to settle today: not *Did Pietro kill Luca?* but *Who killed Pietro Gallo? Was it Luca Pozzetti or Willard Hawkins?* Thank God, I don't have to defend myself against a charge of murder, gentlemen! It's my business to give aid and comfort, and the law has yet to teach me that there's a place where a doctor has to draw the line, stopping to say: 'This man's a felon. Let him bleed to death.'"

"I object, your honor," said the prosecutor. "All this is immaterial."

"Objection sustained. Stick to the facts, doctor," admonished the judge.

"The facts are these," said Doc, "and I'll be damned if anyone has brought them out. A knife was found sticking out of Pozzetti's ribs, obviously Pietro's knife. But has that been established? Where is the knife that caused Pietro's wound? Shouldn't it have been in Luca's hand? Gentlemen, I believe that there was only one knife, and that it belonged to Luca Pozzetti. He came to this girl's house to make an immoral demand upon her. Fortunately her affianced husband was there to protect her. The two men quarreled and Luca Pozzetti drew his knife and slashed Pietro's arm. It was one man's life or the other's. Do you blame Pietro for wresting the knife away from his attacker and thrusting it to Pozzetti's heart? He killed in self-defense, gentlemen, and at the same time he was defending an even higher cause. Is there any man among you who wouldn't kill to protect the woman who bears his child? If there is such a man in this courtroom, let him stand up and show himself, and let us hound him out of town, fellow citizens. This is a new state, but, praise God, it is full of red-blooded men who are not afraid to risk their own lives to protect the lives of their women and their unborn babes!"

Someone at the back of the courtroom cried, "Amen, doctor!" and there was a sudden gust of applause.

Judge Hoffman rapped for silence.

"Dr. Hawkins, have you any further testimony?"

"Yes, your honor. I'd like to explain my own subsequent actions. I have been upbraided for not reporting a death. So far as I know there is no law in this state which requires a physician to report a death. I've never before been badgered for failing to report a death."

"But that's for a simple death, doctor," cried the prosecutor, "not murder where the escape of the accused is involved."

"I'm coming to that, sir," Doctor said. "I was faced with a dilemma that night, gentlemen. I had to make a rapid decision, and

I decided wrong. As I saw it that night (erroneously, gentlemen) a scoundrel was dead and beyond all help. A man and a woman, whose only sin was to love a little precipitately, were going to find themselves in a kettle of hot water. There was an unborn child involved. Every child that is born in this state is a potential citizen. Let him grow up with a father in prison and an unwed mother, and you not only have a potential citizen; my friends, you have a potential criminal. I wanted that baby to have a fair chance at a decent life. That's why I walked out of that cabin that night and did not report a death. Unfortunately, gentlemen," Doctor paused and smiled naïvely at the jury, "unfortunately I forgot my surgical needle, and abstract justice has overtaken me. Gentlemen, what I did in my own unenlightened way was to try to deal out justice in the particular case. I was wrong. I should have left that to the law. But I believe in individual justice, gentlemen, with all my heart and soul. I don't care for the kind of justice that comes in wholesale lots. Well, I am not God, gentlemen, and neither are you. We can only fall back on the justice of the courts. And so I cast myself upon your intelligent mercy. If I was wrong about this, gentlemen, then I was guilty as hell. Deal with me as you see fit, but remember when you pass judgment upon Pietro Gallo that understanding and mercy are attributes of Heaven."

20

THERE WAS MORE testimony and more pleading, but when the time came the jury was not out long. The members had made up their minds during Doc Hawkins' speech, and the intervening formalities had not effected any change. The verdict was acquittal for Pietro on the ground of justifiable homicide, and a recommendation that the case against Dr. Hawkins should be dismissed.

In the hall outside the courtroom Hawkins and Larkin were surrounded by a laughing, shouting crowd of men.

"Doc, you should have been a lawyer," someone said.

Doc threw back his head and laughed. "The law?" bellowed Doc. "By God, I wouldn't soil my fingers with an inhuman institution like the law! Not by a jugful!"

"Come on now, Willard," Larkin said. "You're still making speeches. The trial's over, man, the trial's over!"

Doc flung his arm around Larkin's shoulders, and they stood in the center of a congratulatory crowd, laughing and shaking hands

Judge Hoffman came by.

"Congratulations, doc, you old scalawag!" he said. "You had quite a boilermaker's holiday with justice, didn't you? I suppose you think that what you got was justice, eh?"

"You bet your bottom dollar that was justice," Doctor said. "When twelve good men and true bring in a verdict, I'm still enough of an American, by God, to call it justice—even if it is in my favor!" He laughed uproariously and handed Judge Hoffman a cigar. The judge laughed with him. Doc was a good man. He had pulled two of the judge's children through the typhoid fever a couple of summers ago. Doctor passed out the contents of three boxes of cigars among his friends that day.

Anna and Constant stood for a few moments on the edge of the crowd, waiting to congratulate Doctor; but he did not see them, and at last Anna said:

"I'll go on home and fix supper. I guess he'll have a good big appetite."

"Let me go with you, then. He will not miss me among so many."

"I'm glad it's all over," Anna said as they walked along. "I ought not to have been nervous, because he always comes out on top, but somehow I couldn't help it."

"He has a great influence over people, a kind of magnetism—"

"And yet he's helpless with his own daughters."

"And also his wife?"

Anna gave him a humorous smile.

"You know what the stories of great men all say? 'He had a true and loyal wife.'"

"Perhaps that is why some men are great."

"No, I don't think so. Men like Doctor really don't need wives."

"You should have seen him the summer you went to St. Louis."

"Just the same it is men like you who need wives, Constant. I am looking for one for you. When I have found her, I shall insist that you accept her."

"*Cela m'amuse*," he said. "You make me laugh, Anna."

"No, really I'm serious. Do you think I don't know that you are drinking again?"

He flushed and looked away from her.

"Do not reproach me, Anna. I had a difficult time after the New Year."

"I know. But it's a thing you had better root out entirely. You know you cannot play with it as some men do."

"No, you are wrong there, Anna. I have reduced it to a method now. I have taught myself to drink with science rather than with passion."

"I think you're pulling the wool over your own eyes."

"No. It is like this: I have laid down rules. My thirst is regulated by clockwork. On a Saturday night when the office is closed, then I go to my rooms and I allot myself a certain number of glasses—no more, you see."

"But you will go out to get more."

"I have not done that yet. I grow stronger, Anna, believe me."

"And what if there is a call for you on Sunday morning?"

"On Sunday morning Doctor is always in the office. That bell of the Presbyterians, it drives him there, *n'est-ce pas?* He says to me: 'Constant, I will take care of what comes in. You may keep your Sunday mornings.' "

"Some day he will find out."

"I tell you, Anna, I am slowly growing strong. There will be no more excesses."

"I hope you are right, Constant. Oh, I hope you are right!"

"Trust me, *mon amie*. Your trust, it is what makes life bearable to me now."

"I am glad if it helps. It is the best I can give you, and it seems little."

"You do not come to my rooms any more to save me, do you, Anna?" He smiled at her quizzically and a little sadly.

"No," Anna said, looking down at her hands. "There are some things I can't do any more."

They had come to her gate, and Constant leaned to open it for her.

"Will you come in?" she asked.

"No, I thank you," he said. But he held the gate for a moment without letting her pass through.

"A trial makes one think a little, does it not? What is justice, Anna?"

"I don't know."

"Doctor knows," he said. "Allerton knows. But you do not?"

"No. Do you?"

"I share your ignorance." His eyes were on the ground, and still he held the gate so that she could not pass through. In a low hurried voice he said: "Sometime I will tell you about a trial, Anna, which occurred some years ago in France. The defendant was also a physician, a very young one, and he was accused of criminal negligence in connection with the death of a patient."

"Yes?" Anna said. He did not go on, and Anna said again, "Yes?"

"He was acquitted," he said, "but I happen to know that he was guilty, and that there are those in France who may still suffer from his guilt."

"I am sorry for that. Has he never gone back to find out?"

"He has never gone back."

"But surely there is something he could do?"

"It is a long time now. The little children who were wronged by him must be grown up. This man would have to be very courageous if anything were to be done."

"And you think he is not?"

"I am afraid so."

"I believe the man will sometime find enough courage to do what he thinks is right."

"I thank you, Anna," he said formally. He opened the gate and allowed her to pass through.

21

JENNY SKIRTED the crowd of laughing men in the hall of the courthouse. She had stopped to speak to Gina and Pietro before she left the courtroom. Few people were interested in them any longer. While the courtroom emptied they stood together, dazed by their good fortune and a little uncertain how much happiness they dared reach out for.

"I'm glad it turned out right for you," Jenny said. She lifted a corner of the baby's blanket and looked at the tiny, sleeping face. "He's lovely, isn't he?" They smiled at her in silence, and suddenly the tears began to run down the Italian girl's cheeks.

As she passed the group in the hall, Jenny heard someone say, "Now, Doc, tell us the one about the two Irishmen."

"By George, I nearly forgot that," Doc said. "Well, there were two Irishmen, just fresh from the auld sod, and O'Toole says to O'Connor, 'Begorrah, O'Connor, me lad . . .'"

Through the courthouse door Jenny saw Dr. Allerton walking away alone, quiet and self-contained as ever. She was touched by his apparent loneliness. She quickened her steps and came alongside him at the foot of the courthouse steps.

"Doctor, you made a brave plea for abstract justice. I'm sorry that it was ridiculed. I'm sorry that both sides couldn't have won."

He turned and looked at her, and there was a kind of lonely gratitude in his steady gray eyes.

"I believe that the trial came out in the best way," he said. "I have no quarrel with Dr. Hawkins. I should have been sorry to see him tried and convicted; but there are principles which are more important than men, Miss Walden, and someone in a town has to stand for those principles, even at the risk of making himself disliked."

"Yes, I can understand that," Jenny said. They walked the rest of the block in silence, and then he lifted his hat very courteously to her and turned the corner towards his office.

At dinner that night Katherine said: "Hugh, you should never have mixed yourself in such a distressing affair, should you, dear? Now that the trial is all over and everybody is acquitted, it would have been better, wouldn't it, if you had never mentioned that dreadful needle? Wasn't there something brought out at the trial about the girl having a baby by the murderer and no marriage ceremony? How horrid and shocking! Hugh! You should have kept aloof, shouldn't you, dear?"

Hugh replied to her kindly, but he did not try to explain his position to her. He had tried to do that many times in the past, and so often she would not or could not understand. She would say, "Yes, dear, of course"; but the next time that the subject came up she would have returned to her original position and would still be asking for an explanation of his. To argue with her was like trying to shape water. The wind might ruffle it, but it would always return to its own level.

Other people understood his motives, he reflected—even Jenny Walden. What had she said? *Yes, I can understand that,* she had said. But in this case Katherine was so blinded by her horror of sex that she could only see that he had mixed himself in something shocking and horrid. Her words seemed somehow like a hot, foul breath blowing across his clean ideals of honor and integrity.

22

A FEW DAYS AFTER the trial Alf Stevens came back from the asylum. Kessler stopped by Doc's office to tell him that he had seen Alf in town.

"What in all tarnation did they let *him* out for?" Doc wanted to know.

"He looks perfectly sane," said Kessler. "I saw him in the butcher shop the other day. Butcher Neischmidt said to him, he says, 'Say, Alf, I t'ought you vass crazy. How come they turned you loose?' 'Hold your damn tongue,' says Alf, 'or I'll show you who's crazy in this town.'"

"By George, that was a pretty smart comeback," said Doc, laughing. "I hope he behaves himself. I'd like to have a look at him."

"He's got some kind of paper you have to sign, they tell me. Funny he hasn't been around."

"He'll come," said Doc.

That afternoon when Doc returned from a country call, Alf was waiting for him in the office.

Doc came in by way of the back door and the little back room. Duval heard him coming and met him in the back room, closing the door into the front office as he did so.

"Alf Stevens is here, doctor," Constant said. "He has returned from the asylum. He will not talk to me."

"All right. I have been expecting him," said Doc. "Leave us alone a few minutes. I can handle him." Duval shrugged his shoulders and went out the back door. Doctor entered the front office, smiling cordially.

"Well, Alf, they sent you home again, did they? That's mighty fine. I guess your old mother was mighty glad to see you."

Alf sat still in Doctor's swivel chair, his heavy shoulders hunched a little forward, his eyes on the yellow flicker of fire behind the isinglass of the baseburner. Doc saw that he was a man now in all his proportions. He had still had the look of a youth when he went away, but now he was heavy and strong, and quick when he shifted his hands or turned his head. He had lost the deep tan of the farmer for an unhealthy institutional pallor.

"You going to shake hands with me, Alf? We're old friends, you know. Your father and I were brother Masons. Did you know that?"

Alf gave him his hand. It was unexpectedly hard and resolute.

"You feeling pretty well now, Alf?"

"I always been feeling well," said Alf. "Look! I am strong. Nothing ails me at all. You are a pack of fools."

"Now, now," said Doc, "I wouldn't go so far as that. You want to be careful what you say, Alf. Folks might misunderstand you."

"Let them," said Alf.

He thrust a paper into Doc's hands.

It was a letter from the doctor at the Asylum. *Can't find anything specific wrong with him . . . seems normal in all of his reactions . . . overcrowded here. We can't take care of doubtful cases. Be glad to have you keep an eye on him. . . .*

Doc finished reading and turned with his back to the stove, warming his hands behind him.

"Now, Alf," he said, "I'm going to talk damned plain to you. You're here on probation. We're all glad to have you back, and we'll do everything we can to help you. But, by Gad, you begin threatening folks again or peeping in their windows—you start horse-whipping your animals or mistreating your mother like you did before, and we'll have you right back at Orofino! I mean every word of it. You've got it in you to be a good citizen and a fine farmer. You do that and you'll find every hand in Opportunity stretched out to help you. It's up to you now, Alf, and don't you forget it!"

Alf looked at the floor. It was impossible to know what was going on in his mind. He got to his feet now, and stood shifting from one foot to the other, swinging his hands slightly in rhythm with the swinging motion of his body. Suddenly he caught up his hat from Doc's desk and bolted out of the door. His horse was standing with dropped reins beside the hitching post in front of the bank a few yards up the street. Alf did not alter his pace but, half running, leapt lightly into the saddle, caught up the reins, and set the animal into full gallop. People looked out of the store windows along Main Street as he clattered by. Alf's eyes went from side to side as he galloped along, and he knew that people were watching. They hadn't seen anyone gallop on Main Street like that since the day he left for Orofino!

When he had passed the last houses, he slowed the horse to a trot. He did not look at the snowy fields or the dark mountains, but let his head hang slack, his eyes on the deeply rutted road.

Alf's horse was still breathing hard when he turned into the barnyard at his mother's farm. He dismounted and led the horse into its stall. A shepherd dog with shaggy hair and yellow spots over its eyes came creeping on its belly, cringing and fawning on Alf's feet—a bondslave in the lowest agony of humility. Alf pushed it aside with his foot, not looking at it. His eyes were raised to the square opening into the haymow. When he stood beneath it, he could just see the rope hanging from the rafter of the roof. His mother had taken the rope down while he was away, but he had fastened it there again on his return. It hung black and still in the gray loft. In the end of the rope was a noose.

23

WITH THREE DOCTORS in town, it did not often happen that none of them was available in an emergency. But the afternoon that Mrs. Walden was taken ill the minister ran first for Allerton, then for Hawkins and Duval. When he found that Hawkins and Duval both had been called out on a runaway accident south of town, he returned to Allerton's house. His face was gray-white with anxiety as he spoke to Katherine.

"Send Dr. Allerton as soon as he comes, won't you? I don't know what it is. She's in most awful pain."

"Oh, yes, I will," Katherine said. "I don't know where he is. I don't know why he should not be here. Would it help if I should come?"

"No. I am going right back. Jenny's gone out somewhere. I had to leave my wife alone. But send him right away when he comes." He almost ran down the street, looking suddenly old and anxious and bewildered.

Katherine went on preparing supper, but her hands trembled with tension and anxiety. When an urgent call came in for Hugh and he was not at home, Katherine always fretted. That he should be late made it even worse, and that it should be his minister who needed him! She thought of poor Mrs. Walden suffering so terribly. *She's in most awful pain,* he had said.

The thought of pain made Katherine's head begin to throb. Pain seemed to her unbearable—*unbearable!* Why must God visit it upon His children? And all day long Hugh dealt with pain. He was calm and reasonable about it, as her father had been. After she had thought of pain, she thought of the hypodermic syringe. It was like a sigh of relief, the release of floating on soft clouds above jagged peaks. She was frightened now lest she was going to have one of her headaches.

When she heard Hugh's step on the front walk, Katherine ran to the door and flung it open.

"You must eat your supper quickly, Hugh. It's all ready—and you've to go out again at once. It's the minister's wife. They don't know what it is, but she's in terrible pain. Pain, Hugh—they don't know what it is." Unconsciously she pressed her hands to her own breast as if she felt the pain herself.

"Mrs. Walden?" he said incredulously. "Who came to tell you?"

"It was the minister himself. He looked frightened. His daughter was not at home. He said she had gone out somewhere. Mrs. Walden was taken suddenly with this pain, he said. Come, Hugh, you must eat. You're late already, and you may be there a long time."

He took the plate which Katherine thrust into his hands and sat down at the table. He did not like sitting down with the buffalo coat on the back of his chair, and without washing his hands. Mechanically he took a few bites and then pushed the plate back.

"No," he said, "I'll take something to eat when I come in tonight. How long ago was Walden here?"

"Only about an hour, but I expected you at any moment then. What made you late this time?"

"I drove home by the ridge road from Sampson's farm."

"Wasn't that the longer way?"

"Yes, it was."

"What possessed you?"

"It was a beautiful sunset. I like to see the town lights come on from the ridge road."

Katherine looked at him with disapproval and surprise. He went to the sink and carefully washed his hands. Then he thrust his arms into his coat sleeves again. What he did not tell her was that he had picked up Jenny Walden in the country for the second time that winter, and that some folly in him had made him want to show her the view from the ridge road at twilight when the lights of Opportunity began to rival the stars. He had seen it so many times alone. The folly of his action filled him now. Her mother had been needing her—and him—while they had sat in that strange, warm silence looking at a fading sunset and a kindling town. His scorn for himself was deeper than anger or sorrow.

"I wish you would eat," begged Katherine.

"Honestly, I'm not hungry, my dear," he said. "I'll be back when I can. Don't wait up for me." He hunched his shoulders into the buffalo coat and was off again. A kind of sick disgust filled his mind as he hurried along.

Jenny opened the door for him, and he could see that she had been crying; but their eyes did not meet.

"She was all right when I left," she said in a low voice.

He went directly into the bedroom and set his bag on a chair. After Katherine's draped and ornamented house the parsonage looked bleak and austere. Everything was a little threadbare; but one could read by the lamps, and there were books on open shelves. Jenny brought him a basin of warm water for his hands. He could hear the minister's wife moaning and gasping for breath, and almost before he looked at her he knew what it was. The heart that had carried her valiantly through all the hard years had suddenly begun to falter. Simple heart failure was so much better, he thought. There was little difference in the final result, and angina pectoris was pathetic to watch and horrible to suffer.

Mr. Walden sat by the bed holding her hand, and his blue eyes which usually twinkled were filled with bewilderment.

"She was never sick before, doctor, not for a day in her life, except when the little girls came—" His voice was asking Dr. Allerton to remove this strangeness and restore her to her former invulnerability. "Never sick a day!"

"That's a good record, isn't it?" said Hugh quietly, leaning over the bed. "Quite a remarkable record." *One must always say something easy and quiet in these first moments. They have to be reassured first, and the real truth let out to them gently, bit by bit, as they can bear to take it.* That was a thing he had learned almost as soon as he had begun to practice: honesty tempered by kindness. There was another thing he could do, even more important, perhaps. After the examination had been made, he could deaden the pain with narcotics. Then there came a sweet peace after the crying of anguish. There was a silence of rest after pain. He had come to value his power to give sleep.

"She will be easier now," he said at last, straightening from the low bed. "Miss Walden, if you will stay with her a moment, while I speak with your father."

The minister went ahead of him into his study. There was a fire in the little Franklin stove, but the lamp had not been lighted; and when the match was struck Hugh saw that notes for a sermon lay in disorder on the desk. A daguerreotype and two framed photographs were among the books and papers. The daguerreotype was a wedding picture of an earlier day, and Hugh recognized Mr. Walden in the optimistic young man seated by a table with his hand on the Bible. The bright-eyed young bride who stood beside him with her nosegay of white roses was the elderly woman who fought now for each painful breath in the next room. The other two photographs were of young girls, and one of these, he saw, was Jenny, holding in her hand a scroll tied with a ribbon. It was a good likeness, and she was smiling. It came to him suddenly: *She will be old, too, some day, and when that day comes I shall probably be gone and be forgotten.* It was not often that he thought of himself in connection with a case.

Mr. Walden fumbled the lamp chimney, and the high-turned wick streaked it with smoke. He turned the wick down and thrust another stick into the stove. His hands were trembling.

"These things happen quickly, when they come, Mr. Walden," began Hugh. "She has lived a full life. She may have some time yet to enjoy life, but—"

It was the hardest thing he encountered in his profession, to extinguish hope. When he had said all that he could, he did not know how well he had succeeded. The minister sat heavily in his desk chair, lifting and measuring a paperweight from one hand to the other, and his eyes were more dazed than comprehending. Hugh laid his hand quietly on Mr. Walden's arm.

"Have Dr. Hawkins look at her, too, if you like. I think he will make the same diagnosis, and in the meantime I'll do all that I can for her," he said.

Mr. Walden still sat in his chair when Hugh went back into the hall. Jenny came softly to the bedroom door with the lamp in her hand. She looked deeply at him, and her eyes asked a question.

"She's quiet now," she whispered. "What you gave her has helped."

"I am sorry sometimes," he said, "that so much of what I do is not curing—only relieving."

"But to give peace!" she said. "Peace after pain."

"There is only one real peace, Miss Walden," he said. He had not meant to tell her. Let her father do that. But the question in her eyes had to be answered.

"Death?" said Jenny in a low voice.

He saw the change in her face as she uttered the word, and how the color drained away and drained away, leaving the sensitive face dead white. The question had gone out of her eyes, and she looked at him strangely; but still her eyes were wide and unfrightened. Realization was in them now, but not fear.

Hugh saw for the first time that he had underestimated her. He saw that she was shaken, but that she was one of the select few whom death does not terrify. Every day in his profession he worked with people who feared death either for themselves or for those they loved. He knew their loose mouths and blotched faces. He knew the abject and craven horror in their eyes, the struggling and striving against what is at last inevitable for every human being. But there were a few, and he had learned to recognize them, who could look at death and not be afraid. It was a thing he sometimes thought of in the night when he lay awake, and he wondered about himself. Would he be afraid when the time came?

24

JENNY LOOKED FAIRER and younger than ever in her long black dress. The little yellow curls on her neck seemed even more rebellious and turbulent, escaping as they did over the high black collar with its severe edging of white.

People in Opportunity talked about Jenny more than ever now, and she was giving them just cause. After the first crushing weeks of mourning for her mother, she began to fling herself into any sort of frivolity that she could find or invent. Her laughter echoed mockingly through a disapproving town.

They discussed her in the drugstore and the saloon and the church parlor. The Presbyterian ladies took her case up individually after the business of foreign missions had been settled and the coffee and jelly roll were being served.

"It's simply disgraceful and irreverent, the way she carries on," said Mrs. Kessler. "You'd think the death of a saint like her mother would have toned her down some."

"I think she's putting on a bold front," said Anna slowly. "I've seen children like that. They don't want anyone to know how deep they're hurt inside, so they go around making a lot of noise."

"As far as I'm concerned, there's no explanation for it. It's time she began to take over her mother's duties with the sick and poor. It's too bad for her father and the Methodists that Della's teaching school this year and Jenny at home. Della's a serious girl."

"Give Jenny time," said Anna. "I think there's a lot to her."

"Well, I'm glad we don't have her in the Presbyterian manse. That's all *I* have to say." The other ladies agreed with Evelyn Kessler.

Certainly the town was divided on Jenny Walden. She did not follow the prescribed pattern, and that is fatal in a small town. The older ladies cried shame when three weeks after her mother's death she accepted an invitation to the Odd Fellows' ball and danced every dance. The younger ladies, looking through their lace curtains at the sound of the fire bell, were scandalized to see her running bareheaded down the street behind the men who pulled the hosecart. The married men sided with their wives at home, and in the street they took off their hats to Jenny with a large gesture. The young men were mostly in despair over her, because she never hesitated to tell them how dull they were; and yet her eyes always gave them the hope that a little self-improvement might turn the trick.

After her mother's funeral Dr. Allerton avoided Jenny as much as possible. He was sorry for her, because he had seen her drawn, white face at the graveside and he knew that she had loved her mother. People in town said that she was too light to care, but he did not think so.

Yet the fact that he had taken her to look at a sunset on the afternoon of her mother's first attack troubled his conscience; even more, it troubled some inner sense of security and trust which he had in himself. He was too old and grave and reliable to let unexpected impulses rear their heads in the reasonable daylight of his life. There was something about this little girl which might play the fool with him. He determined to be careful.

There was only one thing about Jenny's conduct after her mother's death which seemed normal and appropriate to the ladies of Opportunity. Now her long rambles in the country appeared to have achieved some purpose, for they took her often to the cemetery with a bunch of wild flowers which she had gathered along the way. As the spring came on it was not unusual to see her sitting in the long grass on the cemetery hill, her eyes dreaming, the wind whipping her hair about her face. There was a wonderful silence on the cemetery hill, a silence which was accentuated by the lyrical questions of the meadow larks and the wind which made a harp of the pines.

Alf Stevens used to watch her go by the farm, and sometimes he followed her and lay in the long grass up in the potter's field where he could look down and watch her sitting there without being seen himself. Only once did he speak to her. She had been sitting still for a long time, and finally she lay back with one arm flung over her eyes to shield them from the sun. She had been quiet for so long that she seemed asleep, and Alf went closer to look at her. There were lamb's-tongues and little blue grass flowers blooming here and there in the green place where she lay. Her hair was spread out all about her head, and only her black dress seemed incongruous.

Alf could go very quietly when he wished. It was only in town that he made a great noise of clattering hoofs. That was to make people look at him. But when he did not wish to be seen he could creep under people's windows with the stealth of a cat or lie for long periods with the patient inertia of a rabbit under a bramble.

So he had come quite close before she heard him. Then suddenly she flung down her arm, and her eyes were looking into his, startled but not terrified. She did not move to get up nor open her mouth to cry out. Finally Alf spoke in a voice that sounded angry: "Get up off there, why don't you? That ground is wet."

"Leave me alone," Jenny said. "This is my place."

"It wouldn't be, if I said not."

"I guess you wouldn't do that, would you?"

"No, I guess not."

He went on down the hill and left her alone.

Half an hour later when she came by the farm, Alf saw her pass from one of the little windows in the barn. He stood very still, and only his eyes followed her down the road as long as he could see her.

25

"Dr. Allerton," Jenny said, "aren't you coming to the May Day choir party?"

Spring had come on, hot and yellow. The church was uncomfortably warm for choir practice.

"No, Miss Walden. A doctor's social life doesn't amount to much. We're more or less on duty for twenty-four hours a day, you know."

"You could bring your wife, of course. I think that Mrs. Allerton would have a good time. You weren't at the meeting, so I don't expect you know what we've planned. The ladies are all bringing basket lunches; and the baskets will be auctioned off to the highest bidder, and the money will go into the fund for new music. It was my idea. Don't you think it was a good one?"

"Yes, indeed."

"Then why don't you come?" She was laughing and sparkling at him. "You might even bid in my basket, and then I should eat supper with you. Think of that!"

"Now, Jenny, that's no fair!" cried Lester Davis, who was always at her elbow during choir practice. "You know that *I'm* going to buy your basket."

"But you won't know which it is, Lester. I intend to keep it a perfect secret. Dr. Allerton has as good a chance as you to get it."

"Thank you, Miss Walden, but I won't deprive the younger men of their chances," said Hugh in his quiet voice. He put his hand into his pocket and drew out a five-dollar gold piece. "Put this into the music fund, please, and consider it a bid on the prettiest basket if you like."

"The prettiest basket will be mine, doctor," said Jenny, laughing. "May I consider it a bid on my basket?"

"If you like." He gathered up his music, and prepared to go. He usually came late to choir practice and left early. He did not care for the preliminary plans and chatter, nor for the pairing off to walk home. Singing was a joy for him, but he avoided the social contacts which belonging to the choir seemed to entail.

After Hugh had gone Jenny kept turning the small yellow piece of money in her fingers without saying anything.

"Wow! What a lot of money!" said Grace Murphy, the alto with the prominent teeth. "He's funny, isn't he?"

"He's kind of stiff and formal," said Lester. "Not like old Doc Hawkins. And that English accent of his!"

"I rather enjoy it," said Jenny. "It's different from the rest of this town."

"You don't like this town, do you?"

"Of course I do. But sometimes I'm bored."

"*You* bored! Jenny, you're too beautiful to be bored."

"Beautiful—beautiful! It bores me to hear you say that again, Lester. Now, if *you* had an English accent—"

"Why, Jenny, he's an old man."

"I'm not talking about him. I was just thinking how well an English accent would go with your new mustache."

After that Lester Davis began to drop his *r*'s and soften his *a*'s; but, try as he would, Jenny never seemed to notice that he had made the slightest change in his method of speech. She could be quite annoying, that beautiful little girl could, and Lester knew it all too well.

The first of May came around, and Hugh sat at the desk in his office writing up notes on some recent scarlet fever cases. He had pulled three families through the disease without the loss of a single child, and he felt that his methods of treatment were worth recording. He was feeling rather happy and absorbed. He had left the front door open to the street, and the evening air came in softly, warm for the first of May. When he raised his eyes to look out of the door, he was struck by the deep blue of the twilight. It lent magic to the plain brick front of the real-estate office across the street. He knew that he ought to go home now, because it was time, and Katherine would be fretting over him. He wondered if Katherine would have thought to open the windows. She lived indoors so much herself that she never minded a stuffy house, and throughout nine months of the year she stanchly maintained her middle-class English belief in boiled potatoes and cabbage as the backbone of a dinner. Sometimes, when she could get them, she varied the cabbage with cauliflower or Brussels sprouts. "Veg," they called it, in English lodging houses, and the smell was always the same.

Hugh thought: "I dare say I'm not a domestic sort of man. Sometimes I'd rather have a sandwich at the office than go home. But Katherine wouldn't understand."

He was reaching for his hat when he heard laughter and voices outside the office, and Jenny Walden came through the blue doorway with several of the choir members behind her.

"Well, you were the highest bidder."

"Four and a quarter was the nearest bid," cried the alto with the prominent teeth. "Jenny says it belongs to you, because you gave her five."

"It isn't fair, doctor," said Lester. "You should have been there yourself to bid. We didn't know which basket was Jenny's, and all of us fellows feel cheated."

Hugh looked at them and smiled. He didn't quite know what to say to all of this. He had put the choir dinner out of his mind when he gave Jenny the five dollars.

"Fancy!" he said. "I really had no intention of competing for Miss Walden's basket."

A shade of the vivid brightness went out of Jenny's face. She held out the basket to him. It was covered with colored tissue paper and trimmed with wild flowers, and it was really very pretty.

"I hope you haven't had your dinner," she said. "It's got fried chicken in it and potato salad."

"She wouldn't tell *us* that," cried the second tenor in a neat falsetto.

They had all rushed in on the impetus of a merry idea; now suddenly they began to look self-conscious and embarrassed. Hugh wanted to put them at their ease, but he could not think quickly of a way to do so; and the grinning faces of the two young men made him unreasonably annoyed. Their young male voices, one a little nasal, the other sometimes slightly off key, to the right of him in the choir loft, had often jarred upon his nerves. Now he knew that he disliked them intensely. Jenny was still holding out the basket, and the brightness continued to fade from her expressive face.

"It was just a joke," she said.

"I'm sorry," Hugh exclaimed, taking the basket. "You surprised me, you know. I'd forgotten I was in competition. But it's beautiful, really."

"I—I thought Mrs. Allerton might like it," said Jenny, "since you were too busy to bring her to the party."

"Oh, yes," said Hugh awkwardly. "Yes, indeed. Katherine will be delighted. I—really, I can't thank you."

"Don't try."

"But what are *you* going to eat? You and Mr. Davis? This was your basket."

Jenny looked at him, and now her face was impudent.

"I bet Lester a dinner at the hotel that you wouldn't ask me to eat out of the basket with you, and he bet that you would. He's lost; so I'll have a nice dinner at the hotel at his expense. Good night, doctor."

Hugh went after her to the door.

"Oh, I say! Miss Walden—"

But she was gone as quickly as she had come, and he could hear them laughing down the street. He felt angry and somehow hurt. It was youth that was hurting him, the youth which he had never fully experienced himself.

He put the basket in the back room of the office. He couldn't take it home because Katherine would not understand it. Perhaps he did not want her to understand it.

The doors and windows were all closed when he let himself in at home, and there was buttered cabbage.

"Oh, Hugh!" said Katherine. "You are so late again, dear."

"I'm sorry, Katherine. It couldn't be avoided."

26

"By GEORGE!" said Doctor. "That damned property of mine is eating us out of house and home. A new picket fence here, wallpaper there, the cesspool has caved in on the place on Seventh Street, and old man Darley fell through a board in the sidewalk in front of the Ash Street place. Fixing over just about eats up the damned little rent I get for those hovels!"

"The town will grow, doctor," said Anna with a twinkle in her eye. "You'll make your fortune out of that property yet."

"She's making fun of you, Uncle Doc," said Gene.

"Women!" snorted Doc. "They know so damned much more than the men."

"No, doctor," laughed Anna, "they don't know any more really. They just get so little chance to exercise their knowledge, that you can't blame them for loving to say 'I told you so.'"

After Doctor was gone, Anna looked across the table at Gene, who was still occupied with a bowl of oatmeal.

"How would you like to have supper with your father, Gene?"

"You mean he's coming here?"

"No, I thought you might go there."

"Well," Gene said, "I have my rabbits to feed, and Uncle Doc said he was going to bring a big, thick steak for supper."

"Yes, but there will be other times for steak. Your father will have something nice."

"It's Saturday night—the boys will be playing out. Why do you always want me to go on Saturday night?"

"I know it's Saturday night," said Anna, "but I think you should go sometimes to your father. I'm sure he's pretty lonesome."

"All right," Gene said. "I'll feed my rabbits before I go."

"Feed them early then, Gene. I'd like you to go for him before the office closes. Tell him you're going to have supper with him. Then he'll take you with him to do his shopping. Maybe he'll get steak. I think it might be fun if you were to spend the night there, too, don't you? You could take a little bag with your night things, as if you were traveling."

"Uh-huh," said Gene.

"That way you would have a chance to talk with him. During the day he's so busy."

"What would we talk about?"

"Oh, all sorts of things, of course. What you want to be when you grow up—"

"I want to be what Uncle Doc is."

"But you could plan for it with your father. He is a doctor, too, Gene."

"I know. My father is a damned good doctor, Uncle Doc says. But Uncle Doc is the boss."

"I don't like to hear you say 'damned,' Gene. That's something you can take up when you get whiskers and begin to smoke a pipe."

Gene grinned sheepishly.

"Well—" he said.

"And that about being boss. It's not always the best thing, I think."

"I would rather be boss than not, though, when I am grown."

"First of all you must boss yourself then," Anna said. "To be honest inside yourself, to say 'Yes' and 'No' to yourself when you should, that's what makes a strong man."

Gene was a little bored.

"What else shall I talk about with my father?" he asked.

"You could ask him about your mother," Anna said.

"He doesn't like to talk about her."

"I think he does really. You try him. Ask him to tell you how she looked. She had golden hair, and she was very beautiful. He will tell you."

"Am I like her?"

"No. I think you are more like your father—at least, your hair and eyes are dark like his."

"She was English, wasn't she? I hate the English."

"Why do you hate the English?"

"I don't know. Doc Allerton is English."

"And why do you hate Dr. Allerton?"

"Because Uncle Doc does."

"Nonsense!" cried Anna. "You're big enough to have your own thoughts. Never hate because someone else does. Besides, Doctor doesn't hate Allerton. He's a little jealous, that's all."

"Well, I'll go," said Gene, "but I'd rather wait until Monday."

"No, it's tonight, Gene," Anna said. "This is the best time to go. I know you'll have a good time."

About five o'clock Gene departed for the office with his nightshirt in a little straw-matting satchel. His reluctance had been overcome by a fleeting sense of importance. He was nine years old now, and a tall, good-looking boy.

Anna watched him going down the street with pride and anxiety in her eyes. She knew that Gene's coming had somehow failed of its purpose. She had made several sincere efforts to establish Gene and Constant together in a house with a housekeeper; but no one favored this arrangement except herself. Gene, Constant, Doctor, all three preferred things as they were. Only she herself seemed to see and fear the danger of their situation. She loved Gene very much, and it was hard to be the only one who realized that they were not doing him a kindness by keeping him with them, and that Constant was being cheated of something he should have had, yet seemed to prize not at all. Watching Gene walk away, she thought:

"I wish he were really Doctor's boy. His being here hasn't worked out the way I planned it."

She turned to pick some Thousand Beauty roses from the trellis on the front porch. She would have them in a bowl on the supper table. Just Doctor and herself at table! Lita was spending a month at Mary's again. She had met a young man down there who had a captivating blond mustache. The house would be very quiet with Gene away for supper and the evening.

But Anna did not have long to savor loneliness, for in half an hour Gene returned. He had run all the way up the hill, and his cheeks were red, his eyes dancing. He flung his cap on one chair, his satchel on another.

"Hello!" he shouted through the house.

"Gene!" Anna cried. "Why did you come back? Why didn't you stay?"

"Papa said to tell you," said Gene impressively, "that Monday night suits *both* of us much better, Auntie Anna."

"Gene! You told him you didn't want to stay?"

"We told each other."

"Oh, Gene, really it was important for you to go tonight!"

"No, papa said not, and now I can play out after supper with the boys."

27

JENNY WAS haughty with Dr. Allerton after the May Day party. Hugh thought: *This is the best way*. He went on pouring his soul into the plodding hymns on Sunday morning, and sometimes the offertory music gave him unexpected pleasure. He did not share in the laughing and bickering of the younger people which went on at choir practice. If sometimes he was acutely aware of it, he gave no sign. Outwardly he smiled a little as from another sphere at the antics of children.

The summer seemed hot and dry to an Englishman, but still the air had a lightness and the nights were cool. Katherine made herself some muslin and calico dresses, marveling that even in the mountains here one could not wear woolens in the summertime. She did up her housework in the early morning hours and sat crocheting behind drawn curtains in the afternoon. In the evening, she moved to the porch where she sat in freshly starched muslin, rocking and watching people pass on the dusty sidewalk. A few of them nodded to her, but for the most part she had made little impression upon the social life of the town. Sometimes Anna came and sat with her, and they talked as they rocked. The trial had made no difference in their friendly relations.

Hugh had long hung away the buffalo coat in favor of a linen duster. His horse wore little nets over her ears to keep out flies. The unpaved streets were heavy with dust, and in the country oxalis and wild lobelia blossomed in the cracked mud of dried stream beds. The water supply ran low as it usually did in August, and typhoid fever was rampant again.

During the first days of the outbreak Hugh happened to meet Doc

Hawkins in the drugstore. They had had very little to do with each other since the trial, but they were extremely civil when they met.

"Well, you fellas have got your work cut out for you now for a month or two, I guess," Skogmo said good-naturedly. "Too bad the typhoid season has to come during the best vacation weather, eh, doc?"

"You're damned right," Doctor said; "but typhoid's a summer sickness, like diarrhea and cholery morbus. I've been a physician for a quarter of a century, and, by George, I've never yet had a full-fledged vacation when I wanted to take it!"

"Do you mean to say," Allerton asked, "that you have a typhoid epidemic here every summer?"

"Well, not quite for a quarter of a century," Doc laughed. "Twenty-five years ago the only sickness here was caused by the premature removal of a hunk of scalp."

"This typhoid business has been going on about four or five summers now," said Skogmo. "It keeps the doctors sweating, but it pays their taxes for them."

"And you let it go on from year to year without doing anything?" asked Allerton.

"Without doing anything?" repeated Doctor, his sideburns beginning to bristle. "By God, I'll tell you we do something! We work night and day, without sleep, sometimes without food, in the hottest infernal weather. We lose pounds of healthy flesh every summer struggling to keep folks from dying. Ask anybody in town if we let the typhoid season go by without doing anything!"

"Preventive, I mean," said Hugh. "Surely there's something wrong with the water supply or the milk. Do you make them boil their milk?"

"Sure I make them boil their milk, and our water comes down from God's green mountains. You won't find better water in any of your damned little prairie towns—nor England either, I'll bet. Typhoid's a summer sickness, I tell you. You'll find you've got your hands full giving cold baths and administering stimulants to failing hearts without worrying about milk and water. It's all right to get your theories out of books, but a doctor's got to be a realist, too, by God! He's got to deal with individual cases."

"That is true, doctor, and yet the long view is quite as necessary, I believe."

Doctor was angry now.

"Are you accusing me of being shortsighted, doctor? Ask Skogmo here if I haven't taken the long view in this town. Who started the Academy in this town? Who got them to put up a decent courthouse and an opera house? Who's put all his investments into the real estate of a town whose future he believes in?"

"Doc's all right," said Skogmo. "He's got the interests of this town to heart."

"Nevertheless," said Allerton doggedly, "the sewage and water supply will be none the worse for our inquiring into them."

"You can take my word for it, they're all right," cried Doc, "and my word is as good as any other man's in Opportunity."

"I see no reason for making this a personal matter," Allerton said coolly.

"Yes, by God! it *is* a personal matter, when a young upstart comes in here and tells me what's wrong with the way I've taken care of this town. Then that *is* a personal matter."

"Good morning, doctor," Allerton said, and he went out of the drugstore quietly, closing the door very gently behind him.

So, although there was no reason why it should have been so, Dr. Allerton's investigation of the fever situation in Opportunity became at once a personal matter between the two doctors. Both of them were busy from morning to night fighting the onslaught of the fever in individual cases, but Hugh also concerned himself with the dwindling water supply. He suspected that the sewage disposal of the town must be at fault, and that the low water must have a direct relation to the rapid spread of the disease. It did not take much investigation to discover that most of the residential part of the town was dependent for its water supply on outmoded pumps and wells, and for its sewage disposal on overworked cesspools. Hugh Allerton was not a fighter as Doc Hawkins was, but he never turned back, once he had set his face forward. Now, in addition to the extra burden of caring for so many sick, he undertook the task of reforming sewage and water conditions. It would have been better if the two men could have worked together. Hawkins would have made a powerful ally. As it turned out he had somehow become a powerful opponent. Hugh blamed himself for having failed with Dr. Hawkins.

"I've never been good at managing the proud. Perhaps I've not been good at managing anyone but myself. What is it I lack? Tact? Determination? A loud voice?" He smiled a little bitterly. But he understood without resentment that, whether his cause was right or wrong, Dr. Hawkins would now oppose it with all the violence of a headstrong nature. Yet Hugh meant to make what effort he could. In the mayor's office, the courthouse, all up and down Main Street, his calm voice went on and on, questioning, warning, begging for improvements.

One evening, a week or so later, he was talking to a little group in the drugstore when Skogmo came around the counter and put a hand on his shoulder.

"You ain't a swearing man, are you, doctor?"

"No, I'm not," said Hugh.

"It's too bad, doctor. What you need is to cuss the hell out of this town. Yell at 'em, and wave your arms. Maybe you'd get some action. The town's used to that method. That's the only kind of talk they understand."

"I'm sorry, Mr. Skogmo. That's never been my way. I dare say I shall be slower doing it my way, but I won't give up easily."

"Well, if you keep at us long enough, maybe you can tire us out; but a few well placed blasphemies wouldn't do your cause no harm."

Hugh thought this over as he walked home in the summer darkness, but he disliked violence of any kind. Whatever he had done in the past, had always been done with reason. He thought of God. *This is the time when I should pray for divine guidance,* he said to himself. The words were on his lips, but they went no deeper in him. In Manchester, God had lived in the chapel, warm and secure from the fog of the streets. One could supplicate Him and feel intimately near Him. But in Idaho, God sat on the blue hills; He passed high over the earth in the huge chariots of cumulus clouds which moved swiftly with the wind. God was majestic here, but also detached. One could not help feeling that it would be useless to ask Him to interfere in a matter of sewage. Hugh thought that somehow he was nearer the earth this year than he had ever been—and farther from heaven. But the thought did not dismay him as it should have done. Through his physical weariness the thought of his nearness to earth ran like a thin, bright stimulant along the whole course of his blood. He raised his eyes to the night stars, and the thought came to him that earth was too beautiful to barter for an unknown heaven. He did not chide himself for the thought; and, since he had left the door open for that thought, another followed it unbidden. *If earth is the most important—the all—am I getting as much of it as I want?* He closed the door of his mind after that and walked more quickly towards home. He knew that he was becoming very tired physically. It was better not to think when the body was weary. *Keep your mind on the typhoid problem, and don't generalize,* he told himself.

He looked again at the sky, and as it arched above his house it seemed to him to contain more stars than he had ever seen before. The milky way was a fine broad band of shining dust, and the rest of the heavens were so powdered and studded with brilliants of all magnitudes that they were like a broad celestial daisy field. As he stood watching, two stars fell with a brief swiftness that transfixed the heart.

"August," he said, "the month of falling stars. The August Perseids."

Someone was on the porch with Katherine. He could see the gleam of two white dresses, and he thought at once of Mrs. Hawkins; but then he remembered that she would not be sitting on the steps at Katherine's feet. The white dress on the steps swooped upward and came quickly towards him as he entered the gate. The swiftness and the grace of the movement made his heart pause as the falling stars had done.

"Miss Walden," he said.

"I wanted to see you," said Jenny, "but I knew you were too busy to bother with me at your office. It's this awful typhoid. I wanted to help some way. I know there are so many people sick and dying, and I thought if I could help to care for them—I'm not a nurse, but I could do the ordinary things, especially with children. I'd like so much to help. I thought you could tell me." Her voice seemed to rush ahead of her, encircling him and pulling at his sleeves. He stopped where he was on the walk. He could see her face now, a pale, luminous oval in the starlight.

"And have *you* sick, too?" he asked in a rough voice. "You might nurse for a week, and then I'd have another patient. Maybe it would kill you."

"I'm very strong," she said with dignity. The voice had stopped, too, where she stood, and it no longer ran and plucked at his sleeve. "I have never been sick, and I am not afraid. I think it is a help, not to be afraid, don't you?"

"Yes, it is something not to be afraid."

"I wasn't boasting. I just meant it seemed like a kind of protection against catching the disease."

Katherine's rocker had ceased creaking on the porch.

"I told her that you'd not let her do it," she said. "For a young girl to run such a risk!"

"Oh, please, let me, Dr. Allerton," begged Jenny. "My life is so useless, I sometimes think. I want some purpose—like—like this."

"No," he said flatly. "I can't let you do it. It would be quite absurd. There are plenty of practical nurses and relatives of the families where there is sickness."

"I think my mother would have been helping now," she said in a low voice.

"But that's a different matter."

"You think I wouldn't be steady enough to help, doctor?"

"I can't go into that tonight, Miss Walden. I'm dog-tired, and I only know that I don't want to have you unnecessarily mixed up in this epidemic."

"I hope you mean that kindly, doctor."

"Yes, I do." He paused, then he added roughly: "If you want to do something, why don't you go out and tell people to clean up this town? Tell them to fill up their cesspools and their old wells, and get a decent water and sewage system into use. That's going to do more good than nursing where typhoid is concerned."

She stood very still, looking at him in the starlight. Her face was pale above the pale dress, but he could see the sudden lift of the delicately pointed chin.

"Good night," he said.

She went without saying good night.

After she had gone, with her quick, darting way of going, Katherine's chair began to creak again.

"I trust you didn't offend her, Hugh," she said. "After all it was kind of her to offer, even if she couldn't do anything, and she's our minister's daughter."

He went into the dark house and lay down on the couch by the window. A cool breeze, laden with the acrid sweetness of blossoming geraniums, blew across his face, and between the lace curtains he could still see the multitude of stars. Now and again one fell with a breathless trickle of gold, but he was too tired to feel a lift of heart.

28

"WELL, YOU'VE GOT at least one supporter in your cesspool fight, doctor," said Skogmo, winking at Hugh across the drug counter. "She may turn the trick for you, at that. I wouldn't even put it past her to swear a little if she felt like it."

"I don't believe I understand you, Mr. Skogmo."

"It's Jenny Walden, doctor. You know, the Methodist minister's gal. I don't know where she picked it up, but yesterday she gave the female literary society quite a spiel on cleaning up this town, my wife tells me. You been workin' on her, doctor?"

"No, I haven't," said Hugh shortly. He felt himself flush with something which must be anger, and he was even more angry that he should have been childish enough to have changed color. He turned and went out of the store.

He heard rumors of Jenny's crusade wherever he went.

Two weeks later, when he saw the mayor, Hugh was surprised at his changed attitude.

"Doctor, I'm going to call a meeting to discuss both sides of this sewage question. Will you present yours?"

"I shall be glad to, Mr. Balch. I hope you are beginning to see the need for some reform," said Hugh. His gray eyes were deeply serious in his tanned face. He had grown thin in the last few weeks from anxiety and loss of sleep. The fever epidemic was still in full swing.

"Well, doctor," Balch said, "there's a growing demand for some kind of action. It's funny, but the women of this town seem to be on your side. That little Walden girl is quite a pusher. She's been up and down Main Street into every store and office pouting and looking through her lashes at the men, and for once she's got the women back of her, too. They ain't giving their menfolks any peace until we tear up the streets of this town and lay down sewer pipes. I hope to God you know what you're doing, because if we've got to do it, it's going to cost us a sight in taxes."

"I know what I'm doing," said Hugh quietly. "It's the best way to fight typhoid. You'll never regret putting decent sewers in this town, no matter what the taxes are."

The mayor looked at him curiously.

"You're quiet, doctor, but you're smart. I wouldn't have thought of taking it to the women. But they get things done their way once they start to move."

"I didn't take this campaign to the women. If they took it up themselves, it was their own doing."

"That Walden kid's a worker," said the mayor admiringly. "If she wants a thing she'll get it. People make idle talk about her, but she's got what it takes."

Hugh tried to think of Jenny Walden going unasked about his business, and he was angry and puzzled and ashamed. Yet he *had* asked her, too. He had not really meant to ask her. He had thrown it out as a challenge from the depth of his own irritation and despair of any result, and she had gone right ahead and made a cause of it. When he thought of her, he was angry; but when he did not think, there was something warm in him that he felt.

It was true that for the moment Jenny had found a cause, an outlet for the boundless energy and enthusiasm which seethed, unsatisfied, within her. She felt strangely happy while she was making her crusade. The crusade would have been easy, she reflected, if at every corner she had not met Dr. Hawkins' opposition. Wherever she went Doc Hawkins seemed to have been there before her, joshing and telling jokes and heaping good-natured ridicule on the necessity for costly reform. Jenny knew Doc Hawkins as only a person who has loved another can know; and now, for some reason which she did not herself understand nor care to scrutinize too closely, she found herself hating him and wanting to see him put down. He had always stood for the best interests of the town, and now she felt that he was suddenly, inexplicably against them. Her idol had completely fallen. She thought that any method of discrediting him would be fair according to his standards.

29

TRAVELING SHOWS did not often come as far west as the Opera House in Opportunity. The mountains shut them off. For amusement the people had only themselves: the gossip, the bits of scandal, the politics, the trials, the Academy graduations, the histrionics in the many churches, the public meetings. When the mayor called his meeting to discuss the question of a public water and sewage system, the Opera House was packed with people. He had asked both Allerton and Hawkins to present their views, and the audience expected something in the nature of a debate. Typhoid had become a serious scourge; it brought death and disaster during the hot months when life was hard enough at best. Yet, on the other hand, a modern water system would cost the town a small fortune, plunge it perhaps into a temporary depression, and Doc Hawkins laughed at the idea that such a drastic measure would improve the typhoid situation. What was one to believe? It was easier, of course, and much less expensive to believe Doc Hawkins. People were used to believing what he said. He had never yet betrayed them. They did not know the Englishman very well, and his quiet voice did not make a loud, authoritative noise in their ears.

It was so again on the night of the meeting. Hugh Allerton spoke with a quiet man's restraint, and the passion which burned so hotly in him did not warm nor fire his listeners. As always he seemed to be a lonely figure, unable to communicate his deeply felt convictions. Jenny listened to his logical marshaling of facts and figures and basic truths with an emotion she had never felt before. She could have wept for him. She could have washed his feet with ointment and dried them with her hair.

And old Doc Hawkins was so easy and so confident. He started out with a funny story, and he had the audience roaring and ready to eat out of his hand before he ever got around to typhoid fever and the sewage problem. There was only one way to fight Doc Hawkins, Jenny thought grimly, and that was his own way.

Anna Hawkins was restless, too, listening to Doctor's superb flow of oratory. Most of his stories she had heard before, and she did not laugh. She saw that he was reducing Allerton's earnest struggle for reform to something light and comical. He was dismissing something grave with a wave of the hand. Leaning towards Duval, she said in a low voice:

"It's the first time I ever saw Doctor on the reactionary side. I've tried to reason with him. It's been his greatest glory that he was always ahead of the bandwagon."

"The first speech I have heard Doctor make," said Duval, "it was for the good of the town; the next one, it was for himself; and now, I think, it is against the town that Doctor speaks."

"And you do nothing, Constant?" Anna asked.

"Nothing," he replied.

"You are the third doctor in town, Constant. A word from you might turn the argument."

For a moment he did not reply. Then he said to her quietly:

"You and I, Anna, we are spectators, I think, not actors. Is it not so?"

"Perhaps," Anna admitted reluctantly. They did not say any more.

Dr. Hawkins was concluding his remarks in a jovial vein:

"Well, friends, what are you going to do about it? Dr. Allerton doesn't like the odor of our cesspools; he's been peeping in the doors of our privies, and he's come to the conclusion that they have more stylish privies in England than we have in Idaho. He doesn't like the taste of our clear mountain water that comes rushing down from God's high summits. No, friends, Allerton is all for pumping our water up from the infernal regions. It's going to be damned expensive, friends, but maybe we can afford to humor an Englishman once in a while. God knows, we did our best to put the Englishmen out in 1776, but there's something about our country they like, cesspools or no cesspools.

"But, whatever you decide to do tonight, my friends, I'm convinced that our typhoid problems will remain the same—and that reminds me that I've got my evening rounds to make. I'll bet I've lost more sleep this past month over the typhoid fever question, my friends, than any of you have. I'll tell you the honest truth. Last week I hadn't had my pants off for three nights, and just as I was about to get a wink of sleep, some feller called me out again on a chronic heart case. I went over there, practically walking in my sleep, and took the feller's pulse and temperature. There didn't seem to be much wrong, but I put my head down against his chest to listen to his heart.

" 'Start counting very slowly, will you please?' I says. 'And keep right on.'

"Well he did: 'One, two, three—'

"The next I knew, a shaft of sunlight hit me in the eye, and I could hear the patient's voice kind of faint and far away: 'Twelve thousand, eight hundred and ninety-one,' says he, 'twelve thousand eight hundred and ninety-two—' "

Doctor left the platform with a roar of laughter filling the hall.

Suddenly Jenny Walden was on her feet and going like the wind up the aisle to the platform.

"Ladies and gentlemen," she cried, "may I have a word?"

People were enjoying themselves.

"Go ahead," they shouted.

By this time the whole town knew which side of the water question she was on, and those who were for reform began to applaud. No one had expected her to have the effrontery to speak out publicly in a men's meeting, but they welcomed the diversion. In her own way Jenny was as good a show as old Doc Hawkins.

She began to speak rather rapidly in a clear, loud voice, the color coming and going in the bewitching face.

"You've heard some amusing stories," Jenny said. "You've had a lot of fun, but Dr. Hawkins hasn't given you any facts. Let me give you a few facts that neither Dr. Hawkins nor Dr. Allerton has brought out. Dr. Allerton is too much of a gentleman to give them to you; Dr. Hawkins would rather not call attention to them. Yet, if you think them over, you will all know that they are true.

"Dr. Hawkins owns at least twenty old houses in this town. There are enough defective cesspools on Dr. Hawkins' old properties to keep this town supplied with typhoid germs for years to come. Doc Hawkins owns property on Oak Street, on Ash Street, on Seventh Street, on Main Street, on Poplar, on Washington, on B Street, and

Third, not to mention the pieces he owns in Swedetown and out near the Academy. Doc Hawkins has been investing in this town for years. We might call Doc our leading citizen in more ways than one.

"But now Dr. Allerton proposes to have us tear up all of our streets and put in a modern sewage disposal and water system in order to clear up the typhoid situation. No wonder Dr. Hawkins is against it! Doc Hawkins will have to pay sewer and water and paving taxes for property on Oak Street, Ash Street, B Street, Third Street, Seventh Street, Main Street, Poplar Street, Washington Street, Jefferson Street, C Street, Swedetown, Shantytown, Academy Hill—" People began to laugh. Jenny laughed with them, and spread her hands.

"Doc Hawkins is our leading citizen," she cried above the sound of laughter. "Should we do this to him? Should we remove one of his best sources of income, the annual typhoid fever business, and burden him with all these taxes? We love Doc Hawkins in this town. He's always done what's best for it. Now, hadn't we better sacrifice our children's health for his good? Hadn't we better do as he asks us to, and leave the situation where it is? Surely we don't mind losing a few of our children through typhoid fever every summer, if we can keep our leading doctor prosperous and happy? Think it over, ladies and gentlemen. This is your opportunity."

Jenny returned quietly to her seat and sat down. She was such a little girl, and her face was so innocent; but in the uproar of discussion which followed, Hugh Allerton reflected that it was a pebble from a small sling which slew Goliath.

30

BEFORE THE END of August they were already tearing up the streets of Opportunity to lay down modern pipes, and drilling for artesian water. For the first time Doc Hawkins had lost his fight. Somehow he had never expected to lose, and he was a little bewildered.

"What the devil happened?" he asked Duval. "I thought I had them all sewed up."

Duval only smiled.

"By Gad," Doctor said, "this thing is going to ruin me, if nothing else ever does. Do you know how much taxes I'm going to have to pay?"

"Yes, doctor," said Duval, "that leetle Walden girl, she told us."

"Well, she's a kid," Doctor said. "I don't hold it against her, but I'll get Allerton for this—you see if I don't."

"Perhaps he has done a good thing for the town. I think that he was right, doctor."

"Maybe—maybe. But I don't love him any more for that. He's so damned sanctimonious, it's hard to get at the fellow. He don't have a handle to get hold of. But I'll find one. There's one way you can get these damned goody-goody men—they'll always fall for a woman. If I could catch him with a woman—" Doctor laughed.

There is nothing that will unite a community in common brotherhood like high taxes. With the fickle inconsistency of the public mind, the people of Opportunity disliked Dr. Allerton for bringing on them a costly reform, and loved Doc Hawkins the more, because the poor old buzzard was paying more taxes than any of them were. They greeted him on the street, "Hi, doc, how's taxes?" and Doc took it all in good part.

"They used to say that there were two sure things—death and taxes," Doc replied with a grin and a wink. "Now that Allerton has got rid of death for us, we only have one sure thing left." He laughed as loudly as anyone, and he could not help succumbing to the excitement of what was happening to the town. The sound of pumping, the fuss and fury of tearing up the quiet streets, the shouting of teamsters, the backing and plunging of horses, the jets of dirt that appeared to be flying up from the bowels of the earth wherever a person turned—all these were fascinating to Doctor. As if it had been his own idea, Doc turned plumber and had a figurative finger in every ditch. He advised and denounced, swore and praised, and he was the first one called when there was a cave-in or a crushed hand.

But once the project was under way Dr. Allerton seemed to lose interest in the practical mechanics of it. Meeting him on the street one day, Anna said to him:

"Dr. Allerton, I want to congratulate you on the success of your fight against typhoid."

He looked at Anna with his reserved gray eyes.

"Thank you, Mrs. Hawkins. But other people in the town really deserve the credit for it. I hope it serves the purpose we anticipate."

"Well, they're certainly making a hash of our streets," laughed Anna.

"That's so. I notice it when I'm driving. I dare say the inconvenience and expense will scarcely seem worth the trouble, since people never think of an absence of disease. It's only the epidemic that moves them to action."

Anna watched him walking away, vigorous but self-sufficient. She thought: "Maybe other people can get closer to him—I don't know. I was never one to make friends easily, but it does seem as if he's awfully reserved. People like that suffer more because they can't blow off steam. He's a nice-looking man, too, but I don't think he has what he wants of life."

Weeks had gone by, and Hugh had not seen Jenny Walden alone to have a word with her. He knew that people talked about her more than ever now because she had dared to speak publicly in a men's meeting, using a man's weapons to strike at an opponent. She was in his mind a great deal, and that shamed and annoyed him. He saw her swooping towards him through the darkness in her white dress. He felt her sitting quiet beside him in the cutter watching the lights of the town prick out of the winter dusk. These images were very deep. When he tried to think reasonably of her, he was rough with irritation.

He knew that he must thank her. The whole town shared the knowledge that he was obliged to her for espousing his cause. He could not pass it off without a word. But he did not make the opportunity. He waited for it to present itself. So it happened to be a choir practice evening at the beginning of autumn. He saw her walking ahead of him, alone, and he hurried to overtake her.

"Good evening, Miss Walden," he said.

They both felt awkward and constrained.

"Good evening, Dr. Allerton."

"Miss Walden, I must say something to you. I want to thank you for talking to the women about the sewage condition in this town."

"I talked to the men, too," she said proudly.

"I know. I want to thank you personally."

"I didn't do it for *you*, Dr. Allerton," she said. "I did it for the little children."

"Yes, I know. I'm thanking you for them as well as myself. I'm not a very good pleader. Evidently I needed your help."

"Evidently you did."

"I am grateful, Miss Walden."

"Maybe I shouldn't have done it," she said. "Maybe they'd have voted for reform anyway. I don't know. But I could see that you didn't know how to fight Doc Hawkins. I did, because I used to love him."

"Why did you fight him then?" he asked.

"Because there are things I love more."

"Truth?" he said after a pause.

"Yes." She held her head high and a little averted.

They walked on in silence, and even the realization of his hopes for the town did not make him feel happy. Silently he held the church door open for her, and as she passed through he saw by the light within a sudden glitter of drops on her lashes as if she had been near tears. She was so young, and yet she was somehow not happy, and neither was he. Was there no happiness here on earth for anyone? Was all the beauty of the mountains and the sunset and the moving clouds only a promise of what must be fulfilled in heaven? But heaven had become a name, and the ache of unhappiness was a daily reality. A few moments later he saw her laughing with the young people of the choir. Whatever the cause of her wet lashes, she could soon forget it; but his unhappiness went on, and somehow it was deeper when he saw the others laughing. He was becoming a fool. The difficult summer had made a weakling of him. He braced himself to be strong for the coming winter.

PART III

1895–1896

1

LITA CAME HOME from Mary's that summer with an engagement ring on her finger.

"He's wonderful, mama. His father's in the banking business with loads of spondulix, and he's so refined—not like papa, you know. And, oh, I hope we can impress them all a little at the wedding, mama! So they won't think we're just a little country doctor's family, but real people, mama."

"We'll do the best we can, dear," Anna said. "He's rich and refined, you say. But is he kind, too? Is he broad-minded? Does he love you?"

"Of course, mama. How silly!"

"There's just one thing about the wedding, Lita. I think we ought to make it simple, nice but simple. You know your father's going to be hard hit financially this year."

"Well, surely he has something saved!" cried Lita. "Look at all the real estate he has."

"I'm afraid that's just the point," Anna said.

"Mama, you shouldn't have let him be improvident. He's just been selfish always, always! He's never treated you as if you had a bit of sense."

"Listen, Lita. Your father is not a man to be ashamed of. He's been a great man in this town, and he still is. It's not he who's asking you to have a simple wedding. I'm the one, my dear."

"Well," Lita said. "I'll talk to *him*."

"A wedding?" Doctor said. "Of course, you'll have a wedding, Lita. It comes at an awkward time maybe, but we won't skimp it. No, by George, we'll have a wedding that will open the town's eyes. I've always promised myself that much when my girls got married,

283

and Mary cheated me out of it, by Gad! Now we'll make twice the fuss for you, baby, twice the fuss! You understand that? We'll show those damned Oregon bankers what Idaho can do. You love your papa, Lita?"

Lita threw her arms around his neck.

"Oh, papa, you're an angel, honestly you are! And what about clothes, papa? I've got to have a trousseau, too, angel. Honestly I have."

Doctor put his hand in his pocket and brought out a gold piece.

"Well, here's a starter," he said.

Anna labored with Lita that autumn to make every gold piece go as far as possible. She knew now that there would be a big show if it ruined them; but she meant to get the most out of every dollar.

After the sewage reform came in, Doctor had tried to sell off some of his property; but real estate was at a standstill that year in Opportunity—nobody wanted to burden himself with more taxes than he already had. Anna did not see their way clear to a big wedding, nor beyond it to the day when the taxes would fall due; but all her life she had let Doctor have his own way, and somehow in the past she had made ends meet. So she continued to move serenely with the confidence that somehow they would come through.

But her confidence and serenity did not prevent her saving pennies and cutting corners wherever she was able to do so. Little things that she had never had to notice before became important to her now. Without asking Doctor's consent she sold the surplus fruit from their orchard that year instead of giving it away as they had always done; sometimes she sold eggs and chickens, too, when Neischmidt, the butcher, was willing to buy them or to trade a beef roast for them.

The chickens had once been her whim and pleasure; but now they had become economically important, and when they were not laying well the cost of their feed was something to think about in the wakeful hours of the night.

Doctor did not suspect these small contrivances of Anna's. They would have irritated him if he had known, for he thought in large terms and had no patience with petty economy.

Katherine Allerton stopped by one day while Anna was feeding her chickens. She watched Anna scattering the feed and talking to the chickens as if they were children:

"Don't crowd there, Cocky. Give the little ones a chance, Spot. My, but you're greedy, you!"

"You sound as if you knew them all, and liked them," Katherine said.

"Oh, I guess I do. I like most anything alive—and young. Babies and calves and colts, or young dogs leaping and cats fawning against my legs. I guess it's being young again in the hopefulness of their youth."

"And you've got a daughter getting married!"

"That's right," said Anna, smiling. "She's getting too big for me to baby her, so I have to baby the chickens and the cats and Gene now."

"I'm so alone!" said Katherine.

"I've thought of that," Anna said gravely. "You need something young to look after, too—almost anything. It would take you out of yourself and give you a wider horizon."

"I have my house to keep," said Katherine.

"I know. But, since you feel so much alone, why don't you have a pet to keep you company? Take a puppy, for instance. I could get you a half-spaniel pup. There are some in the next block that they want to give away."

Katherine had introduced the subject, but now she was vaguely upset.

"Oh, no, Anna! There would always be mud tracks on my nice floors."

Anna thought of Katherine's spotless floors. Where they were not covered by flowered carpet, Katherine had had Buchanan paint her floors dark brown and finish them with a simulated grain of wood in lighter brown. Over this had gone a high coat of varnish, so that they shone with a hard bright surface that was kept spotlessly clean. Anna could imagine how each imprint of a dog's foot would show on floors like these, but still she persisted.

"You could train the dog to keep to certain rooms and sleep where you wanted him to. That's the pleasure of handling young things— to train them up with kindness and love until they justify your care for them. It takes you out of yourself and lifts you up—even to train a young dog."

"You mean," said Katherine in a low voice, "because I have no children. You're reproaching me."

"No, Katherine, I mean no more than I say. It's good to have something young in the house, something alive and growing, even if it's only a pet of some kind."

Katherine was silent a moment.

"Once Hugh wanted a dog," she said. "He brought a little puppy home in his coat, but it wasn't housebroken at all, Anna. It spoiled my carpets and my floors. I told Hugh that I couldn't have it. I just couldn't have it, Anna. He doesn't care about a dog any more."

"Why don't you try again?"

Katherine looked dubious. "No," she said. "I wouldn't want a pet. I don't like to be responsible for things. It would bother me and—it would only be a compromise."

"You have to learn to compromise," said Anna. "I don't think I'd have got so much out of life if I hadn't been willing to compromise. The older I get, the more I see the virtue of a little give and take. But we're all different, I guess."

"It's only my floors—"

Katherine was apologetic, and Anna did not press the matter further.

2

TOO MUCH TOMFOOLERY went on among the young people at choir practice, Hugh Allerton thought. Before Mrs. Kempel, the choir leader, came in to take charge, they were running up and down the worn old carpets to the choir loft, making the church ring with secular jests and outcries. Mrs. Kempel's mother was invalided with rheumatism this year, and Hugh knew that it was difficult for the choir leader to be on time; but he wished she might have made the attempt more often. He had the habit of carrying one of Harper's Half-Hour Series in his pocket, or some other small book that he could have conveniently with him for the odd few moments between calls or whenever he had any waiting to do. There were miniature volumes of the poets, too, and lately he had begun to read those, finding to his surprise that they gave him as much pleasure as the Psalms.

Now, when he had to wait a few moments at choir practice, he sat quietly in one of the front pews, reading Lord Macaulay or George Eliot or Robert Browning, and trying to be oblivious to the noise of the young people. If he had not had a book, he might have felt obliged to talk to Miss Isaacs and Harry Seward, the two members of the choir who were older than he; but this had become as impossible to him as entering into the heedless chatter of the young people.

Miss Isaacs and Seward were against the young people, and Hugh was trying to preserve an open-minded neutrality.

"Look at them!" Miss Isaacs would say, drawing her breath in sharply. "Just look! Carrying on like that in church. I've said all I can say, but they just laugh at me. It's all the fault of Jenny Walden. She's the daughter of the minister, and she could stop the flirting and running up and down if she wished; but she's the wildest of the lot of them."

"She's been spoiled with too much attention," acquiesced Seward.

"We wouldn't have that riffraff of boys and girls in the choir, if it wasn't for her."

"I dare say the choir would be rather thin with only the three of us to sing in it," observed Hugh mildly.

"More levelheaded people might join it, if it weren't for Jenny's beaux," said Miss Isaacs sourly.

She could continue in this vein almost indefinitely, and Hugh preferred his books. But between the lines he couldn't help hearing the laughter and the running feet. The young organist, who was as scatterbrained as any of them, was pumping the organ up to play *Sweet Marie* or *The Band Played On,* and Lester Davis was leaning over the choir rail towards Jenny to sing: "Oh, promise me that some day you'll be mine."

As soon as Mrs. Kempel came in and clapped her hands the foolishness stopped, and practice continued with a reasonable amount of decorum. Hugh might have said something to them himself, for the antics of the young men particularly filled him with disgust; but he wouldn't align himself with Miss Isaacs and her antagonisms. Better to read and pay no attention.

One evening in October Mrs. Kempel was unusually slow in arriving, and the scatterbrained element had started a game of Hide and Seek. Hugh was trying to read Lord Macaulay on William Pitt and he found concentration difficult. He saw Jenny flying by him up the aisle, her mouth open with laughter, her cheeks red. Their eyes met for an instant as she sped by. The alto with the prominent teeth was hiding her eyes against the front of the pulpit and counting audibly.

"15, 20, 25, 30, 35, 40—all who aren't ready holler 'I'!" They were like a pack of half-grown children. He continued doggedly to read, but there was a quick rush from the other aisle, and Jenny had come back to crouch in the seat beside him.

"Go on reading," she whispered. "They won't look here."

She was breathing quickly, and he could see the rise and fall of her breast. The excited blue eyes included him in the conspiracy.

"You are a little fool," he said under his breath, but making a pretense all the same of reading his book.

"The hopeful thing is that I know it," she retorted.

"Then why do you go on being one?"

"I don't know. Maybe it amuses me."

"You're easily amused."

"No, on the contrary."

She had crept closer to him between the pews, and he could look past his book and directly into her upturned face. He had never seen before how smooth and delicate the skin was nor how velvety black the dilated pupils in the clear blue irises of her eyes. She was laughing and audacious.

"Call me a fool again, doctor. You have such a nice English way of saying it."

"I won't oblige you, Miss Walden."

"Do you never oblige anybody?"

He couldn't help smiling. "Not if I can avoid it."

Suddenly he noticed that the church had fallen silent, and then he heard Mrs. Kempel clapping her hands.

"No more nonsense now!" she said. "I'm sorry to be late. Practice is beginning."

Hugh rose uncertainly, and Jenny darted out of the pew, still laughing. She ran down the aisle and started up the steps to the choir loft. It was the old worn carpet that did the mischief. Hugh, coming more slowly behind her, saw her catch her foot on the worn place on the second step and fall, clutching at the curtain on the choir railing as she went down. They were all around her in a moment.

"Jenny, are you hurt?"

"Goodness! That old worn carpet at last!"

"Look, dear, can't you get up? Help her, one of you boys."

"Oh, please," cried Jenny. "No! No! Just let me be a moment. Oh, dear! I'm really hurt."

The delicate face was suddenly twisted with pain.

Hugh came forward quickly and bent over her. He was a doctor now, and that put him more at ease with her than he had been a moment ago. Still he felt the sharp sensation of anxiety that only his earliest accident cases had used to arouse in him. He was short with the others.

"Stand aside a bit, if you don't mind. Thank you, that's better. It's in the ankle, isn't it, Miss Walden? No, don't try to move it if it's very painful."

She made an attempt to laugh again, but he could see that she was gritting her teeth and blinking back tears. He made a hasty examination and he knew that the ankle was either badly sprained or broken. He did not attempt to undo the high shoe with the silly little high heel. He said:

"I think we must take you home before we do anything further."

"Let me carry her, Dr. Allerton," cried Lester. "Russ and me will be ever so careful, and it's only a step to the parsonage."

"Thank you," said Hugh coldly. "I'll carry her myself if you'll be so kind as to open the doors for me. Will you go ahead, Davis, and warn her father? Miss Isaacs, may I have her coat to put around her?"

Jenny lay silent in his arms, her lips pressed tightly together and her brows contracted with pain. She was soft and warm against his breast. She let her head rest upon his shoulder, and he felt the slender roundness of her body in his hands. The bright, disordered hair brushed against his cheek. She was lighter than he had supposed she would be.

"Is it very bad, Miss Walden?" he asked in a voice that sounded odd to him. She did not reply directly, but flashed a quick look up at him from wet lashes.

"You think I'm more than ever a little fool, don't you?"

"I think you are behaving bravely."

Her voice had a querulous note. "I'm sorry this had to happen to me, Dr. Allerton! Now you have me on your hands, and you hate me, don't you? If only Dr. Hawkins had happened to be here instead of you!"

"I shall be glad to call Dr. Hawkins."

"And let me die of pain while we are waiting for him to hitch up his horse? No, I'll put up with you, Dr. Allerton, if you can bring yourself to put up with me."

"You seem to imagine a much more personal relationship between patient and physician than is likely to exist, Miss Walden."

"You've never liked me!"

"Don't be tiresome. This is a question of an injured ankle, not of likes and dislikes."

"I think I could walk."

"I think you could not."

Mr. Walden met them at the door of the parsonage, his hair in disorder and his blue eyes full of anxiety.

"Jenny!" he said. "My little Jenny!"

"It's nothing, papa," said Jenny, making up a little face at him. "Just the old torn carpet on the choir stairs, and I was running. Maybe they'll get you a new carpet now."

The girls ran ahead, throwing open the door of Jenny's bedroom and laying back the covers on her narrow bed. Hugh followed them more slowly with Jenny in his arms. It had not seemed far from the church.

When he had put Jenny on her bed, he straightened and looked around. The room was poorly furnished, but there was somehow a look of clean gayety about it, from the crisp red and white gingham curtains and cushions on the chairs to the bookcase which had obviously been homemade from a couple of packing cases and painted red to match the curtains. He saw that the books were well worn with loving use, and his eye picked out a pocket Browning which was a match for his own.

"I'll undress her, doctor," said Miss Isaacs, impatient for the proprieties.

"I can undress myself," cried Jenny passionately.

"I'll have off her shoe first and take a better look at the ankle," said Hugh. "I think we'll need splints and bandages. Lester, will you go to the office for me? There's no reason why the rest of you should not continue with your choir rehearsal. I'll look by and let you know how she is, when I've finished. Mr. Walden and I can take care of everything."

"But she has no mother—" began Miss Isaacs.

"It's all right," said Mr. Walden. "Jenny and I know how to manage."

"I'm glad you got rid of them," said Jenny with a sigh that was almost a sob. "Hold my hand, papa, like a good dear. My shoe is killing me."

Hugh cut the laces on the shoe and worked it gently off her foot. The shoe was scuffed on the toe from much running up and down, and it had that foolish little high heel.

"Why women wear such things!" said Hugh, tossing it on the floor.

"Instead of high heels, you'd have us all in strait-jackets, doctor!" She couldn't keep the tears from running down her cheeks, but she still had her spirit.

"Now, honey, don't be impudent," said her father. "Doctor's doing all he can for you. It's wonderful that he was there when you fell."

"Yes," sobbed Jenny, "it *was* wonderful, wasn't it? I know how much he enjoyed it."

"Be still, Miss Walden," said Hugh. "Your ankle is broken, and it's going to be difficult to set. I shall rely upon your best cooperation."

"Go ahead then. I may be a fool, but I'm not a coward."

"Thank you."

He had never seen finer, whiter skin than the skin on her leg. It was a beautiful foot, too, slender and small and delicately arched. He felt the broken bones slipping back into place beneath his fingers. He knew how much it hurt her, but she was too proud now to make a sound.

3

DELLA CAME UP the next day from her school to spend the week end at the parsonage. Things ran smoothly while she was there. Hugh had never had much acquaintance with Della. She had been at home during the summer, but she did not sing in the choir nor run about town. He saw that she was an admirable girl with little of Jenny's wildness.

"I wish I could stay, Dr. Allerton," she said; "but schools are hard to get, and I just can't lose this one now. Old Mrs. Mills two blocks over has promised to come in every morning to tidy the house and get Jenny ready for the day, and father does quite well with the cooking. Besides, people will send in things to eat. How long do you think Jenny will be off her feet?"

"Five or six weeks, with luck," said Hugh. "Sometimes an ankle is trickier than a broken leg, but Miss Jenny is young and healthy."

"It's so hard to know where one's duty lies, but really we need the money from the school teaching so badly. It's horrid to be poor."

"Don't let this worry you, Miss Della. I shall be in every day to see that things go right. You can trust me to let you know if you are needed, but I'm sure you won't be. Mrs. Allerton will always be glad to come in, if a woman is required; and your father and I can surely keep things running smoothly."

"I can't thank you enough, doctor, for all you've done. You were so kind during mother's illness, too. Father and I often speak of it. I hope you won't mind Jenny's impudent way of speaking to you. She's grateful, too, but in lots of ways she's still so young."

"Yes," repeated Hugh absently, "she is still so young." He went slowly upstairs to her room.

"So you have come at last!" cried Jenny. "I might die of anguish here while you were grinding up your powders or stewing your horrible concoctions."

He took an orange out of his pocket and held it up for her to see.

"This is what I carry in my pocket for good children who don't scold the doctor when he is late."

"Really? You're nicer than I thought. I fancied the only things you kept in your pockets were pills or bits of flesh you'd amputated and pickled in formaldehyde."

"You have a nice imagination."

"That's only a sample."

"I don't think you should exercise it too much."

"No, no! You're not going to put my imagination into splints, doctor. Then I *would* be a cripple! But aren't you going to give me the orange?"

"I keep them for *good* children."

"I'm not good, and I'm not children; but I know you brought it for me. Can you look me straight in the eye and say that you didn't?"

"No honest man could stand that test." He tossed the orange on the coverlet.

Jenny took it in her hands and turned it softly over and over.

"It's still warm from your pocket," she said. One of her sudden silences fell upon her.

The second day after Della went back to her school, Hugh found the house full of young people when he came to call. Mr. Walden opened the door for him. The minister had a pencil behind his ear, as a grocer might, and a half-written sheet of foolscap in his hand.

"Try and write a sermon with this going on!" he said, his face wrinkled in mild protest. "I believe that all the young people in the congregation have been to see Jenny today, and they've brought enough pies and cakes to start a bakery—but not a bowl of soup in the lot."

Hugh laughed shortly. "How is the patient standing it?"

"Well, she's laughing and carrying on with the rest of them, but I don't think it's very good for her. What do you think, doctor? I can't very well turn them out when they come in kindness and charity—"

"Kindness and charity!" grunted Hugh.

"—but maybe you could, being the doctor."

"I can, and I will."

Mr. Walden watched the doctor taking the stairs two at a time with a chuckle of relief. It was fine to have a responsible man like Allerton take over the authority which he always disliked to exercise in his own household. When his wife was alive she had attended to all matters of tact and discipline, and left him to the calm realm of contemplation in his little study. All he asked was to be let alone with his books and the building of his sermons. He could even shut his ears to the noise if he knew that someone else had assumed the responsibility of ordering the house. He heard Dr. Allerton's voice lashing out like a whip in the midst of the good-natured uproar, and he didn't wait to see the culprits come filing downstairs and out the front door. Still chuckling, he went back to the study.

"Let's see, where was I? Second chapter, Deuteronomy, seventh verse." Yes, it was a good text.

For the Lord thy God hath blessed thee in all the works of thy hand: he knoweth thy walking through this great wilderness; these forty years the Lord thy God hath been with thee; thou hast lacked nothing.

These forty years—yes, it had been longer even—nearer sixty years that the Lord had been with him, Mr. Walden thought. *Thou hast lacked nothing.* He folded his hands on his desk, and his faded blue eyes were dreamy and tender. There had been small material lacks along the way, clothes for the girls, sometimes even food and shelter, but the joys of the spirit had been heaped upon him. He had lacked nothing. He closed his eyes for a moment.

"O God, Thou hast been kind. I thank Thee. Amen."

He took the pencil from behind his ear and began to write. The house was very peaceful now, and he smiled as he wrote. How comforting was the thought: *he knoweth thy walking through this great wilderness.* If he could make the congregation understand that in next Sunday's sermon!

4

IT WAS THAT nasal quality in Lester Davis' tenor and the slight devi-
ation from key in the voice of the other young man whose name
Hugh could never remember, that made Hugh hate them so. When
he heard them harmonizing *Juanita* in the upper hall outside Jenny's
open door, the simple irritation he felt at seeing one of his patients
subjected to too much company blazed into blind anger. There were
two girls sitting in Jenny's room, one in the rocking chair and the
other on the foot of the bed where the covers should have been loose
and light over her injured foot. Whenever the serenaders paused for
breath, the girls burst into laughter and applause.

Hugh took it all in at a glance as he ran up the stairs.

"What is the meaning of this?" he cried. He was white with anger.

The boys looked startled and abashed. "Well, we were serenading
her," they said. "Just a little music. We thought she'd be bored lying
here."

"*Bored!*" cried the doctor. "You thought she might be bored!
Do you know that what she needs now is rest and quiet and a chance
to get well? Have you nothing inside your skulls but fat meat?"

"Well, we thought—" began Lester, his blond mustache beginning to tremble with a species of anger, hardly so tempestuous as the
doctor's but equally sincere.

"*You* thought! What about Miss Walden's thoughts? Did you
consult those? If you haven't given her at least two degrees of fever,
I shall be much surprised."

"She could have sent us home whenever she got tired."

"Is that all the consideration you have for her? To try her politeness to the limit of being obliged to ask you to leave?"

"Well, we didn't mean—"

"Clear out now," said Hugh, "all of you. If I find the lot of you
here again, I'll resign the case to Dr. Hawkins."

They went quickly and without any lingering farewells.

Hugh did not speak to Jenny, but he went in and took her wrist in his hand. His fingers were hard and steady on her pulse. He dragged out his big, loudly ticking watch and looked at it while he counted. There was no doubt that her pulse was high. Her cheeks were flushed, and her eyes dilated with excitement. She looked at him with a devil of humor dancing about her eyes and mouth.

"That was a lovely storm you raised, doctor! I didn't know you could do it."

He did not answer her for a moment. He could see that she was tired as well as excited, and he was ashamed.

"I was as bad as any of them—worse," he said in a low voice. "I hope you will forgive me."

"Yes, I will."

"Do you like that sort of thing?"

"No."

"I'm sorry I lost my temper."

"I'm glad you did, and that they are gone now. But"—her eyes sparkled at him—"if you will not let me have any company, what shall I do with myself?"

"You are going to rest."

"But I can't sleep. It's tedious lying here alone."

He went to the window and half pulled the shade, shutting out the long glare of light that lay across the bed.

"I haven't slept through the whole night a single night since I broke my ankle. I lie awake and think, and there's no good in that."

"You are going to sleep *now*."

"How?"

He stood looking down at her. Then his eyes ran along the home-made bookcase beside her bed. He leaned down and drew out the pocket Browning that matched his own.

"I shall read to you," he said.

"Is that how you put yourself to sleep?"

"Yes."

"I always read to keep awake."

"Listen to the sound and not the sense. If you like music, this will rest you."

He sat in the little rocking chair with the red and white checkered cushions.

"My chair is too small for you," said Jenny.

He smiled at her apologetically. "I feel small."

"Please don't. You were going to read."

"If you'll try to sleep."

"Yes, I'll try."

He turned the pages of the pocket Browning, noticing that here and there a passage had been marked. His voice was rich and deep and very quiet. He had always enjoyed reading aloud, but there were so few occasions when anyone cared to hear him. When he had sometimes tried to read aloud to Katherine she had either dozed or interrupted him with irrelevant remarks. Miss Walden lay very still with her large eyes wide and alert, watching him. He selected something at random:

> *But do not let us quarrel any more,*
> *No, my Lucrezia; bear with me for once:*
> *Sit down and all shall happen as you wish.*
> *You turn your face, but does it bring your heart?*
>
> .   .   .   .
>
> *And autumn grows, autumn in everything.*
> *Eh? the whole seems to fall into a shape*
> *As if I saw alike my work and self*
> *And all that I was born to be and do,*
> *A twilight-piece. Love, we are in God's hand.*
>
> .   .   .   .
>
> *Ah, but a man's reach should exceed his grasp,*
> *Or what's a heaven for? All is silver-gray,*
> *Placid and perfect with my art: the worse!*
>
> .   .   .   .

In this world, who can do a thing, will not;
And who would do it, cannot, I perceive:
Yet the will's somewhat—somewhat, too, the power—
And thus we half-men struggle. At the end,
God, I conclude, compensates, punishes.

.   .   .   .

I am grown peaceful as old age tonight.
I regret little, I would change still less.
Since there my past life lies, why alter it?

.   .   .   .

Again the Cousin's whistle! Go, my love.

He had been reading for a long time. There were eight closely printed pages. She was not sleeping when he finished, but her eyes were full of quiet.

"Will you read to me again?" she asked. "Tomorrow?"

He did not know why he answered so, but he said:

"Yes."

5

SKOGMO KEPT several shelves of books in one corner of his drugstore. He had started the book corner to take care of the demand created by the new Academy, but, since Dr. Allerton had come from England, it was he who patronized it most. Allerton used to smile in his serious way and say it was odd how pharmacists in the States felt called upon to sell so many things besides drugs. Yet, almost every time he came in to leave an order or fill a prescription, he paused for a moment to see if Skogmo had anything new on his shelves. The doctor subscribed to some of the English reviews, and, knowing what was being read in the world beyond the Idaho mountains, he used sometimes to advise the druggist what books to buy.·

Poetry had never sold very well until the doctor came to town.

Occasionally a student at the Academy or some member of the Ladies' Literary Society asked for a copy of Longfellow or Tennyson or Robert Browning. But Tennyson and Longfellow didn't appear to satisfy the doctor, although it seemed to Skogmo that either of the books was thick enough to give a man poetic indigestion for the rest of his life.

During the typhoid siege, when Allerton was on the go from morning to night with patients and using every spare moment to talk sewage reform to the healthy citizens of town, he had come into the drugstore one day, looking white and dog-tired, and had laid down a list on the counter.

"Order those for me, will you, Skogmo?"

Skogmo had expected it to be a list of drugs, but it had turned out to be a list of books, books by poets of whom Skogmo had never heard. Crazy, foreign names they had: Dante Gabriel Rossetti, Algernon Swinburne, Percy B. Shelley, and two that sounded like a minstrel-show team, Keats and Yeats. Keats and the others had been easy to locate, but Yeats had been a sticker, and had held up the whole order for a long time.

Dr. Allerton kept coming in and asking for the books after the epidemic died down. When they hadn't arrived he was always quiet and polite in that way of his, but Skogmo could see that he was disappointed. It seemed as if those books were really important to him in some odd way.

"It's that Yeats book that's holding up the order, doctor. You sure there *is* such a poet and you weren't just seeing double with Keats?"

"Yes, I'm sure," said Allerton, looking as if he might have burst out laughing if life hadn't been quite so serious to him.

Along towards the end of October the books arrived. It was a fresh blue and gold day, and Skogmo could see the yellow leaves blowing outside the window of the back room as he unpacked the box. He heard the bell on the front door jangle, and before he could go to see who the customer was, Dr. Allerton came striding into the back room. The fresh mountain air seemed to come in with him.

He had certainly got over the strain of the typhoid epidemic. He looked full of life and vigor today and almost like a boy with the fresh red in his cheeks.

"I don't suppose those books I ordered have come in?"

"They sure have, doctor. I'm just unpacking them."

"No!" cried the doctor incredulously. "After all this time, they came *today*!"

"You sound as if today was Christmas, man."

"No, no. Not Christmas. But it's a day when I can use one of them. I'd almost call it a coincidence, their coming today."

Skogmo opened one of the books at random and held it at arm's length from his farsighted eyes. He read with the expressionless monotone of the unaccustomed and the skeptical reader:

> *"Fair youth, beneath the trees, thou canst not leave*
> *Thy song, nor ever can those trees be bare:*
> *Bold Lover, never, never canst thou kiss,*
> *Though winning near the goal—yet, do not grieve;*
> *She cannot fade, though thou hast not thy bliss,*
> *For ever wilt thou love, and she be fair!"*

He looked up with a bedeviled air, scratching his head. "It's such a damned complicated way of stating facts. I hope you make more of it than I do."

Allerton took the book and ran his eye down the page.

> *What little town by river or sea shore,*
> *Or mountain-built with peaceful citadel,*
> *Is emptied of this folk, this pious morn?*
> *Ah, little town, thy streets for evermore*
> *Will silent be; and not a soul to tell*
> *Why thou art desolate, can e'er return.*

The doctor had been inexplicably content all day, and now his spirit lifted with a thrust of happiness. He closed the book gently and put his hand in his pocket for his wallet.

"It's a different kind of language, Skogmo," he said. "Some people never care enough to try to understand it. I think perhaps it comes from a marriage of mountains and of music. I'm just beginning to get the notion of it."

"Well, doctor, I'm glad your books came. You're sure looking fine today."

"I'm feeling fine, thank you."

He took the books to the office and unwrapped them to gloat a little while. When he had looked them all over, he hesitated a few moments, and then he took his pen and wrote rapidly on the flyleaf of the Keats:

Miss Jenny Walden

He set the other volumes on the shelf with his *materia medica* and his professional journals; but he carefully rewrapped the Keats in the paper from Skogmo's drugstore and laid it on top of his desk.

6

ON TUESDAY afternoon Hugh read to Miss Jenny Walden from the new book.

"It's for me? You want me to keep it?" she had asked, holding it in both hands in that eager, possessive way she had.

"If you like," he had said carelessly.

"Oh, thank you!" she had said.

But then she had lain very silent to listen to him, and her little elfish face had been secret and full of mystery.

All the rest of that day he had felt uplifted with a strange elation, going about his business with a detachment that still listened mentally to the beautiful words and phrases he had been reading. When he had read poetry before, it had always been to himself; to read it aloud to someone who cared to listen was to give the words new significance. They burned now with the clear white light which the poet had felt when he wrote them.

Hugh felt relaxed that night, and completely at peace. He walked awhile in the crisp, windy evening, and came home to find, as he had hoped, that Katherine was already asleep in her bed. He went to his own with a feeling that he would sleep well because of the unaccustomed happiness which he felt.

He slept well, but in the night he had a dream. In his dream he and Miss Jenny Walden were walking together in the windy October weather. The leaves blew and whirled about them, and it seemed that there was something which threatened her, and that he must protect her from it. There were fallen trees and brush in their way, and suddenly it seemed that they were not only walking together but fleeing together from something which pursued them. And then there was a moment when she paused and looked at him, and the delicate small face was pale with the secret and mysterious look which he did not understand. But then she put her hand in his, and they were together, running and stumbling together, away from some unknown fear.

The fear and urgent hurry of his dream awakened him, and he lay still, listening to the wind which blew about the house, now loud and weighted with flying leaves, now sunk to a murmur. After the fear and the hurry, he was flooded with an exquisite sense of physical delight at the memory of the touch of her hand. He lay in a state between waking and sleeping and savored the bliss he had known in the dream. She had looked at him and given him her hand. They had gone on together. Presently he slept again without dreaming.

On Wednesday morning Hugh came wide-awake with a strong feeling of revulsion. He could not bear to think of the books of poetry he had bought; and that he had actually sat with a patient and read aloud, as if he had been an old lady's companion, made him turn red with mortification. He did not want to think of going to see Miss Walden today after making such an ass of himself. She was better off with her caterwauling young men than with a fatuous old doctor who read poetry to her.

He was silent at breakfast, and Katherine said:

"Oh, Hugh, is anything wrong?"

"Of course not, my dear. What should be?"

"I don't know. Hugh—"

"Yes, Katherine?"

"You won't forget to settle the butcher's bill, will you, dear? I could go down and do it, but you'll be right on Main Street, and it's quite a walk for me with the wind switching my skirts about on a day like this."

"It's a lovely day. It would do you good to get out."

"It's such untidy weather," said Katherine. "Look at the leaves under the apple tree and in the fence corners! I'll have to get a boy to rake. Perhaps Anna will know of one. But about the account at the butcher's, dear?"

"I'll take care of it, of course," said Hugh.

"Oh, I'm so glad. Thank you, Hugh."

He was annoyed with Katherine, too, this morning. Why need she be so afraid of the wind and weather? Sometimes he thought that wind and weather and the change of seasons were all that made life bearable. Sometimes he thought— She disliked the wind switching her skirts! What did it matter? Katherine's ankles would never be of interest to the pool-hall loiterers. When he had gone this far, he was appalled. His mind was sinking to the lowest depths of vulgarity. This was worse than having his head immersed in clouds of poetry. There was only one thing that gave him any pleasure this morning, and that was the feeling he had had in his dream when Miss Walden had put her hand in his; but he wouldn't allow himself to remember it. It was out of the question.

He did not want to see Jenny Walden today. There was no reason why he had to call upon her every day for a broken ankle. Certainly he had already spent too much time upon her in proportion to her need.

He opened the butcher-shop door and stepped into the clean, damp sawdust. Neischmidt came forward to the counter, heavy and blond and with spots of blood on his coarse white apron.

"Somet'ing I do for you, doctor?"

"I'd like to settle Mrs. Allerton's account."

When the bill was paid, the butcher looked at Hugh with a quizzi‑cal smile.

"Say, doctor, ain't you tired of boiled beef?"

"Yes," said Hugh. "Why?"

"I yust t'ought. You order out a nice piece of ham. I have my boy tell Mrs. Allerton how to fix him."

"Thank you," said Hugh. "I'd be glad to have you do that."

He thought angrily as he went out:

"Katherine has no imagination. Even the butcher knows it and laughs about it. Boiled beef, boiled potatoes—and veg!"

The word "imagination" rang another bell in his mind. He heard a lilting, girlish voice saying, *You're not going to put my imagination into splints, doctor. Then I would be a cripple!*

He was sick with disgust and weariness of himself.

One thing he could do, and that was to keep away from the Waldens' for twenty-four hours, at least.

7

IT WAS THE continuous sound of wind that made him restless, Hugh thought. By Wednesday night he had come a long way from the tranquil sense of well-being which had uplifted him on the previous evening. He would not indulge himself by going out to walk again, but sat with Katherine in the lamp-lit parlor. He had tried to resume his reading of Macaulay, but the local paper was simpler to comprehend and larger to hide behind. Still Katherine's voice went on, even with the barrier of paper between. Her fingers flew with her crochet as she talked.

"I was so astonished, and I must say I thought it rather impudent.

BUFFALO COAT

The boy just thrust the package at me, and he said, 'Ham, ma'am, and I'm to tell you how to fix it.' I never can become accustomed to the American fashion of saying 'fix' when they mean 'prepare,' and I was really quite at a loss to know what he meant."

"I dare say you were."

"Yes, you may imagine! But, when he said *you* had ordered it, I was even more surprised, because you seldom take an interest in such things. I do try to give you wholesome food such as we had in England. I never thought of ham. It seems such an American thing somehow. But I know now I was wrong. You must have been longing for it, Hugh. I am so sorry."

Hugh put down his paper with more outward patience than he felt.

"No, Katherine," he said. "Can't I make you see that it was the butcher's idea, not mine? He just said, 'Why not try some ham, doctor?' and I said: 'Very well. Send it out.' It was as simple as that."

"But it was so odd—the boy telling me how to prepare it."

"Did you know how?"

"No, but I could have asked Anna Hawkins. I'm sure she would have known."

"Well, let's forget it, my dear. It made a very good dish for a change."

"But that's just it, dear. I haven't been giving you what you want. I know it so well, and it worries me so. If only I knew what to do to please you!" She began to cry, and her crying was a sight that never pleased him. If he had only gone to walk! Tonight his nerves were beyond enduring Katherine's twaddle.

"Now, dear," he said quietly, "please don't cry. It's utterly ridiculous." He folded the newspaper and rose. Then he went to the kitchen and fetched her a glass of water. "Don't be silly now."

"You think I'm silly, Hugh!"

"Yes, when you cry."

"I'm so alone!"

"You needn't be, if you'd go out and meet people—stir yourself up."

"That's dreadful, too. I don't like strangers."

There was a sound of quick steps on the porch, and the bell was turned with its shrill grating sound of urgency. A wave of relief swept over Hugh. He went to the door and opened it. On the threshold stood the Reverend Mr. Walden with a look of mingled anxiety and shame on his pink-cheeked, wrinkled face.

"Doctor," he said, "I'm most sorry to trouble you when you are at home with your wife at night like this. I can't think it's really very important, but I had to come, doctor. My daughter has worked herself into quite a state. Her ankle's very painful, and she doesn't sleep well. She looked for you all afternoon and when you didn't come—"

"Hugh!" said Katherine reproachfully. "You did not go to see Miss Jenny today?"

"No," said Hugh roughly. "I thought she could wait until tomorrow."

"She would have, doctor," said the minister apologetically, "but I guess I'm a foolish old man with no womenfolks to advise me. I couldn't bear to see her so upset."

"She was upset?" repeated Hugh slowly.

"Yes, terribly. She's kind of a high-strung girl, and her ankle's very painful. It seemed as if she had to have you. I'm sorry to bother you."

"I'm sure he doesn't look upon it as a bother—do you, Hugh?" cried Katherine. She had dried her eyes now for the minister.

"It is no bother," said Hugh.

Katherine made a supreme gesture.

"I could come, Mr. Walden, if you think it would help."

"No, Katherine," said Hugh. "It is windy and cold outside. This is my business."

He took down the buffalo coat from its hanger in the closet and slipped his arms into it. It was the first time he had had it on that season.

"I don't know what's come over Jenny," said Mr. Walden in the windy street. "She's never been afraid of pain, but this accident seems to have made her very miserable."

"I think it is a very painful break. I reproach myself for not having visited the house today."

"It was only that she expected you, I think."

Dr. Allerton began to whistle. He often whistled to himself when he was alone. Something about the wind tonight made it seem appropriate.

"I can't seem to make my sermon come right this week," said Mr. Walden. "It's being worried about Jenny, I guess. I've been getting the evening meal, too, and I'm not a very good hand at that."

"Did she eat her supper?"

"Not very well."

"Do you have some milk and eggs in the house?"

"Yes, of course."

"Will you let me take charge of your house for half an hour or so?"

The minister laughed. "That's why I let her talk me into getting you, doctor."

"You can have a clear half-hour to work on your sermon, and then I trust she'll be ready for sleep."

8

JENNY LOOKED at him with wide eyes that were no longer blue but dark with their dilated pupils. Her hair was spread in a wild, beautiful disorder on the two pillows that propped her.

Hugh stood in the doorway returning her steady look, and the happiness which he had wanted all day came flooding back to him.

"You are a bad patient," he said.

"I thought you would never come again. It wasn't right of you. I heard you promise Della that you would look in every day. With all your faults, one thing I believed of you was that you were a man of your word."

"I have no excuse."

"You had forgotten me—and I have been here less than a week!"

"I have a few other duties. You are a conceited young woman."

"I think it is unkind of you to abuse me further."

"I think so, too."

He smiled at her and came to stand by her bed with his watch in one hand and his fingers on her wrist. She lay quiet, but he felt the movement of her heart against his fingertips. One minute, two minutes—the watch scarcely mattered, so long as he could make pretense of having business with her hand. It was like the dream he had been in last night, and he had to battle with a sudden numbness of his mind. He laid her hand back on the coverlet.

"You are needlessly upset—Jenny," he said.

"I never liked my name."

"It would be too bad to change it. Somehow it fits you."

"Jenny—Jenny—Jenny!" she raged. "It's what they call a female donkey."

"Let me see your ankle now. Your bedding's disarranged. No wonder you are having extra pain. Where is the little trestle I arranged to take the weight of bedding off your foot?"

"It fell on the floor. I wouldn't let them put it in again."

"Who is 'they'?"

"Father, of course, and that Miss Isaacs was here. She came when I was fretting for *you*."

"Not a good substitute?"

"No."

When he had made a satisfactory arrangement of the weight over her foot, he asked, "Why didn't you eat your supper?"

"I wasn't hungry."

"You are going to eat now."

"Why?"

"Because I say so. You can't behave to me as you do to Miss Isaacs and your father."

"Why not?"

"I won't have it! It's time you grew up."

"I am older than you are, doctor."

"By what calendar?"

"My own reckoning."

"Very well. Lie still and think again. I am going to get your supper."

The minister was not a very good housekeeper—he had left the greasy dishes and pans in the kitchen for the woman who would come in the morning; but Hugh found what he wanted. He assembled milk and eggs, sugar and nutmeg, and made a heavy eggnog. He emptied a sedative powder in a small glass of water and put both glasses on a tray.

When he went upstairs again, she had managed to braid her hair. She looked demure now instead of recklessly disordered.

"I never have liked eggnogs."

"Isn't that too bad!"

"But I shall drink this one to please you, and to put you into a better temper with me."

"First drink the water in the little glass."

"You want to settle me, don't you? I don't blame you. You are dying to get home again and put on your slippers."

"No, I'm thinking of staying here until you are asleep."

"Really? I've never been watched to sleep before. I shall be self-conscious."

"That isn't necessary. Most patients consider the doctor only a part of the bedroom furniture."

"Then sit down. That way you look more like a chair."

He tilted the eggnog glass for her. Her throat was white and rounded above the high-yoked nightgown with the embroidered ruffle. When she swallowed there was a delicate, convulsive movement of the throat that somehow stirred in him a yearning pity. She lay back upon the pillows, relaxed and quiet.

"Of course you are too eager to get home to read poetry to me."

He sat forward in the little rocker with his elbows on his spread knees, and his eyes on his hands.

"Miss Walden—" he began gravely.

"I don't mind your calling me Jenny."

"*Jenny*—" His eyes flickered up to hers for a comprehending instant, but it was better to look at his hands now. "I realize that it was rather silly of me the other day to send away the company of your own age and substitute myself. I was angry because there were too many of them and they were too noisy, when you needed rest. But I need not have gone so far as I did. It seems to me that I have just discovered poetry after a lifetime without it. However, that is no excuse for involving you in my belated enthusiasms."

"I love poetry," said Jenny in a low voice. "You are the first person I have found in this town who loves it too."

He did not look up, but went on in his serious tone:

"I should tell you, perhaps, that that is why I did not come today. I was as angry with myself for my lack of perception as I had been the day before with the lack of perception of Lester Davis."

"Oh, Lester Davis!" she said scornfully.

"He is your own age—Jenny, and very fond of you."

"Why do you make such a point of age?"

"Because—No, I don't know why."

"I think it is absurd to crystallize people into layers, according to age!"

"We live by a great many absurd conventions. It is not safe to defy them."

"Do you really believe that?"

"I always have."

"Now you are being fatherly tonight. I much prefer you when you read poetry."

"I'll send Lester in to read to you tomorrow."

"I won't endure that. He reads through his nose, just as he sings."

"Very well—the contralto then with the front teeth. What's her name?"

"Look! Have I worked myself into a frenzy tonight for nothing at all? You come and give me a powder in a glass of water and expect that to put me to sleep, when all I wanted was to hear you read."

"You are making fun of me."

"If you would look at me, you'd know that I was serious."

He raised his eyes to her face. One could go very deep into her eyes; one could lose consciousness and drown. There was no bottom to them, only a blissful descent into something that took the breath. He reached out his hand for the book. His own voice sounded strange to him and as if it came from a great distance when he began to read:

"*I stood tip-toe upon a little hill,*
The air was cooling, and so very still,
That the sweet buds which with a modest pride
Pull droopingly, in slanting curve aside,
Their scantly leaved, and finely tapering stems,
Had not yet lost those starry diadems
Caught from the early sobbing of the morn."

Presently he dared look up again. Her wide eyes were still upon him, but now they were a little heavy and not so bottomless.

"You must close your eyes," he said.

"It is too bad to sleep."

"No, it is good."

She slipped her hand under her cheek and closed her eyes.

"*The clouds were pure and white as flocks new shorn,*
And fresh from the clear brook; sweetly they slept
On the blue fields of heaven . . ."

He read on quietly for a long time. There had been no sound, no change, but presently the words seemed hollow to him as the sound of footsteps in an untenanted room, and he knew that only he heard them. He closed the book and laid it on the shelf beside the bed. Then he arose very quietly and took up the lamp. For a moment he looked down at her, seeing the faint blue shadows under her eyes, the delicate relaxed droop at the corners of her mouth, and the regular, slight rising and falling of her breast. Holding the lamp carefully, he tiptoed down the stairs and along the passage to Mr. Walden's study.

"Eh? Eh? Asleep, is she?" said the minister, smiling and jerking his head up quickly from his own dozing. "You've a fine touch with patients, doctor. I remember how you were with my dear wife, and how she trusted you. Thank you for coming! Thank you for coming!"

Hugh walked quickly home in the turbulent night, and he thought angrily: *It's not right that a girl like Jenny Walden should have such an unworldly father. He trusts me because I'm the doctor and nearly twice her age; but he'd trust anyone else equally well.* The thought was almost unbearable.

Katherine was still awake when he let himself in. She called from her room: "What a long time you were gone, dear! Was she very bad?"

Hugh stood still in the center of the room, thinking rapidly. There was nothing of this evening which he wished to share with Katherine.

"After she was asleep," he said, "I talked with her father."

9

ALF STEVENS watched the cemetery road that fall, but he did not see Jenny Walden walking along it. The goldenrod and black-eyed Susans bloomed in heavy masses of yellow and orange outside the fields which were golden with ripe wheat, but she did not come to pick them. Where the wild roses had blossomed along the fences in the spring, there were red and orange hips set like colored beads on the green bushes. Asters were a purple mist at the roadside; the berries of the mountain ash burned red on the dark mountains. But Jenny did not come to look at them.

Alf worked in the fields at harvest time beside the other men, the sweat running down his back and staining his faded blue shirt, but he did not laugh with them nor share their common talk. His thoughts and feelings were his own, withdrawn and secret, tinged with strangeness like the thoughts of a man from another planet. He frowned as he worked, and he was quick to take offense and strike out with heavy fists. The other men held back from him, glancing at him out of the corners of unfriendly eyes.

"He's been in the asylum. His old man hung himself. There's a crazy streak all through them. The old woman, too—she looks like a witch."

At the threshers' table he ate heavily and in silence, staring at his plate, his shoulders hunched, his elbows on the table. A strange smell hung about him, tainted with savagery, like the smell of an animal. He was deeply tanned now except for the little lines about his eyes which had been puckered together with squinting in the sun.

Unless someone crossed him, he was docile and lethargic. But once when an old horse fell in the traces, overcome by heat and fatigue, he seized a whip and beat it to death before the other men could intervene. When harvest was over he returned to his own place, and people seldom saw him except at such times as he rode breakneck to town. He rode the old route he had used to take, through Swede-town over to Elm Street and down past the Kesslers' and the Peavys' and the Methodist parsonage to Main.

Mrs. Kessler complained of it to Mrs. Peavy.

"That fellow who killed my little dog is back again. I don't know why they ever let him out of the asylum. He simply terrifies me."

"I know," Mrs. Peavy said. "Mother sits by the parlor window all day with her fancywork, and she notices him every time he gallops by. She says, 'There goes that boy that killed Evelyn's little Bonnie.'"

"My darling, darling little Bonnie! I still cry for Bonnie on days when I feel low."

"You know, Evelyn, the queerest thought crossed my mind the other day. We're just kitty-corner from the parsonage, and that Stevens boy is always gawking in there as he gallops by. I wonder if he's *sweet* on Jenny Walden."

"I shouldn't wonder," Mrs. Kessler said. "He isn't the only male in town who's crazy in *that* direction. Well, he can have her for all of me. How's her ankle coming on?"

"I guess it's pretty bad. Mama says the doctor's still calling every day. I haven't taken anything in to her yet. It seems like there are enough Methodists to keep them in cakes and pies."

"I'm going to have my husband speak to Dr. Hawkins about that Stevens boy again. He ought to be sent back where they had him."

"Well, I hope you can do something."

But Doc was not very responsive to Kessler's suggestions.

"What's he done?" he asked.

"Why, nothing, Willard, only he's riding up and down the streets the way he used to. I don't think they'd ought to have let him out."

"Maybe not," Doctor said, "but they're overcrowded and they don't think he needs confining."

"If you said the word, doc, they'd probably take him back."

"Look here," Doc said, "so far as I know the fellow's been behaving himself. You can't put a man in the crazy house for galloping his horse. I'd be there myself if that was the only qualification." They laughed, and Kessler said apologetically:

"You're right, Willard. The fact of the matter is, I came because my wife insisted."

Doc threw his arm affectionately about Kessler's shoulders.

"Never let your wife insist, man. When a woman begins to insist, take her across your knee. It's a sure cure."

"Well, I tried that once—a long time ago," said Kessler a little ruefully.

They both began to laugh.

"I know! I know! They're all alike! Now *you're* the one who gets spanked, eh? And I'll bet you like it!"

"Well, not especially," said Mr. Kessler.

They slapped each other on the back, and parted in the friendliest manner.

10

HUGH DID NOT TRY to avoid calling on Jenny Walden again. It was very much easier to cease struggling. The day after the minister had come for him, Katherine said: "Now, Hugh, you won't forget to call on Miss Jenny today, will you? Even if she isn't very sick, you must go to see her for her father's sake. Since it's service that doesn't pay, it would seem niggardly if you skimped it."

"Yes, Katherine."

"Hugh, you are so good."

"I wish you would not say that."

"You never like to be praised, do you?"

"No," he said.

His quiet voice was almost savage, Katherine thought, the way he spoke to her. It was so difficult to please him!

He went about his morning duties with his usual methodical care. It was only towards afternoon that his pulse began to quicken and a fever of anticipation began to shake him. He would not admit to himself how, as the days went by, he was living more and more for the hour of the afternoon when he slipped into his coat and took up his medicine kit and swung briskly up the street to the parsonage. If he had been driving just before his visit to Jenny, he left the horse and buggy at the livery stable, for there was no use in advertising to the neighbors how long he cared to stay. They might not understand how innocent it all was. His visit to the Waldens was always the last one of the day, and, if the company was pleasant, there was nothing to which he need hurry away, except one of Katherine's English suppers. He did not allow himself to think of what he was doing, because for the first time in his life he had begun to feel rather than to think. The novelty of happiness was too magnificent to be tainted by thought. He no longer questioned his presumption in taking so much of Jenny's time, because her eyes told him that he was welcome—and expected. It was tedious for her, lying there. If he could do anything to make her happier . . .

After a while Jenny was sitting up in bed with pillows at her back, and there was scarcely any need for taking her pulse or looking at her ankle, but they went gravely through the pretense of a daily examination as a prelude to the talking and the reading. There was not so much pain now, and she was sleeping and eating well. There was a warm color on her lips and a kind of bloom or luster on her cheeks which was difficult to describe. Someone had knit her a little bed jacket that was the color of her eyes, and sometimes she did surprising things to her beautiful hair. Now it was piled high on top of her head; now it hung heavy and bright about her shoulders; now she made it into a sleek circlet of braids like a crown.

"I see the hairdresser has been here today."

"I'm practicing on myself. I think I shall be a professional hairdresser. Wouldn't that be fun? Then I'll get a job as lady's maid to a beautiful and famous actress and she will take me with her on all of her tours."

"Fancy how the Ladies' Aid would react to that!"

"That's one of the most delightful aspects of the thing!"

One day, when he came, he saw that she had been writing something, and that she hastily folded the paper and put it under her pillow.

"You are hiding something from me."

"How clever you are!" she mocked.

"Very well, if you insist upon having secrets."

"I don't mind telling you—I was trying to write a poem. It's harder than it sounds."

"Will you let me read it?"

"I don't think so. It isn't very good."

"How shall I believe that unless I read it?"

"You must accept my word."

"But authors are rarely the best critics. At least you might tell me what it is about."

"It is about what all poor poets first begin to write of."

"What is that?"

"It is about love. I don't think that that would interest you."

"What do you know about—love?" he asked.

"Not so much as you, I suspect," said Jenny, flashing him a quick glance, "because you are married."

His face darkened. "You are mistaken," he said. "I know nothing about love."

"Does not marriage teach one?"

"Some marriages do not."

"I think it would be a pity never to know love."

He turned his head aside and said nothing.

"Perhaps I shall write a poem to spring some time, and then I'll let you read that. Aren't spring and love the two things amateur poets write of?"

"I should rather hear what you had said about love."

"It doesn't even scan very well. You'd think it is silly."

"I promise not."

"Before you read it?"

"Before I read it."

"But, of course, that's the wrong answer, because I wouldn't want you to read it with your mind made up in advance."

"You are hard to please."

"Do you care whether or not you do?"

"Yes."

There was a silence. Then he said in a low voice, "Was *that* the right answer?"

"Yes."

"Then I may read the poem?"

She reached over and put the crumpled bit of paper in his pocket.

"When I am not with you," she said. "I couldn't bear to see your face when you read it. You might be amused."

When he was alone in the office, he took out the crumpled paper and read what she had written. Some words had been crossed out and others written above them. It had not sprung like Athene from her brain, but had been labored over with evidences of care.

Today there is not a wing in the sky
Not even the wing of a dove.
November is outside the window,
But I should be warm with love.
Like fire against a winter world,
Burning with clear, white light,
Love should warm my coldness
And star my night.

He read it three or four times, and then he folded it carefully and thrust it deep in his pocket. He thrust both of his hands in his pockets, too, to keep them from trembling, for it was suddenly as if he had been struck with a kind of palsy that shook his whole body with a violent trembling.

11

"I LIKED YOUR poem very much, Jenny." His voice was formal, and he had tried to make it fatherly. "The last line is short a foot, but I do not object to a slight irregularity of meter. It seems to me to emphasize the thought, making a climax to the last line."

She flushed. It was not the first time he had seen that delicate flood of rose rush up her cheek.

"Of course, you understand it's something I made up," she laughed. "I've never been in love, and I never intend to be. I shall go on keeping house in parsonages for years and years and years, making thin ends meet and struggling with bad plumbing. Then I shall probably take in boarders, or maybe I'll keep cats. Yes, that will be it! I'll have dozens and dozens of cats. How many would you consider a good number?"

"I am not attracted by cats," he said gravely.

"Cats are very nice," chattered Jenny. "I understand that they are quite a solace to loveless old women."

His eyes rested with a deep gravity upon her flushed face, and he spoke in a low, intense voice.

"Someone will love you very much some day, Jenny. And, if you return his love, he will be happy. But I do not think that he will ever be able fully to realize how fortunate he is. It is only those standing outside in the snow who can appreciate the feast they see spread beyond the lighted window."

The flush had all drained away from Jenny's cheek, leaving it transparently pale. When she spoke again her voice was still light and hurried.

"You must learn to be facetious, really you must. It helps one over so many awkward situations."

Their eyes met for a long, still look of understanding, but the color did not return to their white faces. Still dwelling in her eyes, he reached for one of his books of poetry, which stood now, all of them, beside Jenny's bed. He opened it at random, and then, as travelers from unknown seas returning to ports which have been charted, his eyes came reluctantly to the page.

"But the trees grew taller and closer, immense in their wrinkling bark;

Dropping; a murmurous dropping; old silence and that one sound;
For no live creatures lived there, no weasels moved in the dark:
Long sighs arose in our spirits, beneath us bubbled the ground."

He broke off and said roughly:

"Continue to be facetious, Jenny—it is safe and becoming; but never abandon your dreams."

"I never intended to."

There were so many days when they trembled on the verge of the forbidden knowledge. They had learned to step very carefully, for instinct, or some inner wisdom which was not quite drowned by the dark surge of happiness, warned them of a border beyond which they must not go. There is a moment at the end of winter when the chill air trembles with gold. Could one but hold the perfection of that moment, before spring precipitates her unbridled torrents!

12

Mr. Walden came out of his study, his thin gray hair standing in untidy disorder above his brown, wrinkled forehead.

"I'm glad to catch you, doctor. Maybe you can give me a bit of advice."

"I shall be very glad to, if I can," said Hugh.

"By the way, how do you think Jenny's coming along?"

"Very well. I dare say that by Sunday she might sit up in a chair. It will be a change for her."

"She's a little fly-up-the-creek, doctor, as you've probably gathered. I think we've done pretty well to keep her in bed so long. It *is* a long time, isn't it?"

"I hadn't thought. An ankle mends slowly. She has been a good patient."

"You think she won't be lame?"

"I see no reason why she should be."

"I shouldn't like her to be handicapped in any way."

"No, that would be too bad."

"You have been good to us, doctor."

"Not at all."

"But what I wanted was not medical advice. I heard you coming downstairs and I thought: 'Here's a valued member of the congregation and a leader in the choir. I'll ask him.' You see, I'm wondering about the propriety of my next sermon."

"Indeed?" said Hugh uneasily.

"I am going to preach my next sermon on divorce, doctor," said Mr. Walden. "Do you consider that a proper subject for the pulpit?"

Hugh gave him a quick, startled look, but it was impossible to ascribe any ulterior motive to the owner of that gentle, innocent face.

"I suppose any topic is fit for the pulpit, if suitably treated."

"That's what I thought," smiled Mr. Walden. "You wonder why, out of all the fine inspirational matter in the world, I should select a disagreeable subject such as that, don't you, doctor?"

"I do not question your wisdom, Mr. Walden."

"No, but I feel I must justify myself a little, and I value your opinion, doctor. Divorce used not to be a thing to consider at all, but now one continually sees instances of it in the eastern papers. It seems as if the twentieth century which we are about to enter is to be an era of disregard for the marriage vows. Of course, there are times, God forgive us, when it is better not to mention a new sin for fear of fixing it in the public mind. But it seems now that it is time we spoke out from the pulpits against divorce. You agree with me, don't you, doctor?"

"Yes," said Hugh slowly. "I agree with you. Yet, sometimes one wonders in particular cases, when two people are wholly unsuited to each other and there can only be unhappiness on either side—"

"Well, but look closely at most of those cases, doctor. Isn't it true that the unhappiness usually arises with the advent of a third person and the consequent thrusting up of an ugly lust of the flesh? Pardon me for using strong words, but you are a medical man and understand such things."

"Yes, I understand them," said Hugh, "but they are not always ugly. I think they might be beautiful."

"You are broad-minded, doctor, and I admire you for that; but I believe that there are not a half-dozen people in this town who would take so liberal a view of divorce."

"Then perhaps you need hardly preach a sermon on it," said Hugh, trying to smile, while he felt a kind of empty sickness at the pit of his stomach.

"Well, that is what I am thinking. Is it necessary to discuss an unpleasant problem before we are aware of it in our midst? But I think we should be fortified against it, doctor, before the evil appears."

"Perhaps you are right," said Hugh. "I was always against it—I have only wondered sometimes—"

"I think I shall definitely use it," said Mr. Walden, dreamily retiring to the pleasant inner pastures of his mind. "Lines from the marriage service would make an admirable text, yes, an admirable text. *Whom God hath joined together, let no man put asunder.* You can see it, can't you, doctor? A good text, an admirable text."

"Yes, I dare say."

"There is only one other thing. We do have one divorced person in town. I should not like to appear to point the finger of scorn at an individual. But that all happened a long, long time ago. An old scandal. I don't think my sermon would seem to point to any particular case. It would be simply a preventive measure."

For no reason at all Hugh felt sick and shaken. He bowed formally to the minister and took his departure. *I must have an errand in the country next Sunday,* he thought. *I cannot sit in the choir looking down into Katherine's face and listen to a sermon on divorce.* He did not know why this was so, but it was so. He was familiar with the narrow view which the town took of unfaithfulness in marriage and of divorce. It had always been his own view, and, but for a blinding light that had recently filled his mind to the exclusion of all else, perhaps it still was. He was suddenly a stranger in his own mind. In a few weeks he seemed to have traveled far in an alien land.

13

ON SATURDAY NIGHT it rained, and on Sunday morning it was cold and dark with low clouds in the sky and wet leaves lying dark and sodden on the brilliant green of the lawns.

"I don't see why you must go just at church time to dress Mr.

Colver's leg, Hugh," complained Katherine. "With Miss Walden still absent from the choir, the music will be very thin."

"I am first of all a doctor, Katherine. They knew they would have to accept that when I joined the choir."

"But why couldn't you put off the long drive until after dinner?"

"Colver is a bachelor. He's all alone out there since his mother died. The dressing should be attended to. I don't like to leave him alone out there for too long."

She knew that it was of no use to argue with him. On the surface he was so mild and pliant, but she could never sway him if he had made up his mind.

"Well, please don't be late for dinner. I've a roast in the oven, and I shall make a Yorkshire pudding in the pan as soon as I come in from church."

"Yes, certainly, I shall be here."

He had an unexpected sense of freedom as he left the house. He went to the livery stable, and stood in the thick scent of horses and harness oil and hay while they put his horse into the shafts for him. He stood quietly warm with a secret knowledge yet unnamed, and he did not let himself think ahead. When the horse was harnessed he got into the buggy and took up the reins. He drew the lap robe about his knees and spoke quietly to the horse.

Mud was heavy on the country roads, and the wheels continually flung particles of it against the side of the buggy with a fine staccato sound. Under the heavy clouds the mountains were the deepest purple, and they had come close about the town today and looked down upon it like docile giants.

Hugh's breath and the breath of the horse made little fitful clouds of gray mist that faded into the chill air. Behind him in the town he heard the church bells ringing. Under the heavy sky they had an ominous sound, like the voices of the righteous pronouncing sentence upon the unrighteous. They swelled and faded upon the air, varying only the volume of their sound, not its reiterated warning. But still he felt free and glad in the fresh November morning.

It did not take Hugh long to dress Colver's knee. The man had been peeling fence poles in the wooded land at the back of his farm, and the ax had slipped on a knot and given him an ugly cut. Hugh felt a little stab of guilt as he removed the dressing. It could have waited until Monday, and his honesty told him so; but his honesty was not equal this morning to penetrating any deeper into his own motives. He spent a few moments chatting with Colver. The man was a clean-faced, upright fellow with a mind uncomplicated and at peace. Hugh had sometimes envied him that. When he came to town, Colver used to bring around his best eggs and sometimes a dressed chicken to sell to Katherine at her back door. He was like the countrymen of England: simple and upright, with a dignity of his own which never presumed above its station. The inside of his house was as neat and tidy as if he had had a woman in it.

"Your floors are almost as shiny as my wife's, Colver," said Hugh.

The farmer smiled. "Yes, I see Mrs. Allerton is a good housekeeper, doctor," he said. "She's never afraid to let a fellow in her back door. My mother was a good housekeeper, too. When she was old I used to keep things up for her the way she liked them. I guess I got the habit."

"A good habit, I dare say, but you ought not to live here all alone, Mr. Colver. I'm surprised a man who loves his home as you seem to do hasn't married long before this."

"Well, you see, doctor, I had my mother with me until last year. That's why I didn't marry before. My mother had had a hard row to hoe, doctor, and for twenty-five years I tried to make it up to her. I'll tell you how it was, doctor . . ." The farmer launched into a long recital of family misfortune to which Hugh only half attended. He was thinking: *I'm going to be early in town. Church won't be over yet.* When at last Colver had finished he looked expectantly at the doctor for some comment.

"I understand," said Hugh absently, "but I still think it must be lonely for you. Perhaps you will marry yet."

"I've thought of it," said Colver; "but then again, maybe I'm too old now."

"Old? I'd say you were about my age—not much older surely. Is that too old for love?" Hugh was interested at last.

"That's what I wondered. You're happily married, doctor. You ought to know."

"Yes," Hugh said. "Yes, of course." He arranged the contents of his bag carefully and neatly and snapped it shut. Then he said: "But I do not think it entirely too late, Mr. Colver. Many men make the mistake of marrying too young—before they know what they want."

"Well, I don't know," the farmer said. "I haven't seen the right woman yet, I guess." He laughed apologetically.

"The right woman," Hugh repeated. "You believe that there is a right woman for every man?"

"That's what they say," Colver said. "I guess it's true."

"I believe you are right."

Hugh felt happy as he went away. It was as if he had been able to speak to someone of Jenny. It was as if he had said: "Look at her. Isn't she beautiful? Isn't she gay and good? Is there any woman more perfect?" And the other person had replied: "No, there is none above her."

It was only a quarter after eleven when Hugh again reached the outskirts of town. He knew that he had timed his excursion badly. There was still time to slip into the back of the church for the sermon if he had been determined to hear it.

A little pulse began to throb in his temple, for he could not avoid the thought that Jenny would be alone and later today she would be sitting up in a chair. There were not so many more days left when he should have the right to visit her. He did not stop to leave the horse at the livery stable and walk to the house. There would not have been time enough for that. He tied the horse to the hitching post in front of the house, and ran up the porch steps. He no longer stood on ceremony at the parsonage, but gave the bell a quick twist and walked in. From the bottom of the stairs he called: "It's your medical adviser, Miss Jenny Walden. May I come up?"

"Oh, do!" cried Jenny. "How wonderful to see you when you weren't expected! What gave you such a beautiful idea?"

"A flash of inspiration."

"You have brought the outdoors with you!"

"I'll take off my coat. It's enough to chill the house."

"No, let me touch it first, to see if winter has really come."

Smiling at her, he went near the bed, and she laid her little hand on the worn buffalo fur. "Yes, winter is here."

"Do you mind?"

"No. What do I smell? Is it antiseptic or horses?"

"Both," he said, laughing. He was very happy.

"I like that combination."

"Because it reminds you of old Doc Hawkins?"

"No, there are other reasons."

"You have your wrapper on."

"I made Mrs. Mills give it to me this morning before she went to church. I was waiting for you to come and help me into my chair. Think of being out of this dreadful bed for an hour."

"You have been a good patient, but soon you will be walking everywhere. You will have no more need of a doctor."

They looked at each other for a long moment.

"Will you help me up now?" Her eyes fell away from his, and she began to lower her feet experimentally to the floor.

"Wait. I must put a blanket into the chair. Where are your slippers?"

"At the foot of the bed."

"May I help you with them?"

"Yes."

"You have little feet like a child's. Did I ever tell you that?"

"No. Are you making fun of them?"

"I do not make fun."

"Why not?"

"If I had met you a long time ago, I might have learned how."

"How odd it feels to have my feet on the floor again! How shall I do this? I feel as helpless as a baby."

"Put your hand on my shoulder. I'll help you to support your weight. You need only take a step. Soon it will all seem natural again."

"How horridly weak I feel! What is the matter with me?"

"You have been in bed a long time. Would you rather wait another day or two?"

"No, of course not!"

She put her hand on his shoulder and he half slipped his arm about her to help her to rise. When she had taken her first step, she swayed a little bit against him.

If the tongue touch winter steel, if the hand make contact with a live wire, there is no undoing either. They must cling together with the terrible necessity of forces stronger than flesh.

So now Hugh took her in his arms, and they were together like one thing with a strong, hot current flowing through them. So they stood together for a long time, and it was for this that she had waited, and for this that he had crossed the sea from England to Idaho. It was for this that they had been born so far apart and had been traveling through dissatisfaction and unhappiness and darkness for so long.

At last he felt her tremble, and he put her gently into the chair.

"Oh, my dearest, forgive me! Forgive me, Jenny. I have lost my reason."

"No, no, Hugh. It had to be. Sometime. Sometime."

He knelt beside her and laid his head against her breast.

"Jenny, I love you."

She held his face close to her with her two hands.

"What lovely words!"

"Can you say them?"

"I love you! I love you!"

"Keep saying them forever."

"Like a parrot?"

"No. But I can never hear them enough."

"We have been starving."

"Kiss me. There is only a moment and we are insane to do this."

How quickly the clock ticks off a kiss!

"No, not insane, Hugh. It is the first beautiful thing I have had."

"I am older than you are."

"Does that matter to you?"

"No, but it must to you—"

"Nothing matters but that we have found each other."

"You are the thing I have wanted all my life, and I did not know until I met you what it was."

"Hugh, when did you first begin to love me?"

"Does it matter?"

"Yes, I must know."

His turbulent mind went back, and suddenly he knew when.

"It was the first time we rode together in the sleigh, and you told me about being lost in the snow and riding home in Dr. Hawkins' coat. I was jealous of Hawkins then."

She drew his head against her breast again. She was laughing softly.

"But I loved you long before that," she said. "It was the day you were hanging your sign, and the wind blew your hair, and you looked so sturdy and sure and yet so sort of unprotected, too. I couldn't help loving you after that."

"And you thought you would protect me?" he whispered.

For a moment she did not answer, and when she did her voice had become serious.

"No, I knew that whatever I could do for you would not be good, but I couldn't help it. Oh! I couldn't help it!"

"Nor I, Jenny—dearest!"

They heard the clock striking twelve.

"Go quickly," she said. "They will be coming from church."

"Yes, I will go."

"When shall I see you again?"

"I must think, but it will be soon."

"Oh, don't forget me for a moment, will you?"

"I could not if I tried. You are around my heart and soul."

"But you will not think that we are wrong? Not today, Hugh?"

"Not today, Jenny—not today."

He was just driving down the street to the livery stable when the church doors opened to let out the final strains of the postlude. So much can happen in so short a time! As he drove down the street he saw nothing of the muddy wooden sidewalks, the dusty store windows, the dull-eyed people who walked in Sunday clothes; but in a kind of amazement he kept saying over and over to himself:

"I have never known what it was to be happy before this. Nothing must happen to spoil it for a few days. Only a few days more for all the meaningless years I've had and the ones that will come! What if I shut my eyes for a few days more! When she is well, she will forget me, and I shall have had this. The one thing in my life worth living for."

14

THE NOVEMBER DAYS were short, and twilight was the sweetest time of the day, before the lamps were lighted and Mr. Walden came out of his study to make supper with a great clattering of pans and skillets in the kitchen. It was such a brief time—only a few moments in which to express the unsaid things which lay like shining waters between them.

On the Monday afternoon Hugh found Jenny sitting in a chair downstairs.

"Look at her!" cried Mr. Walden. "You'd never know she had been hurt. You've done a good job, doctor, and never lost the roses from her cheeks. You'll pardon a doting old father if I say she's pretty, won't you?"

"I'm afraid I shall have to agree with you," said Hugh. "But how did she get down the stairs?"

"I carried her myself," said the minister. "Bad as my knees are, I thought she wanted a change of scene. I've done without her long enough. We must have her up on crutches now, and without them as soon as possible. You won't have to give us much more of your valuable time, doctor."

"No. She will not need me much longer."

"But it's not right that papa should have to carry me," cried Jenny. "I told him so today, and how he is to get me up the stairs again is more than I can imagine."

"Now, Jenny, don't exhibit my infirmities. I can still go up and down stairs."

"But not carrying me."

Hugh said: "I can at least do that. I can carry her up and down stairs for you, Mr. Walden."

"You've done more than enough already, doctor. If you would let me pay you—"

"I have been paid," said Hugh.

Mr. Walden sat with them that day, chatting as garrulously as a child on a holiday.

"Papa, you don't seem to be worrying about your sermon this week."

"No," laughed the minister, "I think I'll dip into the barrel of old sermons this time. I gave them such a stinger yesterday, 'twill take them a week to recover."

"You preached—on divorce?"

"I did indeed, doctor, and I'm afraid I shocked them just a little. Next week I shall give them *green pastures* and *still waters* to compensate."

"I don't know why you should have encouraged the narrow views this town already holds, papa," said Jenny. "What is so wicked about divorce?"

"Now, now, I got it all out of my system yesterday, dear. I don't mean to preach it all over again to you today. I've never been very good at preaching in my own family, doctor. That's why Jenny here has grown up as wild as a young hare. I deplore the fact, doctor, but the Lord knows that's where my fatal weakness lies."

"Papa, that's why you're so funny and dear," said Jenny. "I'd have run away with the circus years ago, if I'd had a father who preached at me when he was out of the pulpit."

"Hold your tongue, dear, and I'll go and make us a pot of tea to celebrate your being downstairs."

When he had gone to the kitchen with a sound of clattering and banging of cupboard doors and pans, Hugh and Jenny looked at each other in silence.

After the silence had grown long and warm with the unspoken things, Hugh said in a low, husky voice:

"Have you ever gone downstream in a boat, Jenny?"

"No. Is it something I should have done?" Her eyes were quiet on his face, as if she were memorizing his eyes, his hair, the little gentle lines about his mouth, and he saw that she only half attended to his words.

"When I was a student in England, I used sometimes to go boating on the river during a holiday. Sometimes I would stop rowing and let the current take me, and it was pleasant to go like that, making no effort to strive against the current, and seeing familiar landmarks on the shore slip by without minding that they fell behind."

"Why do you remember now?"

"Because we are like that, Jenny. It is so easy to drift with the current and feel the sunshine and the sweet air. But somewhere ahead of us lies the sea."

"So it be deep enough, Hugh. That is all I care."

"Ah, Jenny, there is no one like you—no one in all the world!" His voice had sunk to a whisper.

"You are complaining of me?"

"No, I am complaining of all the years of blindness and darkness when I have gone like a mole without knowing the sun."

"Now they are over."

"Just for a moment. That's why my eyes dazzle so. The dark will close in again."

"We must never let it."

"No, no! We must never let it. But I have not dared to plan, Jenny. What is there for us?"

"Hush! Hush! The boat is still afloat, Hugh. Let it drift as long as it can."

"I'm not very good at brewing tea," said Mr. Walden. "Coffee I can make, but tea seems to need a woman's touch. However, I'll waste no apologies, but let you make the best of it with sugar and milk to suit your taste."

It was any tea party at any parsonage.

"I'm tired now," said Jenny, when they had finished drinking tea. "Dr. Allerton, you won't mind carrying me up to my room, will you?"

"No, Miss Walden," said Hugh.

She was so light, so golden, and her head lay against his shoulder . . .

15

IT WAS ALMOST a week later and Mrs. Peavy, Mrs. Larkin, and Mrs. Kessler were sitting at one side of a circle of ladies in the basement of the Presbyterian church, stitching on infants' garments to be sent to one of the new mission stations in China. Anna Hawkins was there that day, too, although she didn't often come. She had her own private opinion of Foreign Missions, which was all of a piece with her feeling that everybody should be let alone to settle his own affairs in his own way, but she was always willing to stitch diapers and hem

shirts for heathen babies if she were not asked to bend their minds
in unnatural directions. Anna sat on the other side of the circle and
at first she didn't pay any attention to what the three women were
saying.

"It's the queerest thing about Jenny Walden's ankle," began
Mrs. Kessler. "It must be a most difficult break."

"How do you mean?" asked Mrs. Larkin.

"Well, I mean with all *my* record of ill health, I have never kept
a physician dancing attendance on me every day as that little Walden
girl has succeeded in doing with her broken ankle. Dr. Allerton
has been to see Jenny every day since she fell. I mean *every day*.
Isn't that so, Louisa?"

"There was only one day we didn't see him," said Mrs. Peavy
with restraint. "Of course our house is kitty-corner, and mother
spends quite a bit of time by the window with her house plants and
her bird. It's possible she might have missed him that day."

"How funny! I heard she was getting along all right."

"Tell her about last Sunday, Louisa. The whole thing seems so
queer."

"Well, you know mama had a cold last Sunday, and she didn't go
to church; but she wasn't bad enough to be in bed, and she sat there
by the window, and she says Dr. Allerton visited Jenny during
church time. His horse was tied in front of the parsonage for nearly
an hour, and just before church let out, he came out of the house and
drove away. Jenny must have been all alone there, for mama saw
Mrs. Mills leave for church before he came."

"I thought he sang in the choir."

"He must have had a country call." The three ladies laughed.

The part of the circle nearest to them had fallen silent to listen.
Anna, who had been silent before they began to talk, went on stitching with lowered head.

"Jenny sings in the choir, too, you know, when she's up," observed
Mrs. Larkin.

"There's another funny thing," said Mrs. Kessler. "My hired girl is a Methodist, and what do you suppose Mr. Walden preached about last Sunday according to her?"

"What?"

"Divorce!"

"Well, you mean—"

"Oh, nothing, of course. Only how funny, as if he thought there were any need to preach about divorce in this town! There's only Mrs. Shanley, and it's late to begin on her. He must know someone else who needs such a sermon."

"No!"

"Well thank our Heavenly Father, that kind of thing don't go on among the Presbyterians."

"It's a dreadful thing for Mrs. Allerton, though. Someone ought to warn her."

Anna's voice cut in sharply. Her eyes were blazing.

"You are making a mistake to let this talk go so far, ladies," she said. "Dr. Allerton is a very high-principled man, and Jenny a good girl. Because she is an independent piece, it's quite silly the way folks make talk about her."

The three women looked at Anna with lifted brows. Here was another independent piece. Anna Hawkins had never been one of them, in spite of her husband having so many friends in town. Her own reputation might bear a little watching, the way she was always being seen with her husband's assistant.

"Where there's smoke, Anna, there's apt to be fire," said Mrs. Kessler coldly.

The three women said no more that afternoon, but perhaps they went over it more thoroughly in their minds for having their tongues silenced.

It was odd that Anna should have been one of the first to hear it, because she so seldom went out in the feminine hotbeds where gossip flourished.

She folded her sewing and put it neatly in her bag, and, brushing the lint and ravelings from her skirt, she stood up to go.

"Aren't you going to have coffee with us, Mrs. Hawkins?" asked the minister's wife.

"I don't believe I will today, thank you," said Anna.

She had not thought of it before, but now that she had heard the women talking several things came into her mind. Twice she herself had seen Hugh going to the Waldens', and she remembered that after the first week Doctor had never had to give much attention to his fracture cases. And there had been that day a few weeks ago when Katherine had told her how Hugh had forgotten to make a call, and how the minister had had to come and fetch him in the evening.

"I was so mortified," Katherine had said, "because, you know, Hugh never charges a fee of the minister. And how awkward that he should have seemed to be negligent! And it seems that Miss Jenny was dreadfully upset." But, of course, if he had forgotten, it meant that there was nothing to the women's gossip. Yet Anna feared gossip for its own sake.

Shut in on all sides by the mountains, she knew how deadly gossip in Opportunity could be, how fast it could run. It was not the women's facts which troubled Anna. The most incriminating facts could often be explained away, but it was the tone and the malicious light in the eye which alarmed her.

She did not want Katherine to hear this gossip, because it would hurt and humiliate her; and she did not want Doctor to hear it, because she was afraid that he would use it as a weapon against Allerton. She had heard him say: "Just you wait. There's one way you can get a damned goody-goody feller like Allerton. Some day he'll go sweet on a woman." But she reflected that Doctor was fairly impervious to gossip. He was too engrossed in himself, and in the panorama of life which unfolded every day in his practice, to give ear to rumor.

With Katherine it was different. She lived an isolated life, but her mind was sufficiently empty, so that a suspicion would have room to grow.

It was not in Anna's nature to interfere in other people's affairs; but she couldn't help thinking how defenseless Katherine was—and how pitiful. Anna had seen the gossips of town in full cry before, and she had seen sturdier women than Katherine go down under the impact of neighborly suspicions.

Anna did not sleep very well that night. She never liked to act on impulse, and it took her all of the next morning to make up her mind to see Dr. Allerton. But by afternoon she had decided. She put on her coat and hat and went down Ash Street to Main and down Main to Dr. Allerton's office.

It seemed odd going into another doctor's office—like being in the camp of the enemy. She had a guilty and embarrassed feeling. She noted that his window curtains needed washing. Perhaps she could drop a hint to Katherine some day. Katherine did not think of such things.

Dr. Allerton had just come in. He was hanging up the buffalo coat on the rack behind the door and whistling softly to himself. The sight of the old coat brought an unaccountable lump into Anna's throat. She tried to fix her mind upon the fact that he was whistling. She hadn't known he was a whistling man. Somehow it surprised and disarmed her. There was a secret look of happiness upon his face that faded as he turned to her. Anna was sorry to see it fade. It changed his face completely.

"Why, Mrs. Hawkins!" he said. "Is there something I can do for you?"

"I came," she said, "about—about Katherine."

"About Katherine?" he repeated. Then he said: "You have been kind to her, Mrs. Hawkins. I appreciate that very much. She needs friends. I think you are the only one she has here."

"I'm fond of Katherine. I believe I understand her. You'll think I am a busybody, doctor, but I've come to try and help you both."

"Yes?"

She saw the guarded look on his face, and she was almost sorry that she had come. She knew that he was surprised at her visit, perhaps even a little alarmed. Doctor would have damned any woman to hell and back who had come interfering in his affairs. But she was less afraid of that than of this man's cool reserve. She began to speak rapidly, to get it over with.

"You're from England, Dr. Allerton. I don't know how they are in small towns there. But here in Opportunity folks' amusement comes pretty largely from watching other folks' affairs. I thought you ought to know that this town is a hotbed of gossip, doctor."

"A hotbed of gossip?" he repeated stupidly, as if he did not comprehend.

"Dr. Allerton," she said desperately, "maybe it's none of my business, but I thought you ought to know. They're talking about *you*."

The color had drained from his face, but he was not angry with her. His voice was quiet.

"Mrs. Hawkins, gossip can no longer touch me."

There was a constrained silence in the office. At last Anna said hesitantly, "It can still touch your wife, Dr. Allerton."

"My wife?" he said.

"I think the people who talk have not reached her yet. I wanted you to know before they do. That's why I came."

"I thank you, Mrs. Hawkins."

Anna found that she was trembling as she walked up the hill towards home.

"Don't be a fool," she said to herself. "That's what you get for interfering in other people's business. It's as Constant says: we're not actors, he and I. I should have left it as it was." She kept seeing the look of secret happiness on Dr. Allerton's face, and how it had drained away. She had not realized that his face could hold as much life and beauty as she had seen in that unguarded moment. He had stopped whistling, too. It was fanciful of her to think so, but she felt as if she had awakened him from a beautiful dream to a cold reality.

16

THAT AFTERNOON Katherine received a letter. It was not often that she had one with an American stamp, for most of her letters came from England. She tore this one open and read it two or three times before she began to realize what it meant; even then she could not really understand it.

Dear Mrs. Allerton:

Do you know that your husband is still visiting a patient who isn't sick any more? This is just a word of warning from

A well-wishing friend.

Frightened and confused, Katherine thought over all of Hugh's patients, and Jenny Walden was the only one she could think of who might fit. But Jenny was just a little girl, and Hugh was—Hugh was nearly forty—and Jenny was the minister's daughter. And why did the person who wrote the letter not dare to sign a name? There could be nothing to it at all. It was utterly ridiculous. Someone trying to throw suspicion upon a good man whose faults were so few that the malicious must invent them.

Still it was horrible to think that there might be something in it. Hugh—continuing his calls when there was no need for them! But, if it were Jenny Walden they meant, then, of course, he went to see her father. They were the best of friends, and Mr. Walden was a fine, good man. But why did he not tell his wife that he still went to the Waldens'? The answer, of course, was that it seemed so unimportant to him that he had never mentioned it.

Katherine began to cry, and then she took the letter and burned it in the stove, and then she washed her face and felt momentarily better. But the very uneventfulness of her life made this small, malicious puzzle loom large. Should she tell Hugh about the letter and ask him what it meant? But she could see the cool scorn in his eyes and hear the quiet voice. *"You would believe that twaddle, Katherine?"*

"Oh, no, Hugh! Never! Never!"

"Then why should you mention it?"

Oh, no, she could not speak to him about the letter. She must simply forget about it herself, for it was nothing, nothing at all. Hugh had always been good to her and he always would be. There had never been anything in the past. She knew that she could trust him. She felt that little angry pulse of pain beginning to throb in her head.

By the time that Hugh came home Katherine had gone to bed with one of her devastating nervous headaches. The table was set for his supper, and everything laid out where he could find it. When she heard him come in, she called to him from the bedroom.

"Oh, Hugh, you'll find your supper. I had to go to bed, dear."

"You are ill, Katherine?"

"Oh, yes, it's my head again, Hugh. I've been vomiting dreadfully, and the pain is so awful. You must give me a little morphine, dear; otherwise I can't bear it through the night."

"You know that I don't like to do that, Katherine."

"Oh, please, dear, please! I can't bear it without."

He came and stood beside her bed. He hated her when she was like this. She was so frightened of pain, it filled him with disgust.

"Katherine, you are not very brave."

"You don't know," she cried. "You've never had pain like this yourself." She turned her face away from him, the tears running unheeded from under the heavy eyelids.

Could it be true? she thought. *Oh, surely, surely not! Oh, my head, my head is killing me!*

He stood very still looking down at the blotched white face, the straying black hair, and the purple blemish which at these times seemed always to take on a deeper hue. Then he went back into the dining room and fetched his bag. Slowly and deliberately he laid out a clean towel on the bedside table, and on it he put the little bottle of alcohol, the vial of morphine, and the hypodermic syringe. As he made these familiar preparations for relieving pain, a clear white thought illumined his mind with a sudden intense vitality. It was the strangest thought that he had ever had, but it took him so unaware that he did not immediately draw back from it.

If he gave her too much morphine, he thought, she would die very easily and comfortably. She would never know how little he had loved her—he could spare her that. No one else would know either. Say she had died in her sleep, a stroke perhaps, or a failure of the heart muscle to contract. He was the doctor, he could say what he liked. No one would know.

He saw it all very simply. It would solve so many problems. He and Jenny could be happy—and no one would know—no one would ever know. And then he thought: *Doc Hawkins would know!*

Hugh's hand began to tremble. The luminous moment passed, and he was filled with a deep sense of fear and horror. A doctor's business was to save life, to give life. He had never before trembled on the verge of the desire to take it. Now he looked at that desire yawning beneath him, black and bottomless, and a physical sickness went over him. He thought, *There is only one life that a doctor can take—only one that belongs to him.*

"Hugh," she cried fretfully, turning her head upon the pillow. "Hugh, why are you standing there? Why don't you do something to ease my suffering?"

"I'm just filling my syringe, Katherine," he said.

After she was asleep, he went out in the back yard, and paced up and down the brick walk that led to the woodshed. Through the black horror in his mind was a flaming column of shame. He had thought first of Dr. Hawkins. Before the awakening of his own conscience, of his own moral sense, had come his fear of the other doctor. His guilty personal fear of discovery had rushed forward before his sense of honor and of duty. He could scarcely believe it of

himself. The blades of grass that had grown up between the bricks
of the walk were stiff with frost. There was an apple tree beside
the walk, and one of its branches grazed his head as he passed under
it. Absently he reached up and broke the branch and threw it aside.
He walked back and forth in the cold starlight and he tried to reach
out once more to God as he had done in the past.

*O God, show me Thy face. In the depth of my iniquity, give me
a sign; if it is only to smite me, God, in my sin and my misery. O
God—O God Almighty, who knowest our sin and our unhappiness—*
But there was no sign, and the hand of vengeance did not fall.

When he was tired with walking, he went back into the house.
He went and stood beside Katherine's bed and looked at her, and the
tears ran down his cheeks. His heart was very heavy.

Finally he went into the parlor and sat down beside the marble-
topped table. The family Bible lay there between the pressed-glass
paperweight and the shell which some missionary had brought to
Katherine from the South Seas. He had not opened the Bible for a
long while; but now, with some idea that it would give him help, he
took it in his hands and held it closer to the narrow circle of rose-
tinted lamplight. He held the Book a moment in his hands, almost
afraid to open it. He remembered that his mother in the tenement
near the mills had taken the Bible thus into her hands in times of
stress and opened it at random for a sign from heaven. He had not
remembered her for a long time now.

Hugh put his finger between the pages and opened the Book. The
lamplight fell upon the page and the heavy type glittered and swam
before his eyes.

*By night on my bed I sought him whom my soul loveth: I sought
him but I found him not. . . . Saw ye him whom my soul loveth?
. . . I held him, and would not let him go, until I had brought him
into my mother's house, and into the chamber of her that conceived
me. . . . Thy lips are like a thread of scarlet, . . . thy temples
are like a piece of a pomegranate within thy locks. . . . Thy two*

breasts are like two young roes that are twins, which feed among the lilies. . . . I sleep, but my heart waketh: it is the voice of my beloved that knocketh, saying, Open to me, my sister, my love, my dove, my undefiled . . . Who is she that looketh forth as the morning, fair as the moon, clear as the sun, and terrible as an army with banners? . . . How fair and how pleasant art thou, O love, for delights! . . . His left hand should be under my head, and his right hand should embrace me. . . . Set me as a seal upon thine heart, as a seal upon thine arm: for love is strong as death . . . Many waters cannot quench love, neither can the floods drown it.

When he had finished reading, he sat on, white and trembling, and there was a rushing sound in his ears like the beating of wings. He turned the lamp low and half rose to blow it out, and then he sat on in darkness, alone and despairing, in a house without light.

17

BY MORNING KATHERINE's headache had gone, but she was still pale and querulous. She saw that Hugh had not slept in his bed last night, and this frightened and confused her.

"Hugh," she said, "you went out after you gave me the morphine. You left me all alone here!"

He came to the bedroom door from the kitchen where he had been starting the coffee. The smell of the freshly ground bean came poignant and clear, and there was the smell and crackle of twigs and kindling stirring in the cookstove.

"No, Katherine," he said gravely, "I did not go out. I was here all night."

"You didn't sleep in your bed. That seems very odd."

"I sat by the table reading. I fell asleep in my chair."

"How am I to believe that? You could go away and leave me while I have the morphine, and I would never know."

"I can only give you my word, Katherine."

She began to brush her hair. She could not bear to look at her own face in the mirror this morning, knowing its pallor, the circles under the eyes, the ugly welt of purple. A wave of futile anger swept over her, and words rushed out that she had meant to hold in.

"Hugh, you aren't going to see that Walden girl again, are you? Isn't she well now? Must you keep visiting her?"

He showed no surprise at her words. His voice was as quiet and steady as ever.

"Yes, she is quite well. I shan't see her again after today."

"But in the choir! You'll see her in the choir."

"Do you want me to give up the choir, Katherine?"

"Oh, no! no!" Suddenly she began to cry. "No, I don't want you to give up the choir; but, I don't know, I feel so badly this morning."

"A cup of coffee will help you. You must pull yourself together now, Katherine."

They ate breakfast in silence. Outside they could hear the rushing of the wind and see the last leaves hurrying by the window on their way to winter.

After her coffee Katherine felt better. She was desperately sorry for what she had said. When she saw Hugh putting on his coat she went to him, twisting her hands.

"I didn't mean what I said, Hugh. Will you forgive me?"

"There is nothing to forgive, Katherine," he said. "I think that you have fewer faults than most of us."

He did not pat her shoulder or lean to kiss her cheek as he used to do.

As he went out the door a rush of dead leaves came in and whirled about her immaculate hallway in a kind of frenzied dance.

"Oh, we are getting old," thought Katherine, "and what have we had? Oh, what have we had?" She left the leaves lying where they were, for this morning she did not care if the hall was untidy or not.

18

THE COLD AIR BRACED Hugh for the day. All of his muscles felt tired as from a long test of physical endurance, but the wind was a tonic to them. He made his usual rounds and attended the office routine with methodical care, but at the back of his mind he left untouched and unexplored the warm, bright spot that burned there. He had formed a resolution which must be carried through, and he knew that the warm, bright spot must be walled up and forgotten. There was only one last time when he could see her alone—that was a necessity for both of them.

He did not try to conceal his last visit to Jenny, although he knew that the neighbors must have been watching him or Mrs. Hawkins would not have come to his office and spoken as she had. And even Katherine must know, from what she had said this morning. He went up openly with his black bag in his hand, but he *did* know that Mr. Walden would be out, for he had seen him go by the office. Jenny was up now all day, getting around the house by herself.

He did not rap and walk in as usual, but rang the doorbell and stood waiting on the porch. Jenny came to the door, limping. Her eyes went suddenly soft and strange when she saw him.

"Oh, it's you—it's *you*! When I heard the doorbell I thought it was someone about hymnbooks or the church supper—something unimportant. Oh, Hugh!"

He closed the door and set his bag in the hall. He kept looking into her strange eyes and neither of them spoke.

Open to me, O my sister, my love . . .

"Jenny," he said at last in a husky voice. "I have come to say goodbye to you."

"Oh, no!" she said. She looked at him with fear now. "No, Hugh."

"There is no other answer, Jenny. I have faced them all."

"We could go away together. It is ours—our own."

"You would face that with me?" he said.

"Oh, yes!"

My dove, my undefiled.

He took both of her hands, and now he looked at them instead of into her eyes. They were small and soft. It was almost as if they had no bones under the soft skin as they lay in his. He held them securely with his fingers, and his thumb moved along her wrist feeling the smoothness of it.

"We couldn't do it, Jenny," he said, "at the expense of other people."

"You are not afraid, Hugh?" she asked.

"Yes," he said, "I am afraid for two reasons. I am afraid for your happiness, Jenny—that I should be a blight on it."

"No, Hugh! *No!* My happiness will be you."

"I am thinking years ahead for you, Jenny—not now; and I am thinking of Katherine. Last night I had a terrible idea about Katherine. I thought that I might kill her and perhaps nobody would know."

She did not try to draw her hands away, but a tremor went through her. There was more firmness in her soft hands as he held them. She was thinking now as well as feeling.

"You see what I am afraid of, Jenny. We must end this now before we make a horror of something beautiful."

"Yes, it must be beautiful," said Jenny in a whisper. "It has always been beautiful to me, Hugh."

"To me, too, until last night, when there was—*that.*"

"Oh, yes!" she said. "Yes, we must say goodbye. But how are we to bear it? to see each other on the streets of town and know that we do not belong to each other?"

"We do belong to each other, ~~Jenny.~~ Can I make you understand that? That you are my first love and my last. That I am yours forever, ~~Jenny.~~"

"Sometimes it will be hard to remember, ~~Hugh.~~"

"When it is hard for you to remember, Jenny, then I want you to forget. I want you to have your own life."

"That wasn't what I meant. I meant, I'll want you, and I'll forget what you have said—I'll think you never loved me."

He had no answer for a moment. They stood close together in the cold hall, holding each other's hands, and darkness and pain crowded in upon them from all sides.

"Oh, Hugh," she said, "how strange that it should be just the two of us in all this world to come together like this and love each other!"

"Yes," he said, laying his cheek against her hair. "But, even if we can never have each other, I am glad it was so."

19

THAT WAS A LONG, bleak winter. The snow drifted and blew in the hollows and ridges of the mountains, and the dark days were without hope, and the clear, blue days when the light lingered on the high places were beyond enduring.

At Christmas time Lita Hawkins was married, and the town had never seen such a wedding. There were hats and laces and bolts of material from Spokane and Portland and Seattle; while hampers full of smilax and orange blossoms and calla lilies and freesias came up from California.

"Mama," Lita said, "I wish we didn't have to have the farmers and the plumbers and butchers and those long-haired, dirty old homesteaders at the wedding. I don't know what the Abercrombies will think."

"My dear, your father's giving you a splendid wedding. You must let him have the people he wants," Anna said.

"But after all, mama, I'm the one who's getting married—not papa."

"You're getting married, Lita, but I think it's your father's wedding. You wouldn't be having one like this if it weren't for him."

"It looks like he's trying to drum up practice, having all those horrible people in."

"No," Anna said, "it isn't that, Lita. He loves this town and all the people in it, and this is a kind of gesture to them. It may be his last for a while until times are easier and taxes lower."

"Mama, this wedding isn't really going to make a difference to you and papa, is it? We've always had everything. You and papa are going to be all right, aren't you?"

"Of course we are, Lita," Anna said. She put her hands on Lita's shoulders and kissed her.

Christina and Anna worked together over the details of the wedding reception. There were chicken salad and deviled eggs in chicken jelly and cold baked ham and tongue; pickles and relishes and preserves of all kinds; little soda biscuits stuffed with potted ham and a variety of warm raised breads and rolls; a huge wedding fruit cake and a crock of caraway-seed cookies, pound cakes iced with brown sugar frosting, and three freezers full of rich frozen custard. There were gallons of coffee, and Doctor had two big hampers of champagne packed in straw and shipped to him from the Coast.

Two of Christina's sisters came from the farm to help with the serving.

"Mis' Hawkins," Christina said shyly to Anna when they were alone in the kitchen for a moment on the morning of the wedding, "you t'ink you like one of my sisters to vork for you maybe?"

"Why, Christina? You're not thinking of leaving me?" asked Anna in surprise.

"Maybe I should get married, too, sometime, like Miss Lita."

"Christina!" Anna said. "Did Olaf get around to asking you?"

Christina buried her face in a convenient dish towel.

"Vell, vat you t'ink?" she cried between muffled bursts of laughter.

Anna left the biscuits she was cutting to put her arms around Christina and kiss her.

"I know you'll be happy, and he'll have the best little cook in town!"

"He ain't much good," said Christina happily, "but neither am I."

Anna denied this vigorously.

"You're the salt of the earth, Christina, both of you."

"You vant my sister, Mis' Hawkins? You have vich vun you vant. I teach her everyt'ing."

Anna thought quickly for a moment.

The weight of Christina's future was off her mind.

"No," she said. "There'll be only Doctor and Gene and me— maybe Gene will be going to his father. I think I'll get along alone, Christina. There are other good places in town for your sisters."

Christina understood.

"Sure, you get along," she said. "My sisters ain't vorth much anyway. Sometimes I'm not busy, I come in and help you, yust for fun, Mis' Hawkins."

It was a busy day with so many people coming and going, so much food to prepare, the doorbell ringing with presents being delivered, the groom's family arriving, the flowers to be arranged, the banisters twined with smilax, and Lita's dress and veil to be adjusted at the last moment before leaving for church. Anna put on her black silk dress and the diamond earrings, but she did not take time to look herself over carefully in the mirror. Too many more important things needed her attention.

Lita looked beautiful, and the church was filled; it was a successful wedding, and Anna was pleased for Doctor and for Lita. For herself she felt a little sad. Although she found that she liked the young man whom Lita was marrying, it was still hard to see another daughter going away to an unknown life in another town. But Anna was used to rationalizing things, and she thought: *It's better for her to be in another town. She'll be more independent and successful if she can't run in and borrow or get advice from me.*

As the reception drew to an end, Lita went to her room to prepare for the journey, and when Anna went in to say goodbye she found her in tears.

"What is it, Lita? I thought you were so happy."

"Oh, mama, look at yourself in the mirror—just look! You forgot to put on your lace collar. Everybody at the wedding could see your black dress turned in at the neck and the pins sticking in it."

Anna looked at herself in the mirror.

"I'm sorry, Lita," she said. "I guess you are right. I was so busy, I forgot."

"Oh, mama, honestly, how could you, dear? How could you?"

"I don't know, dear. I'm awfully sorry."

After Lita, in her handsome wine-red velvet suit with the short jacket and the big sleeves and the yards and yards of soutache braid around the skirt, had driven away with her husband in the station hack, Anna went back to the bedroom and picked up Lita's things. Sometimes she felt a pang of shamefaced disappointment in her children. It was not the mistakes they made nor the wrong enthusiasms, but the knowledge that they were small in understanding which hurt her. She had witnessed their petty resentments and intolerances with pity and sorrow; for, whatever her own limitations (and she knew that they were many), she had always tried to have a large view. She knew the beauty and the peace of wide horizons, of raising her eyes to the mountains when small things loomed too large, and she blamed herself that she had not been able to open the eyes of her children to the same broad sweep of understanding.

It must be my own fault, she thought. *Somewhere along the line I failed them.*

"A penny for your thoughts, old woman," Doctor said. He was standing in the doorway with his hands in his pockets, beaming at her. Seeing him flushed with the triumph of his splendid wedding, she could not tell him what had gone through her mind.

"Oh, doctor," she said, "I was thinking how well everything went."

"Well, there's a damned big mess to clear away."

"That's right."

"I guess I'll go down to the office and have me a cigar, while you and the girls get it out of the way."

20

HUGH HAD HAD COUNTRY BUSINESS on the day of Lita Hawkins' wedding; but Katherine was invited, and she went to it. Anna had asked her to pour coffee, and it had given her a feeling of importance to be pouring coffee in another woman's house for another woman's guests. She thought of Anna's daughter going away with a young man to be his wife, and she wondered how Lita felt: was she glad, or terribly afraid? But at that point Katherine's mind drew back, because there were certain barriers beyond which it rarely ventured. Safer to pour coffee and not think about the fear and the shame which a modest young woman might feel, after the few words a minister said had so intimately changed her relationship to a man.

Katherine had had a new dress made for the wedding, and she had turned the marked side of her face away from the guests as she sat to pour, and she had felt for an hour or so as if she belonged here with these people and were one of them.

After the wedding Katherine ran in and out almost every day. Anna's calm friendliness filled up that want in her life which she could not explain. Sometimes she trembled again on the verge of talking intimately with Anna and trying to tell her about the awful emptiness of her life, about the ache of privation which she could not understand, because after all she had a good home and a good husband. . . . Sometimes she wanted to tell Anna about the letter she had received. But then again she remembered Anna's words that first time she had tried to utter the unmentionable things, and it seemed that they were better friends and somehow understood each other better, too, when they walked on the firm surface of generalities.

Hugh was very kind to Katherine that winter; but his kindness

was detached and made him more unapproachable than ever. It was
a winter of la grippe and pneumonia and diphtheria, and he never
spared himself a night call or a long drive in the country. Some of
the calls might easily have been put off or avoided, Katherine thought,
but he was meticulous in going beyond the limit of his duty. Was
he going beyond the limit of his strength, too, she wondered, seeing
him, pale and tired, sit staring at his plate of food, weary beyond
appetite?

But she did not try to reason with him, for they were past that
now, and it was enough to have the surface of their life smooth
and untroubled. When he was not on call, he read a great deal, going
through strange books, which she did not understand, with incredible
rapidity; and he came late to bed, usually after she was asleep. But
sometimes she only pretended sleep, and then she heard him tossing
and turning for a long time in the silent darkness of his room. How
strange a man he was—and he was her husband!

She studied his face as he sat in the choir loft on Sunday morning,
and he seemed different somehow from the man with whom she
had breakfasted. He looked thinner and more intense, and the light
from the high, uncurtained windows picked out new hollows at his
temples and new shadows about the mouth and nostrils. Sometimes
she looked at Jenny Walden, too, sitting so sleek and small in her
beauty a few rows below him, and she was sorry that she had ever
mentioned Jenny's name to him, for she was sure that Hugh had
not seen her since her ankle had healed, and she was so much younger
than he was—and he was so honorable. There had been moments
after that letter came when she would have believed anything. Those
were horrible moments which she put away from her, together with
the other things she could not bear thinking of. But it was all over
now—all over! Thank God, she could look at Jenny Walden now
and see her as a silly little small-town flirt, and not as a woman
Hugh might love!

But Jenny was not so flirtatious this winter, nor so outspoken and provocative. "She's beginning to realize her position as her father's daughter in his church," Mrs. Swanson said to Mrs. Gibbs, the plumber's wife.

"Well, the giddiest girl will settle down after a while. What she needs now is a nice, sober young man, and wedding bells—that's what I think."

It was true that Jenny was taking over some of her mother's duties among the women of the church; but she performed them perfunctorily with a mind in abeyance. She was like a sleepwalker, lost in some deep abstraction.

Mr. Walden consulted Dr. Allerton concerning her health during the winter.

"She seems so listless," he said, "and she's lost a good deal of her color. We've had some consumption in our family way back, and I wouldn't have that lay hold of my Jenny. I wanted her to come and see you, but she wouldn't hear of it."

A little pulse began to throb in Hugh's temple.

"You think she's really ill? You want me to see her?"

"Oh, no, I didn't mean that. It isn't that serious—maybe it's only a fancy of mine. But I thought, if you knew of some tonic, I might get her to take it without telling her I'd seen you."

Dr. Allerton was awkward about writing out the prescription. He seemed uncertain about the amount of iron with the wine on the first one, and he blotted the second one. The third prescription was all right, and he handed it to the minister with an apologetic smile.

"I seem to be a bungler today," he said. "I hope that she will be benefited by it. Will you—tell her— But you didn't want her to know that you had seen me?"

"No, since she forbade me. Not that she has anything against you, you know, doctor, with all your kindness to her last fall; but she's an independent child, and now that she's on her feet she won't admit that she might ever need medical assistance again. You understand, I guess?"

"Yes, I understand," said Hugh. "I understand very well."

"Thank you then. I'll see what I can do with her. She's all I have left, you know, doctor, since her sister's away and her mother—left us. Jenny's very precious to me."

"Yes, I know, Mr. Walden."

Dr. Allerton did not look again at the minister's face. It was as brown and wrinkled as an old apple with still a trace of healthy red in the cheeks, and it was also full of a simplicity and gentle innocence which could not be looked upon with equanimity by the troubled heart.

On the long drives into the country and back in the steel-blue twilight, Hugh took meager comfort from being able to name his loneliness. Before he had known Jenny, it had been vague and nameless—a sense of something of vital importance to his happiness which had been left out of his life. But now his want had a name and a face and a body that was warm to the touch if he would allow imagination to present it warmly to him. In a sense he was no longer alone, and yet the pain was greater than it had been before he knew Jenny. He was always on the lookout for her straight back and her little fur hat on the roads about town, and in his imagination they rode together again, side by side, and spoke together or were silent. But this winter he never met her on the road. Coincidence had conspired against them, both in bringing them together alone when it was not necessary, and, now that they hungered for a sight of each other, in keeping them apart.

So, when he beat his mittened hands against the old buffalo coat, it was sometimes not from cold but from the anguish of his spirit. He had shut himself away from all help until his trouble, like a Spartan fox, fed upon his own vitals.

It was a long, dark winter, and much snow fell, burying the mountains and the town deep under many layers of silence and loneliness.

21

CONSTANT SAW how it was going with the Hawkinses that winter. He knew that Doctor was property-poor and loaded with taxes, that Lita's wedding and trousseau had been a ridiculous and a fabulous expense; he knew that little by little Allerton was encroaching upon Doctor's practice. Anna's diamond earrings disappeared after the wedding, and Constant understood that they would not return. When Christina was married and Anna began to do all her own housework, he was stirred out of his inertia to take some action.

He had plenty of money himself, for he lived in the very simplest manner, and the things he wanted were not available on the open market. Yet Doctor was still "boss," and there was no way in which he could share with them or offer to tide them over without giving offense. There was only one thing he could do to ease the situation, and that was to relieve them of his son.

He thought about it for some time before he reached a decision, because it would mean a complete change in his way of living, and he was settled now into a routine which suited him as well as any. He thought it would be best to take a small house and hire a house-keeper, and there would be the old question again of trying to give up the drinking just when he thought that he had it under a moderate control. He suffered a good deal of doubt and mental discomfort before he finally came to a decision about Gene. But when at last his mind was made up he began to anticipate having the boy with him, and to think that perhaps he could do better with this life than with the others which he had tried. He thought how he could bestir himself to father the boy, to be to him all that Doc Hawkins had been and more besides.

Elizabeth will be with us, he said to himself. *I must make her live again for Gene.*

He took up her workbasket and opened it, fingering the spools of colored silk, the emery bag shaped like a strawberry, and the little silver thimble. The mountain air had blackened the silver so that it was not pretty. He took it to the kitchen and polished it until it shone again, but still he felt cold and unmoved. Sometimes now Elizabeth seemed a long way off in England, not a warm breath in the room with him. She had become the heroine of a story which he had read.

Gene shall bring her back, he thought savagely. *Gene shall bring her back.*

On a Sunday afternoon in February he arose and bathed himself and dressed and cleared away the glass and bottles that stood on the table from the night before. It was snowing, and he bent himself into the storm to go up the hill to Doctor's house.

Gene's sled was on the porch leaning against the wall beside the front door with snow still clinging to it. Before he rang the bell Constant could hear Gene's eager voice holding forth inside the house, and the rumble of Doctor's laughter.

Anna came to let him in, and her hand rested lightly for an instant against his sleeve, her eyes deep and questioning on his face.

"It snows," he said.

"Yes, let me take your coat. You are very wet."

Gene and Doctor were sitting by the dining-room table with a checkerboard between them.

There was a warm fire in the dining-room stove, and Gene's mittens and muffler hung to dry behind it. He and Doctor were having an animated but friendly argument about a move which had just been made. They looked up, but without bothering to make formal recognition of Constant's entrance.

Constant went to stand beside them and watch the progress of the game.

"Some day I must teach you how to play *trictrac*," he said to Gene.

"Is that a French game?" Gene inquired. His voice indicated that, if it were, he was not very much interested.

"Yes. It is what you call backgammon here perhaps."

"Checkers is a good game. I'm getting so I can lick the stuffing out of Uncle Doc."

"You are not!" roared Doc. "Why, you little so-and-so, you've only beat me twice, and look at all the times I've tarred and feathered you!"

Gene shouted with laughter. "You wait and see!" he cried. "You wait and see!"

"They're terrible opponents," Anna said, but she continued to watch Constant with a kind of gentle pity.

Constant began to speak.

"I have taken a great resolve," he said. "Tomorrow I shall sign a lease upon that little shingle house two blocks from the office, and one of Christina's sisters shall come to be my housekeeper. Then Gene and I, we shall live together in our own house."

There was a sudden silence, and Gene and Doctor both looked at him, the game completely forgotten.

"No!" Gene said. "Why, papa?"

"I have wished it for a long time, my son. Now it seems the good time."

"Oh, I am so glad!" Anna said. "It will be the best for both of you."

"Well, Anna," Doctor cried. "You sound as if you were glad to turn the boy out! My Lord, he's lived here a long time. Let's not do anything hastily."

"We have not been hasty," Constant said. "When he was little, that was different. I did not feel capable, and you were more than kind; but now—now he is a big boy, I think. He is ten years old. It is time we should be together, like father and son."

"*No!*" Gene said again. There was a kind of unhappy violence in his voice. "I'm all right here. I help, don't I, Uncle Doc? I curry the horse, I shovel snow, I do a lot."

"You're my right-hand man," Doc said.

"You hear him, papa? I'm his right-hand man!"

"Nevertheless you are my son," Constant said. He had not meant it to sound didactic. It was difficult for him to know how to speak to a child.

"You've been a long time waking up to the fact," cried Doctor, and Gene sprang up, scattering the checkers all over the floor.

"I won't go away from here," he said. "I won't go away from Uncle Doc."

"Listen," said Anna. "What a fuss you're all making! Gene will go to live with his father, but he'll see Uncle Doc every day. It's not a question of going away or losing old friends."

"No," said Gene. "I would rather be here."

"Then I must insist, Eugene," said Constant. "If you have never learned to obey, then it is time that you began."

"I'll obey Uncle Doc," cried Gene. "I won't obey you!" He burst into tears and rushed into the kitchen, slamming the door behind him.

"Well, now you've kicked over the applecart for sure, damn you!" said Doctor. "I'll go and see what I can do with him." He followed Gene into the kitchen.

Constant spread his hands helplessly. "What is it that I have done then? I have no tact or knowledge of children, perhaps, but I do not see where I was in the wrong." He went and stood by the window, watching the falling snow with absent eyes.

"You were not in the wrong," Anna said. She came and stood beside him.

"What is it then?" he asked. His voice was hurt and bewildered.

"He has taken your son," Anna said. She was full of sorrow and anger.

"Yes, I see that. But how did it come about? When? I do not understand."

"It has been going on for a long time. I have tried to tell you."

"Yes, I know. I think I did not realize."

"And you are not angry?"

For a moment he did not speak. Then he said: "No. I find I am not angry. I wonder why? Is it, perhaps, because I also—I have taken something of his—"

Anna did not reply. They stood for some time in silence, looking through the screen of falling snow to a gray, distorted world beyond. The flakes beat upon the outside of the window glass with a tiny, crisping sound which had nothing to do with the firelight and the mixed emotions within the room.

After a while the kitchen door opened softly and Gene came in.

"Papa," he said, "Uncle Doc says that I must say I am sorry. Well, I am sorry."

Gene continued to stay on at Dr. Hawkins' house. He was Doctor's shadow, running his errands, laughing at his jokes, driving his horse for him. And Doctor, too: *Where's Gene?* he wanted to know whenever the boy was not around. It was as if the momentary threat of separation had driven them more irrevocably together.

Constant insisted now on paying monthly room and board for Gene, but Doctor would not touch the money.

"I'll put it in the bank for Gene," he said. "This ain't a matter of money. He's like my kid. I've still got my head above water so I can support a boy."

But Anna was not surprised when one day at the end of winter Doctor came home without his beautiful beaver coat. He laughed about it in a loud voice.

"By God, I made a marvelous deal today! A drummer was in the drugstore, and he bought the coat right off of my back. The poor devil was a sucker. He offered me twice what the thing was worth and I couldn't pass up a deal like that. The damned coat was always too hot. It ain't healthy to wear a coat that makes you sweat. A mackintosh is better with spring on the way, and by next fall I'll have another beaver—a better one."

Anna did not say anything. She let Doctor laugh.

22

THE PARSONAGE was well kept that winter. Jenny's slapdash methods of housekeeping were improving, but the town scarcely saw her. Her broken ankle seemed to have made her afraid of the slippery streets, and she did not go to the Odd Fellows' ball this year, nor run to fires. But when people met her in the stores, doing her ordinary household errands, she seemed the same Jenny, beautiful and smiling, her cheeks stung to a warm rose-leaf color by the cold.

Jenny looked at herself in the mirror and felt a vague stirring of wonder that the face showed no more change when the heart had curled like a frosted leaf and blown away.

The winter light fell bleakly across the parsonage floor where Jenny swept; the frost made fantastic pictures of fern and jungle on the window pane; and Jenny tried to keep her mind inactive and obedient. There is less suffering when the mind is numb.

From what seemed a great distance she observed the agitation for women's suffrage in Idaho which resulted before the year was out in triumph for the women's cause; but now it mattered not at all to Jenny that her state was one of the first in the Union to put women on a theoretical equality with men.

I wasn't so far ahead of them after all, she thought. *To vote?* she said to herself. *What's that? It's what men think of us that really counts, and if we can't be free to live as we like and to love where we must— Well, let the women vote if they want to, maybe they'll work out something some day for the ones who come after. Men are what they think they are, and we, we are what they think we are, too. It's not so much because we can't help ourselves, as it is that we don't want to. I am like the rest,* she thought. *All I want is to be married to him, safe within the law and the conventions.*

So all of her thinking inevitably came back to Hugh, and she was desperately unhappy. Sometimes there was nothing to do but put on her hat and walk in the snowy streets until she was tired.

As she went down Elm Street she saw Mrs. Shanley shoveling the snow off her front walk and piling it in heaps on either side where the roses and snapdragons and bachelor's-buttons had been. Mrs. Shanley's movements were brisk and birdlike. Her short gray curls glistened in the winter sunshine. She seemed not to have changed at all in appearance since the day she had given Jenny the rose. But Jenny had changed. She had grown from a little girl to a woman, from careless well-being to conscious despair. She saw that one grew and changed very rapidly in youth, but that, when one reached the broad plains of middle age, one went on forever and ever without change. The sight of Mrs. Shanley gave her a sudden devastating premonition of the years which lay ahead of her. The loneliness, the emptiness were just beginning.

She stopped and leaned on Mrs. Shanley's gate, watching the woman's energetic movements.

"Once you gave me a rose and hoped I would be happy," Jenny said.

"Did I? I don't remember. Well, have you been?"

"I think so," Jenny said. "It didn't last long enough for me to be sure."

"It don't," said Mrs. Shanley. She went on shoveling, the jets of loose snow sparkling like diamonds as they shot up in the blue air.

Jenny continued to lean on the gate.

"I'd like to ask you something, Mrs. Shanley."

"Yes?" Mrs. Shanley said. Her black eyes were defiant.

"It's about your divorce," said Jenny.

"Well, what do you want to know about it? You got some reason? Is your old man going to preach another sermon?"

"No," Jenny said. "I want to know for myself."

"All right, I'll tell you," Mrs. Shanley said. She stuck her shovel into the snow and came to stand inside the gate with her hands on her hips. "*I* got the divorce, see? It wasn't him, it was me. I wanted to be free of him. He ran off and lived in sin with another woman, and I thought: 'Well, I'll be free again, like I was as a girl. Maybe he don't love me, but anyway I'll have my freedom.'"

"It must have taken courage."

"No, I was just a fool," Mrs. Shanley said. "I thought I could get along without people. I didn't know what a hell on earth decent people can make for a woman with a divorce."

"But it wasn't your fault?"

"No, it wasn't my fault. If I'd have gone on the way I was, with him hoodwinking me, I'd have had my shame, but I wouldn't have been cut off. This way what have I got? I haven't slept with a man since mine went off and left me, but that don't make no difference to this town. I've had a divorce, and they put me lower than the chippies over the other side of the tracks."

"But what about the other woman?" Jenny said, "the one he ran away with?"

"I dunno. I guess she's had her hell, too; but then she had *him* to go along with it."

"Yes, she had him," Jenny said. "All they wanted was each other, I guess. Maybe they were willing to pay for that. But it was cruel that you had to suffer, too."

"I wish they'd died of it!" Mrs. Shanley said passionately. "Everybody's hand is out to help a widow, but a woman with a divorce has got a hard row to hoe. I'm telling you that. If they'd died, I'd have been all right."

Jenny was silent. She wanted to go now without saying any more, but Mrs. Shanley reached across the gate and put her hand on Jenny's arm.

"You're like I was. I know. I've watched you. I've seen you running bareheaded to fires and standing up in front of the town making speeches. You think you can buck the world. So did I, but I've found out different. You keep away from divorce—and men, too. He used to think I was cute and smart, going my own way. Then what did he do but take up with this clinging vine of a woman? After the divorce I kept coming west, thinking to get away. But there's no use running away. Gossip runs faster than trains. No, it don't do to go against society. I've learned it the hard way, but I've learned it."

"Thank you," Jenny said.

She walked quickly away down the street. She had a sudden impulse to see Katherine Allerton and talk to her, not about Hugh but on some safe, general topic. She turned into the next street and walked towards the house; but as she drew near she saw Mrs. Allerton standing by the small bow window looking out. As soon as Katherine saw her, she moved quickly behind the heavy lace curtains so that she would not be seen. The movement was instinctive and furtive, and it filled Jenny with disgust. She walked quickly by the house with her head averted.

At the next corner she turned and struck out to the country where she had not walked for a long time. The road was hard-packed and icy; the sky, a cold, hard blue. She did not look at the mountains. *I'll walk until I'm tired,* she thought, *until my ankle hurts again.*

When she was coming back, she heard a horse behind her. Her heart leapt with a wild, fierce trembling. She kept on walking without looking around, but when the horse drew in beside her it was only a saddle horse and the rider was the crazy Stevens boy.

"I could run you down," he said, "walking in the road like that."

"Well, why don't you?"

"Maybe you wouldn't care."

"Maybe not."

"Why don't you look at me sometimes? I'm not dirt. I'm not the dirt under your feet."

"Don't I look at you? I'm looking at you now."

"You think I'm dirt."

"No, I don't. I'm sorry for you. I'm sorry for lots of people in this town. I'm sorry for myself."

"You can have anything you want."

"No, that's not true. I haven't anything."

"Who has taken it away?"

"This little, hateful town, I guess," said Jenny, trying to laugh.

"If I knew, I would kill him," Alf said.

"You are always full of big talk, aren't you?" Jenny said, "to talk of killing."

"Well, there are lots of people better dead."

"Maybe you're right," said Jenny.

"You'll see. Some day I'll show you."

"Go on now, Alf. Ride along. I came out here to be alone."

He continued to ride along beside her for a moment; then he whipped up his horse and galloped away. The horse's iron shoes struck sparks from the frozen road.

When Jenny returned to the parsonage the fire had gone out, and her father was away. Twilight had begun to replace the winter sunshine. The only sound in the house was the ticking of a clock. She stood in the cold, bleak hall staring with vacant eyes straight ahead of her. Her walk had done her no good. There was an indescribable pain all about her heart, and her throat was choked with something hard and dry, but no tears would fall.

23

IN WINTER THE frozen earth lies dormant, insensible to pain. The sap in the trees sleeps deep and still, and there is no sound of running water. It is easier to be hopeless in the winter, to forget and to be forgotten. Winter is a leveler, a giver of narcotics; it asks nothing beyond patience and endurance. Hugh was patient, and he endured. Sometimes a thought came to him which he had had for the first time on the night he had wished to kill Katherine. *There is only one life that a doctor can take—only one that belongs to him.* That thought was secret to him, and somehow it was sweet. But he put it to the back of his mind. He could still go on for a long time on his strength.

Early in March the chinook wind blew out of the mountains. It blew for three days, and it was Hugh's first experience of that warm wind which comes suddenly out of the mountains in the midst of winter. There are no such winds in England.

Hugh felt the wind warm and violent on his face while the snow was still cold under his feet. His ears were full of the sound of its blowing and of the tinkle of falling icicles. Wind was like wine to him. He had loved Jenny to the sound of October blowing.

From the snowbanks and the long ledges of ice upon the sides of the mountains began the gentle seepage and flow of water. As the chinook blew, tossing and twisting the branches of trees, the water ran faster and faster. Seepage became trickle, and trickles joined and ran together to meet rivulets and streams. Under the ice, water gurgled and rushed, breaking its bonds and crying to be free. Air and earth were full of movement and the excitement of change. The iron bands of winter were being broken with violence and with joyousness. There was a great pagan sound of delight in the air; and the streams and rivers ran full to the brim with waters which were never to return.

"Never to return," Hugh said to himself. "Never to return."

Katherine went to bed early the third night.

"The wind makes my head ache a little," she said. "You won't mind if I go to bed, will you, dear? You may leave the door open and have the light. I dare say I shan't sleep much at first. I dislike wind so much, but I shall be better if I lie down."

"Yes, Katherine, go to bed. I'll read a little longer, I believe."

But the type blurred to his eyes, and he found himself reading the same sentences over and over without understanding their meaning. Presently he abandoned his book, and began to walk softly back and forth across the flowered carpet.

"What are you doing, Hugh?"

"Prowling," he said with a short laugh. "Does it disturb you?"

"No, it just seemed odd."

"There are so many odd things in the world."

"I suppose you are right. I didn't mean to find fault."

"Try to sleep. I'll stop prowling."

He sat again in his chair, but now his heart walked for him, back and forth, back and forth, beating violently with the warm violence of the wind outside.

At half past twelve the doorbell rang. He never went to the door at night now without seeing Mr. Walden's face and hearing him say: *Yes, terribly upset. It seemed as if she had to have you. She looked for you all afternoon and when you didn't come—*

It was a young boy with a frightened face.

"Doctor, it's my grandmother—Mrs. Mills, you know. She's had a stroke or something. I heard her making this queer kind of gurgling noise, and her eyes looked, but she couldn't speak to me. I think you better come."

Hugh took his coat off its peg in the hall.

"You live there alone with her, don't you, Tom?"

"Yes, but I got someone to stay with her first before I came."

Hugh went to the bedroom and spoke reassuringly to Katherine. "It's Mrs. Mills. Probably a stroke. I may be out most of the night. Don't worry about me."

"No, but I wish you had got some sleep before you had to go."

"I don't mind. The wind makes me wakeful. Good night."

"Good night."

He and the boy were walking quickly in the dark street. The snow was rotten underfoot, and there was a singing and surging of life in the gutters.

"Do you think she's going to die, doctor?"

"I can't tell until I see her, but we'll hope for the best. If it's a stroke, she may recover completely. She's not an old woman, if I remember. Wasn't it your grandmother who took care of the Waldens' house for them when Miss Jenny was ill?" It was best to speak easily to the boy in this way as they walked along; at the same time the utterance of Jenny's name gave Hugh a fleeting personal delight.

"Yes," said the boy. "We live near them. It's Miss Jenny I got to watch her while I ran for you."

"Miss Jenny is there with your grandmother?"

The doctor's voice was so strange that the boy was frightened.

"Yes. Was that all right?"

"It was all right," said Hugh.

Hugh was glad that he had had warning; otherwise he might have made some kind of fool of himself when she came to the door.

"Good evening, Miss Jenny."

"Good evening, doctor."

He let her take his hat and coat. She said in a low voice: "I didn't know what you would need, but I put a kettle of water on to heat."

"Thank you. It was thoughtful of you."

They stood looking at each other, as two people who meet for the first time but have often heard of each other from mutual friends and are curious about each other's appearance.

"Grandma is in here," said the boy.

"Yes, yes, of course," said Hugh gently. "Thank you, Tom."

He went into the bedroom and bent over the old woman on the bed. Jenny had come into the room behind him, and he could feel her presence there, although she said nothing. He felt suddenly very strong, and his mind clear and lucid to deal with the obscurities of sick flesh. As he worked over the old woman, the feeling of power and lucidity grew in him. He could be skillful tonight. He could have performed the most delicate and intricate of operations if there had been need. It was because Jenny was there watching and believing. The thought went through his mind, *I could have been a great physician, even a great surgeon, if I had found Jenny before Katherine.*

Mrs. Mills was very near death that night, and, whether or not it was the borrowed skill and confidence he had of Jenny, Hugh brought her back during the silent watches. When he was sure that she was back again on the side of life, he rose and went to the window. Young Mills had fallen asleep on the lounge in the front room, and the house was very quiet. Jenny came and stood beside him at the window. There was a lightening of dawn coming in the eastern sky, and the eaves still dripped with the melting snow.

"You are not angry that I was here, Hugh?" she said in a low voice. "Tom came for me."

"Angry, Jenny? No. This is the first happiness I have had since we said goodbye." He turned to her and drew her to him, kissing her gravely and gently on her lips. She clung to him passionately for a moment, and her cheeks were hot with tears.

"I can't go on, Hugh, without you," she said.

"I know, dearest."

"I see you in the choir. You are so close—and so far away."

"I know. It is too much."

"What shall we do?"

"Jenny, there must be some honorable way out of this for us. But what it is I do not yet know."

"And must you still have honor, Hugh?"

He looked at her steadfastly for a moment, and when he spoke his voice was heavy with regret.

"Yes, I think that I must."

There was a clear lemon-colored light growing in the eastern sky, and the mountains had changed from black to deepest violet. Hugh went to the bedside table and put out the lamp.

"You will be here tonight again?"

"Yes, I shall be here tonight."

"You must get some sleep now, little one. Your eyes are dark with weariness."

"I am so happy, Hugh."

"Why, Jenny? We dare not think beyond tonight."

"But there will be tonight. Yesterday I could not have imagined it."

"No, yesterday was still the dark pit of loneliness. When we are together, we are on the mountaintops. Does it seem so to you, Jenny?"

"Yes, Hugh."

He took her hands and, turning them over, kissed each one in the warm, cupped palm.

24

KATHERINE WAS starting the kitchen fire when he came in. She looked as if she had not slept well.

"I thought I should find you still in bed, Katherine."

"You know I don't rest well when you are out of the house at night, dear—and then the wind! I'm thankful it has gone down this morning. Mrs. Mills must have been very ill."

"She was. Most of the night I thought I might not save her, but now she has a good chance to live."

"For what?" asked Katherine in a heavy voice. He looked at her in surprise.

"I don't know. It's a doctor's business to save life, not to ask why."

"Of course," said Katherine. "I dare say I need my coffee."

He threw himself down upon his bed until Katherine should call him to breakfast. When he closed his eyes he saw Jenny's face, and he said to himself: *Tonight again. Tonight.* He could not help being happy.

When they sat at breakfast Katherine asked: "Who is looking after Mrs. Mills, Hugh? They are too poor to hire a nurse."

He hesitated for just an instant, but his voice was matter-of-fact.

"Young Tom had gone for Miss Jenny Walden before he came for me."

"Miss Jenny was there last night?"

"Yes. They are close neighbors. Mrs. Mills took care of the parsonage in the fall when Miss Jenny's ankle was broken."

Katherine was silent. He could see that her face was alert, and that she was thinking. When he was ready to leave for the office, she followed him to the door.

"Who is to sit up with Mrs. Mills tonight?" she asked in a choked voice.

"Tom will doubtless arrange for someone."

"You think that it will be Miss Jenny?"

"Possibly. I shall leave that to them to arrange."

"No!" she said. "No, that would not be right. Miss Jenny must have her sleep tonight. I shall go and watch with Mrs. Mills, Hugh."

"You, Katherine? There is no need for that."

"Yes, I must go," said Katherine. "I do not do enough of that sort of thing. I am so useless. But it is time I started. I will go and watch, and, if you must be there, too, we shall watch together."

"This is quite unnecessary, Katherine," he said roughly.

"No, Hugh, you must let me do this—really you must. I'll write a note to Miss Jenny and send it around by the grocery boy telling her she need not watch tonight. She is so young, she needs her sleep. It will be much better for me to go."

"Very well, Katherine," Hugh said.

He knew that he must see Jenny and tell her himself, before she got Katherine's note. For a moment the door had been open to happiness, and now it was closed again. There was the old dark wall where the glimpse of paradise had been. The wall had never seemed to him more unendurable.

He did not go until afternoon, for he hoped that during the morning Jenny would be sleeping. He had looked in at the Mills cottage and found another neighbor in charge.

"Who will stay with her tonight?"

"The minister's daughter."

"My wife has suggested that she relieve Miss Walden. Perhaps I had better leave word at the parsonage."

"That would be a good idea."

He went to the parsonage and rang the bell. It was Mr. Walden who answered it. *Was there no kindness for them in the world?*

"Well, doctor, it's nice to see you."

"It's about Mrs. Mills—"

"She's worse?"

"No. I had a message for Miss Jenny."

"Oh, Jenny! It's Dr. Allerton to see you. Sit down, doctor. This is like old times."

Jenny came quickly down the stairs, and he could see the joy and the anxiety struggling in her vivid face.

"Miss Jenny—" He came forward, awkwardly turning his hat in his hands. His eyes were dark in his white face.

"Let me take your hat, doctor."

"No. No. There is something I had to tell you. Mrs. Allerton— she wishes to stay with Mrs. Mills tonight—to relieve you, Miss Jenny."

"That's good of her," said the minister, "but Jenny would have been glad to do it, wouldn't you, Jenny? I like Jenny to assume some responsibility among the sick and poor. She's just beginning to take an interest."

"You mean—I'm not to come?" asked Jenny in a low voice.

"Yes."

He kept turning his hat, while they looked at each other.

"Well, perhaps the night after—" said Mr. Walden cheerfully.

"I don't know," said Hugh slowly, "but I rather think that Mrs. Allerton will also arrange for that."

"Well, Jenny my dear, you must thank Mrs. Allerton for her kindness and try to make yourself useful elsewhere. Any other sick folks who need her services, doctor?"

Hugh paused. His voice was thick when he said: "There is an Italian child sick in one of the boxcar houses near the brickyard. It is just beyond the railway station on the bank of the creek, you know. I hesitate to ask Miss Walden to visit such an out-of-the-way place, but they are very poor and the child has nothing to play with. I remember, Miss Jenny, that you once told me you were good with children."

"Yes, I think I am. What hour would be best for visiting the child, doctor?"

"I should say about four tomorrow afternoon, Miss Jenny."

So, there was that to look forward to, he thought. Thus drowning people grasp at twigs.

25

KATHERINE HAD PACKED her crochet work and a sandwich in her workbasket, and Hugh walked with her to the Mills cottage.

"Now you must tell me just what I should do, dear," said Katherine. "You know I've never taken much responsibility."

"It should be very simple, Katherine. I believe there will be nothing for you to do but see that she is comfortable. You will notice at once if she takes a turn for the worse and can send young Tom for me."

"You are not going to stay then, Hugh?"

"Why should I? It was necessary to be with her last night. Tonight it is not. Someone must be at home if other calls should come in."

"Yes, of course," said Katherine. He could see her thinking: *Perhaps I should have let Miss Jenny do it after all. There was no need to worry and put myself out.* His heart felt very cold tonight, and he was not sorry for her.

When he had done what he could to make the old woman comfortable for the night, Tom said to him, "Oh, doctor, if you ain't too busy, Mr. Peterson next door asked me to have you stop in and have a look at his ingrowing toenail."

"Very well," said Hugh. One thing was as good as another to keep his mind from Jenny and himself. For an hour or more, after he had dressed Peterson's toe, he sat and listened to the man's political views. "Yes" and "No," said Hugh, "and I should hardly go so far as that, perhaps"; but his mind kept repeating: *Tonight I should have seen her again. What are we to do? How are we to go on like this? Is there any answer?*

It was late, when he left Peterson's, and dark, with the warm wind still in the air but less noisily insistent. There was a smell of uncovered earth and coming spring. He went around by the parsonage and leaned against the gatepost like a lovesick adolescent. He had the mad idea of going in to look at Jenny and to hear her voice. But how could he do that? Her father would come to the door, surprised and cordial, and perhaps he would ask Hugh's advice about next Sunday's sermon. It would be worse than nothing.

There was a light in her bedroom window, and as he looked at it, sick with desire for her, he saw her shadow swoop across the drawn shade with one of those quick, light movements which she made.

Oh, Jenny, Jenny! All that is beautiful on earth! All that is wild and precious! And we cannot have each other.

As he stood there in the darkness, pressing his breast against the hard wooden ball of the gatepost, he suddenly knew how far he had strayed from the wide, plain road which he had laid out for himself. He had so firmly believed that the intellect could direct man's life. As he thought back now, he saw the life he had planned, the careful turnings he had made, all neatly finished like a map with scale of miles and contours done in colors. But now he had lost his way in trackless regions, and his map no longer served him. For the first time he realized that there were forces in life which were beyond his control and understanding. He was no longer the map maker, the disinterested planner. He was not his own master. Something older and deeper than the intellect had taken hold of him and was moving very swiftly with him through the trackless dark towards some unforeseen denouement. He felt a deep despair, but it was tinged with ecstasy. There was only one question now: how to retire from the old planned life with the least dishonor and disaster. He could not think clearly any more—only he knew what he must have.

While he stood there Jenny came to the window and drew up the shade and opened the sash. She leaned for a moment on the window sill looking out at the dark sky.

"Jenny," he said in a low voice.

She started and looked down at him. "Wait," she said. "I will be with you."

He saw her quick movements in the room, heard her light, running footsteps on the porch and walk, and then he held her.

For a long time they walked in the dark streets of the town, speaking little because there was little they could say. They did not know or care who saw them, and sometimes they stopped in the heavy, dripping shelter of the fir trees and clung together and kissed. Water rushed and sang in the gutters, and they were wet to the knees with slush and rotten snow.

Once when they stopped in the dark clump of pines at the foot of the Presbyterian hill, a man passed them going up the hill. It was old Doc Hawkins returning late from lodge meeting, but they did not know or care.

At last they found their way back to the parsonage, and Hugh said: "You will come tomorrow, Jenny? It may be the last time." And Jenny said, "Oh, yes!"

26

"By God," Doctor said, "I'd have sworn it was Allerton kissing a woman on the street! It seems too damned good to be true, but I couldn't have been mistaken."

"You have talked so much about catching him with a woman," Anna said. "I expect your imagination supplied the rest."

"Imagination nothing!" said Doctor. "I tell you, I'm sure!"

"Doctor," Anna said, "leave it alone. Please do."

"That's a funny attitude to take. I thought you were his wife's friend."

"I am. That's one reason."

"Maybe *you* were the woman," said Doc with heavy jocularity. "You seem so damned anxious to hush it up."

"Didn't you find me in bed when you reached the top of the hill? Doctor, sometimes I marvel at your lack of understanding. Now leave well enough alone, do!"

All day Doctor was filled with unreasonably high spirits. He thought to himself that he would not be hasty, he'd wait for the right moment. It was becoming increasingly important to him to smash Dr. Allerton, to hold him up to ridicule and hound him out of town. And now some benevolent Fate had put the longed-for weapon directly into his hands. He had seen it with his own eyes—Allerton, a married man, carrying on with some light woman. You could break a professional man in Opportunity with a thing like that. Doctor wanted to go and shout it up and down Main Street; but this was like handling a speech: you had to get the temper of the audience and pick the moment for a revelation of this kind. He held himself in with considerable difficulty.

27

HUGH WAS filled with a recurrence of dark remorse, after their night of walking through the town. Yes, it must end, somehow it must end. Yet he could not help living for the afternoon, when he should see Jenny in the Italian shanty town. He tried to summon his mind to the making of plans, and all he could think was that he should see her once again.

When he came into the dim interior of the boxcar house, he knew that Jenny was there. It was as if her body gave off a kind of light or a perfume of early violets.

"Lookit, doctor. Here is a lady. She bringa my leetle boy some pencil' and some pape' for draw." The Italian mother was smiling, her arms folded across her ample bosom, scratching her elbows with satisfaction and nervous delight.

"And orange! See?" cried the little boy, his dark face beaming from the dirty pillow. He held up an orange in his thin, brown hand.

"That is what I carry in my pocket for good children who do not scold the doctor for being late," said Jenny, smiling at Hugh. She wore the little fur hat that she had worn the day he had stopped the cutter for her.

"And is the orange still warm?" he asked in a low voice.

"You have a good memory, doctor."

"Only for things that are precious."

"You know dis lady, doctor? Isn' she a pretty lady?"

"Yes, Mrs. Sacconi, she is the prettiest lady I have ever seen."

"Me, too," said Mrs. Sacconi, nodding her head until her gold hoop earrings bobbed, and showing her white teeth in a wide smile.

Jenny held her little muff up to her face.

"You make me blush," she said.

"It's becoming."

"I was just going, doctor, as you came in."

"Don't let me keep you, Miss Jenny." He went to open the door for her. "By the way, they tell me that the pussy willows are out along the creek bank. Upstream, I believe, just around the next bend. Perhaps you would like to gather some. How are you shod?"

"I wore my old shoes, doctor. Thank you for the suggestion."

He did not hurry. Since last night, since he had ceased to struggle against this thing, there seemed time for everything. He left the Italian woman and child happy and smiling. When he had closed the door upon them, he turned quickly towards the creek and went along the bank upstream beyond the bend.

The creek which died away to a thread in summer was rushing now with a great noise of freshet. Branches and pieces of ice swirled downward upon its tempestuous current. The high bank cut off the view of town, and across the stream was an open meadow and the brickyard. It was so noisy that Jenny did not hear him coming. She sat on a ledge of rock above the water half screened by the fringe of willows, with a bunch of pussy willows across her lap. But as she sat there, thinking herself alone, there was a sadness in the droop of her shoulders that wrung Hugh's heart. He came beside her, and he said in a rough voice:

"Jenny, I have ruined your life for you. I should be horsewhipped out of town."

Her shoulders lifted then, and she turned the full light of her face around to him.

"Sit beside me," she said. "How silly you are, dearest! What makes you say a thing like that?"

"Because you were sad just now. I couldn't help seeing it. Sadness should never touch you."

"I was only thinking, Hugh, that I cannot go on like this without you. My life was a kind of wilderness before you came, and now it is pure desolation when I am not with you. Last night everything was different. If it could be like that, without the fear and pain!"

He sat beside her and took her hand. Her glove was cold to his touch. He pulled off the little glove and warmed her cold, small hand in both of his.

"No, we cannot go on like this," he said.

"I would rather be dead," she said in a low voice.

He turned and looked very strangely into her eyes. "Now you are speaking wildly, Jenny. You do not mean what you say."

"Yes, it is true. You don't believe me, perhaps, but it is true. I stood on the bridge back there as I crossed over this stream, and I thought that I would be better to be rushing away in it, dead, than alone without you."

"'Alone' is the one bitter word."

"When the snow came down so steadily this winter, I didn't dare go far out in it, for fear I should keep on going. I think it would be easy that way—just to keep walking into the storm and thinking of a golden gate and a blue dress, maybe, the way I did as a child. But for all my hopelessness, I couldn't leave you behind. It is too difficult alone."

"We are going to be together now," he said quietly.

"How, Hugh?"

"I have tried to think of all the ways. There is this way—arranging odd meetings when we can in secret places. We might have nights like the one last night, but it will be more and more difficult."

"Yes, I know," she said, "and that is not enough."

"No, it is not enough."

He hesitated, then he said heavily: "We could go away together, and perhaps Katherine would give me a divorce. That way I should bring you shame and dishonor, Jenny, but we should have each other. At first that would be enough, but some day, if the flame burned lower, you might hate me for it."

"No, Hugh, I would never hate you."

"We must face the possibilities."

"One of those would be the loss of your practice, wouldn't it?"

"I could give that up. There are other things I can do to put bread into our mouths. I used to work in a mill. I am good at using my hands. What would be harder would be to see you scorned and battered by the righteous women."

"I have thought of all that," she said. "I believe I would not care."

They sat in silence listening to the sound of the creek. A boy came slowly downstream at the edge of the water. He had a chip boat which he was shepherding with a long stick. At first he did not see them. They sat apart, and Jenny put her hands in her muff. When the boy looked up, he was at first startled and then mildly curious. He grinned.

"Hello, Dr. Allerton."

"Hello, Jim."

"It's sure kind of like spring today."

"Yes."

"My sister's all over the chicken pox now. I never got it like you thought I would."

"I'm glad you didn't."

"I guess you're glad you were wrong, aren't you?"

"Yes, I'm glad I was wrong."

"Well—goodbye, doctor."

"Goodbye, Jim."

When he was gone around the bend, she said, "We might have—children, too."

"We could not give them an honorable name, Jenny. We might not care, but they would."

"It would be hard for them, wouldn't it?"

"Yes."

"Hugh, what are you thinking?"

"If we should go together, Jenny? Not the river or the storm—quietly, I mean, without pain?"

"Yes, I could face that."

"We could give ourselves a day together first. Something perfect, Jenny, with no regrets afterward, no feeling of shame, no gradual cooling of this wonder we feel."

"Yes, Hugh. I think that is the answer."

28

DR. ALLERTON was so engrossed in his own narrowed field of thought and feeling that he did not at first notice the tension in the atmosphere of the drugstore. Doc Hawkins was in there, and several others standing around or leaning against counters. When he came in, they ceased speaking. Hugh went directly to the prescription counter and gave Skogmo his order.

"You use a lot of morphine in your practice, don't you, doctor?" Skogmo said, beginning to fill the order.

"It eases pain when nothing else can," said Hugh absently.

"Maybe he takes it," Dr. Hawkins said. "I've known doctors get the habit when there's something they want to forget. It's more damned subtle than alcohol."

Hugh turned and saw Doc Hawkins lounging against the cigar

counter, his eyes very black and bright under the shaggy brows. The other people in the drugstore were watching them with a kind of expectancy.

There was a boy who ran errands for the Bon Ton Store, and a student from the Academy; there was old man Gaultrud in for his patent medicines, and the crazy Stevens boy, leaning against Skogmo's new glass showcase and looking at the hand-painted pillow tops and cut-glass objects which the druggist had recently added to his stock. The green and blue bottles in the window shone, translucent with the hard light from the street.

Hugh answered slowly and guardedly:

"No, I have never been an addict, doctor."

"I beg your pardon, Allerton," Doc said with mock politeness. "I didn't mean to imply something that's not true, but you never know how far a man will go when he starts on the road downhill."

"I am not quite sure that I follow you, Dr. Hawkins."

"God! When you see a married man kissing another woman in the open street, he might as well be taking dope, too, it seems to me." Doctor's voice was loud and authoritative.

Hugh flushed scarlet, and then all of the color drained away from his face, leaving it dead white.

"Do I understand, doctor," he said, "that you are making some sort of charge against me?"

"No," Doc said. "Only there's a place in this town for illicit love-making. There's a house out beyond the depot."

"I do not patronize such houses."

"Obviously not, doctor. I'm just suggesting that you might well do so, and keep our city's streets above reproach."

Hugh stood by the prescription counter, white and trembling. Waves of physical sickness went over him. The winter had been very hard to bear, and the sublimities and depressions of the past two days had shaken him to the core. He saw that they were all watching him as people watch a stricken animal, and they were expecting him to defend himself. But he had no defense.

"Dr. Hawkins," he said at last in a low voice, "you must do what you see fit with my reputation, but I beg you to keep the name of any woman out of this."

"By God, Allerton, I don't have to know the woman's name to ruin you. You're a married man. The fact that there *is* another woman is enough. I'm going to hound you out of town with this."

Hugh's color had begun to return. His voice was still low, almost gentle, when he spoke.

"As one professional man to another, doctor, do me one favor, will you, please?"

"What is it then?"

"Give me three days, will you? before you start this, what you call, this hounding out of town."

"All right," Doc said, "all right. I'll give you three days before I tell the town what I saw. But think fast, doctor—three days ain't a very long time to hush a scandal in."

After Allerton had gone, Skogmo said, "Not much fight in him, doc."

"No," Doc said, "not much fight in him. I can't make the fellow out. I never could. But he asked for a few days. I'll give 'em to him, and then, by thunder, I'll raise such a stink it'll blow the roofs right off of the churches."

29

IT WAS STRANGE that in the next few days Hugh should have felt happy and at peace. Happiness and peace had not been with him for a long time. He thought kindly of Katherine during this time, and he tried to plan for her as well as he could. He was troubled that she had not made more friends. He could think of only one, and that one was the wife of Dr. Hawkins. But he could even view Dr. Hawkins with a certain detachment, and he thought: *He will be merciless with me, but he will not persecute Katherine.*

Hugh had always been prudent in laying away money for the

future, and his conscience was clear in the matter of Katherine's financial situation. With a lucid and a logical mind he spent the last day in setting his affairs in meticulous order. But beyond the logic and the lucidity there was a chaos which he did not try to explore.

There was only one time when he felt anxiety, and that was when he was walking to the train with his bag. He had allowed only just enough time to catch the train, for he had not wanted to be seen with her at the station, or during the long wait before the train left. Now, walking quickly, he thought: *If I should miss the train, and she should have to go on alone!* And then he thought: *No, it will be the other way. She will not be there. It will be I who must go alone. If she is not on the train, it will be better so. O God, what am I doing to Jenny, to the one person in the world I have loved with my whole soul and body? The one beautiful thing! Oh, it is better if she does not come!* But even then his heart differed from his mind, and he fell to trembling with anguish that she might not love him enough to come.

He could see the train standing at the station platform, and he ran the last half-block, full of the panic certainty that something must go amiss. The throbbing of the engine was the throbbing of his heart. He could feel all through his body the long creaking shudder of the train's experimental start, and the jolting impact of its stop. The "All aboard!" went through him like a knife; and then he swung himself up on the platform of the last car and was struggling with the door in the entry. The train had begun to move in earnest now with a sound of herculean anguish and regret that gradually changed into the steady, rhythmic beat of emerging purpose.

He flung open the door of the car and supported himself against one of the seats while his eyes ran the length of the aisle. She was not there. There was not a woman in the car. She had changed her mind and not come! And then he saw the spittoons, the matting-covered seats, and the traveling man puffing on his cigar. *Oh, God!* he was in the smoker.

He pushed on down the aisle and into the next car. The fields were flying by now, and the town of Opportunity already lay behind him, folded among the hills, something past and gone like a buried city in a forgotten land.

Hugh felt suspended in time and space, a soul already severed from its body. For a moment he dared not look down the aisle of the second car. His nostrils were full of the reek of close air and coal smoke, under his fingers he felt the grit of cinders in the red plush of the seat back.

Oh, Jenny! Oh, my dove, my undefiled! You have not come! You have forsaken me.

And then he looked up and saw her at the other end of the car. She had half risen and was looking at him with wide eyes whose blue was lost in the dark velvet of her distended pupils.

There were only a few passengers besides themselves, and even had he known them he was beyond caring what they thought. He went quickly and took both of Jenny's hands.

"Oh, you came, Jenny!" he said. "You are here. I can hardly believe that it's true."

"Sit beside me. We are on a great adventure."

Confidence and happiness flowed back through his veins like warmth after ice. This was right. He had no more doubts. This was the ultimate good of his life. He could only look at her and smile, some of the color beginning to return to his white face.

"Do you notice anything strange about me?" asked Jenny. Her voice was a little tremulous, as was the light in her eyes. He knew that she was giving him time and an extended hand.

"You are more beautiful than ever. Is that strange?"

"Look again. I have really gone to great pains."

"You have a new dress!"

"Oh, you are clever! I was afraid you wouldn't notice."

"You need not have had a new dress. Whatever you wear is beautiful."

"You mustn't say that or you will disappoint me."

"Then I am glad that you have a new dress, dearest. You lend it great distinction. It is a fortunate dress, Jenny, a happy dress. How did you manage it?"

"You would never believe that I had had a bank account of my own, would you?"

"Nothing about you surprises me now. There is no more room for wonder."

"Once I won a hundred dollars in an essay contest. Can you fancy that?"

"An essay contest? It should have been poetry, I think."

"No, I was quite grave and thoughtful in those days—at least sometimes. It was an essay contest."

"And what was the title of the essay?"

"I think I won't tell you."

"Please."

"You would try to draw an analogy—or something—I don't know just what I mean."

"Then tell me."

"It's very silly. I called it *Our Future Is Full of Promise.*"

He turned his face towards the window, gazing with unseeing eyes at the flying blue and purple and gray of mountain meadows. When he spoke his voice was a hoarse whisper.

"You were wrong, Jenny."

"I am willing to give up the future for the present, Hugh. Let's not be sad when the time is so short."

"And the dress, my little one?" he said at last. "You have been saving the money for this?"

"Oh, I spent a good deal of it, here and there along the way. But one bit I put in the bank—for a special purpose. And yesterday I thought I would use the money, because it really was my own, and not enough to matter greatly to anyone else—afterwards."

"And what was the special purpose, dear?"

"My trousseau, Hugh."

"I am glad that you spent it," he said. He fumbled awkwardly in his vest pocket and brought out an old, thin wedding ring. "Give me your hand, Jenny. This was my mother's ring, and this is my first true marriage."

When the train stopped at the next station, they got off together. The name of the station was Custer. They were still surrounded by mountains and the wild rushing sound of newly liberated waters. Hugh carried their bags to the Traveling Man's Haven, the one hotel in town, which sprawled in an unpainted confusion of wooden out-houses and annexes at the corner of the main street.

Jenny looked over Hugh's shoulder as he signed the register:

Dr. and Mrs. Hugh Allerton—Opportunity.

"It is done now," she said, smiling at him.

"Not all done."

"No."

They held hands like children as they followed the slow-moving Scandinavian proprietor up the stairs.

The window shade was broken behind the starched machine-lace curtains, and the mirror had been dimmed and spotted by damp weather. The edge of the brown and white crockery washbowl was chipped, and a dark crack ran from the chipped place down to the center of the bowl. The pitcher was of gray and white crockery in a different pattern. But over all the ugliness of the room there was a magic that nothing could dispel.

Jenny went to the window and looked out while Mr. Johnson brought in the bags and gave Hugh the key. When the door was closed and the man on his way downstairs, Hugh came behind her and put his arms about her.

"What do you see?"

"The sun is coming out. I think there are buttercups in that meadow across the stream."

"Impossible."

"No, the early ones come out close to the ground as soon as the snow is gone."

"Shall we go and pick them?"

"When you have kissed me."

He turned her around to face him, looking deeply into her eyes.

"Welcome home, Jenny."

"Oh, Hugh!"

"Shall we be happy today?"

"Yes."

30

"WHY THE HELL should Allerton's wife be spending the night with us?" asked Doctor in the kitchen.

"Be still, doctor," Anna said. "She was all alone for the night. She's afraid to be alone, and I was glad to have her."

"And why the devil should she be alone? Has Allerton skipped the country?"

"Be sensible," said Anna patiently. "He was called out of town on a consultation. It's all been explained and is perfectly clear."

Doctor grunted. "It's funny," he said. "He asked for three days—" He felt a vague uneasiness, he didn't want to miss out on his revenge. If Allerton had just slipped out of town— But surely the man would fight.

It was just before noon the next day that the boy from the telegraph office pedaled up the Presbyterian hill with the yellow envelope. Doctor had gone on a country call and would not be home until late afternoon.

Anna and Katherine were in the warm kitchen cutting and rolling carpet rags while Anna's bread baked.

"I don't understand quite why he had to go," Katherine was saying anxiously as she had said so many times. "It's the first time he's ever been called out of town, but he said it was this consultation. The only thing about which he was quite definite was that I was to stay with you."

"Well, it's a treat to me," said Anna. "With Lita married I get very dull here by myself. I'm glad he didn't want you to stay alone."

"Your house is so cozy, Anna. Sometimes I hate my house."

"Nonsense. You ought to get out more!"

"You're a nice one to talk," laughed Katherine.

Anna laughed, too. "I know. It's ridiculous. I'm the worst homebody in town. Doctor is always after me to get out into society. But I'm like a calf with five legs in society. I've always loved my own house best."

"Anna, there's someone at the front door."

"I believe there is," said Anna.

She got up and put her half-rolled ball in her chair. Her skirts rustled through the dining room to the front door. A little stab of ice went through her at the sight of the messenger. Her first thought was always for the girls. She tore the envelope open and read the message through several times before she could comprehend it.

"Should I wait for a reply, Mis' Hawkins?" asked the boy. He was a little curious about the message he had carried, because the operator had looked puzzled and excited when he gave the envelope to him.

"That's damned funny," the operator had said. "I thought I saw Mrs. Allerton on the street with Mrs. Hawkins yesterday. Try and find out if she's there, if you can without saying anything."

So the boy craned his neck around the door now, and saw Katherine coming from the kitchen with a ball of carpet rags in her hand.

"No, don't wait," said Anna. "I must think a moment first."

"There was a message came for Reverend Walden, too," said the boy. "I just delivered that." He threw his leg over his wheel and went coasting down the hill to Ash Street.

"What is it, Anna?" asked Katherine. "Is anything wrong?"

Anna sat down in the chair beside the dining-room window and began to rock. Her face was quite strange. Presently she stopped rocking and leaned forward to pick a yellowed leaf from one of the geraniums on the window sill.

"Anna, for God's sake, tell me!" cried Katherine. The birthmark stood out suddenly dark and purple on her white face. "It's something about Hugh."

"I don't understand very well," said Anna in a low voice. "Perhaps it is a mistake. Someone named Johnson at the Traveling Man's Haven in Custer is asking me to—to come and identify the bodies of Dr. and Mrs. Allerton."

They looked at each other, dry-eyed and silent. Their faces were terribly intense.

Katherine said in a hoarse voice: "Of course it is an error." Then she added with a kind of cry: "What—what did the boy say about the other message?"

"For Mr. Walden," repeated Anna.

Katherine stood very still, with her fingertips just touching the table, like a wooden figure which will stand upright and rigid if it has only a little support.

"You had better go, Anna," she said in a half-whisper. "I would go if I could, but I don't believe—I could get through it. There's a train that leaves in half an hour. It's the one he—they took yesterday."

It was harder to tell Mr. Walden than Katherine, Anna thought. He had seen her in the train and had come to her with a grave, troubled face.

"I wonder if you are on the same errand as I am, Mrs. Hawkins? I had a wire from Custer just now. It seems that Dr. Allerton and his wife are dead there in a hotel. I cannot understand it, for I had not known that they were out of town."

"It was only Dr. Allerton who went to Custer," said Anna in a low voice. "Mrs. Allerton has been staying with me."

"Then the whole thing must be a mistake. The telegram said *Dr. and Mrs.*"

"Mr. Walden," said Anna, "I am not good at saying difficult things. I know no more than you do, but I wonder— Is Jenny at home today, Mr. Walden?"

A strange look crossed his face.

"No," he said. "No, she isn't. She went for a little visit with her sister over the mountains. She left on this train yesterday. You don't think— But I don't understand—"

"Neither do I," said Anna. "I only know that there was some sort of attachment between them. I think they loved each other, Mr. Walden."

It was hard to see his valiant face crumple into lines of old age. They rode in silence for a long time. At last he said in a shaken voice:

"Thank you for telling me. I don't know how I could have been so—unprepared."

31

SEVERAL IMPORTANT persons met them at the train. The little mountain town which had been wrapped in anonymity the day before was stirring now with identification and importance. Something of note had at last occurred in it.

Anna's heart had never troubled her; but as she climbed the hotel stairs its heavy beating was painful to her, and she felt a suffocating sense of breathlessness. But anticipation is worse than reality. When she had seen them, her heart grew quiet again.

"Yes," she said in a steady voice, "it is Dr. Allerton; but the other is Miss Jenny Walden."

Mr. Walden rested his hands on the foot of the bed, and she could see that he was shaken by some inner convulsion which could not escape in sound. She wished that she might comfort him, but she did not know how. When he spoke, his voice was high-pitched and uncertain.

"She was such a good little girl," he said, "always smiling and laughing."

"Yes, she was," said Anna.

Her eyes went from the quiet, sleeping faces to the chair beside the bed. What it contained was familiar to her—the clean towel, the little bottle of alcohol, the hypodermic and the empty morphine vials. Beyond the towel was a glass of water, and in it the first buttercups of the season lifted their small shining cups. Not one had begun to wither.

Anna was filled with pity, not for the two who were dead, but for herself and all the world of mankind. Pity for those who had never known the ecstasy that these had known. Pity for the middle-aged world which could impale its youth upon the sharp fence of its conventions. Pity for the waste, the lack of thrift, the profitlessness of death in youth. But most of all her pity was not for those who die young but for those who have never lived richly, nor consciously been happy.

32

MR. JOHNSON HAD PASSED from shock and anger that such a thing should happen in the Traveling Man's Haven, to a kind of garrulous contentment. He had begun to tell the story that was to be the principal conversational achievement of his life.

After they had seen the bodies, he offered them coffee and rolls in the dining room. Mr. Walden could not eat, but Anna was glad of the coffee.

"They sat over there at that corner table," Mr. Johnson said, "and they were laughing most of the time. I never t'ought they looked suicides. Honeymooners, they looked like, that's what I t'ought. First they went up to the room for a while, and then they was out most of the afternoon—picking buttercups, it seems like. They come in laughing and their feet all muddy, and they eat a good supper. Before they went upstairs he come to me at the desk, an' he says, 'I'd like to settle my bill tonight.' So I told him what it was, and he gave me a twenty-dollar gold piece. 'I guess I ain't got the change.' 'Never mind,' he says. 'Just keep the change.' 'I'll have it for you in the morning,' I told him. 'We have been very happy here, Mr. Johnson,' he says. I might have t'ought that was funny then, because most I get is complaints, but I says, 'Well, sir, I'm glad you was pleased,' and then I says, 'Do you want I should call you in the morning?'

" 'Yes,' he says, and then he was quiet a minute, an' he says: 'We're both hard sleepers. If no one answers your knock, open the door and come in.' 'You're sure you want me to do that?' I asked him.

" 'Yes,' he says, 'I do.' "

"How did you know who to notify?" asked Anna.

"Oh, it was this," he said. He pulled a crumpled slip of paper from his pocket. On it a tired hand had scrawled:

Wire Mrs. Anna Hawkins } Opportunity
Rev. Charles Walden }

"It was in a poetry book," Mr. Johnson said, "like a marker, sort of. I'll show you the book. I know the page it was in." He brought a book and thumbed through it. Anna took it in her hands and read:

Even as a bride, delighting and delighted.
The hour is come:—the destined star has risen
Which shall descend upon a vacant prison.
The walls are high, the gates are strong, thick set
The sentinels—but true love never yet
Was thus constrained. . . .

"It's queer, but it seems like he must have been reading to her there at the last," said Mr. Johnson.

33

RETURNING ON THE TRAIN Anna and Mr. Walden sat opposite each other. His ruddy, innocent face had turned gray and old. His chin trembled spasmodically, and every now and again he took out his handkerchief and wiped away the tears that kept welling into his eyes.

Anna wished that she knew what to say to him, but she was not one to speak of "God's will." And how could she say that it was "for the best"? There was Katherine, too, to think of. How could she help her and explain to her? There had been so many things to arrange. Anna felt very tired. She felt a sickness of the world today, too, which did not often trouble her.

At last Mr. Walden began to speak.

"I never preached much hell-fire, Mrs. Hawkins," he said. "That's why I'm out here. They moved me on from church to church in the East because they wanted to hear more about hell. I'm wondering if this is a judgment on me for neglecting my duty. Does it seem to you that God would condemn my little girl to hell to punish me for withholding the threat of it from my congregations, Mrs. Hawkins?"

Anna leaned forward and laid her hand on the minister's knee.

"I have never believed in hell-fire, Mr. Walden," she said quietly. "I wonder if an unbeliever's view would be of any help to you now."

"I should be glad to hear it, Mrs. Hawkins."

"I think there is a God," said Anna, "and I think that He is good, because He has given us a good and bountiful earth for us to live on. But a good God should be like a good father. He would not condemn His children to the tortures of hell-fire because they were weak and erring on this earth."

"And the eternal life?" asked Mr. Walden. "You do not believe in that?"

"It's only the view of an ignorant woman, Mr. Walden—maybe

it's the view of a woman who has loved the earth too well. But golden streets and golden harps—they don't have any beauty for me. Sometimes it seems to me better that things should end, and not go on eternally. Heaven and hell are all here in ourselves, it seems to me, locked in our own breasts. We bring them into the world with us when we are born; and when we die I think they go down to earth with us and are lost in dust. I don't look forward to dying with any fear, Mr. Walden. I've always loved the earth, and it doesn't frighten me to sleep and be lost in it. I thought today when I saw their peaceful faces: 'They've had their heaven, and less hell than they would have had if they had lived. They can sleep very quietly now and go back to earth whence they came.' Yes, Mr. Walden, Jenny has had her heaven, and let's think only of the smile that was still on her face."

Mr. Walden did not reply. He turned his face towards the window, and the tears ran unheeded down his cheeks. But he reached out and patted Mrs. Hawkins' hand, as a child will pat the hand of someone who has brought it comfort.

34

EVERY HUMAN BEING has his days of doubt and self-appraisement, but Dr. Hawkins had known comparatively few of them. He was not given to reminiscence nor regret, and the silent anguish of introspection was foreign to his nature. Yet now, for the first time in his life he experienced a glimmer of doubt about the rightness of his own actions.

There were moments that summer when Doctor awoke in the night and sat up in a cold sweat, thinking: *Good God, it was the little Walden girl! The woman—it was Jenny Walden!*

He had things his own way in the town once more. He and Duval had all the practice, and those who had strayed to the camp of the enemy returned with contrition to Dr. Hawkins, for they saw now that they had put themselves into the hands of a man who would betray his wife and seduce a young girl and murder and commit suicide. It was a scandal that shook the town and beat against the insensible mountains with waves of malice and revulsion.

Katherine bore up under the horror of it with surprising strength and fortitude. She did not even succumb to one of her headaches. Anna was surprised, but on the whole it made the situation very much more tolerable; and she was glad to see that Katherine had some unexpected reservoir of strength. There were two things which Katherine did not want to do. She did not want to go back to her house, and she did not want to see people. Anna helped her in that way, breaking up the house for her and packing away Hugh's things and seeing to the auction of the furniture. Anna helped her to decide what things to keep and what to pack in boxes and barrels for the return to England; for Katherine now had only one thought: to return to her father and the place she knew.

"Perhaps they won't have heard how it happened, there in England, Anna. Would it be wrong to let them think he died of—of a railroad or a hunting accident?"

"No, I think it would not be wrong," Anna said.

When the curious came running to the back door with a glass of jelly or something under a napkin, and peered inside for sight of the widow and how she was bearing up, Anna was polite but short with them. She was able to spare Katherine a good deal.

But after the auction there were some things left which Anna did not know how to dispose of. She brought them to Katherine for her final decision. Among them was the old buffalo coat.

With admirable fortitude Katherine made the necessary decisions about the various objects. When she came to the coat, she said:

"I don't know what to do with this, Anna. There would be no place for it in England. Once someone told me that it used to belong to your husband. I wonder—"

"Yes," Anna said, "I think he could use it again. How much would you like for it, Katherine?"

"Oh, I couldn't take money for it, Anna. Surely you understand that. It's only that I want to be rid of it—to be rid of everything that makes me think of Idaho."

Anna left the coat hanging in the hall closet. One day after Katherine had gone away, Doctor found it and brought it out. He held it up, and for a few moments neither he nor Anna said anything. At last Doctor said, "What the hell is this doing here?"

"It has come home, doctor."

Doctor went back to the closet and hung it up; when he returned to the dining room, he remarked with a curious intonation in his voice: "That was a damned good coat—when it was new. Maybe I'll wear it again next winter, for country driving."

35

It was a hot, dry summer, even as it had been a cold and bitter winter. It was also a good year for crops, and the valley was carpeted with a magnificent stand of wheat.

After school was out, Doctor took Gene with him whenever he drove out of town. He seemed to have need of a boy now more than ever, and Gene was happy to go. They chattered together about everything, about what they saw along the road, and how many bushels of wheat to the acre there would be, and what was the best cure for ringworm or St. Vitus' dance. Gene was learning a lot, and he was good company.

Anna went quietly about her routine; but the heat and the dust were unusually trying to her, and the quietness of the house became a positive rather than a negative thing. Perhaps it was only the singing of grasshoppers through the open windows that made the quiet so compelling and concrete. The sunshine lay undisturbed beyond the doorsill. Even the dust was quiet on the road before the house. Her flower garden was a riot of color.

Sometimes Constant stopped for a moment during the somnolent morning, but only once did he mention the suicides and Anna's connection with them. His mind was used to retreating from the unpleasant and the unsolvable.

"Anna!" he said gently. "That you should have been the one to have to go on such an errand, *ma chère!* No, it was not right."

"Yes, I was the one to go," Anna replied. "It was best, because I understood."

"Yes, you would understand. It is that which I have most appreciated in you. But I am sorry that your understanding was obliged to stretch so far."

"They loved each other, Constant."

"Yes, I know. . . . And we have loved, too, Anna, have we not? But not to such lengths."

"If we condemn their love, we take the bloom from ours. They were younger than we are. What we feel for each other is something quiet and mature, I think. It's more an appreciation of mind and character, maybe, than a hunger of the flesh."

He was quiet a moment, as if he were evaluating this, and then he said:

"But suicide, Anna—no! No!"

"You are right," Anna said. "I see their point of view, but I could never go so far. I am too much in love with life. The more I see of life and all its cruelty and strangeness, the more I am devoted to it."

"You accept without trying to change, Anna. That is why you have been very good for me."

"I like things as they are. Perhaps I'm too lazy to struggle against them."

"I appreciate that, Anna. You alone have seen me as I am, with all my fatal weaknesses, and yet you have found heart to care for me."

"Oh, my dear," Anna said, "knowing what you had done or left undone didn't make any difference. It was knowing what you were that mattered to me."

36

DOCTOR SAT IN HIS OFFICE on a Saturday afternoon in August and answered letters. He didn't like secretarial work, and it was particularly annoying when his mind was disturbed. It was ridiculous how he kept thinking: *Did I drive them to killing themselves? Was it my fault?* Futile, of course, to let his mind dwell on it; but he kept recalling what he had said to Allerton in the drugstore that day, and, in the light of what had happened later, his words seemed, even to him, cheap and tainted with self-interest.

Mrs. Kessler, driving by in her phaeton, saw the open door and drew her horse in to the hitching post. She was almost out of her capsules, and she wanted to share her latest bit of gossip. Dr. Hawkins' conversation stimulated her as well as did his capsules.

"The dear, good man is busy with his books!" she cried, her large, dark shadow poised with tremulous lightness on the threshold. "May I come in, good man?"

"Yes, indeed," said Doctor heartily. "Come right in, Lady Kessler!"

"And may I sit in the swivel chair and turn myself about?"

"The office is yours, ma'am. You were my first patient."

Mrs. Kessler laughed girlishly. "You know, doctor, I'm ever so grateful to you for keeping me going. I think I should have passed on years ago, without you."

"Now, no gloomy thoughts, my dear lady! No gloomy thoughts!"

"But there's one black mark on my conscience, doctor. I might as well confess it to you, because it haunts me now since last spring."

"Yes, Mrs. Kessler?"

"Doctor, I went once to that Allerton, when he first came to town. Just to see, doctor—just to see."

"You don't mean it!" said Doctor, feigning innocence.

"Yes, I did! And now it's out, I hope you'll give me absolution. I've lived to see my error. What a dreadful thing that was: a middle-aged man like that running off with a young girl—and the daughter of a minister! Of course she was no better than she should be, but one expects something more of a physician."

Doc's voice had a tinge of irritation. "Physicians are human, ma'am," he said. *Good God! Was he defending Allerton?*

"Speaking of *them*," said Mrs. Kessler, "you know I heard the funniest thing the other day—I mean odd, not funny the other way, of course. They say her grave has always got a bunch of wild flowers on it. They say that crazy Stevens boy, the one we put into the asylum and they wouldn't keep him— I said to my informant, I said: 'Only an insane person would put flowers on *her* grave.' "

"Oh, damn!" said Doctor. "Did you want something?"

"My capsules, of course, and now I've made you angry somehow. But I've been so concerned about this whole affair. I knew there was something wrong there 'way last fall. I wrote Mrs. Allerton a letter. She should have put a stop to it, before it made the whole town reek. I warned her, and she should have stopped it."

"You warned Mrs. Allerton last fall?" Doc asked, surprised out of his irritation.

"Yes, I did," said Mrs. Kessler. "Someone has got to take the decency of this town to heart; someone has got to try and keep such things from happening. If I am the only one with enough feeling of moral obligation to do it, then I must be the one."

Doctor was unaccountably angry. It was a combination of the heat and the letters, and the self-imposed necessity of being polite to a woman whom he knew to be a fraud.

"My God!" he said. "That's what I call playing the busybody, Mrs. Kessler."

Mrs. Kessler's mouth fell open just a little. The tip of her tongue was red and healthy. She began to breathe more quickly, and a sudden cold gleam came at the back of her eyes.

"I've thought of *you* sometimes, doctor," she said in a soft, gentle voice, "and felt so sorry. Everyone in town but you has seen what was between your wife and your assistant."

Doctor sprang up with his eyes blazing.

"Get the hell out of here, Evelyn Kessler!" he roared. "And don't come back. There's never been a damned thing in your capsules but sugar and baking soda, anyway, you fool!"

"Oh," cried Mrs. Kessler, "oh!" And she ran out of the office and climbed into her phaeton with her handkerchief before her face.

After she had gone out of the office Doctor sat down in his chair, and his brown, hairy hands shook as he pushed the litter of papers back and forth upon his desk.

"The damned old scandal-toter!" he said. "The damned old slut!" He had known for a long time that Anna and Duval enjoyed each other's society; but there was nothing wrong there, nothing wrong. And that old buzzard had to lay her dirty fingers on it!

He thought that he must warn Anna against this woman. And then he wondered if he could. It was strange how he had always been with Anna: they lived so close, and he loved her more than he had ever loved any other woman; but still there were things that he never said to her, wild land between them which he had never explored. She was probably the only person in the world of whom he sometimes felt shy. Doc had never felt much need of women; he was a man's man, as they say. And yet where would he have been without Anna?

Yes, by God, I'll have to face her with it, he thought heavily, *but not today, not today!* . . . And Duval, too! The fellow had gone for his Saturday afternoon. He wouldn't put in an appearance for a good twenty-four hours. What did he do with himself all that time? Did he go to Anna? But no, he was never around the house on a Saturday night; it was the one night when he didn't come. Suspicion and distrust made Doctor's heart beat heavily and his head ache—give him another stomach upset, like as not.

It was the August heat as much as anything. It was clamped over the valley like a bright glass oven. The wheat had headed up early this year, and even in town it seemed that you could smell it and hear it rustling. Doctor had pulled down the front window blind so that the office was reasonably cool and half dark, with the open door a yellow rectangle through which he saw in vivid detail the dusty street, the hitching rack on the other side and a dark block of shadow thrown by the side and back of the Bon Ton Store. Crickets and grasshoppers sang even here in town, almost on Main Street.

Sitting at his desk, Doctor felt an unaccustomed sense of discouragement. Had he handled the affairs of the town more cleverly than he had handled his own? But even the affairs of the town . . .

By this time in other years the typhoid epidemic would have been in full swing. This summer there had not yet been a single case. Doctor made himself face these facts. The town, his town, was better off this year because he had lost his fight with Allerton. He had fought against the town, and lost, and Allerton had been in the right.

Doctor stood up and began to pace back and forth, the length of the office. He had let himself slip into an awful frame of mind. It was better not to sit down and think. Go out and make calls, wrestle with other people's troubles, and keep your mind off your own. That's what it was to be a good doctor—lose yourself completely in your patients. That way you got rid of yourself; and a damned sight better off you were when you had yourself off your hands. That was the trouble with Duval. He always had himself first before his patients. Duval? *And Anna! God!*

A shadow fell across the doorway.

"Hi, doc! May I come in?"

"Hi, Larkin! Sure you may! Walk in. You're just in time to rescue me from a passel of letters. They run me ragged, Larkin, they run me ragged."

"Well, doc, here's something else that's going to run you ragged. One of the farmers from out cemetery way was just in with a long tale about Alf Stevens. It seems he's been beating his mother. The fellow said he heard her crying last night as he drove by on the road. He stopped to see what was the matter, and there she was with welts on her back as big as your finger, and trying to cover them up and hush her crying so he wouldn't say anything to Alf."

"Where was Alf?"

"Off riding hell out of that horse of his."

"He's got to stop that," said Doc. "We'll have to go out and see him."

"That's what I thought. His father was a Mason and all. We can't let him go on like that."

"No, we can't."

"I wish they'd kept him at the asylum where we sent him. Why didn't they?"

"There are times he seems perfectly sane. I dunno. Sometimes I think it's just damn meanness with him, more than it is insanity. I warned him when he came back. I said: 'Alf, we want to help you, but you've got to help yourself, too. You give us any more of these mean actions, and back you go to the asylum.' I talked straight to him."

"Well, do it again, doc. You're the one to do it. Half the men in town are afraid to talk up to him. By Golly! I think you're the only fellow in town who isn't afraid of *anybody*!"

Doc laughed uproariously.

"Larkin," he said, "I'll let you in on a secret. I was just sitting here wondering what is the matter with me. I think I'm afraid of my wife!"

"Willard, you're a card," laughed Larkin, "a regular card!" He clapped Doctor on the back. "Well, I s'pose this means a drive out to the Stevens place, eh? When shall we go? Tonight?"

"It'll be cooler then."

"How about getting Peavy and Kessler to go with us? They're all brother Masons, and four makes it kind of official. Sort of a delegation like that ought to impress the fellow that we mean business."

"All right. Will you ask them? If Kessler's wife has had a chance at him, he may not want to go. I gave her the devil this afternoon."

"More power to you, Willard! Some of these females need the devil once in a while."

They laughed.

"Well, Sam, after supper then, when it begins to get cool. I'll take you in the phaeton, and Kessler can drive his span of blacks."

"All right. But you're to do the talking, Willard. You've got the gift of gab."

"Leave it to me," said Doc.

But after Larkin was gone, Doc became serious again. He thought: *I must handle this carefully now. I mustn't make any more damned mistakes like I made with Allerton.*

37

THE FOUR MEN drove out to the Stevens place in the cool of the evening. After sunset the sky was a clear luminous green for a long time and seemed to be very high-arched like an inverted dome of glass. Beyond the wheat fields the mountains were deep purple and remote as if they had no concern with what went on in the valley. The nights were rarely hot here even in August, and now a coolness, as disinterested as the mountains and the glassy sky, settled over the roads and fields. No wind stirred, but two little puffs of dust followed the two vehicles on the road towards the cemetery.

"Damned finest crop of wheat I ever saw here," said Doc, pointing his whip at the fields as they went by.

"Ought to go twenty-five or thirty bushels to the acre," said Larkin. "It's God's country, doc."

"Yep, it's God's country all right," said Doc, "but *He* didn't clear it and put it into wheat. You've got to give the credit for that to man. God's a mighty fine provider, Larkin, but, by George! I'm a great believer in humanity."

They hitched their horses to the fence in front of the Stevens house and went up the path to the front door. Alf was sitting on the narrow porch in a weathered rocker, and he did not get up when he saw them coming. The shepherd dog rose stealthily and began to creep forward, growling, the hair rising along his neck and back.

"Lay down!" said Alf.

The dog slunk back and lay behind Alf's chair, peering between his legs at the strangers and growling.

"Well, Alf," said Doctor, "it's a mighty nice evening after the heat of the day. We've been admiring your wheat as we came along. Looks like a good crop this year."

"Ya," said Alf, "it'll do. It got to be harvested like the rest."

"We haven't seen you in town much lately, Alf."

"There ain't nothing to come for."

It was difficult to begin, but Doctor took the plunge.

"Alf," he said, "you remember we had a little talk in my office after you'd been away. I said we all wanted to help you, Alf. That's mighty true. We do. But we'd have a better chance if we saw you more often."

"I never wanted no help. I told you that. I can mind my own business."

"Look here," broke in Kessler, "we know something about the way you mind your own business. Night before last they heard your old mother crying way out to the road. When it gets that bad, it's everybody's business."

"Let Doc handle it, Kessler," said Larkin.

Alf sat silent, not looking at them, his elbows resting on his knees, his big hands hanging loose between.

"Alf," Doc said, "Kessler's speaking the truth. Folks in town know that you've been mistreating your mother again."

"She deserved what she got," said Alf.

"You admit you struck her, don't you?" cried Peavy excitedly.

"Ya, sometimes I hit her, but not too much—only when she needs it."

"Look here!" cried Kessler. "The town won't stand for that kind of thing. The Masonic Lodge won't stand for that kind of thing. Your father was a Mason, and your mother deserves our protection. Even a renegade like you can't do that to his mother. We're going to see that it stops!"

Alf spat into the dirt beyond the porch. He began to rock himself rhythmically back and forth. The rocker had one kind of squeak, and the porch floor another. The dry grass around the porch was full of the shrilling of crickets.

Doc didn't like the tension in the air. He sat down on the edge of the porch and crossed his legs. His voice was easy when he spoke.

"Let's not get excited," he said. "We're five men here together: let's keep calm and reasonable. We all know that women are foolish sometimes, but it's a man's bounden duty to be gentle with them. They're not as strong as we are. Your mother's a little bit of a thing, and if it weren't for her where would you be today?"

"I'd still be in the womb of time."

"There you are! She gave you the gift of life. She's cared for you all these years when you were fatherless."

"Don't talk about him."

"All right, we'll leave your father out of it. It's your mother we're concerned with now. She's little and helpless, and she needs you to protect her, Alf, not to punish her. Let God do that."

"God is no good. He don't punish any more."

"That's not for us to say. We've all got to do the best we can in this world. The strong have got to take care of the weak."

Alf did not reply. He continued to rock backward and forward, backward and forward.

"This beating has to stop, Alf," said Larkin. "We won't have it, that's all. If you continue to be cruel to your mother, you'll have to go back to Orofino."

The rocking ceased.

"You think I'm crazy," said Alf in a thick voice. "I know. The butcher said so. He said I was crazy. No, it's you that's crazy, all of you in town, all of you."

Doctor stood up. His voice was clear now and incisive.

"Alf," he said, "Mr. Larkin is right. This is a civilized town now, and no man in it can beat his mother, just because the whim takes him. If I beat my wife, you'd have a right to come to me and tell me I must stop. You'd have every right to put me in the jail or the asylum. It's the same with you. You act sane, and we'll treat you like a sane man. This is the last warning we're going to give you, Alf. The last warning."

A dark light suddenly blazed in Alf's eyes. He said:

"What do you come bellyaching at me for? Just because I hit my old woman. It was you killed the preacher's girl."

"My God, no, Alf! It was Allerton who killed the little Walden girl."

"Ya, him. But it was you, too. I heard you talking that day in the drugstore. I heard you talking to him."

"I didn't know then who the woman was," said Doc. "I never knew it was the little Walden girl."

"I didn't neither," said Alf. "I'd have killed him then, if I did. He ought to have been killed before he did that to her. But it's you, too. It's all you folks in your little, stinking town."

"No, Alf! No! I tell you I didn't know about the girl. None of us did."

"It don't much matter what you tell me," Alf said. "She's come back to the hill now where she used to like to lie. That's all right. That's where she ought to be, I guess. Only it wasn't your business to put her there. But it don't much matter, because the end of the world is coming pretty soon now. Maybe you didn't know it, but it's so; and there won't be no sinners left on earth. The flowers can grow then and the wheat go to seed. There won't be no threshers or harvesters to reap an' mow."

"Let's get out of here," said Peavy.

But Doctor kept standing there.

"Alf, it isn't true."

Alf did not answer him. He sat as before with his hands hanging between his knees and his eyes on the worn boards of the porch. The rocker creaked back and forth rhythmically.

"For God's sake, doctor, come away!" said Larkin.

"Good night, Alf," Doctor said.

The four men turned and went down the path to their horses. The shepherd dog followed them, growling, and the man in the chair did not call him back. When they reached the hitching post, Peavy turned and shook his fist and shouted:

"We mean every damned word of it, Alf, about the asylum and everything. You put that in your pipe and smoke it!"

The only answer from the porch was the creaking of the rocker and the shrilling of the crickets.

It was almost dark now, and the early stars were beginning to shine. Doc and Larkin were quiet driving back to town, but just before they parted Larkin said: "Well, doc, I guess that fixed him for the time being. But we've got to get him back in the asylum before he does anybody harm. All that talk about the end of the world: he's plainly out of his senses."

"Yes," Doc said absently. "Yes, we'll have to make out more papers and put the fellow away."

"He talked you right down, Willard," Larkin said with an attempt at laughter. "It's the first time I ever knew anyone to do that to you."

"I don't know," said Doc seriously. "Those fellows are kind of tricky to handle. I wish I knew a little more what went on in their heads."

"Don't worry," said the lawyer. "He'll be on his good behavior for another few days anyway. By that time we can put him away. Thanks for your help."

38

Doc FELT TIRED and low in his spirits tonight, and there was Anna still on his mind. But he wouldn't speak to her about Duval just yet. He unhitched in the barn and turned the horse into the box stall. Seeing no light in the house, he knew that Anna would be sitting in the dusk on the porch as she often did in summer. When he came around the house he could see the gleam of her white dress.

"Well, doctor, you were gone a long time."

"We've been out haranguing that Stevens boy."

"Is he bad again?"

"Looks like it. Don't you want a light?"

"No, I like it this way. But I'll get one for you."

"No. I'll just sit on the step awhile before I go to bed. Is there any cake or pie in the cupboard?"

"Yes, there's quite a bit of that spice cake. I'll get you a glass of milk from the cellar."

"Not now. I'll help myself on the way to bed."

"Did you have any trouble with Alf?"

"Not exactly. He talked a lot of nonsense. I'm damned sorry for the fellow."

"I wish you didn't have to mix up with him, doctor."

"My Lord! Anna, there's hardly a soul in Opportunity I haven't had to mix up with one way or another. It's my business."

They sat in silence. A full moon was coming up and checkering Anna's white dress with a pattern of leaves.

"You're a quiet woman, ain't you?" Doctor said.

"I guess I am."

"Still water runs deep, they say."

"Maybe so. I don't know."

"You been happy here, Anna, since we came to Idaho?"

"Yes, I have. And how about you, doctor? Have you been happy here?"

"You bet I have!" said Doctor. "But there's a lot yet to do before we're finished with this town. I kind of slipped up a little there last summer, this spring, but I'm going to make it up to the town now in other ways."

Anna put out her hand and touched his hair lightly with her fingers. "I'll get you your glass of milk. The evening's milk will be nice and cool by now."

"Get me that big tall glass full, Anna. I talked myself dry tonight."

"The big tall glass full, doctor." She paused in the doorway and added: "Gene didn't want to go to bed before you came. I think he's asleep now, but he was hurt because you didn't take him with you."

"It wasn't any place for him tonight. I'll let him go to the office with me in the morning."

39

DOCTOR WAS LATE with his shaving on Sunday morning. He had nicked himself with the razor, and it took a few minutes to staunch the tiny beads of blood upon his chin. Doctor was in a hurry, but he was not in a bad humor. He had been thinking as he dressed that he must have had a little dyspepsia the day before, to see things so darkly. The world was a pretty good place, after all, with clear yellow sunlight drying the dew on the lawn and the smell of coffee and bacon coming from the kitchen. He thought that, with such a crop of wheat, it would be a good year for collecting old bills, and that the times were looking up again for him.

"Can I go with you, Uncle Doc?" cried Gene. "Can I go?"

"You bet your life! But hurry up. That damned church bell will begin to ring before we get off the hill."

"Doctor, Gene ought to go to Sunday school," said Anna.

"Not this time," Doctor said. "This will make up for last night."

After breakfast he and Gene went out to the barn and put the horse into her harness.

"Look at her," said Gene. "She'll go and put herself right in the shafts. If she could handle the buckles, I believe she'd put on her own harness."

"She's a smart old gal," said Doc, rubbing the mare's nose. "She knows the way to the office better than I do."

As he drove out by the house he saw Anna sitting on the side porch in her black silk dress for church. She had a checkered gingham apron tied over it and a tin pan in her lap. She had just begun to shell the peas for dinner, and when he stopped the horse by the porch he could see the businesslike way she had of snapping open the pods and chasing the peas out with her thumb, and he could hear the *plop! plop! plop!* of peas in the empty pan.

"By gum!" he said. "This isn't the first time I ever caught a smart-looking girl shelling peas on the back porch."

"I guess you kissed the other one," said Anna without looking up.

"Guess I did," said Doc.

"You weren't too lazy to get out of your buggy in those days, doctor."

"Darn your hide, Anna! That bell's going to start to ring before I'm off the hill," said Doc. But he stepped out of the phaeton and came up to the porch and kissed her on her cheek.

Anna put her arms up around his neck. "Well, doctor, you haven't forgotten how."

"No," said Doc, laughing, "there's fire in the old dog yet."

He got back into the phaeton beside Gene and slapped the reins over the mare's neck. When he reached the end of the driveway, he looked around and waved his hand. He saw that Anna was watching him, and that she put up her hand in a gesture of farewell. He certainly felt better this morning. It did not seem now that Anna could have stopped loving him.

"You're funny," said Gene, "you and Auntie Anna."

"Wait until you're old enough to have whiskers—you'll see," said Doc. "It mows down the best of us."

They reached the bottom of the hill as the sexton started to ring the first bell for Sunday school. The mare turned into Ash Street and began to jog along towards the office. There was a solitary horseback rider galloping up Ash Street towards the phaeton.

"It's Alf Stevens," Doctor said, "riding hell-bent as usual." An unaccountable stab of anxiety went through him, but it was not until the rider was almost opposite the phaeton that Doctor comprehended his intention. Then he saw Alf's face, and he knew that Alf was out to kill. Doc's instinct was not only for self-preservation, but to strike out, to fight back. He snatched the driving whip and stood up in the phaeton to lash out with it as Alf came abreast. Gene caught the meaning of the situation, too.

"Uncle Doc!" he cried. "Uncle Doc!" And he flung his small body in protective frenzy against Doc's breast. That was how it was that the one shot pierced the two of them.

Nobody heard the sound of the shot because of the Presbyterian bell. The horseman wheeled and galloped back to Main Street. Dr. Hawkins just slumped a little into his seat and the whip and reins relaxed in his hands. Gene had fallen forward, crumpled between the dashboard and the seat. The mare flinched at the shot, but then she went on as usual, down Ash Street to Washington, over a block to Elm, and down a half-block to the hitching post in front of the doctor's office. There she stopped and stood waiting, switching the flies with her tail.

On Main Street there were cries and people running.

"Someone's been shot. It's Neischmidt, the butcher. No, it's Peavy —shot in the arm. It's both of them! For God's sake, get the doctor!"

They were running along the board sidewalks towards the doctor's office.

"There's his horse. Thank God, he's in! No, the door's locked. Oh, look! He's in the buggy. He's bleeding. The boy's there, too. Get them out and lay them down. Get his key off the chain and open the office. Run for his wife. Go for Duval. Duval's the boy's father, he's Doc's assistant. He'll know what to do."

"God! What an awful thing!"

"Well, run, damn you! Can't you see Doc Hawkins is dying?"

"Who shot him?"

"Don't know. There's a killer loose in town."

"Open the office. Carry him gently. The boy's light, but Lord, the doctor's heavy! Do you think he's dead?"

In a moment there was a crowd around the office door, around the phaeton where the blood still dripped from the seat to the floor and thence to a thickening pool in the dust of the street.

"The little boy's dead, I think, but Doc's still breathing."

"Put him on the operating table."

"No, we better not lift him. Lay him on the floor. Where's his wife? They ought to get her here before he's gone."

"Skogmo had his buggy tied behind the drugstore. They've gone for her in that."

"Damn that bell! Won't it ever stop ringing?"

"Has anybody got some brandy?"

"Here, take some of this cotton and try to stop the bleeding."

"What do you do for a wound like that?"

"Nothing. It's the end of everything."

"Look! He's moving a little. Did you hear? He's starting to moan. Maybe it'll be all right. If we could get hold of Duval! In God's name, where is Duval?"

A man came running from Duval's rooms.

"He's still in bed," he said. "We couldn't get him awake. It looked as if he'd been drinking all night. They're trying to dress him and get him here. Somebody better go for old Doc Schilling."

There was a movement in the crowd along the sidewalk, by the office door.

"Here's Skogmo's buggy. They've got Mrs. Hawkins. Stand back, everybody. Get out and make room. Let Mrs. Hawkins through. That's right. Stand back, everybody. It's his wife now. Let her in."

Anna came in quickly. Her face was as white as chalk above her black silk. She still wore her gingham apron, and her fingers were stained with the juice of the pea pods. She went down on her knees beside her husband.

"*Doctor*! Oh, doctor!"

His eyelids fluttered a little; then they opened, and he looked at her with strange eyes as from a great distance; but he could not speak. The Sunday-school bell stopped ringing, and all around them there was a heavy, pulsing silence. Out of it began to emerge the smaller sounds—crickets in the August sunshine outside the office, the shuffling of feet on the board walk, the buzzing of a fly on the ceiling.

"Duval's coming," someone called. "Up the street. They're bringing Duval!"

The name Duval stirred something in Doctor's fading brain. He opened his eyes again and looked into Anna's eyes, his lips forming desperate words.

"Anna—you—and—Duval?"

Anna understood what he meant. She put her face near his.

"No, doctor, no!" she said. "There was never anything you couldn't have seen or heard."

"All right—my—girl—"

There was a little silence. Anna had her fingers on his pulse. His eyes flickered open once more.

"Gene—where's Gene?"

Anna looked at the pathetic form stretched on the floor beside him.

"He's with you, doctor," she said.

He closed his eyes again. She continued to keep her fingers on his pulse, but presently she laid his hand gently upon his breast, and sat back on her heels, turning her face away from the many curious eyes which were watching her. There was something thick and dry in her throat and a heavy kind of pain across her chest. She did not look up to see Duval standing in the doorway, half dressed, his eyes heavy with sleep, his white hands trembling.

40

JUST OUTSIDE the office door in the sunny street, a man began to speak in a high, excited tone of voice.

"I saw him when he came into town. It was Alf Stevens. I never thought there was anything wrong. He stopped to water his horse at the trough in front of the blacksmith's shop. I noticed his horse was sweaty, but he always rode hard. He had a couple of revolvers strapped to his belt, but he used to go that way, too—I've seen him often. I said, 'What are you doing in town on Sunday morning?'

" 'Paying my debts,' says he.

" 'The better the day, the better the deed,' I says. 'Who do you owe?' He took out a piece of paper and held it out for me to see.

" 'I've made a list,' he says. 'Read it, and remember who was on it when I've paid up.'

"He had about a dozen names on it. There was Dr. Hawkins and Peavy and Kessler, Neischmidt and Larkin—I don't remember who all."

"He showed you a list?"

"Yes, it's true. He showed me a list. He says, 'The end of the world is coming,' he says. When someone told me Neischmidt was shot out behind his shop, I started to run for the doctor. I didn't think then about Alf. And then they said Peavy was shot, too. When I saw Dr. Hawkins I thought of the list."

"You say Kessler and Larkin were on it, too?"

"God, yes! Where are they? Are they dead?"

"I think they're both at home."

"And the others on the list?"

"I don't know. I don't remember."

"Was I on the list? Think! Remember!"

"I don't know. It doesn't matter. We've got to get him before he gets us."

"Where did he go? Which way? Did anybody see him?"

"I did. About a quarter of an hour ago. He was riding like hell out of town."

"Which way?"

"Out the way he lives—towards the cemetery."

"Get every able-bodied man in town. Someone get Swanson and see if he'll open his hardware store and give us arms."

"Keep the women and children indoors. Don't let any more bells ring for church. Go up and down the streets, and get every man who can handle a gun."

"Shouldn't we leave it to the sheriff?"

"Sure. Get the sheriff, but don't leave it all to him. The law's too slow and uncertain. This is a matter for the town. It's got to be done quick."

Presently Anna was alone with Doctor and Gene and Constant Duval in the stillness and the strangeness of the office.

41

THERE WERE NO more church bells rung in Opportunity that day. The Sunday clamor of bells, too many for the size of the town, that echoed back and forth against the hills, was still. The August sun lay hot and golden over everything. The heavy-headed wheat rippled a little when a breeze passed by, and it was like a golden face of innocence and tranquillity.

Will Swanson unlocked the back doors of his hardware store and gave out arms. It was cool and dark inside the big store, and the men swarmed in, still hot and sweating from the August streets, their mouths dry and their eyes red; and each one armed himself in the best way he could. They were like hounds who have caught the scent of the fox. They were savages running to the kill.

When they had left the town, it lay silent and deserted, transfixed with apprehension. Those who could get horses and rigs from barn or livery stable drove; the others trudged in the road, full of strength and purpose.

The sky was very clear and blue overhead, and here and there in its clearness floated white galleons of cloud which had come across the mountains and were unconcerned with movement in the valley. On the road to the cemetery dust rose and hung a long time on the air.

About a half-mile from the Stevens place, the men tied their horses to the rail fences and spread in a large, encircling movement through the wheat on either side of the road. Much of the wheat was breast-high to a man, and they crept through it, so that their heads were not seen. Some crawled on their bellies across the roads or gaps in the wheat, crouching like animals in the shelter of fences or ditches. The foremost of them continued on the flank of each wing until they met, having made a complete circle. The Stevens place was surrounded, and there had been only a little undue rippling in the wheat where they had gone.

Then the sheriff and two deputies rode up to the house, and the sheriff knocked on the door with the butt of his gun. The house was gray and silent, and it was a long time before he had an answer. When he had knocked and bellowed for a long time, the door was opened a little way, and the thin, gray face of the old woman who had been beaten by her son looked out.

"What do you want?"

"Your son. He's murdered the doctor and a little boy. The butcher and the postmaster may be dead by this time, too. You must give him up."

"He isn't here."

"I've got a warrant with me. We'll have to search the house."

"No, no. He's ridden away. It's no use coming in."

"I have to see for myself. Open the door now. Don't try to prevent us."

"No! No! It's better for you if you go away. Believe me what I tell you! It's better you go away!"

The sheriff thrust open the door, and a bullet from Alf Stevens' gun caught him in the right shoulder, so that he fell back against one of the deputies, dropping his gun on the worn boards of the porch floor. Crying, the old woman slammed the door shut, and they could hear her locking and barricading it with furniture.

The deputies half carried the sheriff to a ditch across the road and laid him down. Then the circle of men began to close in about the house. And now they stood up, showing themselves here and there in the wheat, and crying out to Alf to surrender.

"Give yourself up now—we'll take you alive or dead. Which will it be?"

There was no answer from the house. Alf's shepherd dog ran up and down the barnyard, frantic and hoarse with barking. Inside the barn the horses whinnied shrilly and stamped their feet. Then as the foremost man in the circle approached the yard fence, there was a shot from an upper window which clipped the hat from his head. They crawled in the wheat after that, kneeling and taking aim between the heavy heads. They peppered the house with bullets. The bullets crashed through the windows, and the thin sound of splintering glass mingled with the sharp crackle of the firing. There was a meadow lark, too, that kept giving his lonesome call from a fence post over by the cemetery.

"Come out, damn you, Alf! Give yourself up, and we'll take you to jail without hurting you."

But the only answer was a shot that grazed Buchanan the sign painter's cheek as he knelt to take aim.

Once they heard the old woman's voice rising to a kind of shriek of supplication within the house. That and the firing gave them Alf's location in the upper room. They poured volley after volley of lead through the weathered clapboards. The house, standing up so stark and alone without shed or tree, made a perfect target. A bullet struck the dog and he ceased his plunging and barking to slink under the house with glazing eyes.

Little wisps of blue smoke drifted above the wheat from the discharge of many guns. Here and there the wheat was trampled and the ripe kernels spilled on the ground. Dust had settled thickly on the men's faces, and now it was furrowed by rivulets of sweat and blood. Still they kept reloading and firing for quite a while after the firing from the house had ceased. No one noticed that at first, and the sharp crackling, the little puffs of smoke, continued all around the house. The number of perforations grew in the gray wood. They were all over the upper story of the house—holes a little larger than a woodpecker would make.

Then there was a dreadful crying in the house, and the old woman ran onto the porch, her arms spread wide, her gray head shining in the beating sunshine.

"Stop it! Oh, stop it!" she cried. "He's dead now. Oh, God! don't shoot no more. My boy is dead."

They came up then, all of them, slowly and cautiously at first for fear that she was lying. But when she sat hunched over on the porch step with her apron over her head crying and sobbing, and made no move to go back into the house, they came on more quickly. The fever of killing was beginning to leave them now. As they went into the house, they pulled off their hats; but they didn't put up their guns until they saw him lying halfway down the narrow staircase in the abandonment of death.

"I wonder whose bullet?" said one of the men.

"Pray God we don't never find out," said another.

They went through his pockets and he did have a list there, with many of their names upon it. Beside the names of Hawkins, Peavy, and Neischmidt there were little checks, and the whole paper was greasy and wrinkled from long handling. In the same pocket with the paper was a little sprig of dried juniper, all yellowed, as if he had carried it for a long time.

"Well," said Kessler, "I guess the fellow was crazy, but we did the best we could. We've avenged Doc Hawkins, anyway."

Driving back to town, Larkin said suddenly, "You remember Doc's speech two years ago at the graduation?"

"Sure," said Kessler, "but I remember the one he made in court better. Doc was a fine orator as well as a doctor. This town will miss him."

"It was what he said about mob rule," said Larkin. "He thought it was over in Idaho."

"I don't remember that," said Kessler. "I know he cracked a joke about the undertaker. He was great for cracking jokes."

"H'm!" said Larkin. "The undertaker won't be idle today, I guess."

They drove along in silence, and Larkin kept his thoughts to himself. They were all late for dinner, and they had had a hard morning. Heat waves shimmered in the blue air above the golden wheat. It was a strange Sunday.

42

IT HAD BEEN difficult for Anna to know what to say to Constant. She pitied him, but her very love for him made it impossible for her to think of any words with which to comfort him. Together they settled the things which must be settled; they sat beside each other in the church during the funeral and rode together to the cemetery, past the gray, shattered house at the foot of the hill. But somehow they could not break the awkward silence which made them strangers even when their shoulders touched.

After it was all over Constant walked with her to the gate of her house, and they stood there for a few moments as they had stood before, his hand on the latch so that she would not go in before he had said what was on his mind to say. They were pale and awkward, and strange in their formal black clothing. He said abruptly:

"Anna, say that you blame me. It will help me somewhat, I think. I think it will help me."

"No," Anna said, "even if you had come sooner, you could not have saved them. All your life, Constant, you have blamed yourself for things that were inevitable. You mustn't do that again."

"If I had been at the office, Doctor would not have been obliged to go down—he wouldn't have taken Gene— If I had not been drinking—"

"Constant," Anna said earnestly, laying her hand on his arm, "you must put an end to this sense of guilt. It is another kind of intoxication to you."

"Yes, I am going to put an end to it," he said. "I have thought it over very much in these last days. Anna, I am going back to France."

"Oh, no! What can you do there now, after this long time? Is it only to make some kind of restitution to the children of a man who died during an operation? Can anything you do now be of any help to them?"

"It will be of help to me. You, yourself, how many times you urged me, Anna! 'Turn backward,' you yourself said. 'Stop here until you can turn backward.' "

Anna was silent for a moment. Then she said: "Yes, I was right, Constant. I should not have forgotten. I only faltered now perhaps because—because so many people I loved are gone—"

"Anna," he said, "it has taken another tragedy to give me courage."

"You have always had courage, I think. What you lacked was resolution."

"Yes, I lacked resolution. You have built it up in me. I think I will not lose it now."

"It is eight years since you came that night in the midst of the storm. It seems a short time, somehow."

"Anna, will you come with me now when I return to France?"

She did not at first reply, and he was obliged to repeat his question. Then Anna shook her head. She was trying to find words for something she felt. "You will find your peace of mind better alone." And then she added quietly as if she were analyzing her own nebulous feelings: "I love this place, but I have always been afraid of it. Now I'm not afraid any more. There is nothing else that it can do to me."

"But it will be hard for you here alone."

"You haven't chosen the easiest way either."

"No."

They were silent again for a few moments.

"It may be a long time before I can come back," he said at last. "But, if I come back? You would still be here?"

"Yes, Constant, I would still be here."

He let her pass through the gate and half turned as if he were going away, letting the gate click shut between them. Then he came back and said in a low voice: "Once we had a kind of argument, do you remember? You were feeding the colt in the barn. I said true love came only once, and you said no, the heart was large enough for many loves. Another time you said that I was stubborn—not faithful, only stubborn. You remember?"

"Yes, I was hurt then and a little angry."

"But you were right, for now I see a little how the best love may come last. It is a love that is mature, and strong enough to face separation with equanimity."

Anna did not answer, but she laid her hand on the gate beside his so that their fingers touched.

"Then I will say goodbye, and thank you, Anna."

"Goodbye, Constant."

For a moment their hands came together, warm and seeking. Then he turned and went quickly down the hill, with his loose, awkward gait, the shoulders thrust forward, the long arms swinging. Anna watched him out of sight, her hand still on the gate. When he was gone, she turned towards the mountains, contemplating for a moment their eternal paradox. Ever changing, now blue, now purple, now pale as silk; sometimes tremendous and threatening the sky, and sometimes dwindled to a gentle undulation around a peaceful valley, the mountains seemed as fickle as water; and yet they were the only permanence. In all of their variety, they were the only certain thing, the serene, unchanging peaks which rose above the quicksands of passing days and of humanity. And birth and death, and gain and loss, and even love itself, these were the shadows and the transiencies. Anna stood for a moment with the smell of the late summer flowers in her nostrils, and then she dropped her hands to her sides and went alone into the quiet house. In spite of all that had happened to her, she felt at peace.